THE WASTE LAND

Tim Hodkinson

An Aries Book

This edition first published in the UK in 2021 by Head of Zeus Ltd
An Aries book

9 7 5 3 1 2 4 6 8

A CIP catalogue record for this book is available
from the British Library.

ISBN (PB): 9781801105514
ISBN (E): 9781801105491

Cover design © Dan Mogford

Typeset by Siliconchips Services Ltd UK

Printed and bound by CPI Group (UK) Ltd, Croydon, CR0 4YY

Head of Zeus
First Floor East
5–8 Hardwick Street
London EC1R 4RG

www.headofzeus.com

For Trudy, Emily, Clara and Alice

Historical Note

This book is the second in a series set during the Scottish invasion of Ireland in the Fourteenth Century.

In 1314, Robert Bruce of Scotland defeated Edward II of England at the Battle of Bannockburn, ensuring the sovereignty of Scotland as a separate country. One year later Robert's brother Edward took an army across the sea to invade Ireland, provoking a war that raged up and down the island for four years and continued despite the onset of one of the worst famines in European history. This was the backdrop to the previous novel in this series – *Lions of the Grail* – and it is at that point in time, 1316, that this story commences.

Some of the characters in this work of fiction are based on real historical figures. For those unfamiliar with them from the previous novel, I am providing this list of the main ones to give some context.

The Scots

Robert Bruce (Robert de Brus/Roibert a Briuis)

Robert Bruce probably needs no introduction. As the names listed above show, he was a man of mixed Anglo-Norman and Gaelic heritage. Through his mother's side he is believed to have spent part of his early life being fostered among the Gaelic nobility of western Scotland or their cousins in the north of Ireland. On his father's side he was related to many of the nobility of England. He began his career as a "young bachelor [knight] of King Edward's Chamber" and fought for King Edward I of England in what is now called the first wars of Scottish Independence. In 1302 he married Elizabeth, daughter of Richard de Burgh, the Earl of Ulster and staunch supporter of Edward I. By doing so he wrapped himself further into the web of allegiances and blood that crisscrossed the north channel at the time. Robert then decided, in his own words that he "must join my own people and the nation in which I was born". Having himself crowned king of Scotland, he embarked on a long war which culminated in his decisive victory at Bannockburn in 1314.

Edward Bruce (Edward de Brus/Edubard a Briuis)

Edward Bruce was the Earl of Carrick, a lordship in south-west Scotland (not to be confused with Carrickfergus in Ireland). He was King Robert Bruce of Scotland's younger brother and supported his brother in the Scottish Wars of Independence. In 1315, one year after the Scots defeated the English at the battle of Bannockburn, Edward invaded

Ireland at the head of an army. Within a year he had taken half the island and had himself crowned King of Ireland.

Gib Harper

Harper was from Edward Bruce's estates in Carrick and seems to have been a key henchman and a formidable warrior, though not a knight or member of the nobility. He is described in chronicles as '*douchteast in deid*' (the most doughty in deeds) and 'without peer' in Bruce's personal entourage.

Syr (Sir) Neil Fleming

Fleming was a young Scottish knight and captain in Edward Bruce's army in Ireland.

Tavish Dhu/Thomas Dun/'Black Thomas'

Tavish was a notorious sea captain and pirate who terrorised the Irish Sea in the early 1300s. As the fledgling Scottish kingdom lacked a navy, in 1315 Robert Bruce hired Tavish to ferry his brother's invading army across to Ireland.

The Irish

Richard Óg de Burgh

De Burgh was Earl of Ulster and Baron of Connaught. Known as the 'Red Earl' he was immensely rich and at one point ruled nearly half of Ireland. He played a key role in fighting against the Scots during the reign of Edward I of England (a personal friend) and his daughter was married to Robert Bruce (who at that time was nominally on the side of the English King). 'Óg' is another Irish title usually interpreted as 'young' and referring to the young age he became earl (twenty). At the time of this novel he is in his fifties and has lost all his lands to the Scottish invaders.

Thomas de Mandeville

De Mandeville was the Seneschal of Ulster. The role of seneschal – an official title in medieval government – in Irish realms was slightly broader than the usual administrative remit and de Mandeville spent most of his tenure acting as a military leader.

Henry de Thrapston

De Thrapston was keeper (or castellan) of Carrickfergus Castle. In medieval life, a castellan was responsible for the running of a castle, overseeing both the domestic staff and the military garrison.

John de Bermingham

The de Berminghams (known in Irish annals as the MacFeorais) were a powerful Anglo-Irish clan who were barons of Athenry. De Bermingham became Justiciar of Ireland, which meant he ruled the island in the name of the King of England. The Lordship of Ireland (*Tiarnas na hÉireann*) refers to the lands in Ireland ruled in the name of the King of England by the justiciar (now called the 'lord lieutenant'). The lordship was created as a Papal possession following the Norman invasion of Ireland in 1169.

The English

Roger Mortimer

Baron Roger Mortimer was a very powerful English nobleman with ties to Ireland through marriage. At the time of this book, he was part of a small ruling cabal of nobles who effectively governed England.

Edward II (Plantagenet)

Edward II succeeded his father Edward 'Longshanks' to the throne of England in 1307. His reign was a troubled one and due to the defeat at the hands of Robert Bruce, the onset of the famine and behaviour generally regarded at the time as not suitable for a king, he became very unpopular and was forced to relinquish a lot of his power to his barons, including Mortimer.

Fictional characters

Of the fictional characters, many have some basis in historical fact. John Barbour, a poet sometimes referred to as the 'Father of Scottish Poetry', wrote an epic account of the life of Robert Bruce within living memory of some of the events described in this book. At one point he listed the names of the chiefs of the Ulster army fighting against Robert Bruce and some readers may recognise a few of the names:

'*Brynrane, Wedounne, Fitzwarryne,*
And Schyr Paschall of Florentine,
That was a knycht of Lumbardy,
And was full of chewalry.
The Mawndweillis war thar alsua,
Besatis, Loganys, and other ma;
Savages als, and yeit was ane
Hat Schyr Nycholl of Kylkenane.'

Brinrans, Weddens, FitzWarins,
And Sir Paschal of Florence,
who was a knight from Lombardy,
full of chivalry.
The Mandevilles were there also,
Bysits, Logans, and other men;
Savages too, and one
named Sir Nichol of Kilkenny

Glossary

Some of the names of characters and places and terms that appear in *The Waste Land* may sound strange to modern ears. In order to help the reader, this glossary of some of the more frequent words has been provided, giving the word as it appears in the book and its modern equivalent.

Galloglaich: Gallowglass – a heavily armed Scots-Irish mercenary
Domnall: Donal
Ui Neill: O'Neill
Tyr Eoghan: Tyrone (roughly equivalent to the modern-day county Tyrone)
Ceannaideach: Kennedy
MacHuylin: McQuillan
Cladh Mor: Claymore
Vikingsford: Larne Lough
Ui Flainn: O'Flynn
Syr: Sir
Le Poer: Powers
Aengus: Angus
Seneschal: A medieval position part judicial and part military. The Seneschal had to keep the peace and defend

a district in the name of the earl and through him, the king.

Béal Feirste: Belfast

Hobyny: A small, highly agile Irish cavalry horse. The lightly armoured skirmishers who rode hobynys were called Hobelars. Hobynys proved so effective in war that King Edward II at one point banned their export from Ireland. They are thought to be the ancestor of the modern Connemara pony and the term "Hobby Horse".

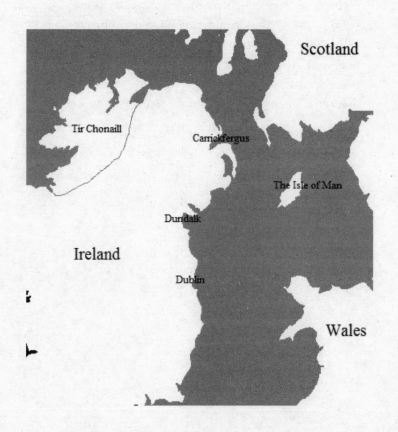

'Whii werre and wrake in londe and manslauht is i-come,
Whii hunger and derthe on eorthe the
pore hath undernome,
Whii bestes ben thus storve, whii corn hath ben so dere,
Ye that wolen abide, listneth and ye mowen here
The skile'

'Why war, destruction and murder has come
to the land,
Why hunger and famine have seized the poor,
Why animals starve, why corn is so dear,
You that will wait, listen and you will hear
The reason.'

From 'Poem on the Evil Times of Edward II', circa 1321

I

27th March 1316 AD, Bordeaux, South-East France

Two men sat high up on a set of tiered wooden benches. In a temporary arena below them another pair of men faced each other, preparing to fight.

The benches surrounded an oval enclosure about thirty-five paces across, its surface covered in a mixture of sand and sawdust. So far that day the arena had seen wrestling contests, quarterstaff fights and finally, sword fighting. Each combat had left its mark. Now, as the dreary winter sunlight faded to the grey of late afternoon, the ground was churned up, the sawdust swept away by feet and here and there clogged by patches of mud and half-dried blood.

The pair watching on the benches were clearly men of violence. Despite the holiday they wore mail shirts over leather jerkins. Their armour was old but well maintained, repaired many times and shaped so they fitted like well-made shirts. They wore wide-brimmed steel helmets sporting dents that showed they had been in conflict, but the armour still was fit for purpose. Their bare arms and faces bore scars and the marks of former fights. Both had badly broken noses. They had the look of professional soldiers but that was not unusual in Gascony. It was a province of France recently taken back by the King of England. It was a frontier fief. Over the border the forces of Louis of France waited like an impatient surgeon to lance this last infected boil of dissent to his rule. To deter that happening, the English kept Gascony permanently flooded with men of war. These men were not in the employ of Edward of England, however.

One of them pointed at one of the combatants below – a bedraggled figure in a stained leather jerkin and rusty chain mail.

'That's him,' he said, speaking quietly in the Gaelic language, his accent Irish.

'Are you sure? He looks like nothing,' the second watcher said. He spoke the same language but with a strong Scottish accent. 'How do you know?'

'I watched him competing in a tournament back in Ireland. We fought against him as well in a forest and again in Carrickfergus Castle. Vicious bastard he is. That's Richard Savage all right.'

'Good.' His companion thumbed the hilt of the kidney dagger sheathed at his waist. 'We'll get him after the tournament.'

'He's a tricky one,' the other man said, a flash of concern crossing his face. 'We'll need to be careful.'

The Scot grunted and gave a wry smile. 'Don't worry. He'll never know what hit him.'

2

To call the day's hastilude a "tournament" was to aggrandise it far above what the paltry fighting competition really deserved. However, the fact that it had happened at all was a minor miracle. It was certainly a gathering of martial games, enough to warrant the title hastilude, but there were no knights, no jousting, no melee. Instead it had been a rather dour affair of quarterstaff fighting, wrestling and single combats: lower-class contests that lacked flair and spectacle. The seats in the arena were only half full and the spectators were not treated to any of the usual treats and titbits that hawkers would normally sell at these events. The few spectators there watched the contests with intent, but their eyes were sunken, their faces pale and their expressions hungry.

Gascony, like the rest of the known world, was in the pitiless grip of famine. The Archbishop of Bordeaux, the sponsor of the hastilude, had insisted that the games go ahead despite the current crisis, on the grounds that the people of the town needed something to divert them from the ongoing misery.

The arena, like everything else in the seemingly drowned world, was drenched by the ever-falling rain. It had been raining for months; a merciless, insistent downpour that had washed all the colour and life from the land and rotted the crops in the fields. A dismal harvest unleashed widespread starvation. To accompany the famine, the next of those terrible apocalyptic horsemen – war – had begun to ride abroad also.

Unaware of the attention he was getting from the spectators' benches, Richard Savage wiped a gloved hand across his helmet visor to clear away the rain drips. He looked down at his hand, noticing the slight tremor, perceptible despite the thick leather gauntlet he wore. He was not scared. He was getting tired. The path to this final contest had not been difficult in terms of opponents, but each contest had still taken its toll in terms of effort and he had not exactly been well nourished to start with. His opponent stood opposite him. A tall, heavily muscled German whose equipment showed he was a professional swordsman, probably a mercenary who made his living fighting in the English or French armies and taking part in competitions like this one for prize money. The German looked to be in remarkably good shape for someone who, like Savage, had been fighting for most of the afternoon through all the previous rounds. Worse, despite the fact that most people in the country were starving, compared to Savage he looked depressingly well fed.

It was hardly surprising, Savage reasoned. If there was one place during a famine where you could be guaranteed a meal it was in one of the armies or bands of brigands that raged across France. Warriors did not heed the ridiculous prices that bread had risen to; they just took what they wanted. When famine and war colluded, children starved but soldiers feasted.

Although himself a soldier, Savage unfortunately did not share the German's conditioning. He had been in France for almost a year now and it was not working out well. His younger self would have thought that God was punishing him for the adventure of the previous year, which had ended on top of a Scottish mountain where he had tossed what was quite possibly the Holy Grail into a bog. His present, less religiously certain self, however, told him his current predicament was just plain bad luck.

The previous May, Savage had fought and beaten the renegade Hospitaller, Montmorency, on the summit of Cnoc Dreann in Scotland. He had rescued Alys, the woman he loved, and Galiene, the daughter he had never known he had, but then he and his new-found family had been left with nowhere to go. Ireland was at war. The Scots would kill him if they found him and England had nothing to offer – legally he was still an outlaw there for maiming the Sheriff of Garway.

Alys and he had found a hermit monk who married them in a handfasting ceremony, unfortunately thirteen years too late to make Galiene legitimate. After some discussion, they decided that Gascony was where they should settle. The English were desperate to encourage allied folk to settle the land there to cement its attachment to England. Manors were cheap and so were rents – it was a land of war after all. The weather was much better than Britain or Ireland and it made the finest wines in Christendom. There seemed to be nothing to lose.

They had not anticipated the famine, however. Savage

had secured a small farm with a manor house, rented from the archbishop, but his crops were washed away by the rain. Life was increasingly hard. What little money they had was gone and the price of bread had risen to become unaffordable. Savage had supplemented their larder by hunting, but when everyone was scouring the woods for meat it too soon became scarce. The only meagre consolation was the knowledge that everywhere was suffering the same weather and dearth. All over Europe the crops had failed and the rain kept falling. No matter where they had chosen to go they would have ended up in the same predicament.

When he had heard about the hastilude being held in Bordeaux, Savage realised this was a way to aid their difficulties. There would be prize money for the winners and that money would mean he could afford to buy food for his wife and daughter. Since coming to France he had come to realise that he was no farmer. The dour, heavy toil of tending the land had soon lost its rustic charm and the boring reality of the life he had chosen became apparent. Famine aside, he just did not have the nature to make a success of raising crops and tending animals. As he had listened to the archbishop's herald announcing the coming competition in the village square, he had felt a surge of excitement within him. Here was a chance to use the skills he had spent years in honing: the skills of fighting.

Alys was less enthusiastic. That morning as he had prepared to leave she had looked at him with a mixture of reproach and anxiety, one hand resting on the gentle swelling of her pregnant belly. Armed combat, even in tournament competitions, was a risky business. Accidents still happened: limbs got broken, men lost eyes. Occasionally there were fatalities.

'It's dangerous, Richard,' she said. 'What if you get hurt? What will Galiene and I do? We can't run a manor on our own.'

Savage had smiled. 'You managed for years without me back in Ireland.'

Alys scowled. 'I thought you were dead. And I wasn't pregnant. And I was at home in my own castle. Promise me you will be careful.'

As he had prepared to swing himself into his saddle a strange thing happened. Galiene came up to him and planted a kiss on his cheek.

'Good luck,' she murmured, eyes averted towards the ground. Then she dashed off towards the barn that stood beside their dilapidated rented farmhouse. Savage, literally stunned by this action, stood open-mouthed and tongue-tied. He caught sight of Alys looking at him, a smile of pure pleasure at both her daughter's actions and her husband's discomfiture lighting up her face.

'Well there's new light from old windows,' Savage said, bemused but awkwardly pleased.

The last six months had proved difficult between him and Galiene. She may have been his daughter but she had grown up through nearly all her life without him. Her mother and she had been forced to survive on their own and life had been far from easy for them. Then suddenly, Richard Savage had landed back in their lives and at the same time they had lost their home and everything they had struggled so long to hold on to. All her life, Galiene's family had consisted of just her and her mother, Alys. Now here was this man – the very man, so her mother had told her had abandoned them years before to go on some ridiculous quest for the Holy Grail – who was suddenly back. Worse: her mother seemed besotted with him.

Galiene's sullen resentment for Savage was something she expressed at every opportunity and Savage had to admit he did not do much to help matters. Six years as a Knight Templar, followed by seven years in prison had not exactly given him the necessary skills to deal with a young girl.

'She's thirteen, Richard,' Alys had explained recently. 'It's a bad age for a child,' she checked herself, 'a young woman like Galiene. She's jealous of the attention I give you. She was the same with John Bysset at the start too. You just need to stick at it. She'll come round eventually.'

'You stabbed Bysset to death,' Savage said, frowning.

'Let's hope it doesn't come to that.' Alys smiled.

For the first time in a very long time his belly had been full. He needed energy for the tournament so Galiene and Alys had sacrificed their own breakfasts so he could have the egg from their one remaining chicken. They also used the last piece of salted pork they had been saving for when the famine became really dire. As she cooked it, Galiene had sung. Her voice was pure and clear as the waters of a mountain stream and she could hold a tune like no one Savage had ever heard. He was immensely proud of her singing voice. It evoked memories of his mother who, many years before, had sung as she sat at her needlework in the draughty old Savage castle back in Ireland.

On the morning of his departure for Bordeaux and the tournament, Galiene's voice filled their meagre kitchen as she sang an old Irish song. It evoked in Savage a bittersweet feeling of longing for home, which took him by surprise. He had not felt any attachment to the place for years. This was compounded by a pang of guilt as his wife and daughter looked on at him with longing in their hollow eyes while he ate the feast of ham and egg, but he reasoned that if he won the tournament the prize money would mean their worries were over. They would have enough to buy a whole pig and a new flock of chickens – and he knew he could do it. Fighting was his business.

So far the day had gone well. The expected band of half-starved farmers and part-time warriors he had beaten on the way to the finals had been no match for a knight. And Savage was not just any knight: he had been a Knight Templar, trained to fight under the baking sun of the Holy Land.

Unfortunately, now this well-honed German professional swordsman, named as Syr Heinrich von Mahlberg, and who, like Savage, had enjoyed a reasonably easy path to the final round, stood between him and the prize money. Unlike Savage's, his lightweight body armour was in excellent condition, and he did not look as if he had missed too many meals recently.

The German squinted in the gathering late winter afternoon gloom to get a better view of his opponent and from the slight smile that flickered across his lips it was clear what he thought of the challenge posed by the bedraggled figure in the rusty chain mail on the other side of the arena.

Savage looked down at his sword, nicked and blunted from earlier rounds. In his other hand he bore a buckler, the small shield used in these combat contests, and it also bore the marks of the battles it had been through that day. Its leather was slashed and split and the handle Savage gripped was noticeably loose. It would not last much longer.

Still smiling, the German pulled his padded leather cap onto his head and strode to the wooden weapons' rack that stood at his side of the arena. He set down his own sword and buckler and lifted a huge two-handed longsword from the rack. The weapon he chose was a specialty of the Germans. Its blade was so long it required both hands and great strength to wield it. Because of this, the fighter could not hold a shield as well, but the length of the blade and the crushing blows it could deliver made up for that. Von Mahlberg clearly believed that this, combined with the unusual fighting style involved in wielding a longsword – a style that was uncommon outside the Holy Roman Empire – would make the fight a short one. A single blow from the massive steel blade, even though blunted for the tournament, would shatter Savage's battered buckler to pieces. From there victory would be an easy step.

Glancing back at the rack of weapons on his own side of the arena, for the first time since seeing his opponent Savage smiled. At last here was a bit of luck.

3

Richard Savage strode to the rack. He was slightly disappointed that in turning his back to the German he missed seeing the expression on his opponent's face when he tossed his buckler to the ground and lifted the *claidheamh mòr* sword – the great sword – from the rack. Every inch as long and lethal as von Mahlberg's longsword, the claidheamh mòr was its Gaelic cousin and when used in anger could slice a man in half like a butcher's cleaver halving a leg of roast pork.

Years before, in his former life before the adventure in Ireland that had changed everything, Savage had spent many hours training with one of these weapons in the drill yard at the Templar priory in Cyprus under the stern gaze of another German. That one – a fellow Templar – was a *Fechtmeister*: a sword master. If von Mahlberg thought that picking the longsword would give him an advantage, he could not have been more wrong.

A murmur went around the spectators in the arena as Savage walked forward with the massive sword hefted over one shoulder. Here was finally a decent competition to watch. The last sword-fighting match of the day promised to be a true struggle of equals instead of the one-sided thrashings that had marked each finalist's path through the competition.

Both combatants turned to look up at the special dais where the archbishop and his retinue sat, along with various nobles and counts of Bordeaux. *A Roman emperor and his senators must have looked much the same when watching gladiators fighting in the arena*, thought Savage with a wry grin. The archbishop was sumptuously dressed in a checked gown of red and green, its sleeves deliberately cut wide so as to reveal a lining of silk. He was a large man who somehow had managed to maintain his weight despite the famine. A heavy, black bearskin was wrapped around his shoulders and the only thing that denoted his clerical position was the large, bejewelled cross of gold that hung around his neck on a silver chain.

As Savage tipped his hand to his temple, a gesture of salute that mimicked a knight raising his helmet visor, he noted with a wry smile that the Lady Genevieve de Aumale, one of the richest widows in Bordeaux and rumoured to be the archbishop's mistress, sat demurely among the retinue of Archbishop François.

Savage narrowed his eyes as his gaze locked with the handsome young man sitting on Genevieve's right. In his late twenties, he was expensively dressed in furs and like the rest of the nobility showed none of the signs of being famished that the common spectators displayed. His straight brown hair was combed and cut fashionably long. He wore his upper lip hair in an extremely fashionable long, drooping style, what the Italians were beginning to call a *moustacio*. His ice-blue eyes regarded Savage coolly from beneath hooded lids. Savage had met that arrogant gaze before, but could not immediately recall where he had seen him. As if to confirm the recognition, the man nodded to him.

At that moment, the heralds of arms raised their trumpets to signal that the final sword-fighting contest of the day was about to begin. There was no further time to speculate who the man was; there was a tournament to be won.

4

Several miles to the south, a young girl was wondering how to fill the rest of her day. She had finished all her chores and now Galiene wanted desperately to be busy, to find something to fill her mind and blot out the knot of anxiety that gnawed in her belly. To make matters worse, she resented the very fact that she was feeling worried about her father at all.

Her mother was in the kitchen grinding herbs for the potions she made and sold to bring in extra money. The kitchen was the largest room in the house. The shutters of its tall windows were open, filling the room with sunlight. A fire burned in the hearth and over it a black iron cauldron hung, filled with a bubbling concoction that might do anything from ease pain, fight sickness or perhaps make someone fall in love. A rich herbal aroma filled the air, mingling with the scent of freshly cut leaves. Bundles of fresh-picked herbs were stacked on the long, wooden table where Alys stood, working the iron pestle around the stone mortar with deliberate, swift strokes that smeared the green plants to paste.

'Do you need help?' Galiene asked, walking through to the kitchen.

Alys looked up and Galiene was dismayed at how tired and anxious her mother seemed. She was still a beautiful woman, but it was impossible not to notice the small streaks of grey that had crept into her raven-black hair, the gauntness of her cheeks and the new lines that were creeping out around her eyes. To Galiene, it seemed that these had all appeared in the last year since her father had unexpectedly re-entered their lives. Life had been difficult and she could perceive the toll it was taking on her mother. On top of it all, Alys was now with child and Galiene feared most of all the potential consequences of that. Bringing new life into the world was the way many women ended theirs.

'You shouldn't be working in your condition,' Galiene said. 'Sit down at least. I'll work for you.'

Alys smiled and shook her head. 'I need to keep busy. It takes my mind off… things. If you want to help then you can chop those bunches of woundwort.'

Moving to the table, Galiene took up a knife and began slicing the herbs, but though her intentions were good she felt a surge of renewed anger at her father for putting her mother through such concern. 'You're worried about him, aren't you?' she said. 'You're worried he might be injured in the tournament.'

'Aren't you?' Alys returned, her head cocked, one eyebrow raised.

Galiene scowled and tutted. 'As if I would worry about him! Does he worry about us when he goes off enjoying himself at the tournament while we stay behind and work? He couldn't wait to ride away this morning.'

Alys smiled at the transparency of her daughter's false denial. 'Galiene, your father is risking life and limb so we can buy food.' Her voice took on a tone of gentle admonishment. 'At least give him that credit. Don't worry about him anyway. He's a big lad and can take care of himself.'

Frowning, Galiene went back to work and after a little time she began to sing. Alys listened, always amazed at the beauty of the music her daughter was capable of making. On long, lonely nights in the castle back in Ireland, Galiene's singing had been her one source of comfort. As she worked, Alys contemplated those times and their current situation. Galiene had always been a fiercely independent child, quick-witted and self-reliant and as she got older those traits were becoming stronger. Alys knew that adjusting to their new life was hard for her. Since her birth there had been just the two of them in their castle in Ireland. But then Richard Savage had returned and suddenly Galiene had gained a father, but lost both her home and her newly married mother's sole attention.

Now, on top of all that, there would be a new baby and Galiene may find herself further edged out. Alys worried constantly whether Richard and she had done the right thing for their daughter by taking her away from all that was familiar and planting her in France. Still, Alys was also resolved that life was better here. The famine was hard but it was striking Ireland as well and at least they were away from that war-riven island and the poison it seemed to instil in the hearts of those who lived there. The manor house they rented in France was spacious and way beyond anything they could have afforded back home. The precarious nature of Gascony's political status meant that it was difficult for the archbishop to get tenants in a region that could at any moment be overrun by the French. However, it was peaceful at the moment and that was more than could be said about Ireland. Not that they had the choice to go back anyway. Her castle was now in the hands of Edward Bruce and the Scottish army. Richard had nothing. Alys concluded that even if they stayed here for only a short while, it would be good for the child to be away from Ireland for a time.

Child? As always, Alys checked herself. It was so hard to think that Galiene was really no longer a child. She was approaching a very difficult age: less biddable than she used to be, argumentative and often distracted. Her breasts were fast developing and any day now her courses would start. It would not be long before Galiene would find a boy of her own. If not, a husband would be found for her. Alys bit her lip, hoping that they could put that day off for a little longer.

After a while Galiene's attention began to wander once more, her knife poised over the growing pile of cut herbs, her gaze turned to the window. Noticing the drop in her daughter's productivity, Alys commented, 'I don't see much chopping going on over there.'

Galiene did not reply but she started slicing herbs once more, though her movements were far from enthusiastic.

'I need some more sorrel,' Alys said, judging that Galiene could be more productive in another way. 'Will you go down to the clearing near the brook and pick some for me?'

The look on Galiene's face suggested she had just been asked to walk to Jerusalem and back instead of to the bottom of the garden, but she put down her knife and walked towards the door.

'If you're lucky, maybe you'll bump into that boy who

seems so keen on you,' Alys added, a hint of mischief in her voice.

Galiene, her face flushing, glared at her mother. With an exasperated cry she turned and left, slamming the kitchen door behind her. Smiling to herself, Alys went back to pounding her mortar.

Galiene wandered past the empty sty that had once contained their pig; the barren, muddy patch that had failed to yield any vegetables this year; and the coop where their lonely hen pecked forlornly at the dirt. Beyond, a thick hedgerow and trees marked the edge of a river that flowed behind the manor house.

Enjorran, the boy her mother had referred to, was an annoying creature whose father owned the next manor a few fields away. Recently he had begun hanging around their property, trying to talk to her, asking if she wanted to go for walks and such. He was a gangly boy, full of his own importance and she found his attention irritating, though at the same time and in a way she could not express, strangely interesting.

Ducking to go through a gap in the hedge, she entered a glade surrounded by trees and bushes. The ground sloped down sharply to a little river, barely more than a stream that meandered between the manors. Galiene, crouching, carefully slid her way down the slope to where the wild sorrel grew in abundant clumps beside the water.

She froze.

Galiene felt tingles of shock coursing through her body.

Her chest was tight and it was hard to breathe. She wanted to turn her eyes away but could not.

Enjorran was indeed in the glade. However, he lay face down on the ground, a large puddle of dark red blood spread beneath him and dribbled into the stream, causing its brown waters to tinge with pink. The ghastly white pallor of the skin on his neck and hands told her all she needed to know.

He was dead.

Galiene gasped. Panicked thoughts ran through her mind. She must go. She must get back to her mother.

Three men stepped out of the bushes. Hard-faced, broken-nosed, they wore chain mail shirts and iron helmets. They were men of war.

'Get her,' one of them said. Galiene recognised the tongue he spoke in; it was Irish.

She turned to run but they were on her in seconds. Strong arms grabbed her and she was lifted off the ground, her legs thrashing uselessly in the air. A sour-smelling, hard-skinned hand clamped over her mouth and nose.

From the manor house she could hear her mother's screams.

5

The hastilude was a contest for sport, not to the death, therefore it had a set of strict rules designed to avoid serious injury. To determine the winner there was a scoring system: five points for a hit on the body, ten for a head strike and none for anything below the waist. Points were deducted for fouls. Victory could also be achieved by incapacitating or knocking an opponent out, but only by using one's sword. To enforce the rules, four sergeants in full armour and armed with heavy quarterstaffs stood equidistant to each other around the edge of the arena.

'Gentlemen,' the herald said, 'on your guard.'

In the centre of the ring, the German set himself into the *vom Tag* defensive position, one that enabled the swordsman either to attack or defend from above his head; hence known as "the roof". His right leg was straight and extended forward, left leg bent and ready to spring, sword blade pointing straight up to the sky, both hands holding the hilt beside his right ear.

Conversely, Savage assumed the Alber, the swordplay stance known as "the fool" because it appeared the swordsman was actually dropping his guard. His right leg was forward and bent at the knee. Both hands grasped the hilt of his sword, its point trailing downward towards the ground. He tried to regulate his breathing, emptying his mind of all thoughts and preparing himself for the coming battle. The words of his old Templar sword master came back to him: "Do not think. Act. Feel the opponent's attack and react to it."

After a brief pause, von Mahlberg suddenly sprang forward closing the gap between them in an instant. He attacked with an *Oberhau* – over-hew – one of the five master cuts taught in the German sword schools. His sword swung in an overhead arc designed to come down right on top of Savage's head, the great blade sweeping through the air with a noise like a swan's beating wing. Clearly he meant to finish this as quickly as possible.

Savage just had time to raise both hands up and to the right of his head, pulling his own blade into a defensive position. The German's weapon smashed down onto it with a dull metal clang. Savage felt his shoulders jolted by the impact. The blow was heavy enough to repel his own weapon so that von Mahlberg's blade struck Savage a glancing blow on the forehead before it slid off down the length of the claidheamh mòr towards the downward-held point. There were no sparks, both swords having been blunted for the tournament, and the wet metal merely slithered along its foil.

Savage broke the clinch of weapons and sprang backwards away from his opponent.

'Cinque,' the herald called out, announcing that the German had just scored five points.

Savage swore at himself. He would not be able to sustain this fight for too long. Fatigue and hunger had sapped his body and his tired mind had failed to react as he was trained to do. The sword master's words echoed in his mind once more: "Oppose hard with soft; strong with weak. Flow with your opponent's attack and use it against him." He had simply blocked instead of counter-attacking.

Von Mahlberg grinned, clearly seeing victory within his grasp. Savage took a different defensive stance, this time choosing the *Pflugh* – the plough – both legs crouched, the hilt of his sword grasped at his rearward left hip, the point raised and aimed at the German's face.

His opponent settled back into the vom Tag guard, though he bounced on his thighs, threatening to strike at any moment. When the attack came it was another over-hew, his blade scything through the air directly towards the centre of Savage's head.

This time Savage responded. Instinctively he reacted with another of the five master cut strokes, the *Krumphau* – crooked hew. His weapon came up hilt first, bringing the blade forward to meet the German's sword as it came towards him. This time, instead of simply blocking, Savage moved his sword diagonally, diverting the path of his opponent's blade away from its target and at the same time sending the point of his own rattling towards the German's hands.

Von Mahlberg's eyes widened in surprise. He was forced to leap backwards, breaking the bind of the blades as he did so, to avoid Savage landing a blow on his hands or lower arms. The expression on his face betrayed that this came as a shock to him. He had obviously not expected to meet someone here who knew the secret master cuts of the German sword schools.

As he and his opponent settled back into their guard stances, Savage caught a glimpse of movement in the seats at the top of the stands. Two rough-looking men-at-arms rose from their seats and began making their way to the stairs that exited the arena. *The audience must be getting bored already*, Savage thought. It was time to liven things up.

He swung a *Mittelhau* – middle hew – a sweeping attack designed to hit the left-hand side of his opponent's midriff. It was a risky move, as hitting below the waist was strictly forbidden, but he had to take the chance. Savage could not afford to lose. If von Mahlberg lost, all he would miss out on was a night of debauchery in the brothels and taverns of Bordeaux. If Savage lost, his family would not eat.

The German swung downward, his longsword connecting with the claidheamh mòr before it struck his body, forcing it down and away from its target. At the same time he quickly swung his hips to the right, out of the way of Savage's blade, but he also took a step outward with his left leg so that it very deliberately fell into the descending path of the claidheamh mòr. Carried on by the momentum of his swing, Savage was unable to divert its path before his blade struck the German midway down his left thigh.

The blow was far from substantial, merely bruising, for not only was its initial venom deflected by the German's counter-blow, but in the last moment Savage had tried to pull back. As well as that, von Mahlberg wore thick, padded leather breeches that protected his legs and the blade had been blunted for the tournament anyway. Despite all this, the German let out a gasp, dropped his sword and yelled loudly as if in acute pain. His left hand grasping his thigh he sank to one knee, his right hand outstretched towards the herald in mute appeal.

'Foul blow!' the herald shouted. 'Syr Savage hit below the waist and so loses fifteen points.'

'Oh come on!' Savage turned to the herald, his eyes ablaze with indignation. 'That was deliberate. He moved into my swing to make sure I hit him!'

The herald at first frowned, not quite understanding what Savage had said. To judge from his disdainful expression he saw only a scrawny, black-haired knight in ragged clothes and dented rusty armour. Worse, while Savage spoke in French, ostensibly the same language as the herald, it was a much harsher, altogether more guttural version of the tongue, not just with the Norman accent but also tempered and twisted by its having spent over a century in Ireland. The Frenchman's face cleared as his mind finally deciphered Savage's complaint. He gave a condescending smile, betraying the fact that he was well aware of what the German had done, but was unsympathetic, presumably thinking that if Savage was naive enough to fall for the tricks of a professional fighter then that was his problem.

At Savage's display of disobedience and insolence to the herald, the bored sergeants-at-arms moved forward, quarter-staffs raised, eyes aglitter with the possibility that they might be about to get the chance to deliver a beating.

Glancing at them, Savage shrugged, shook his head and turned back to his opponent. The sergeants hesitated, disappointment etched on their faces, then relaxed back to their original positions.

Quick as a viper, von Mahlberg attacked. Sword held high above his head, quad muscles bulging, he sprang forward from his thighs, rushing in close to Savage and inside his guard.

Knowing he could not bring his sword down to protect himself, the only thing Savage could do was try to get out of the way before the blow landed, but in that instant he felt a crushing weight on his right foot. The German had intentionally planted his iron-studded boot on Savage's instep to prevent him jumping away from the descending blade.

Savage's reaction was instinctive rather than malicious, born not of years spent playing in tournaments, but in real battles where there were no rules: situations where only instinct might save you from certain death.

He dropped his grip on his sword and lashed out with his bent right arm in a vicious elbow punch. The blow was so fast and his opponent so close that von Mahlberg stood no chance. The point of Savage's elbow smashed into the right side of the German's jaw with an audible crack of bone. His eyes rolled up into his head and the weight of his unconscious body crashed into Savage, forcing him to take a step backwards. Still descending, the longsword dropped from von Mahlberg's unfeeling hands and fell to the ground wide of his intended target of Savage's head.

As Savage stepped away, the German slid down the length of his body onto the muddy sawdust, a dribble of blood running from the corner of his mouth.

Chaos erupted among the spectators. A few stood to applaud Savage, but most roared their disapproval. Shouting and arguments erupted as citizens tried to work out if the bets they had placed were still valid. The sergeants rushed forward again, quarterstaffs raised once more, but this time they formed a custodial ring around Savage. The herald blew his trumpet repeatedly to try to gain attention while the archbishop, like the rest of the crowd, was on his feet, pointing and shouting in protest at such blatant disregard for the tournament rules.

'Shit!' Savage spat into the sawdust, realising that his chances of winning the prize money were now lying in the mud with the unconscious German.

Up on the nobles' dais, the archbishop was gesturing for calm and soon the general hubbub died down. Once a modicum of decorum had been restored, the cleric waved a commanding hand to the herald, signalling that he could now proceed with whatever judgement he wished to declare.

'Use of anything but the sword as a weapon is not allowed,' the herald announced. 'Syr Savage is disqualified for cheating. The winner is Syr Heinrich von Mahlberg.'

Another furore erupted as those who had bet on Savage to win voiced their objections. It was not as long-lived or as loud, however, as a lot fewer spectators had believed the scruffy, starving, Irish knight with the poor equipment and straggling black hair stood much of a chance against the tall, professional, well-nourished German swordsman.

As the noise died away, the archbishop turned down his mouth and nodded in an exaggerated way to show he agreed with the decision. At that moment, the young man Savage had recognised but not been able to put a name to at the start of the match, leaned over and touched the cleric's sleeve.

'Surely von Mahlberg does not deserve to win either,' he said loudly. He too spoke Norman French, but with the accent of those who ruled England. 'He allowed himself to be knocked out. He should not be rewarded for that.'

Savage now knew exactly who the young man regarding him with arrogant blue eyes was: Baron Roger Mortimer, one of the most powerful noblemen of England and rumoured lover of Queen Isabella, wife to Edward II of England. The last time Savage had seen Mortimer they had both been in the presence of King Edward of England. Savage, as a condemned heretic, was anticipating death at the hands of his captors. The king, swayed by his barons – Mortimer foremost amongst them – had instead offered him the highly dangerous mission to Ireland to spy on Edward Bruce's army. Having little choice, Savage had accepted. Mortimer had threatened then that if he ran away agents would be sent to kill him. And Savage had done just that.

Staring into that haughty face, Savage reflected that the young nobleman's presence here today could be neither coincidental nor beneficial.

The archbishop seemed surprised. 'Are you sure?' he asked. 'He is your man.'

Mortimer nodded.

'Very well then,' the cleric shrugged. 'No one wins. The contest is void.'

There were general moans of disappointment, some shouts of disagreement and even some howls of laughter from the spectators around the arena. Savage decided that with Mortimer there, he needed to get away as fast as possible. He pushed past the sergeants, who now that the outcome had been decided saw no reason to detain him. With regret he replaced the claidheamh mòr then grabbed his own paltry equipment from the weapons' rack and hurried down the little passageway through which the competitors entered and exited the arena.

The tournament arena for the hastilude had been built in a field just outside the walls of Bordeaux. Around the wooden arena were various booths where hawkers tried to sell what meagre wares they had in this time of famine. There were also corrals holding horses and mules and a little collection of leather tents were set up for the competitors to change in and prepare for the fights inside the arena. Savage, his gear tucked under his arm, headed for the tent where the rest of his belongings were.

Sweeping aside the tent flap he went straight in then stopped dead. Sitting in a folding chair in the centre of the tent was a big, dangerous-looking man in chain mail and kettle helmet. Savage recognised him as one of the spectators he had spotted leaving the arena before the end of the tournament.

'King Edward Bruce sends his regards,' a voice said behind him.

Then Savage felt a massive blow across the back of his skull.

6

Savage pitched forwards. He hit the ground hard, landing face first in the straw that covered the ground in the tent. For a couple of moments his vision dissolved into whiteness filled with multi-coloured stars then it coalesced once more back to reality.

An arm snaked around his neck, a fist grabbed his hair and he was hauled to his feet. As the hand released his hair Savage felt the cold metallic point of a blade digging into his throat, just below his right jaw.

'One move and I'll open your bastard throat,' a voice hissed in his ear. The voice spoke French, but with an Irish accent, and it came from a mouth so close behind him he could smell his assailant's fetid breath and feel his stubbly cheek against the back of his neck.

'You should lay off the garlic, friend,' Savage managed to gasp. 'You smell worse than a French whore.'

'Shut your mouth,' his attacker spat, kicking with his knee up into Savage's right side. Savage grunted in pain as the blow hit his kidney.

He turned his attention to the man who sat in the chair before him. Big, broad-chested and blunt-faced, he regarded Savage with brown eyes like a pair of marbles. His leather jerkin and chain mail armour had the look of a professional soldier, but not a nobleman. Then again, Savage, who was born heir to a manor in Ireland, hardly looked like a lord either. While the man appeared to be in fighting condition, his pale face was slightly pudgy and his hair, which was silvering to grey, was mowed to a stubble. He looked at Savage with an expression of slight amusement.

'Syr Richard Savage,' he said. 'We've come a long way to see you. You're a hard man to find.'

He was Scottish; there was little doubt of that by his accent. Given the events of the previous year's adventure, and the fact that there was a knife at his throat, Savage knew it was safe to assume that this did not bode well.

'My name is Gib Harper,' the Scotsman continued. 'I am King Edward's bodyguard and right-hand man. The man holding the blade at your throat is Aodh of the Clan Eoghan, from the Kingdom of Tyr Eoghan.'

Savage had no doubt now he was in deep trouble. The King of Tyr Eoghan, Domnall Ui Neill, was the Irish King who had invited Edward Bruce to invade Ireland. He had fought against Ui Neill's warriors in a battle at Carrickfergus Castle the year before. He had never heard of Harper, but if he was who he said he was, then whatever message he had would not be a good one.

'The only King Edward I've heard of is the one who rules England,' Savage said. 'What makes Edward Bruce think he can call himself by that title?'

Harper smiled, but it was an unpleasant expression that looked like it actually caused him pain to do it. He drew a long dagger from a sheath at his side and looked at the blade. 'Several things,' he said. 'Firstly, he has conquered most of the island. Secondly, the people of that land have declared him their rightful high king, preferring him – a man of their own blood – to English lapdogs like you. But we're not here to talk politics. My lord Edward sends his greetings and asks for the return of his property.'

'I don't know what you mean,' Savage said then flinched as the Irishman dug his knee into his right kidney again.

'Don't play games, Savage,' Harper said, the "smile" disappearing completely from his face. 'Last year you travelled to Scotland and stole a very precious item from my master's brother, King Robert Bruce of Scotland. We know this and I've been sent to get it back. Now stop pissing me around and tell me where it is.'

Savage's heart sank further. He had hoped the Bruce brothers did not know who had taken their property. How on earth had Edward Bruce worked out it was him who had stolen the Grail? They had left no one alive to tell the tale on the mountain where it was hidden. Someone must have betrayed him. There was no point denying it now, however.

'Oh, you mean the Holy Grail?' Savage said, affecting as nonchalant a tone as he could muster. 'I threw that in a bog.'

This elicited another knee in the kidney. 'Don't mess us about, Savage. I'll slit your gizzard, I swear it,' the Irishman growled in his ear. 'Just give me an excuse, God help me, and I'll do it. You killed my cousin in Carrick last year.'

Wincing, Savage continued to look at Harper. 'If you kill me you'll never find it.'

Harper shook his head. 'Oh, we'll find it, Savage, don't you worry. It'll just take a wee bit longer without your help. Don't worry though. We're not as thick as we look. We know all about you and know you're not likely to respond to personal threats. We're taking other measures to ensure you help us out. So make it easy on yourself and tell us what you did with the Grail.'

The truth was Savage actually *had* thrown Robert Bruce's Grail into a bog. He realised, however, that to insist on that could seriously shorten his life. 'All right,' he said, a plan forming in his mind.

Harper made his painful smile expression once more. 'Good man. It would have been a waste to kill a man with your reputation. You know that Edward Bruce could do with men like you in his army?'

'English lapdogs?' Savage said.

'Trained knights,' Harper responded.

'There's one problem with that,' Savage said.

Harper raised an eyebrow.

'Fighting alongside bastards from Tyr Eoghan.'

As Savage had calculated, this provoked another knee in the kidney. Knowing that the man behind him was now standing on one leg, Savage immediately stamped backwards with his left foot, crushing the Irishman's toes as he did so. Aodh gave a cry of surprise and collapsed backwards. The grip on Savage's neck loosened and he was able to twist himself round. The knife was away from his throat, but the Irishman clung on desperately to him, knowing his life depended on it. Now Savage was turned and bent over, the falling Irishman hanging around his neck and pulling him down with him. He could hear Harper springing out of the chair behind him and he knew his plan had gone badly wrong.

At that moment the tent flap swept aside and Mortimer entered.

All three men in the tent paused, distracted by the newcomer. Immediately after Mortimer came the German swordsman who Savage had beaten in the final. Harper's eyes widened. Savage recovered from his surprise quickest and smashed his fist into the Irishman's face.

Aodh was stunned but still stabbed upwards with his dagger. Savage had to let go of him, throwing himself upwards to escape the blade. Mortimer stepped forwards quickly and stamped down hard on Aodh's head.

Harper, seeing the situation had radically changed, turned and sprinted for the back of the tent. He threw himself to the ground and wriggled out under the tent wall.

The German, a trickle of blood still on the side of his face from his earlier battle with Savage, respectfully pushed Mortimer aside then drove the blade of his own dagger downward into the notch of the supine Irishman's throat. Aodh made a choking gurgle as blood welled up in his mouth and poured out onto the straw on the ground. His eyes bulged then the light went out of them. His body went limp as death took him.

For a couple of seconds there was silence, until finally Mortimer said, 'Now, what the hell is going on here?'

7

'We meet again, Savage,' Mortimer said. 'I've come a long way to see you.'

'That's what the Scotsman said,' Savage replied. 'I seem to be very popular all of a sudden.'

Despite the fact that Savage looked every bit as shattered as he felt, Mortimer plonked himself down on the only seat in the tent, the folding chair that Gib Harper had recently vacated. The German had left, ordered by the young earl to pursue Harper. Savage sighed and sat down on the ground, rubbing the lump that was already rising on the back of his head.

'So they were Scots?' Mortimer said.

Savage shook his head. 'Only Harper – the one who got away. That fellow on the ground is Irish. From Tyr Eoghan.'

Mortimer started from the chair, his normally suave expression replaced by unusual, animated excitement. 'Harper? Gib Harper?'

'That's who he said he was, yes.'

'I'll be back soon. Wait here,' Mortimer said and dashed out of the tent.

Savage sighed and took Mortimer's place on the chair. Things were going from bad to worse. His plan to win the tournament had failed, which meant Alys and Galiene had no food to look forward to. The Scots had obviously found where he had run to and now Mortimer – and with him the authority of the English Crown – had tracked him down too.

Outside the tent he could hear Mortimer shouting orders and from the clattering of arms and armour that responded to his cries there seemed to be a lot of soldiers with him. Right now there would be no point in trying to run, so all Savage could do was wait. As he did so he spotted Aodh's fallen dagger lying near his feet.

His own sword lay on the ground beside the far wall of the tent, presumably thrown there by Harper. Knowing that Mortimer could return at any moment, Savage judged he did not have time to get that weapon, so he jumped out of the chair and grabbed Aodh's blade, concealing it up the sleeve of his jerkin as he sank back into the chair.

It was not long before Mortimer returned, his face still betraying his excitement.

'If we can capture Gib Harper it would be the first stroke of luck we've had in this damned war with the Scots,' he said. 'Harper is Edward Bruce's henchman. I can't believe the audacity of the man that he should come here to an English realm.'

Seeing that Savage was making no attempt to get up from the chair, the smile died away from the earl's face a little.

'Would you like to accompany me to the archbishop's palace? I am staying there for a few days,' Mortimer said. 'It will be more comfortable than this tent. You can get something to eat and listen to what I have to say. I have a proposition for you.'

Savage's eyes widened. 'You aren't here to arrest me?'

Mortimer smiled again. 'I should. However, I received a glowing report of your activities against the Scots in Ireland from my agent there, Guilleme le Poer.'

Now it was Savage's turn to smile as he recalled the young man, a former Templar like himself, who had played the role of an itinerant preacher in Carrickfergus as a cover for his information-gathering activities.

Feeling he had made his point, Savage struggled stiffly to his feet. There was little to be gained by deliberately antagonising a great lord, particularly one as haughty as Mortimer. The man could easily have him flogged for insolence.

'The archbishop's palace sounds nice but I really have to be getting back home,' he said. 'Perhaps you could tell me what this is all about? Why was the German with you, for a start?'

'Heinrich? He's my bodyguard. An excellent swordsman, as you saw. He has a similar background to you; used to be in the *Deutscher Orden* – the Teutonic Knights. When I heard you were competing in the hastilude I thought it would be amusing to pit him against you. I was curious to see what the outcome would be.'

'Now you know; I won,' Savage said.

'Perhaps this time.' Mortimer stroked his moustache. 'In an open battle I'm not so sure. You did cheat, after all.'

'So did he.' Savage shrugged. 'In the last battle I was in, there was no place for fair play or chivalry.'

'More's the pity,' Mortimer said. 'Irish warfare is such a brutal affair.'

'Indeed it is. Speaking of that, how goes the war in my homeland?'

'Not well.' Mortimer's face became grim. 'Edward Bruce has swept all before him and taken most of the north half of the island. Ui Neill of Tyr Eoghan has joined his cause, of course, and twelve more Irish kings and chieftains swore loyalty to Bruce at Carrickfergus in June.'

'Hardly surprising,' Savage said. 'Domnall Ui Neill invited Bruce to invade. It was him who prepared the way for him in Ulster by killing the key people likely to oppose the invasion. The other Irish kings have no love of the English Crown. They may not love the Scots, but they see them as a way of getting rid of the English.'

Mortimer smiled. 'Perhaps it will surprise you then to hear that many of the Irish are not going over to the side of Bruce?'

'Indeed it does,' Savage said, his eyebrows raised.

'Well that is the only thing that is currently stopping all of Ireland from falling into Bruce's hands,' Mortimer said. 'The Irish are not flocking to his cause. In fact the opposite is starting to happen. Two of the kings who submitted to Bruce at Carrickfergus, MacArtain of Iveagh and MacDuilechain of Clanbrassil, switched sides and ambushed his army as they came south through the Innermalane pass. They were defeated but it gave Earl de Burgh of Ulster and the justiciar, le Bottelier, time to raise the feudal army in Dublin. It was too late for Dundalk though; Bruce reached it first. A wine shipment had just arrived in the port there and the Scots took it with the town. Their soldiers got drunk and that led to a massacre. They slaughtered everyone left in Dundalk; it didn't matter if they were English, Anglo Irish or Gaelic Irish. They say the streets literally ran with blood.'

Savage was quiet for a moment. 'Warriors and wine should never mix,' he eventually said.

Mortimer shook his head. 'It's not uncommon in that war, unfortunately. Old hatreds run too deep. And Bruce's army knows no bounds. Everywhere they take, they loot, they burn and destroy regardless of who owns the property. The native Irish, who at first welcomed the Scots as liberators, now hate them more than they hate the English. At least most of them do. Some of them – those with most advantage to gain and who can use Bruce's army to settle old scores for them – stick with him. The problem is that Bruce brought from Scotland a couple of battalions of experienced soldiers, those who'd been with him in his wars against England, most of them battle-hardened veterans of Bannockburn. They win when they stand and fight but when faced with greater strength they just run away. I met them in battle at Kells—'

'You met Bruce in battle?' This was another surprise for Savage. Mortimer was one of the most powerful barons in England and as far as he knew had nothing to do with Ireland. He owned vast estates in the Welsh Marches and along with the Duke of Lancaster effectively ruled England. King Edward II – so unlike his warlike father who had defeated, captured and gutted William Wallace when he hammered the Scots – had made repeated disastrous military decisions. His defeat by the Scots at Bannockburn and several ill-advised and very public love affairs with handsome but unpopular young men had lost him power and influence over his barons and earned him widespread contempt.

'I've inherited considerable lands in Meath through my

new wife,' Mortimer said. 'I must defend both my lands and my honour. I also, unlike some folk in England, realise the danger that Bruce's Irish adventure poses to England herself. If Ireland falls, Wales will follow. England will then be surrounded on all sides by enemy kingdoms. Ireland is the back door to England. Robert Bruce knows this.'

'And how did you fare in battle against Edward Bruce?' Savage asked, genuinely intrigued.

Mortimer reddened. 'I lost. But if I'd had a company of stout yeoman from my estates in Wales instead of the local militia rabble, things would have been very different, I assure you. However, I had another go at them, which went better. Edmund le Bottelier and I met Bruce's army just north of Dublin at Skerries. There was a battle and we fought them to a standstill. No one can say who won or lost. The Scots lost more men but held the field. Anyway, Bruce decided to turn tail and retreated to Ulster for the winter. That's the way things have been ever since. It's a stalemate.'

'So what has all this got to do with me?' Savage said.

'I'd like you to go back to Ireland, Savage,' Mortimer said. 'You did a good job the last time and we have a special mission for someone with your unique background and talents.'

Savage thought for a moment then he shook his head. 'I'm sorry, but no. Ireland is no longer my country. I have nothing left to fight for there. My home and my family are here with me in Gascony.'

'What about your king?' Mortimer said. 'What about Edward of England?'

Savage laughed, but stopped when he saw the genuine

anger on Mortimer's face. 'Understand, Lord Mortimer, that my family are the most important thing to me in the world. Right now I need to find where they can get their next meal, not go running off to Ireland on some adventure.'

'Think about it, Savage,' Mortimer said. 'There's no surer place to find food in times of famine than in a land of war where you can take it from those who are weaker than you. If you work for me you'll be well rewarded. Von Mahlberg can testify to that. I understand your wife held a castle in Ireland that was lost to the Scots? When Bruce is defeated I'll ensure it's returned. I'll also grant you a manor in Meath on my own estates.'

Savage shook his head. 'I'm sorry but you've wasted your time. You have come all this way for nothing.'

Mortimer's face darkened further. Savage reasoned that a lord as powerful as Mortimer was probably not used to not getting his own way. 'Don't flatter yourself, Savage. I came to France on much more important business. It was coincidence that you also happened to be here and this stratagem came to my mind.'

Savage raised an eyebrow. He was about to respond, "Aye, right," risking a potential flogging from the conceited earl, but at that moment the tent flap opened and Heinrich von Mahlberg re-entered. He was red-faced, sweating and out of breath.

'Did you get Harper?' Mortimer demanded.

His bodyguard shook his head while he caught his breath. 'No. He had a horse waiting in the trees nearby. We chased him across a field but there was no way we could keep up once he got to the horse.'

'What about the town garrison?' Mortimer's voice rose

in pitch. 'Order them out. I want the countryside scoured for that rebel!'

Again, the German shook his head. 'Most of the garrison have been called away. There's something going on outside the town. A manor is burning to the west of the city and they've gone to investigate in case it's a French raiding party.'

Savage's mouth dropped open slightly, sudden realisation striking him as he recalled Harper's words earlier: "We're taking other measures to ensure you help us out."

'What's the matter, Savage?' Mortimer said, observing his ashen countenance. 'You look like you've seen a ghost.'

Savage, however, had already picked up his sword, pushed past von Mahlberg and was running out of the tent.

8

Savage drove his wretched, skinny horse mercilessly across the countryside. The small manor he had leased from the archbishop lay a few miles west of the walls of Bordeaux. To call it a manor was to flatter it, for it was little more than a decrepit moated farmhouse surrounded by a few fields, but it was all he and Alys could afford.

A column of thick black smoke was boiling up into the sky from beyond the trees in precisely the direction of his home. As he kicked his unfortunate steed to travel faster, a deep anxiety gripped him and his chest filled with a terrible sense of dread. He hoped desperately that the source of the smoke was not the manor house but at the same time was certain that his hope was forlorn.

He raced along the road that led away from the city then cut across a wide, rolling meadow towards some woods. The rain had made the going heavy and the horse's hooves dug great clumps of mud up from the ground that tumbled through the air behind him. There was a short track through the trees and Savage rode through, ducking branches that threatened to knock him clean from the saddle and urging his horse to jump roots that could send it sprawling and break his neck. After a brief, reckless journey he emerged into another meadow – the one that led to his house.

As he came out from among the trees, Savage's darkest fears were realised. His house was a blazing ruin, the roof completely gone. From every window and the open front door flames roared, leaping high into the sky to merge with the churning black smoke that rose towards the clouds. As Savage approached across the meadow he seemed to be riding into an invisible wall of heat that was almost unbearable, even from fifty paces away. Nothing could survive inside the inferno that his home had become.

Sick with dread, he saw a group of soldiers from the town's garrison, who had ridden out to investigate the cause of the blaze, standing a little way off towards the trees. It seemed they were gathered around someone on the ground. Savage kicked his mount into a final gallop over to them, leaping from the saddle as the exhausted horse skidded trembling to a halt.

'What's going on? This is my house. What happened here?' he demanded, fear making his voice rise much higher than normal.

'Raiders, my lord,' one of the soldiers said. 'They've torched the place. This woman is the only survivor. We managed to pull her out just as the fire was taking hold.'

Savage looked down. The woman lay on her back; her normally beautiful face was a magenta mask of dried blood. Her red dress was torn and ragged; scratches, bruises and cuts ravaged the pale white skin that was visible on her arms, legs and body. Fresh blood oozed from what looked like a stab wound on her shoulder. Her eyes were closed and she was not moving.

'Alys!' he cried and fell to his knees beside her, deep waves of despair overwhelming him at the sight of his wife in such a state.

To his amazement, she opened her eyes. It was difficult for her; blood caked her eyebrows and her pain was evident from her agonised expression. For a moment she looked confused then she caught sight of Savage. A look of relief spread across her face and she struggled to raise her head. 'Richard,' she croaked, 'thank God you're here.'

'I'm sorry I left you, Alys,' Savage sobbed, grasping her head in his hands to support her, tears streaming down his face and dripping onto hers.

Wincing, Alys shook her head. 'Never mind about that now,' she managed with some effort. Her voice was little more than a breathless whisper. 'They were Scottish; soldiers of Edward Bruce. They took Galiene. They've taken her back to Ireland. They said you must…' Alys sighed, her eyes closed again and she slumped against him.

For a moment Savage thought his own heart had stopped, then he saw the slight movement of her breast and realised she was not dead but unconscious. He gently laid her back onto the ground.

'Sir.' One of the soldiers laid a hand on his shoulder. 'You must get her to the hospital. The nuns in Sainte-Eulalie in the city run an infirmary.'

Savage nodded, distractedly. The soldier was right. He had to get there fast if Alys was to survive.

9

Much later, after darkness had fallen, Savage stood in the small grass-covered square that filled the middle of the outer cloistered courtyard of the convent of Sainte-Eulalie. The near-omnipresent grey clouds had for once cleared away and, looking up, Savage could see stars speckling the black sky. The hypnotic, ethereal sound of the nuns singing compline prayers, the last of the day, drifted through the air from the convent chapel.

He had draped Alys across the saddle-bow of his unfortunate horse and ridden the struggling beast back to the city. It was probably the last straw for the animal. Savage fully expected that when he finally left the convent the beast would not be where he had left it, tethered outside. Its heart having finally given out, it would be gone, its corpse now the makings of a feast for the starving citizens of the town.

The ride could have been the end of Alys as well, but he had to take the chance. If her bleeding was not stopped she would have died anyway.

Men were not permitted to enter the convent proper, and so Savage had to wait outside in the cloister with all the other sullen, anxious husbands and fathers who loitered in their own worlds of distracted apprehension. In this case, no news was good news. They would allow him entrance if Alys was dying, and only then, and the longer he waited outside, the more his hope grew. They had been living together for only seven months, but now Savage simply could not imagine life without Alys. The desolate hole her death would leave in him was too painful to contemplate.

But what of Galiene? His anxiety grew again as he thought of the girl in the hands of Gib Harper and a Scottish war band. If he ever got her back, this would be one more thing she would blame him for.

If he got her back? Savage felt a hot surge in his chest and inhaled deeply through his nose, trying to quell the black anger that suddenly boiled within him. It was not a question of if, it was when. He could not think otherwise. And when he caught up with Harper he would make him pay dearly.

As the day drew on, nuns came out to give the waiting men news of their loved ones and either brought them inside to say goodbye or delivered a more comforting message that sent them home for the night with looks of relief on their faces.

As darkness fell, Savage found he was the only man left in the cloister. By now his frayed nerves were worn to overwrought jitters. He felt strung out and dizzy and suddenly remembered that he had not eaten anything since breakfast. Not that this was unusual these days, but he had expended his energy fighting in a tournament, which intensified his gnawing hunger.

Swaying slightly as he looked up at the stars, he heard the door into the convent open. Looking round he saw a young nun glide into the courtyard, the lantern she carried casting her shadow on the grass. Her habit was greyish white, made of simple undyed wool that was disconcertingly splashed with gouts of dried blood. She looked to be in her early twenties and as she approached and looked up at Savage from beneath the black wimple that covered her head, he saw that she had beautiful brown eyes. In her hands were a jug and a scrap of bread with some cheese on it.

'Syr Richard Savage?' she asked.

Savage nodded, swallowing a sudden rush of saliva at the sight of food.

The nun held it out to him. 'I am Sister Etienne. I have been tending to your wife. Here: you must eat,' she said. 'I am sorry but it is all we can spare in this terrible time of famine.'

Savage grasped the morsels and wolfed them down so fast he began to choke. The nun, an expression of slight reproof at his lack of self-control on her face, held out the jug. He took it and drank deep from the watered wine it contained, feeling it wash the bread and cheese down and clearing his throat.

'What news of Alys?' he gasped.

'I bring good news,' the nun said. 'We believe she will survive her injuries, though it will take a time for her to recover. She was beaten terribly. She lost a back tooth, her shoulder was dislocated. Some of her ribs are bruised, perhaps cracked, and she was stabbed. Your wife was extremely lucky the blades did not penetrate any vital organs. As it was, we sewed the wounds and bathed them. She is covered in bruises and cuts but nothing that will not heal.' The nun laid a hand on Savage's arm. 'God has been merciful to you,' she said with a smile.

'What of the baby—?' Savage began.

Sister Etienne dropped her hand from his arm and looked down. 'I'm sorry, but she has lost the child.'

Savage turned away, heaving a huge sigh. His shoulders dropped as he threw his head back, face raised to the dark heavens and the cold, indifferent stars. 'He has not been completely merciful then,' he said in a hoarse whisper.

The nun shot a reproachful glance at Savage then said, 'Alys sent a message to you. She said you must not worry about her. Save Galiene.'

'I must see her,' Savage said through gritted teeth, fixing the nun with a glare so full of intent that the young woman physically flinched.

She quickly recovered herself though and shook her head. 'That is not permitted. If she was in danger of dying we would carry her out for you to see her, but thankfully that is not her fate.'

Savage fixed the little nun before him with a belligerent glare. 'And who is going to stand in my way?'

Sister Etienne looked back at him with what Savage recognised was a will as strong as his own. She was young, but her work in the infirmary had no doubt given her years of bitter experience in dealing with upset, distraught and unreasonable relatives. Her knuckles tightened white around the crucifix that hung around her neck and he knew she would stand firm.

'I will,' she said. There was anger in her voice. 'And the archbishop will hang any man who breaks into a convent. He has done it before. What good would you be to your wife or daughter if your corpse is swinging from the gibbet?'

Savage looked down, the anger dying within him. This

was not a fight worth having. 'I want to be with her. I want to comfort her,' he mumbled. 'She was so excited about the baby...' He stifled a sob, hoping the nun did not notice.

The sister's expression softened. 'It is pointless anyway: she is asleep, and will be for a long while. We have given her a draught of poppies to ensure she gets the rest she needs. Do not worry. She will not be alone when she wakes. I will make sure of it. The best comfort you could give her is to find your daughter. Now it is late and you should go home and get some sleep yourself.'

Savage nodded, realising she was right. Reluctantly he turned away and walked, half in a daze, across the courtyard to the outer gate of the convent. It was only when he was outside in the street that he realised he no longer had a home to go to.

10

Surrounded by high walls, the archbishop's palace lay just off the market square in the centre of the town. Richard Savage approached it along a maze of pitch-black streets lined by ranks of higgledy-piggledy, crowded and overhanging timber-framed houses and shops. The moon was low, providing scant illumination thanks to the overhanging buildings and any light that might have spilled from the town's dwellings was firmly contained behind closed and bolted window shutters. His eyes had become accustomed to the dark, but even so, at times the shadows became so impenetrable that all he could do was run an outstretched hand along the building walls in an effort to guide himself through the pitch-blackness. Thankfully, save for a few drunks staggering home from the tavern, the streets were quiet and largely empty. That was no reason to drop his guard, however. Robbers often stalked their prey on the night-time streets and most decent people tended to avoid the town after dark.

Savage's nose wrinkled at the stench rising from the sewer that ran down the middle of the street. The tiny amount of moonlight cast enough silver glitters on the slow-moving ooze to enable him to make a reasonable assessment of where the edges were. He leapt over it, then banged a fist against the huge wooden gates that blocked the entranceway to the palace. A barred peephole slid open in the gate at head level and the suspicious eye of one of the archbishop's guards glared out.

'What do you want?' the man asked, his breath rushing out of the gap in the door in a haze of garlic and sour wine.

'I want to see Earl Mortimer,' Savage said. 'Tell him Richard Savage has changed his mind.'

The peephole slid shut again. After a long wait a door in the gate finally opened and Savage stepped through into a courtyard where burning torches chased away the darkness. As he squinted, trying to readjust his eyes to the sudden light, he saw to his surprise a sort of large and opulent waggon sitting in the courtyard. Shaped like a rectangular domed box it was suspended from four wheels by leather straps and its slatted sides were brightly painted. He wondered if perhaps this was a *chars branlant* or "rocking carriage", a recent invention that he had heard but never seen. He could see no coat of arms or distinguishing marks, but it surely could not belong to Mortimer or the archbishop; lords of the land and the church went everywhere on horseback. Such a fancy waggon as this could only be used to transport a high-born woman. Perhaps Mortimer had acquired it for his wife Joan and brought her along with him. On the other hand, it could equally belong to the Lady Genevieve de Aumale, but surely the archbishop would not be quite so blatant in his indiscretions?

Standing waiting at the main door of the house was Heinrich von Mahlberg. Despite the late hour he still wore his padded leather leggings and jerkin covered by a chain mail vest. His lips formed a completely mirthless smile that was more a threat than a welcome. Even in the flickering torchlight a dark bruise could be seen where Savage's elbow had connected with the German's chin in the tournament.

'Syr Savage, you have come crawling back, perhaps?' von Mahlberg said. 'Did something change your mind?'

'I'm surprised you're such a sore loser, von Mahlberg,' Savage replied.

'I am not, if I lose fair and square. You cheated. It was not fair,' the German said.

'Life's not fair,' Savage said.

Von Mahlberg took a step forward. He puffed out his chest and drew himself up to his full height. His face was pale in the torchlight. He glared down at the shorter man with eyes that blazed with barely suppressed rage.

'I am the greatest swordsman in Europe,' he said in a voice that was little more than a growl. 'I don't lose, Savage. Especially to a low born cheat from the bogs of Ireland. A heretic, catamite Templar. We will fight again someday, and I will win. And it will not be in a stupid hastilude for the entertainment of fools. It will be *A l'outrance*: to the death. Mark my words.'

Savage met his gaze for a moment, then realised this was wasting precious time.

'Are you going to take me to Mortimer or not?' he said.

Von Mahlberg sneered and held out his right hand. 'First I must have your sword, then I will take you to my master.'

Savage hesitated, realising that the long war sword strapped across his back was his last possession in the world. He had no choice though. Right now there was one man on Earth who could get him back to Ireland fast and give him a chance of rescuing Galiene. That man was Mortimer. With a sigh he unstrapped the sword and handed it to the German.

Von Mahlberg ushered Savage into the house. They entered an impressive though unlit entrance hall with a very high, beamed ceiling. Savage was shown to a room on the right.

'Wait here,' von Mahlberg said, leaving Savage alone in the room.

Looking around him, Savage took in his surroundings. After the stench of the streets the heady, perfumed aroma of spices mixed with rose petals and other fragrant herbs among the fresh floor rushes was overpowering, though infinitely preferable. He seemed to be in a large dining hall, the sort of grand room that wealthy nobles had in their houses and castles for entertaining important guests. A fire burned low in the huge grate and a single torch flickered in a bracket on the wall, but it shed enough light to show the opulence of the surroundings. The walls were panelled with expensive dark yew wainscoting; rich woven tapestries depicting saints' martyrdoms and other religious themes were hung above it. A huge polished wooden table stretched the length of the room.

Savage noted that the remnants of a meal still sat at one end. From the cups and knives it seemed that two people had recently eaten supper there and he wondered that the servants would be so careless as to leave the mess behind. Looking up, he saw that the hall was the whole height of the two-storeyed house, rising up to dark rafters and cross-beams in the roof. At the level of the second storey, the wall on one side of the hall opened up into a minstrels' gallery.

Savage continued to wait, passing the time by examining a particularly gory crucifixion scene that bedecked the wall to the right of the fireplace, complete with an extremely miserable-looking Christ whose bloody, bleeding wounds were vividly outlined in scarlet wool.

After a while the door swung open; von Mahlberg had returned, this time accompanied by Mortimer. Savage frowned. The earl was wrapped in a large woven blanket and appeared to be naked beneath it.

'I'm sorry if I have got you out of bed, my lord,' Savage said, aware that the German had taken up a stance near the door, which he could not help but notice cut off his escape route.

'Don't worry,' Mortimer said with a conspiratorial smile. 'I wasn't asleep... But how is your wife? The archbishop told me about what happened to your house. I'm very sorry.'

'She's going to survive, thank God,' Savage said. As Mortimer had not mentioned it he decided to say nothing about Galiene. 'We were lucky. Alys is under the care of the sisters in the convent of Sainte-Eulalie.'

'She is in good hands then,' Mortimer said. 'Scots bastards! I trust that is what has prompted you to reconsider my offer?'

Savage nodded. 'If your offer still stands. What exactly is it that you want me to do?'

'I will explain, but first would you like a cup of wine?' Not waiting for an answer, Mortimer walked over to the table and lifted a jug. Observing that Savage was eyeing the dirty platters he gave a rueful smile and shrugged. 'Sorry about the mess. The archbishop has kindly let me stay here and has gone with his house servants to another of his manors outside the town for the duration of my stay. Von Mahlberg and my soldiers are not good at keeping house I fear.'

Savage stroked his close-cropped beard to conceal a sly smile. It was inconceivable that Mortimer did not travel with a manservant, nor would the archbishop have left him without at least one domestic servant. The earl was up to something and he had a good idea what. 'So aside from your bodyguards, it's just you and your wife staying here then is it?' he said, trying to make the question sound as innocent as possible.

Mortimer looked puzzled. 'My wife? Lady Joan is at home in Ireland. I hope and pray she is safe there.'

That confirmed it. Mortimer was here to meet a woman and judging by the expensive waggon contraption outside she was a very important woman. Clearly the obliging archbishop had discreetly vacated his home to allow the earl to enjoy this love nest undisturbed.

'Wine would be most welcome,' Savage said, steering the conversation away from any potential awkwardness. 'It's been quite a day for me.'

Mortimer filled the two cups and handed one to Savage who took a deep, appreciative gulp of the rich, ruby-coloured liquid.

'This must be one of the blessings of living in this French shithole,' Mortimer said. 'At least they make the finest wines in the world. That's reason enough alone for us to keep spilling good English blood to hold on to it. Anyway, as I was telling you earlier, the war against the Scots in Ireland is a stalemate. Edward Bruce and Domnall Ui Neill remain secure in the north. We don't have the army to drive them out of Ulster but likewise they don't have the strength to take Dublin. The famine is taking its toll and we've had to stand down our army. We couldn't feed them and men have their own estates to see to and, being Irish, their own feuds to fight. In the meantime the Scots army live off the land: pillaging, destroying and killing.'

'So why not leave the island divided?' Savage asked. 'Come to terms with the Scots. Half the people of Ulster are related to Scottish clans anyway. It's probably the most sensible option if you want peace.'

Mortimer shook his head. 'Peace? It would never last. We've already divided Britain with the Scots king thanks to Bannockburn, and you suggest we give further ground in Ireland? Every ruler and peasant in Europe will think the Crown of England is weak and to be pushed around. Besides, Edward Bruce wants the whole island just as his brother wants to rule all of Britain. Our spies tell us that he has already appealed to his brother for help and when Robert Bruce arrives with fresh troops from Scotland they'll begin a new offensive to complete the conquest. We need to counter-attack before that happens or we'll lose Ireland completely.'

'That might not necessarily be a bad thing.'

'Ireland provides us with soldiers and grain: supplies that allow us to keep fighting the Scots and the French,' Mortimer said. His teeth were gritted and his tone betrayed his annoyance at the tack Savage was taking. 'And that keeps the French off our backs. Do you think Robert Bruce really cares about the Irish? Of course he doesn't. Any more than I or the rest of the English nobility do. He wants to stop a vital source of military supplies for England and it also keeps his overambitious brother busy and out of Scotland.'

'So what do you want me for?' Savage said.

'I'm getting to that. Robert Bruce's war in Ireland means we English now have to fight him in two places. I want to do the same back,' Mortimer said.

'How?'

'We get King Aed Ó Donaill of Tirconnell to attack Bruce in Ulster from the west,' Mortimer said. 'We then advance from the south with the feudal army from Dublin. Bruce and Ui Neill will be caught between us and Tirconnell's forces like an ingot between the hammer and the anvil.'

Before he could stop it, a laugh blurted out from Savage's lips. Tirconnell – or rather Tír Chonaill – was the last remaining free Gaelic kingdom in Ireland. It sat on the rocky, sea-blasted edge of the vast western ocean in the far north-west of the island. It was fiercely independent. The ancient Brehon law was still practised there, not Henry Plantagenet's common law. The idea of them aligning themselves with the forces of the English Crown was surely a joke.

The look of annoyance on Mortimer's face deepened. 'What's so funny?'

'I'm sorry.' Savage regained his composure. 'But there is no way the Clan Connell of Tír Chonaill will fight for the English.'

'You think so?' Mortimer smiled in a way that suggested he was confident that he knew different. 'Aed Ó Donaill is no friend of Domnall Ui Neill.'

'But they're cousins, aren't they?'

'Not kissing cousins,' Mortimer said. 'Ui Neill supported

Aed's half-brother, Tiorrdelbach when they were both vying for the throne of Tirconnell. Aed finally killed Tiorrdelbach and won the throne. He never forgave Ui Neill. He is no friend of the Bruce brothers either. The Scottish part of their clan didn't support Robert Bruce's claim to the Scottish throne and he threw them off their lands in Kintyre. What is the saying? My enemy's enemy is my friend? I think we have enough to find common cause with King Aed. Besides—' Mortimer's smile became almost unbearable in its arrogance '—I have more than enough gold and silver from the Exchequer of King Edward to make it worth his while. In fact I have already made approaches to him and Tirconnell will support us. However, there is one obstacle in the way. What I want you to do is to remove that obstacle.'

'And what exactly is this "obstacle"?' Savage said, his voice laden with suspicion. He remembered the last time Mortimer and King Edward had sent him to Ireland. He had walked straight into a vipers' nest that nearly got him killed the first day he arrived. So far he had heard little to reassure him that the same thing was not about to happen again.

I I

Pulling his blanket round him, Mortimer sat down on one of the two chairs beside the table. As before he made no indication that Savage should join him.

'There is a certain knight who has taken refuge in Tirconnell. He is reputed to be a fearsome warrior and highly skilled in the dark arts. I don't believe in that sort of tittle-tattle but I do know the man is an inveterate villain. Unfortunately, King Aed is deeply under this man's influence.' The earl paused, taking a sip of wine. 'Despite Aed's hatred for his cousin Ui Neill,' he continued, 'he refuses to attack him and his Scots allies, not because of any antipathy to the English cause, but – so my spies tell me – because this knight has told him not to.'

Savage frowned. It sounded implausible. Why should a Gaelic king listen to a knight? Whoever this man was, if he bore the title of knight he was undoubtedly a foreigner, at least as far as the Kingdom of Tír Chonaill was concerned.

'Who is this man?' he asked.

Mortimer looked away, quickly avoiding Savage's gaze. 'Good question. He is known only as "the Leopard" because he wears the beast's pelt around his shoulders. Beyond that we don't know who he is.'

Savage raised an eyebrow. Mortimer was clearly lying. 'So how do you know he's fugitive? A villain?'

Mortimer shifted in his chair. He flashed another angry glance at Savage. 'I can only tell you what my spies tell me.'

'And why does King Aed listen to him?'

'Again, who knows? As I said, this knight is reputed to know witchcraft. Perhaps he has cast a spell on the king? More likely, though, is that he gives King Aed military advice on how to defeat English knights.'

Savage thought for a moment. Mortimer knew more than he was admitting, he was sure of that. However what he was saying did actually make sense. Until the arrival of the Scots, Tír Chonaill had been surrounded by the lands of Anglo-Irish earls like Richard de Burgh, the Earl of Ulster; men who could put heavily armed cavalry, knights and men-at-arms into the field. Having a tame knight to advise him on tactics, or even fight some of his battles, would help Aed keep his kingdom independent from the ever-avaricious grasp of the earl and his barons. King Edward of England, and his royal father before him, had exiled many a knight during the struggles and civil conflicts that had plagued their reigns. This man could come from the ranks of those disgruntled warriors who, banished from England, had sought refuge and allies in the lands beyond the Crown of England's influence, but still close enough to easily return if the Crown changed heads.

'You want me to persuade the king not to listen to this man's counsel?' Savage said. 'He's hardly likely to listen to a knight from the English Pale. I may be Irish, but he regards me and my kind as English as you and yours.'

Mortimer threw his head back and laughed heartily.

When his mirth subsided he said, 'No. I want you to kill this Leopard. I see no point in argument. I simply want him out of the way. Then perhaps the King of Tirconnell will finally see sense and join our side.'

Savage grunted, thinking that even then Aed was hardly likely to make common cause with the English. 'I'm not a murderer,' he said.

'Perhaps not.' Mortimer looked down into his wine goblet, a supercilious smile creasing his face, then he looked up again and locked eyes with Savage. 'But you *are* a killer – my spies in Ireland have assured me of that – and that's what I need right now.'

'Why not send the German?' Savage cocked his head in the direction of von Mahlberg. 'He looks like a workaday killer. It's more in his line of business. I'd say he'd probably even enjoy it.'

Von Mahlberg shot a hostile glance back at him but remained silent.

'Unfortunately, as a former Teutonic Knight my German friend is from the wrong order,' Mortimer said. 'My plan needs a Knight Templar, which is why you are perfect for the job. You were a Knight Templar, Syr Richard. Ten years ago your order was suppressed by the greed of King Philip of France and his puppet the Pope. Many of your brethren died, either by burning or in the torture chambers of Philip's Inquisition—'

'I know all that,' Savage cut him short.

'Many also fled, escaping the persecution inflicted on them across Europe. The Templars had their own fleet of ships—'

'I know,' Savage said again, becoming irritated. 'I sailed

in Templar ships from Cyprus to Egypt on raids against the Saracens.'

'And what do you think happened to those ships?'

Savage shrugged. 'I've no idea. I imagine they were seized by King Philip of France when he took everything else the Templar possessed.'

Mortimer gave a little chuckle and shook his head. 'Poor Philip. He was in debt up to his eyes to the Templars and thought by turning on them he could solve all his financial problems. Philip had the suppression of the order organised down to the last detail and managed to keep it totally quiet until the time came. He thought he had achieved total surprise. However, when his soldiers stormed the Templar headquarters in Paris, guess what they found in the treasury?'

'Gold?' Savage said, his mind thinking back to the fall of the order years before, the arrests and torture that ensued and how he had come to be taken prisoner and flung into a dungeon to rot.

'Nothing,' Mortimer said. 'It was empty. Somehow the Templars must have got word of what was going to happen. The treasure was gone.'

Savage blinked at the thought. At the time the order had been suppressed they had been one of the wealthiest organisations in the world. It was rumoured that they had more money than the Pope. How could such wealth just disappear?

'At the same time King Philip's men also arrived in La Rochelle harbour to seize the Templar fleet of ships,' Mortimer continued, rising to his feet, a look of excitement on his young face. 'Again they found nothing. The entire

Templar fleet had simply vanished from La Rochelle harbour overnight.'

Savage was silent as he contemplated this. He had spent six years in the Order of Knights Templar and recalled the fleet of at least eighteen new and highly capable vessels in their possession. Those ships ferried him and his brethren across the Mediterranean Sea on raids from their bases in Cyprus to wage havoc on the Saracens in Egypt. The memory was burned into his mind because he hated boats and every second of those journeys on that azure sea had been like purgatory.

'Now,' Mortimer continued, 'there is one kingdom in Ireland with trading links to La Rochelle. It has been exporting fish there for centuries and taking wine back. It also just happens to be where the most westerly Templar priory in Christendom was situated.'

'Tír Chonaill,' Savage said, realisation beginning to dawn on him. Aed Ó Donaill's kingdom was literally at the edge of the world and about as far from the authority of the Pope and the King of France as you could get. The trade route to western Ireland must have provided the escape path for his former brethren who had managed to escape the persecution. Had they taken the fleet and treasure with them? If so who knew what religious relics and other secrets they had taken as well? The old yearning awoke in Savage, the original desire for occult knowledge that had driven him to leave Ireland to join the Templars many years before.

'Tirconnell.' Mortimer nodded. 'King Aed has been allowing fugitive Templars to escape through his kingdom for the last decade. He has given them aid and refuge until they're ready to move on to wherever they flee. I don't know what he gets out of it. Maybe military help, maybe he does it for religious reasons. I can't send emissaries or soldiers to Tirconnell. It's officially an enemy of England, and Ireland is so full of damned spies, gossips and tittle-tattles that the news would reach Edward Bruce before whoever I sent reached King Aed. If I sent you officially to treat with Aed, this knight, the Leopard, would certainly hear about it and be ready for you.'

Savage placed his now empty goblet on the table and rested his hand on the back of the other chair. He could feel the effects of the heavy wine already. He was hungry to the point of nausea and his eyes were raw with exhaustion. He stared at the earl, grappling with the implications of the information imparted to him.

Meeting Savage's red-eyed glower, Mortimer gave a wolfish grin. 'No one, however, will suspect a fugitive Templar arriving in Tirconnell because it happens all the time. That is why I need you, Savage. Von Mahlberg was in the Order of Teutonic Knights. He does not know the correct pass phrases, the secret code words and signals. The things you know that will allow you to pass as a genuine Knight Templar, which, of course, you are.'

'I *was*, you mean,' Savage said. He thought for a moment then sighed. What choice did he have? He had to get back to Ireland for Galiene's sake and right now this was his only chance.

'Can I make one request?' he said.

'Go ahead.'

'Will you make sure Alys is looked after?'

'Of course,' Mortimer said. 'She will come and stay here

with me in this house. I will be in Gascony for some time yet attending to some business. Your wife will be safe under my protection.'

Savage took a deep breath, his mind spinning. He did not trust Mortimer but then again the earl needed him to carry out this task. Alys needed somewhere to recover and he needed to be sure she was somewhere safe if he was gone. He knew Mortimer would keep her safe, even if potentially it was as a hostage to ensure Savage complied. Once he had Galiene safe he could work out how to get Alys away from his grasp.

'All right. I'll do it,' Savage said.

'Excellent!' Mortimer positively beamed from ear to ear. 'In that case you will need this.'

The young earl heaved himself out of the chair. Pulling the blanket around himself, he walked to a chest that stood beside the fireplace. Flinging open the lid one-handed he stooped to retrieve a folded bundle of off-white cloth and carried it back to Savage.

Puzzled, Savage unfolded it. He found himself looking down at an equal-armed cross emblazoned in faded red cloth against a white background. With a grunt of recognition, he realised that it was the mantle of a Knight Templar: a garment like the one he had worn over his armour when riding into battle. 'Where did you get this?' he asked, unsure of how he felt to be looking at the insignia that had once meant so much to him but had led to so much pain and regret.

'I have my means.' Mortimer smiled. 'I have everything arranged. You can leave first thing in the morning.'

'How could you be so sure I would agree to this quest?'

'I always get what I want, Savage,' Mortimer said. It was a statement of fact rather than a boast. 'Always.'

Savage paused for a moment, an unsettling feeling of vague suspicion lingering in his heart. Then he realised he had no time for further speculation.

'I'll be here in the morning,' he said, 'but not first thing.' Refolding the Templar mantle he tucked it under his arm. 'There's something I must do first.'

12

Alys opened her eyes. For a moment she was confused as she saw the bare, whitewashed walls of the tiny convent room. Dawn's early light was filtering through the shutter slats of the window, revealing that the nun's cell was not much bigger than the bed in which she lay. Then the pain in her body and head washed over her and the memories returned. Thankfully there was still enough inside her of the poppy draught the nuns had given her to take the raw edge off her physical anguish. It could do nothing, however, for the emotional pain.

The door opened and a nun entered quietly. Alys sighed and looked away as the sister approached the bed.

'I'm not hungry,' Alys said, assuming the nun had arrived to break her night fast.

The nun did not reply and Alys looked back at her. From the size of her, Alys judged that the sister could probably do with missing a few breakfasts herself. Her habit was stretched tight over her large frame and bulged against the rope that tied it together at her waist. She stood beside the bed, both hands hidden by the wide sleeves of her habit, her face completely concealed by the long hood that hung down over her face. A sudden wave of apprehension gripped Alys. There was something not quite right about this nun.

'Who are you?' Alys demanded. 'Where is Sister Etienne?'

The nun withdrew her hands from her sleeves and swept back her hood to reveal "her" face.

'Richard! What on earth are you doing?' Alys said, a confused smile spreading across her face.

'I had to see you, Alys,' Savage whispered earnestly. His face split into a grin and bending to the bed he hugged her close to him. Alys responded and ignoring the pain from her bruised ribs grabbed him tight, wrapping her arms around his chest. Suddenly, gasping, she pulled away again and looked up at him, her face creased with anxiety and her eyes suddenly bright and shining with tears.

'Oh, Richard, I lost the child,' she sobbed.

He hugged her to him. Pulling her close he buried his face in her hair and kissed the top of her head. 'I know. The nun told me.'

Alys returned his embrace for a few more moments then extricated herself from his arms to look up into his face. 'There were nine raiders, Richard. Mostly Scots, I think, but a couple of Irish,' she said. 'There was nothing we could do. I'm so sorry.' A sob caught in her throat, tears spilling from her eyes.

'Dear God, Alys, you mustn't blame yourself.' Savage held her hands and smiled down at her. It was either that or cry himself. 'It's not your fault. It's mine for leaving you and Galiene on your own.'

'You're not our nursemaid. We can look after ourselves you know,' Alys retorted, shooting a fiery glance at Savage. 'We managed for years without you, after all.' The fire in her eyes suddenly died and she hid her face in her hands, her voice muffled. 'Except this time I couldn't…'

Savage hesitated, unsure how to ask the next question. 'Did they rape you?' he said quietly.

'One of them tried,' Alys said, her voice flat. Then a bleak, ferocious grin spread across her bruised face. 'When he came close, I tore half his ear off with my teeth. That put them off. None of the rest of them wanted to try after that and they knew the fire would bring people running from the village, so they just beat me, stabbed me and left me for dead.'

Savage's eyes widened, anger and dread choking his throat. 'What about Galiene?'

Alys shook her head again. 'No, she said not, but they killed that boy, Enjorran. They promised Galiene would not be harmed if you do what they ask and they took her away. They said you must return what you stole from Edward Bruce by the end of Easter week or she will die. They must mean the Grail.'

Savage nodded. 'They do. Their leader ambushed me after the tournament and said the same thing. That's going to be difficult seeing as I threw it into that bog in Scotland. It must be halfway to Hell along with Montmorency's corpse by now.' He grimaced. 'Easter is only two weeks away.'

'What will we do, Richard?' Alys said, her voice hoarse with despair. 'We have to save Galiene.'

'We will.' Savage laid a hand on each of her shoulders and looked straight into her eyes. 'But you will stay here until you get better. Luckily we have an influential friend who wants me back in Ireland: Earl Mortimer. I leave immediately.'

Alys rolled her eyes. 'Mortimer? Can we trust him?'

'I don't know.' Savage shrugged. 'However, he needs me for a special mission that will get me to Ireland. The task requires a Templar Knight so he needs me as much as I need him. I'll just have to take a chance. He has promised to protect you while I am gone and when you are sufficiently recovered, you will stay with him in the archbishop's palace.'

'And what is this "special mission", Richard? Is it dangerous?'

Savage looked away, avoiding her piercing gaze. 'It doesn't matter. It's a job that will help Mortimer in his war against the Scots. It will get me to Ireland and closer to Galiene and that is all that matters right now. Once there I will find and rescue her.'

'I feel like I've just got you back and I'm losing you already.' Alys's eyes darkened. Her deep concern and fear made her shoulders slump. 'Be careful, Richard. Don't let your temper cloud your judgement. Come back to me. Bring her back too.' She sank exhausted back to the pillow, her face white and strained.

'I'll be back,' Savage said, grabbing her right hand in both of his. 'And I'll bring Galiene home too. I vow it.'

Alys looked deep into his eyes. 'You'd better,' she said. 'Or if Edward Bruce doesn't kill you, I will!' She paused then smiled.

Savage smiled back. Then he kissed her; a long, lingering kiss that ached with the pain of their parting.

'You must go,' Alys said finally. 'If you're caught inside the convent walls you could be hanged – influential friends or not. How on earth did you get that nun's habit anyway?'

'In the very early mornings it's the custom of some of

the nuns to bathe in a pool created by the river Garonne beneath the convent,' Savage said. 'They go before dawn in case someone sees them. All I had to do was wait until they were all in the water then I had my pick of their clothes. Thankfully, despite the famine, some of the sisters seem to be quite well fed still and I found a habit to fit me.'

'That will be Sister Isabelle's—' Alys began but a noise outside the door interrupted her. From down the corridor the sound of running feet and voices raised in alarm could be heard. They were coming closer.

'Ah! It sounds like the nuns have returned from their swimming. I hope Sister Isabelle managed to preserve her modesty.' Savage grinned. 'It's time I was away.'

Snatching a final kiss he went to the window and flung it open. He grabbed both sides of the frame with his hands and raised one foot up onto the sill.

'Don't worry. When have I ever let you down, eh?' He smiled, then – seeing the look of indignation on her face and her mouth opening to tell him when he had done exactly that – he winked and pulled himself up onto the ledge.

A moment later he was gone.

13

Savage felt a twinge of resentment when he found that Mortimer insisted on sending the taciturn German swordsman, von Mahlberg, and two men-at-arms to accompany him on his journey. As they rode north from Bordeaux he wondered if perhaps Mortimer did not trust him completely, then reasoned that after the last adventure he probably had good reason not to.

The horseback journey through the famine-ravished interior of Gascony was depressing, at times horrific. As they passed villages deserted and abandoned they saw starving peasants begging for food: men and women little more than walking skeletons, and children who watched silently from hollow eyes as they rode past. Savage lost count of the number of emaciated corpses lying abandoned and rotting at the roadside, fodder for the crows and rats.

In darkness they sneaked like thieves in the night across the uneasy border between English Gascony and French Poitou, and eventually, as the morning brightened, they arrived at the walls of the city of La Rochelle.

As the curfew had passed they rode into the city without a second glance from the men-at-arms who guarded the gates. Inside the city walls they dismounted and walked their horses towards the harbour. Being a port, there was little sign amongst the inhabitants of La Rochelle of the famine ravaging the land, but Savage surmised that they were probably becoming heartily sick of eating fish. There were fish bones everywhere, either heaped in mounds or simply lying trodden into the mire of the streets. As they approached the harbour, von Mahlberg stopped outside a large house. He dismounted, and leaving his horse with Mortimer's two henchmen, signalled that Savage should do the same then knocked on the door.

Savage soon found himself introduced to a fat, weasel-faced Frenchman called Gaston. His size, Savage reasoned, was probably a fair measure of how unscrupulous a man this was. Many people would have had to go hungry for one man to sustain such a girth in a time of famine. Gaston recognised von Mahlberg immediately and ushered them into the house. With an anxious glance up and down the street to see if anyone was following them, he closed the door behind them. It transpired that he was a wealthy merchant, who acted as an agent for Mortimer in business dealings. Savage wondered just what "business" Mortimer had behind enemy lines, but reasoned that war often did not interfere with the dealings of barons like the Lord of Trim.

The German passed the merchant a fat leather purse that was clearly of considerable weight. The dull clank of gold that came from it and the broad grin it awoke on Gaston's face led Savage to conclude that it contained a substantial amount of money.

'Go to the chapel of Mary-of-the-Sea down at the

harbour,' the merchant wheezed, staring at the purse as he might at a nubile young woman and not even looking in Savage's direction. 'Ask for Father Cyrano. He will get you on the ship you want. Now go. You must not be found in my house.'

They took their leave and when once more outside in the street von Mahlberg raised a hand in salute.

'This is where we must part company, my friend,' he said, somehow managing to make the word "friend" sound as unfriendly as it could be. 'My Lord Mortimer's instructions are clear. You must appear as a lone, fugitive Templar so you must go on from here on your own.'

Savage nodded, glad to finally be rid of the German.

'Good luck with your mission,' von Mahlberg said, his voice still cold, his left hand rubbing the bruise on his chin. 'Perhaps we shall meet again. If so I wish to have a rematch of our competition. Next time I will be ready for your cheating. And next time there will be a different outcome.'

Savage grunted and turned to walk away.

'Be assured,' the German continued, 'we will take good care of your woman.'

Savage spun back towards him, eyes narrowed, his hand dropping to his sword hilt. 'What are you trying to say?' he said. 'If you touch her—'

Von Mahlberg held up his hands in mock fear. 'Calm down, Syr Richard, I am merely assuring you that your woman will be safe in our guard while you are away. Lord Mortimer guarantees it. While you fulfil the mission she will be well looked after.'

'Just make sure that is the case,' Savage said, continuing

to glare at the German over his shoulder as he turned to leave again. As he walked away he tried to ignore the uneasy feeling that had crept into his guts.

14

At first Savage had difficulty finding the chapel of Mary amid the bustling wharfs, warehouses, taverns and brothels of the busy port that cowered beneath the imposing walls of the four-towered, white-walled castle that defended the harbour of La Rochelle. Eventually he located the battered wooden door of the little crumbling church in an alleyway just off the main dock. Pushing the door open, Savage walked into the dark, dusty and seemingly empty interior. The quietness of the place compared to the noise and bustle outside settled around him. Motes of dust swirled in lazy circles in a shaft of sunlight cast from the single window high up in the wall onto the altar.

'What do you want?' a harsh French voice demanded and Savage turned to see a wizened old priest with yellow, rheumy eyes approaching him from a wooden confessional on the right-hand wall. 'Visitors are not welcome here.'

Musing that this seemed a most unchristian stance, Savage replied, 'I am told you can arrange a passage to Ireland for me.'

The priest turned away, waving a gnarled, bony hand in a gesture of dismissal. 'Why would I be able to do that?

I am a priest, not a merchant. Get out of my church and stop wasting my time.'

Savage fervently hoped that Gaston had not simply taken Mortimer's money as part of a scam. He had one more thing to try, however.

'Can I speak on the level with you?' he said. It was an innocent enough phrase but held a secret portent. Another member of the Order of Templars would recognise that phrase.

The priest stopped and turned back, his eyes narrowed.

'Is there no help here for a son of the widow?' Savage continued, emphasising the last few words, which were also an old Templar code phrase to identify a brother in need of assistance.

The priest looked at him and to Savage's relief he saw the old man's expression soften. Satisfied that the man at least knew the Templar secrets, Savage had one more risk to take. He pulled up his tunic, revealing the faded Templar mantle that Mortimer had given him. This would provide final proof that he was a Templar and get him the priest's confidence – or if he was wrong about him, get Savage burned at the stake.

The old priest's eyes lit up and a smile softened his face. 'Welcome, worthy brother,' he said, hands spread wide and, Savage thought, the glint of a tear in the corner of one of his eyes. 'I am sorry for my unfriendliness but you of all people must understand the need for secrecy. Now that I know you are genuine, of course I can arrange safe passage to the land of the Fisher King.'

Savage wondered what the man meant by this curious

phrase but decided not to ask as it would probably reveal the fact that he was only playing the role of fugitive Templar.

'Meet me back here in the morning,' the priest said.

Savage spent an uncomfortable night in a dockside inn. Mortimer had given him enough gold to stay somewhere comfortable, but being in an enemy city he saw no reason to risk drawing attention to himself by starting to throw money around. He regretted the decision, however, as most of the night was spent listening to drunken brawls and the sounds of sailors rutting with prostitutes. All the while he constantly checked that his weapons were in easy reach in case of attack or robbery.

Just after dawn he returned to the chapel of Mary. Father Cyrano led him to a ship waiting at the quay. Given his destination, Savage should not have been surprised by the vessel; however, it was with a sinking heart that he regarded the large, sea-going Irish curragh tied up at the quay. It was wide-bodied, with a single mast and large square sail, but it was still just a bigger version of the light, leather-skinned boats that bobbed across the rivers and lakes of his native land. If it had a keel at all, it would be a shallow one and that meant the journey would involve a considerable amount of rolling and rocking.

To make things worse, as he had climbed aboard his nostrils were assaulted by the overwhelming stench of mackerel and herring, which until the day before had filled the hull of the boat before being unloaded and sold in La Rochelle.

To his surprise no more money changed hands. Father Cyrano had a furtive conversation with the captain of the vessel during which there were several glances and pointing in Savage's direction. After that, the captain, a large-bellied, broad-chested Irishman with a mane of white hair and uneven teeth, simply nodded and cocked his head at Savage as if to signal his assent that he should stay.

Turning to leave, the priest grasped Savage's hand. 'God keep you safe, my worthy brother,' he said with an earnestness that almost provoked feelings of guilt in Savage that he was deceiving him.

Once Cyrano had left the boat they set sail.

As they passed the massive fortification towers that guarded the entrance to La Rochelle harbour, their white sandstone walls glaring in the sunlight, the realisation of what he was embarked on finally settled on Savage. Despite the fact that it was less than twelve months since he had nearly drowned in a shipwreck on the way to Scotland, he had been so caught up in worries about Galiene and concerns at leaving Alys that the prospect of the sea voyage and the terror that accompanied it had not impinged on him. Now, as the salty sea breeze tugged at his hair and the boat began to pitch and roll, his old dread of sea travel returned in earnest.

15

Bordeaux

Alys opened her eyes. A frown creased her brow as she looked around. None of the surroundings were familiar to her. She had gone to sleep the night before in the bare, white-walled cell in the nunnery, but now she was clearly somewhere else; the room she found herself in was luxurious.

She lay on a feather-filled mattress; heavy woven blankets pressed her deeper into the soft comfort. Dark wood panels lined the walls. A fire roared in a large iron grate in the fireplace and her nostrils were filled with the scent of fresh rushes on the floor and the aroma of the herbs and perfumed oil that had been scattered among them. A brightly coloured tapestry hung on one wall displaying a scene of a maiden with a unicorn asleep beside her, its head resting peacefully on her lap.

Alys moved to sit up and winced, catching her breath as a scab of dried blood on her stab wound broke away from where it had adhered to the pristine sheets in which she lay.

With a sigh she sank back into the pillows, her gaze roving left and right as she strove to recall her last moments of consciousness. She frowned again. Her mind seemed foggy, as if her head was clogged with lambswool. With some effort she managed to dredge up the recollection of the previous night. She had been in her room in the convent. Sister Etienne had been bending over her, whispering something to her in a reassuring, soothing tone. The nun had moved away and a new figure appeared, features half-hidden in a dark hood. A glass vessel had been held to her lips.

'Drink,' the voice of Etienne had come to her. 'It will help your journey.'

Alys recalled the bitter taste of the thick, sour liquid as she swallowed it. The others in the room had left and quickly a deep, swirling darkness had risen like a river in flood to submerge her consciousness.

She shook her head to try to dispel the grogginess and struggled once more into a sitting position, this time being more careful. As she did so she heard a rattling at the dark wood door of the room. The latch lifted and a plump, simply dressed young woman with a rosy-cheeked face entered. She wore a wimple and hood, but she was not a nun. Seeing Alys sitting up, her face broke into a pleasant, sunny grin.

'Ah, you are awake,' she said in French. There was no trace of an accent and Alys judged her to be a native of the region.

'I am,' Alys replied. Her throat was dry and her voice croaked slightly. 'Where on earth am I?'

The woman frowned at Alys's unfamiliar accent and she took a few moments before responding, as though trying hard to understand what Alys had said. Suddenly her face brightened.

'Ah! Of course. You're Irish!' she said with a delighted beam. 'The Lord Mortimer said you were from Ireland.'

'And where is this?' Alys repeated her question.

'You are in the town mansion of the Archbishop of Bordeaux,' the woman replied, a note of pride in her voice. She looked to be in her twenties and her green-eyed gaze darted around the room as she spoke. 'But you are a guest of Lord Mortimer, who is the current keeper of the house.'

Memories came flooding back to Alys. Richard had said Mortimer was going to get him back to Ireland. They must have moved her from the nunnery when she was in a drugged sleep.

Carrying a clay jug in one hand, the woman approached the bed. She sat on the edge of the mattress and looked down at Alys with an appraising eye. It was an expression Alys recognised: the practised gaze of a fellow person trained in the medicinal arts and herbal lore.

'You have been through a hard time,' the woman said, reaching out to brush a few strands of black hair stuck by sweat to Alys's forehead. 'But you have been brought here as the guest of the Lord Mortimer for your own protection. My name is Eloise. I will nurse you.'

'You serve Mortimer?' Alys asked.

'You must rest,' Eloise responded, ignoring the question. 'You must give your wounds a chance to heal.' She reached forward, lifted a wooden drinking cup from a small table that stood by the bed and decanted green cloudy liquid into it from the jug. 'This is medicine. Drink it. It will make you well,' she said, holding the cup up to Alys's lips.

Alys sniffed at the strong herbal scent of the draught and tried to work out what she smelt, but her brain was still befuddled with sleep and she cursed herself. 'What is it?' she asked. 'I know herbal lore myself.'

A strange look crossed Eloise's face. Alys could not work out if it was concern or confusion. Perhaps she could not work out her accent.

'Drink,' Eloise repeated, pushing the cup to her lips and tipping it so she had little choice.

Alys drank the liquid. As it slid past her tongue she detected its bitterness and the tastes of a combination of herbs she was familiar with, but her groggy brain could not quite recall the names or the effects of them. In a few short gulps it was all gone. She sighed and closed her eyes, letting her tongue run around the inside of her mouth, exploring the last residues of the tastes left behind by the drink.

'Good.' Eloise smiled pleasantly and once more stroked her forehead in a soothing way. 'It will help you recover. Now sleep.'

With that, she rose to her feet and went to the door. Once there she turned and flashed another smile at Alys as she exited, closing the door behind her.

Alys returned her smile as she relaxed back into the comfortable pillows. She closed her eyes once more, surprised at how sleepy she felt, despite the fact that she had just woken up. As she did so her tongue caught a speck of the dregs from the medicine and she pushed it between her back teeth. Crunching it, she detected immediately the bitter taste of poppy seed. The realisation triggered recognition of what the other tastes in the medicine had been too. They were all herbs with diverse powers, but combined all had one common effect: to induce sleep in a patient.

She opened her eyes but the lids were heavy already and her limbs felt as if they were weighted down by stones. Why would Eloise have drugged her? Perhaps she was injured more seriously than she thought and they needed to induce further rest? This made some sense, but then how badly was she hurt?

It was impossible to think or to keep her eyes open and she relaxed once more into the mattress. As she drifted off into sleep the last thing Alys heard was the click of a key turning to lock the door of the room.

16

Carrickfergus, Ireland

Edward Bruce, the newly crowned King of Ireland, glared at the stark stone walls of Carrickfergus Castle. He clenched his teeth, his jaw muscles standing out like balls of stone.

From a little way off, Syr Thomas Randolph, the Earl of Moray, watched his commander, noting the signs of his evident frustration and the simmering anger that seethed beneath the surface. It was something he had become familiar with over the last year of fighting in Ireland. At first, things had gone spectacularly well for them. Their army – all hardened Scots veterans of the long bitter wars against the English – had defeated every force they met from Irish kerns – bare-shanked warriors on foot – to armoured knights mounted on warhorses. Victory had followed victory. The English-backed government, the Lordship of Ireland, cowered in Dublin, waiting for Edward's decisive attack that would finally break their power and send them scurrying to Connaught, Kilkenny or back across the sea to where they belonged. The Scots had taken half the country and the Irish Gaelic kings had acknowledged Edward as *Ard Rí* – High King of Ireland.

Until final victory came, however, Bruce was in reality king of only half the country. As if to emphasise this point, here in the town of Carrickfergus, the first town to fall to Edward's army the year before and the place that he had chosen as his new capital and base of operations, the castle and its garrison doggedly refused to surrender.

Randolph knew the temperament of the new king well, but he still could not resist provoking him further. 'We should have brought siege equipment, shouldn't we?' he commented, in a tone as innocent as he could manage. He did not add – though he could have – "as I advised".

Bruce's eyes swivelled, his gaze alighting on the other man. His lip curled in barely restrained rage, baring more of his teeth than was polite. Randolph noted it, and also noted the slight twitch in the corner of the king's right eye, but he chose to ignore it.

The two men had known each other for years. Edward, like his brother Robert, was Randolph's half-uncle, but despite their relationship they were not that far apart in age because the Bruce siblings were well spread out. Edward and Randolph were both in their thirties, with flecks of grey appearing in their full beards. Both were veterans of Scotland's struggle for independence, a fight that was now approaching its twentieth year. These men were King Robert's two most trusted lieutenants. At the monumental victory at Bannockburn there had been three Scottish battalions: one led by Robert, one led by Edward and the third under the command of Thomas Randolph. Now both

Randolph and Edward Bruce were fighting in Ireland while Robert sat on the throne back home.

Randolph was no fool. He was well aware of the sneaking sense of resentment Edward had for him. Now Robert was king, appointments and positions of responsibility could go to Randolph without danger. He was loyal to the king and his support was not in question. It was for Robert's sake that he was supporting Edward in Ireland. The same could not be said about Edward.

The Bruce brothers had a rivalry that went back to the cradle. Now they had finally kicked the English out of Scotland the last thing Robert needed was his ambitious little brother nipping away at his heels all the time.

Not that Edward was, or ever would be, content with any position subordinate to his sibling. The day the *Slat na Righe*, the Rod of Kingship, was placed in his hands and Edward became King of Ireland, Randolph had witnessed a look of triumph and vindication cross over the younger Bruce's face that could only have been greater if his brother had been there to witness it. At that moment Randolph had realised just what a shrewd move his Uncle Robert had made in putting Edward in command of the invasion of Ireland, though he still had misgivings. Robert was risking much by giving so important a task into the hands of a character as headstrong and temperamental as his younger brother.

Over the last year in Ireland, without the dominant presence of King Robert to keep order, both Edward and Randolph had found each other's company increasingly hard to bear. As time went on it became clear to Randolph that Edward resented the fact that even though his brother had made him commander of the expedition, he had still sent Randolph along to "aid" him. Edward Bruce felt he had no need of anyone to hold his hand.

Carrickfergus Castle had been besieged for nearly a year, from day one of the invasion when the Scottish fleet had disembarked a mere twenty miles away along the coast. The defenders must have run out of food long ago, but somehow they held on and God only knew how they were sustaining themselves. The south lay at Edward's mercy, but he could not move and leave a garrisoned castle with access to the sea at his flanks.

Bruce and Randolph were among the group of fifteen Scottish men-at-arms who stood, sat or lounged around a siege-work barricade, which had been built by the Scottish army at the bottom of the short hill leading up to the castle's obstinately closed drawbridge. They were fully armed in mail and conical helmets and ready for war. Recently, boredom had proved to be their greatest enemy as they took their turn watching the castle: on guard day after day in case the garrison attempted to break out.

A century and a half before, Syr John de Courcy had picked this spot to build his castle at Carrickfergus and he could not have picked a better one. *Carraig Fhearghais* – the Rock of Fergus – was a long, dark promontory that jutted out into the sea. Its black rocks were now almost completely covered by the fortress constructed on it, its high, oyster-shaped curtain wall surrounded on three sides by the sea. Only one narrow end of the castle faced inland and that was guarded by a double-towered gate divided from the land by a ditch that flooded at high tide. When the drawbridge was up, the castle became an island. Incredibly, for a rock sitting in the sea, Carraig Fhearghais also had a natural spring in the middle of it, which provided the castle with fresh water. As Edward Bruce was finding, it was a defensive position that was well-nigh impregnable.

Edward saw a figure appear on the castellated battlements above the drawbridge. 'Hey! Your Highness! Message for you,' the mail-clad warrior on the wall shouted before he turned around, perched himself backwards on the battlement and bared his arse.

Edward Bruce felt a sharp pain in his right lower molar and realised he was clenching his teeth to the point of grinding them. 'One day, Randolph, we will take this castle,' he breathed. 'And on that day I will personally oversee the execution of every last whoreson in that garrison. I will take great pleasure in watching them being strung up at the market cross. I'll even fix the rope for them.'

He turned away and just caught sight of the smirk on his nephew's face. Bruce turned back to him and fixed his chief lieutenant with a glare, incensed that Randolph could find humour in the situation.

The earl returned his gaze and shrugged. 'Come on. You've got to admire their balls.'

'I want to see them strung up by their balls,' Bruce said in a growl.

'We could do with a few more like them on our side,' Randolph commented.

Edward clenched his jaw again, but did not retort. He knew well the loyalty of the Scots veterans who made up his army depended as much on having Randolph as their leader as it did on his own position as King Robert's brother and that galled him. He was king in his own right now, but Randolph's presence and importance was a constant annoyance; a reminder that this expedition was still very much under the auspices of his brother, King Robert.

'Be careful what you say, Thomas,' Edward Bruce hissed, looking around to see who was listening. 'If our Irish allies hear you they won't be pleased. Some of them have sacrificed a great deal for our cause.'

'Some of them, yes,' the earl said, hitching up his belt as he did so. 'It's a pity more of them haven't though. Otherwise I wouldn't now have to set sail back to Scotland to ask your brother for more troops.'

Despite the fact that he was about to embark on a sea voyage, Randolph wore full armour. This was because Carrickfergus harbour, from which he would begin his journey, nestled beneath one of the overbearing walls of the castle and the path to it passed within bow shot of the besieged defenders. Luckily they were woefully short of arrows so the chance of them taking a pot shot was low. Still it was just not worth the risk.

A young nobleman with a pleasant cheerful face, bright blue eyes and black hair, approached them from the path that led to the harbour. He was dressed in mail with a blue surcoat, a red chevron emblazoned on it. He stopped before the two commanders of the army and saluted.

'Your Majesty, my lord, the earl's ship is ready,' the young knight said. 'I also wish to report that Gib Harper has returned.'

'Excellent! Thank you, Fleming,' Bruce replied. 'I'll see you off, Randolph.'

'Sire—' Syr Neil Fleming looked concerned '—it is not safe to go so close to the castle walls.'

Edward Bruce waved him away with an irritated expression. 'Don't be ridiculous, Fleming. I'm not a coward.'

They began the walk to the harbour. As they approached it, a wild-haired, lank-bearded figure dressed in a tattered monk's robe came staggering towards them, his scrawny arm outstretched as he proffered an accusing finger at the defenders on the top of the castle wall.

'Their day will come, Lord! The day when the followers of the catamite King of England will pay for their sins is close!'

Bruce rolled his eyes. When first undertaking his Irish adventure, he had expected to find a country full of people not unlike the vassals in his earldom in west Scotland: Gaelic cousins who would welcome him as a liberator from their English overlords. Instead he had found a strange land of untrusting poets, scoundrels and lunatics, and no one personified all three better than the preacher who now stood beside him. Sometimes he wondered if there was something in the water of his new kingdom that made everyone here mad.

The priest glared at the walls of the castle with a look of rage that matched that of Edward Bruce. He was an itinerant cleric who – as far as the Scots could determine – had been hanging around the town of Carrickfergus for some time before they arrived, preaching about the iniquities of the King of England and railing against Richard de Burgh, the Earl of Ulster and former ruler of the province. His presence in the occupied town was tolerated because it was well known that he was on their side. The few townspeople who had not fled all testified to this and the fact that de Burgh's galloglaich mercenaries had beaten him on several occasions. He was clearly a lunatic, obsessed with preaching that all men should be equal and share their wealth. However he was harmless though annoying and had the added advantage of justifying Edward Bruce's cause in religious terms.

The three Scottish nobles nodded to the preacher as they passed, awkward grins fixed on their faces. 'That's one lunatic I won't miss when I'm away,' Randolph muttered from the side of his mouth, wincing slightly at the unwashed stench of sweat, urine and ingrained dirt that wafted from the preacher.

Bruce's annoyance faded when he saw the group of warriors approaching from the harbour. They consisted of Scots foot soldiers in mail and leather, and Irish kerns in long cloaks. Some swayed awkwardly as they walked, trying to regain balances set askew by days spent aboard a ship. At the head of them was the big figure of Gib Harper, who dwarfed the little girl who walked beside him. Her hands were bound at the wrists and held before her and she was clearly reluctant to accompany Harper, who impelled her forwards, one large fist grasping a handful of her blonde hair.

'Ah,' Bruce said with evident relish. 'This must be the bastard child of Richard Savage.'

17

'Harper!' Edward Bruce hailed his man-at-arms. 'How did you get on in France?'

'Your Majesty.' Harper saluted with his free hand. 'I'm afraid Savage decided to play silly boys, so we had to resort to our alternative plan. He claims he does not have it, so we took something of his.' Harper shoved the girl forwards roughly for the inspection of the nobles.

Bruce eyed the girl who glared back at him with insolent green eyes.

'This is Savage's daughter,' Harper said. 'I told him if he doesn't bring the Grail here by Easter then she dies. I think he got the message.'

Bruce nodded, satisfied that though he had not got what he wanted today, it was only a matter of time until he did. He regarded the girl. She was about twelve years old, with long, curling blonde hair that was now clotted with dirt. Her features were well proportioned and her bright green eyes met his gaze with a glare that brimmed with confrontation and self-confidence.

'Had to discipline her, did you?' Bruce said, noting the cut on the girl's lip and bruise on her left cheek.

Harper grunted. 'Aye she's a real pain in the arse. I nearly broke my knuckles thrashing the wee bitch. Galiene she's called. Show some respect, girl. This is Edward Bruce, King of Ireland.'

Harper lifted his hand and moved to strike the girl, but Bruce gestured to him to stop. 'Galiene,' he repeated, reaching out a gloved hand to stroke the young girl's cheek. He met her insolent gaze for several seconds, finally discerning that there was not just defiance there but also real fear. A broad smile broke out on his face. 'So you are the by-blow of Syr Richard Savage.'

'I am the daughter of Alys de Logan—' Galiene began to say.

'And the bastard whelp of Savage,' Bruce cut her off. 'I know all about you and your mother the witch. Your father stole something very precious from me and my brother. You will be the bargaining piece I use to get it back.'

Randolph sighed. 'I don't know why you are bothering with this,' he said. 'Half of Ireland has fallen before us already and the rest will follow when we have the resources we need to finish the job. We don't need grails and holy relics; we need soldiers.'

Bruce was about to reply when they were interrupted by the mad priest who had followed them down the hill.

'Do not be afraid, little girl,' he shouted. 'That man is Edward Bruce, the flower of chivalry. I am sure he will not harm you. It will be a blot on his reputation and a black mark on his immortal soul if he does.'

'Get away with you, you mad smelly old bastard!' Fleming yelled, aiming a kick in the direction of the priest, who scuttled out of the way to avoid the blow.

Bruce frowned. He was unsure, but he thought he saw

the priest and the girl exchange glances and in that moment an expression had come to her face that she almost instantly hid. Was it recognition? 'Wait—' he said, holding up a hand. He wanted to investigate this further.

At that moment shouts came from the castle gate. An alarm bell began tolling and horns blew. Six men-at-arms came running down the slope towards them, swords drawn. Fleming, Randolph and Harper immediately drew their own weapons.

'Sire, we have to get you out of here,' the lead man shouted, pointing back towards the castle. 'The portcullis is lifting. It looks like the defenders are coming out. It's probably a raiding sortie.'

'My Lord, you must flee,' Fleming said.

'Never!' Bruce shouted, drawing his sword. 'I'm not a coward, sir. I run from no man.'

Randolph laid a hand on Bruce's arm. 'Sire, he's right. Get back to the camp. Get more men while we hold them. This is just a raid to try to get food. It would be ridiculous if you get yourself killed in a minor skirmish. If you return fast enough this could be our chance to finally take this castle.'

Bruce hesitated a second longer, then nodded. Four of Harper's men closed around him and hurried him off into the town. Behind them the drawbridge of the castle opened with a crash.

18

Behind the drawbridge of Carrickfergus Castle was a massive iron and wood portcullis that barred the entrance. Behind that, in the narrow entrance of the castle gatehouse, heavily armed men jostled and shifted their feet, nerves taut in anticipation of the coming fight.

The raiding party was a motley bunch of thirty men. In the vanguard were a group of eleven galloglaiches – Norse-Gaelic mercenaries. They were clad in knee-length chain mail shirts. Their highly polished conical helmets gleamed in the sunlight and the attached face guards almost hid their features completely, though long blond hair and beards flowed from beneath. Their mail and leather gauntleted hands grasped the poles of long-handled heavy axes.

Behind them were arrayed ranks of the castle garrison, a combination of men-at-arms in chain mail and Irish kerns in padded linen overshirts. All of them were gaunt, hollow-cheeked from starvation and in their dark-rimmed eyes was the hungry look of desperate men.

Beyond them, in the inner ward of the castle, others looked on: anxious women who watched as their menfolk prepared to go to fight, and a few children who wondered what fate awaited their fathers outside the gates. The battlements were lined with what was left of the garrison: a few archers and crossbowmen who still had functional weapons and bolts to fire.

'Look out for food, provisions, anything you can grab that can be carried back to the castle,' Henry de Thrapston addressed the soldiers as they prepared for battle. His voice was clear, loud and bore the authority of a man who held the responsibility of being the Keeper of Carrickfergus Castle. In that role he was responsible for closing the gates once they left, so was not dressed for war. Like the others he was thin and haggard and after the long months besieged in the fortress, his once fashionable, brightly coloured clothes were tattered and dirty. 'Don't get sucked into prolonged fighting. Just hit and run. Take what you can and get back here. Stick together and don't get separated.'

In the midst of the galloglaiches was their leader, Connor MacHuylin. Even by the brawny standards of his men, MacHuylin was a big man. He wore russet plaid breeches beneath his chain mail and his long blond hair and full beard, as yet uncovered by his helmet, tumbled around his shoulders. As the portcullis clanked its way towards the roof he was giving a young lad who stood in the middle of the raiding party a stern talking-to, emphasising each word with a poke on the chest from his gauntleted forefinger.

'Just remember the plan,' he said, fixing the boy with a piercing glare from eyes that seemed to blaze with a blue fire. 'Stay out of the fighting. My lads here will do that. You stick with the raiding party and don't get distracted.'

The young boy nodded, his dark-rimmed eyes agog with a mixture of excitement and fear.

'What's your name again?' MacHuylin demanded.

'Conal,' the young lad replied. He was barely fourteen years old, scrawny and in contrast to the heavily armoured warriors that surrounded him, wore only a light leather jerkin and breeches. This was deliberate as it was important for him to be as light on his feet as possible.

'I shouldn't need to remind you, Conal, that the fate of this castle and all of us in it depends on you delivering that message to the seneschal in Dublin,' MacHuylin continued. 'Keep your eye out for a mangy-looking priest. His name is Guilleme le Poer and he is actually on our side. He disguises himself as an itinerant preacher – one of those mad radicals who thinks we should all be equal and share our wealth – so that he can spy on the Scots for us.'

'Didn't we used to beat him up, Chief?' one of the galloglaich commented over his shoulder.

'We did indeed, MacSweeny,' MacHuylin said, 'and it turns out he was actually working for the Justiciar of Ireland all along. That's how good he is at disguising himself.' The galloglaich commander turned his attention back to the boy. 'All you have to do is get into the town and meet up with the priest. He will show you where to hide and how you can get away. After that, go south as fast as you can.'

Again the young lad nodded but he was no longer meeting MacHuylin's gaze and the galloglaich wondered if he was listening or not. He was annoyed but could hardly blame the boy. They were about to charge out of the relative safety of the castle's defences into a town bristling with Scottish warriors. This was probably the boy's first taste of real fighting so he was bound to be a bit distracted and nervous. Hopefully he was not so wound up that he made a shambles of the mission.

MacHuylin had to admit he was quite excited himself. After the long months besieged in the castle, cooped up in the stinking, overcrowded fortress on the receiving end of arrows, stones and other missiles fired at them by the Scots, he was positively itching to come to blows with his enemies and with any luck kill a few of the bastards.

'Prepare for battle,' de Thrapston shouted, pushing his way back into the castle through the packed warriors. 'Good luck to you all.'

MacHuylin pulled his helmet on, the nose guard, eye visor and cheek pieces encasing most of his face in highly burnished iron. 'Good luck and may the Great One look down on you,' he said to the boy, but his words were lost as the portcullis completed its journey into the roof of the gatehouse. The huge metal teeth that held it in place engaged with an audible click. With a harsh rattling of released iron chains the drawbridge crashed open and the raiders surged out over it.

19

The raiders thundered across the drawbridge, screaming wildly as they charged down the hill from the castle gate. Raucous as their war cries were, the galloglaiches in the lead kept disciplined formation. MacHuylin was in front and the others fanned out in an arrowhead behind him. Their heavy boots stomped in unison over the dried mud and gravel; their chain mail clinked as they ran. They charged, but at a measured pace, the weight of their armour alone making a headlong sprint out of the question.

A short hill ran down from the main gate of the castle and at the base of it the besieging Scottish army had built barricades from which they could both hem in the only point at which the castle touched the land and also take cover from missiles launched from the castle walls. The barricades were earth and wood constructions, taller in height than a man and thick enough to withstand stones shot from a catapult or mangonel.

MacHuylin felt a surge of excitement when he saw that the barricade was sparsely defended. With the long, inactive months of the siege the Scots had grown complacent. As food got scarcer they had moved more and more soldiers away from guarding the castle and onto duties pillaging the surrounding countryside for supplies, a task that now required venturing ever further afield.

As MacHuylin charged towards the barricade he counted at most fifteen defenders and the faces of all of them were pale; they looked like rabbits startled by the sound of the hunter's horn. Even before the raiding party from the castle reached it, a couple of men behind the barricade took to their heels. The combination of the surprise attack and the small number of men manning the barricade meant the galloglaiches should take their first objective with relative ease. Just before the drawbridge opened there had been a report from the battlements that Edward Bruce himself was somewhere outside, but MacHuylin doubted they would be that lucky.

As they reached the barricade, the galloglaiches flattened themselves against it while the men running behind them bearing ladders threw them up with a clatter and warriors began streaming up and onto the top. MacHuylin swore as he spotted the boy scrambling up the ladder beside him. He reached out a big hand and hauled him back down.

'By Christ's holy blood, boy!' he shouted. 'I told you to stay back and out of the way, you idiot!'

There was a shout of pain and the man who had been in front of the young lad toppled back off the ladder, blood gushing from a deep slice carved between the base of his neck and his shoulder.

MacHuylin looked up and saw a Scots warrior, a bloody sword gripped in his hand, standing on top of the barricade. The Scotsman raised a foot and kicked the ladder back into the throng of raiders below, roaring some unintelligible curse as he did so. As it fell MacHuylin spun and hewed upwards with his poleaxe, holding it by the bottom of the shaft for further reach. He felt the blade check as it bit into the thigh of the man above him, releasing a shower of hot crimson rain that splattered down over his arms and helmet. The Scotsman screeched in agony and toppled backwards.

Grasping his poleaxe in one hand, MacHuylin hauled the fallen ladder back up with his other and pushed it into position against the barricade. He charged up it and onto the top. The Scottish defenders below looked up in startled terror. They were all veteran warriors but the fearsome sight of the big, mailed galloglaich towering over them, poleaxe in hand, covered in blood and screaming at them made even the hardiest flinch. Within moments MacHuylin was joined by the rest of his men and that was enough for the defenders of the barricade to judge that their position was lost.

MacHuylin laughed with fierce delight at the sight of the grizzled veterans abandoning their post and fleeing as fast as they could back towards the town. He knew this was a temporary victory – they would soon be back with the rest of their army – but it still felt good to finally strike a blow against the men who had held them prisoner in the castle for so long.

'They're running away,' he shouted as he turned and beckoned to the rest of the raiding party below. 'Hurry, we won't have much time.'

The raiders streamed over the barricade and began running towards the short lane that ran into the town of Carrickfergus. They were hunting for food and supplies: anything they could get to help them hold out longer against the besieging forces. A few stayed behind and began hacking at the barricade to dismantle it.

MacHuylin, still atop the barricade waved back to the castle and a few more men exited the gate, manhandling a four-wheeled cart down the hill to carry captured booty back to the fortress. Conal, the young lad who was supposed to be carrying a message to the seneschal, was still standing beneath the barricade, scared to move after MacHuylin's previous admonition.

'Right, you,' the galloglaich bellowed down at him. 'Get up here and let's find that priest.'

The boy scrambled up the ladder and then they both jumped down the other side of the barricade and began jogging towards the town.

The lane from the castle broadened quickly into a wide, octagon-shaped area where the market was held in more peaceful days. A tall stone cross stood at the centre of the marketplace, the biblical scenes carved on it painted in bright colours. Timber-framed buildings – houses, shops and merchants' premises – ringed the perimeter of the marketplace. The whole area was eerily deserted. When the Scots took the town the year before, they had first looted it then set it aflame, a decision they must surely now regret, MacHuylin reflected, since it meant their army was billeted in tents outside the walls and exposed to the dreadful weather, instead of in the relative comfort the buildings of the town could have provided. Some of the townsfolk had fled to the castle, others had fled south. Any who stayed behind had been slaughtered. Some of the buildings had partially survived the burning, but Carrickfergus was now little more than a ghost town.

MacHuylin knew that defenders from the barricade would be running to the camp outside the town for reinforcements. The raiders would not have long to search the surrounding buildings and the siege works the Scots had built for provisions.

At the far end of the market area, on the crest of a little rise, stood the church of Saint Nicholas. Its stone walls had protected it from the inferno that destroyed the surrounding town. As the raiders from the castle started searching the gutted houses to steal whatever they could find and throw it onto the cart, the sound of the bell in the church tower began to ring out.

'MacSweeny,' MacHuylin shouted to his second in command. 'Some Scottish hero has decided to stay behind and use the bell to summon his friends. Get up to the church and shut him up, will you?'

MacSweeny nodded and trotted off towards the church, axe at the ready.

Something, perhaps a sound or a flicker of movement – he was not sure what – made MacHuylin suddenly spin round towards the castle. His mouth dropped open slightly as he saw armed men rushing up from the harbour below the castle. At least three of them wore chain mail and plate armour and bore swords that marked them out as knights or nobles. Along with them were men-at-arms in chain mail and kettle helmets, and there were also a few Irish kerns in padded linen jerkins. He judged that there were probably about twenty of them, more than enough to do real damage to his raiding party.

'Behind you!' MacHuylin shouted in warning. The men pushing the cart looked to where he pointed and saw the attack coming from their flank. They turned tail and fled back up the hill towards the castle gate, dragging the part-filled cart behind them. The incoming Scots swarmed up to the barricade and quickly retook it.

MacHuylin assessed the situation with dismay. The castle, its gate wide open, lay behind them at the Scots' mercy; worse, he and the raiding party were now cut off in the town.

20

MacHuylin swore to himself and promised that if he made it back to the castle alive he would make the idiot who was supposed to be on lookout pay dearly for not spotting the advancing Scots. The raiding party's flank had been left wide open and now the whole plan was going to pieces. They had to act fast if they weren't to lose the castle.

Pulling the large signalling horn from his belt he sounded three short blasts. Members of the raiding party appeared at the doors of the houses they were in the process of ransacking, puzzled expressions on their faces at hearing the recall signal so soon. Their expressions turned grim when they saw that the enemy was now behind them and barring the way back to the castle. MacHuylin blew one more long blast, the signal to attack. There was no time to group or form up, instead the raiders just charged headlong back towards the barricade. The Scots surged forward to meet them. Chaos ensued as desperate hand-to-hand fighting erupted across the market square. Men fought face-to-face, stabbing with spears, countering with swords and swinging axes. The ringing of blades colliding mingled with angry shouts, war cries and screams of the injured.

MacHuylin raised his axe and ran forwards to join the

fray. As he did so he spotted Conal. Frozen by confusion he stood amid the fighting, his face a mask of terror. It was clear he had no idea if he should run forward or turn and flee back to the castle. MacHuylin changed his course and headed for the boy. Before he could reach him, a big, broad-chested, blunt-faced Scotsman beat him to it. Seeing him, the boy let out a screech of horror and raised his arm up over his head in a pathetic attempt to protect himself.

The only result from this action was that he did not see the blow that killed him coming. The big Scot hewed down with his axe, a strike that severed the lad's arm at the elbow and continued downward, gouging a huge slice into his head. Conal simply crumpled to the ground as if all the bones in his body had suddenly dissolved.

'Damn it to Hell!' MacHuylin roared, his frustration boiling over as he watched the boy die on the ground and yet another part of the plan fell to bits. Too late to save the lad, he launched his own assault on the Scotsman who had killed him, swinging the axe in a blow aimed at cleaving the man's skull in two. The Scot countered with his shield and MacHuylin felt the strength of the man in the firmness of the resistance that stopped his axe short of its intended target. The two of them were well matched in all aspects, from height and build to reach, and MacHuylin held no illusions that this would be an easy contest.

The Scot swung his axe in an uppercut and MacHuylin used the iron-bound shaft of his own axe to stop the blow. At that moment a screamed war cry alerted him to another man rushing towards him from the side. He just had time to jump backwards as a second Scottish man-at-arms plunged a spear at him. MacHuylin's movement took him out of harm's way, but only just. To his further dismay he saw a third man coming at him, this time an Irish kern who also bore a spear. Accomplished warrior though he was, MacHuylin had to admit to himself that fighting three men at once was going to be a hard job.

With a clatter of boots and a rattle of chain mail his galloglaich troops came to his aid. They were professional warriors who, after the initial chaotic charge, had extracted themselves from the general melee, reformed into a disciplined formation then started making inroads into the enemy. Seeing their chief outnumbered, they found their first target and waded in to help. MacHuylin watched with some relief as the wave of soldiers flowed past him and engaged the men who had been pressing in on him. In an instant the two Scottish spearmen were dead, felled by MacSweeny's axe. The big man who had killed the messenger boy was hastily withdrawing, putting a safe distance between himself and the rank of snarling, blond-bearded warriors who now formed a wall of iron between him and his intended victim. The kern turned and ran away.

'Thanks, lads,' MacHuylin said, looking around to assess the situation. Thankfully it looked as though the raiding party were starting to get the upper hand against their surprise attackers; however, any chance of taking a worthwhile amount of provisions from the town back to the castle were now gone. It was only a matter of time before the rest of the Scottish army would pour into the town from their camp outside the turf ramparts. It would be all the raiding party could do to defeat their current attackers and fight their way back into the castle. On top of that, the boy who had been supposed to use the raid as cover to escape the castle and get the message to the seneschal in Dublin was dead. The whole plan had turned to shit.

As he surveyed the fighting around the marketplace, MacHuylin noticed two figures running up from the harbour behind the ranks of the Scots. They stood out in the chaos of the battle because neither was armed nor armoured. It was a man and a girl. MacHuylin recognised the wild hair and beard and tattered clothes of the priest, Guilleme le Poer. The girl he led by the hand as they scuttled, bent over and clearly trying to avoid attention, was familiar but he could not place her straight away. Yet again MacHuylin swore to himself as another part of the plan appeared to have gone awry. Le Poer was supposed to be waiting in one of the houses to provide a refuge for Conal. What was the man playing at? That said, it was all moot now as the boy was dead anyway.

Somehow avoiding the Scots, le Poer and the girl hugged the walls of the houses that surrounded the marketplace, hurrying at a half-crouched run. Le Poer held in his free hand a knight's long dagger that MacHuylin could see was splashed with fresh blood, so clearly he had seen some of the action. What was the idiot up to though? He was on the wrong side of the fighting parties and had brought some strange girl along with him. None of this was part of the plan.

At that point, the big Scot who had felled Conal also spotted the two fleeing persons coming up from behind the Scots' lines. He became agitated by the sight and he started gesticulating wildly in their direction and roaring commands that were lost to MacHuylin's ears amid the din of the fighting.

'Push forward men!' MacHuylin roared. 'We have them.'

A loud roaring sound like onrushing water reached MacHuylin's ears and he realised that the rest of the Scots army had arrived and were piling into the town through the gates in the ramparts. In moments they would be flooding into the square to overwhelm the raiding party.

Seeing that they were gaining the upper hand, and spurred on by the knowledge that if they did not clear a path to the castle immediately they would be outnumbered and slaughtered by the coming army, the raiding party obeyed MacHuylin's urging with renewed, desperate violence.

Despite the imminent arrival of help, the Scots suddenly broke under the raiders' re-invigorated assault. With over ten of their number fallen, they decided the best tactic to survive was to withdraw until the rest of the army arrived. As they turned and ran back down the hill towards the harbour, the big Scot, who appeared to be their leader, shouted in vain that they should stand their ground. No one listened and as he found himself standing alone in the face of his enemies, he shot one more frustrated glance in the direction of le Poer and the girl then turned tail and ran back to the harbour after his men.

The raiding party quickly gathered together what meagre booty they had collected while MacHuylin jogged over to le Poer. 'What in Hell's name are you up to?' the galloglaich said, his voice harsh and metallic from beneath the shadows of his helmet.

'I had to change the plan,' le Poer said, pulling the girl forward by the hand. 'This is Galiene, remember?'

MacHuylin looked at the girl properly for the first time

and now recognised the blonde hair and insolent, sullen stare in the bright eyes of Richard Savage's daughter.

'Edward Bruce had her kidnapped,' le Poer continued. 'I happened to be at the harbour when they landed with her. The rest of them ran up to attack your lot leaving only two men guarding her. I couldn't just leave her there.'

MacHuylin glanced around and saw that the rest of the raiding party were running as fast as they could back up to the refuge of the castle. They could all hear the coming rush, the shouting and clattering of the arriving Scottish army, which was now a mere street away and already swarming around the church of Saint Nicholas. The galloglaich briefly considered the options then made his decision.

'Which one is the safe house? The one you would have hidden the messenger in?' he asked.

'The surgeon's,' le Poer replied, pointing to a town house on the market square. It had been scorched by the fire and its thatched roof was gone, but apart from that it was largely intact. Above the front door there hung a painted sign displaying a bandaged human arm. In an attempt at realism that was hardly likely to instil confidence in any nervous patients, the bandage had been painted with several bright red bloodstains on it. 'It's abandoned like the rest of the shops, but the second-storey floor is still there. I planned we could hide up there until dark.'

'The boy got killed in the fighting,' MacHuylin said. 'I'll have to deliver the message to the seneschal in Dublin myself. We can't take the girl though. She'll slow us down.' He ignored the look of consternation on Galiene's face.

'You'll have to go alone,' le Poer said. 'The Scots will

know it was me who took Galiene. My cover here in Carrickfergus is gone.'

'Get to the castle,' MacHuylin said, realising that they had now run out of time.

Le Poer nodded then he and Galiene turned and sprinted in the direction of the castle gates. MacHuylin watched them go for a moment then turned and ran as fast as his heavily armoured body could take him for the house le Poer had pointed to.

Behind him the last of the raiding party made it through the gate of the castle, followed quickly by le Poer and Galiene. There was a roar and a crash as the portcullis dropped to seal the entrance, followed immediately by the rattling, cranking noise of the drawbridge being winched up. The ditch was opened and once more the castle was cut off from the land.

As the first Scottish soldiers from the army poured into the opposite side of the marketplace MacHuylin reached the door of the surgeon's. He shouldered it open and dived through the entrance, pitching headfirst onto the floor inside. Scrambling to his feet again he slammed the door behind him and drew a wooden bar across to hold it shut.

For a few anxious moments he waited in agonised silence. The only sound in the deserted, soot-blackened room was his own heavy breathing. Sweat dripped from his forehead down the inside of his helmet and into his beard. He could hear the Scots outside, but no one came to the door. The sounds of chaos filtered through to him as the marketplace flooded with soldiers who, denied the chance to catch the raiders in the town, pressed forward to assault the castle gate. Clearly no one had spotted him coming into the building and no one was coming to investigate – at least not yet.

The galloglaich commander sighed again, looking up at the cobweb-coated beams in the ceiling as he tried to calm his pounding heart and quell the raging tide of anger and frustration that boiled within him.

'Shit,' he commented to no one in particular.

21

Immediately they entered the castle portcullis, Guilleme le Poer and Galiene found themselves surrounded by a ring of steel. Armed men crowded round them, both guards left at the portcullis and members of the raiding party, their faces angry and sweating beneath helmets and their armour and weapons still splattered with blood from the fighting outside.

'Who the hell are you?' growled a rough-looking sergeant with broken teeth. He wore a dirty surcoat bearing a red cross on a yellow background – the arms of the Earl of Ulster. 'What do you think you're doing?'

Galiene flinched from the man's challenging glare and involuntarily grabbed the arm of le Poer. She dropped it almost instantly as she remembered she hardly knew the man, though he had saved her from the Scots.

A tall, broad-shouldered warrior – mailed head to foot – a conical helmet on his head and a huge, wicked-looking, long-handled axe clutched in his fist, shoved his way through the throng. The long hair that spilled from beneath his helmet and his braided beard were blond, and Galiene recognised the armour as that of the galloglaich mercenaries the Earl of Ulster had used as a personal bodyguard before the war. She felt a surge of hope: perhaps Richard de Burgh, the Red Earl of Ulster, was in this castle too? He may not remember her but he would remember her mother, who had been his astrologer in days gone by.

'Stand back, give them room,' the galloglaich bellowed, sweeping his axe round to push the thronging soldiers back a little.

'These two ran into the castle after the raiding party, MacSweeny,' the sergeant shouted. 'They could be Scottish spies.'

MacSweeny rounded on the man. 'This man is indeed a spy—' he cocked his head towards le Poer '—but he's our spy. He's the man the messenger boy Conal was supposed to meet outside. The wee idiot got himself killed instead.'

'Who's the girl?' the sergeant said.

MacSweeny shook his head. The suspicion and hostility in the eyes of the men around them was clear. Galiene saw their gaunt faces and knew it was driven by the desperation born of starvation. They were probably not bad people but they were in a terrible situation. Her father had told her that desperate people could be driven to commit heartless actions they would not normally even contemplate.

'I know what you're all thinking,' MacSweeny said. 'but the chief says le Poer is on our side. We have to help them.'

'We don't need any more mouths to feed,' the sergeant shouted, giving voice to the so far unspoken concern of the rest of the men in the gatehouse. His words were greeted by a chorus of 'ayes' and nods.

'Where's MacHuylin?' MacSweeny, ignoring them, asked one of his galloglaich comrades.

The man shrugged.

Eyeing the girl, MacSweeny made a quick decision. 'Get me the castellan.'

The galloglaich did not have to go far as Henry de Thrapston, Keeper of Carrickfergus Castle, was at that moment hurrying into the gatehouse tower to see what all the commotion was about.

The long months of siege had clearly taken their toll on him; he was considerably thinner than the last time Galiene had seen him. His face seemed older as well and his long, fair hair was streaked with strands of grey. The reds and greens of his expensive tunic had faded and the elbows showed signs of being threadbare. As usual he carried on his belt a set of huge keys: the keys of the castle that were both the symbol and tools of his position as castellan. At first his relief was evident as he realised that the Scots had not broken in, but the expression on his face changed to concern when he saw the throng of angry warriors.

'What's going on?' he demanded. He had to shout to be heard not just above the hubbub in the gatehouse but against the rattles and thumps of missiles striking on the walls and closed drawbridge as the Scots warriors vented their frustration on the exterior of the castle.

'These two came in with the raiding party, sire,' the gate sergeant said. 'We don't have room for anyone else here. There isn't enough food for the people already here. We can't take in any more refugees.'

'Good God! Is that you, le Poer?' de Thrapston said, suddenly recognising the spy. 'Aren't you supposed to be halfway to Dublin by now with our messenger boy?'

Le Poer shook his head. 'The messenger didn't make it. MacHuylin has gone alone to try to deliver the message to the seneschal. I happened to be at the harbour when I saw Bruce's bodyguard bring Savage's daughter in as a prisoner. When the rest of them were distracted by the raiding party coming out of the castle I killed the two men guarding her and got her away. This was the only place we could go.'

The constable sighed. He looked down at Galiene and his face softened. 'Of course, Dame Alys's daughter. I remember the look of shock on Richard Savage's face when he found out he was actually your father. Well, if Edward Bruce had you as a prisoner then at least we've given him a bit of a bloody nose today.' He surveyed the meagre pickings in the cart the raiding party had returned with. 'Unfortunately it looks like that is about all we achieved today. Sergeant, these two can stay.'

'But, sire…' The sergeant looked far from happy. 'If she is a prisoner of Bruce then he will redouble his efforts to take this castle.'

De Thrapston held up a hand to silence him. 'MacHuylin has gone so le Poer can take his place. The boy has gone as well so there are no extra mouths to feed. I assure you, if she's half as resourceful as her mother then young Galiene will be more of a help than a hindrance in our current predicament.'

With that, the constable laid a hand on Galiene's shoulder and steered her away from the crowd of angry soldiers towards the inner ward of the castle, praying fervently that what he had said would turn out to be correct.

22

At sea

Savage was in Hell. It was not the fiery prison that his former Templar priest had warned him against, but the lurching, spray-soaked decks of a ship as it surged across the open sea.

He hated boats and had done all his life. When he was a Templar Knight, his arrival on the Egyptian coast to embark on what was practically a suicidal raid, had come as a blessed relief to him compared to the purgatory of the sea journey to get there. The shipwreck he had been involved in the year before had simply confounded his terror of travel by sea. For Savage, that experience was not reassuring proof that such a calamity was survivable. Instead it reinforced his unshakable conviction that boats were highly dangerous.

The first days of the journey had mercifully been lost to him in a haze of nausea and vomiting. Seasickness had kept him too busy to worry about the possibility of the ship sinking, but as they rounded the coast of Brittany he had gained his sea legs, the sickness had cleared and his time aboard ship became endless hours of nervous terror, his throat too dry to eat much, his mind too distracted by thoughts of the unforgiving, cold, green depths beneath the hull. Every lurch of the vessel, every bang or sudden crash, sent a jolt of panic through him as he expected to see a rock come crashing up through the deck from below, its wet, black surface heralding inescapable doom.

The ship was a long, wide-bodied, seagoing fishing boat. Its hull creaked and groaned as it lurched its way across the waves. The decks were open and there was very little in the way of cover. Savage spent a lot of time huddled miserably in the little shelter provided at the sides as spray and rain lashed over into the ship.

All the time Savage cursed himself for his own weakness and the fact that this was mere discomfort compared to the very real terror and imminent danger Galiene was in. His worrying was ridiculous.

As the grey dawn light grew on the fourth day of the voyage, an excited shout from one of the crew alerted everyone aboard that the coast of Ireland had been sighted. Savage hauled himself to his feet and saw to the north a line of ragged, black rocks topped with a skim of green grass rising into view between the sea and the sky. The sight brought home to Savage that his journey was nearly over and it was time to start putting his mind to what his next steps would be. Who was this mysterious "Fisher King" and what of the task Mortimer had sent him to fulfil? He needed to find out more about where he was headed and the only source of information available was the crew of the fishing boat. To question them would be a risky move, but Savage resolved he had to make it.

The captain had introduced himself as Cormac Breslin of Tír Chonaill, in a manner that suggested that was an important name to have. The man had so far largely ignored Savage, and the rest of the crew – four broad-shouldered, wild-bearded Irish fishermen – had followed suit. Savage imagined that to them he appeared little more than a miserable wretch wrapped in a black cloak, who spent most of his time either heaving over the side or huddled in a ball under what meagre shelter was available in the open boat. For his part he had kept himself to himself, wrapped in a wet blanket of his own misery, eating what little he could manage from his own supply of dried fish and restricting his interaction with the rest of the people on the ship to mere grunts or nods. He had to take the risk and change this if he was to find out more information.

'Doesn't like sailing does he?' one of the crew said to a colleague, commenting on Savage's pale face, tight lips and dark-rimmed eyes that constantly shot his nervous, over-agitated gaze this way and that. His companion replied with words that were blown away by the wind, so Savage did not catch them. Both men laughed. They were fishermen, wrapped in heavy wool cloaks, their beards were braided and their long hair tied up behind their heads. Both had piercing blue eyes and they spoke in the Irish language.

'If God had meant us to travel over water,' Savage said, responding in the same tongue, 'he would have given us fins.'

Both men started; looks of surprise, consternation and a little suspicion on their faces. This was the first time they had heard him speak on the voyage, but it was not the simple sound of his voice that surprised them.

'You speak Irish?' one of the fishermen said.

'I do,' Savage replied. 'Does that surprise you?'

The fisherman sniffed and looked away. 'We've ferried many like you across this sea in the last ten years and you're the first one who ever spoke our language.'

'Like me?' Savage asked. 'Templars, you mean?'

'Aye. Poor Knights of Christ,' the fisherman responded, a half-playful, half-sardonic light in his bright blue eyes. The last words were said with a definite tone of suspicion and a gaze levelled straight at him. Now the man looked at him with a new attitude and Savage could guess what he was thinking: there was only one sort of knight who would know how to speak the Irish language and that would be one from within the English Pale that marked the lands in Ireland ruled by the English Crown. In short, Savage had identified himself as an enemy.

The fisherman turned and walked off with some purpose towards the prow, leaving his companion to stay watching Savage with silent, challenging eyes. They did not have to wait long as the fisherman quickly returned, now accompanied by the ship's captain.

Captain Breslin's skin was tanned a deep brown by the elements. It had both the colour and texture of the leather of Savage's boots. His heavy wool cloak was loosely bound around his shoulders and the white linen shirt he wore beneath it was open exposing a forest of grey and white hairs that carpeted his chest. His thick, long white hair – bleached by the sun, the wind and the rain – trailed behind his head in the sea breeze. In his hand he carried a wineskin, which from its turgidity, appeared to be about half full of French wine: the cargo that the ship had exchanged its haul of fish for. For a few moments he stood a little way away, regarding Savage, head cocked to one side and with the all-encompassing gaze of a man trying to assess a horse he was thinking of buying. The fisherman who had brought him over stood a little way off, nonchalantly playing with a fish-gutting knife.

Eventually Breslin took a step forward. 'We need to talk,' he said, offering the wineskin to Savage. 'Drink?'

Savage nodded, took the proffered skin and sucked a long pull from it. The lukewarm, cheap acidic wine scorched his throat, but he was glad of it. He needed to keep his wits about him more than ever – so much depended on what they were about to discuss – and the liquid washed away the sour taste of vomit from his mouth and ignited a hot fire in his chest that stiffened his resolve.

'Enjoy it,' Breslin said, watching Savage's throat work as he swallowed the wine. 'It could be your last.'

23

'Niall tells me you speak our tongue,' Captain Breslin said, though the implied question was redundant as he was speaking that very language.

Savage nodded, handing the wineskin back to Breslin. 'Is that a surprise?'

'A bit of a surprise, I admit,' the captain said. 'I've taken many Templars across the sea from France to Ireland, but very few of them were Irish. There used to be a lot more of you a few years ago, back when they were hunting you around France. I've seen this boat packed to the gills – dangerously overloaded at times – with knights desperate to get away from the Inquisition. Lately, however, not so much. I suppose it's been ten years now, and all the Templars must have been either caught or have got away. Except you, it seems.'

He took a long drink of the wine. This time he did not offer it back to Savage.

'Now on top of all that you speak Irish,' Breslin said. 'And you being a knight as well can only mean you are an English bastard from the east of the country. You'd better start talking fast about what you're up to, my friend, or you'll find yourself swimming home.'

Savage smiled. 'You call me English, but my family have lived in Ireland for a century and a half—'

'And mine have lived there for a hundred centuries,' Breslin cut him off. Any last trace of fellow feeling was gone. 'What are you doing on my boat?'

Savage felt the boat rolling beneath his feet. There was a blazing sun in a clear blue sky above. The black, rocky coast was still a mere strip on the horizon. There was no way he would be able to swim that far. He needed to choose his next words carefully.

'It's true, I grew up in Ulster.' Savage nodded. 'My family were vassals of the earl.'

Breslin grunted. 'Richard Óg de Burgh? You're not doing yourself any favours here. The Red Earl of Ulster is a sworn enemy of our king. For years de Burgh harassed us from the east from Ulster and from the south from Connaught. It's not enough for him that he already owns half of Ireland but he wants Tír Chonaill as well. Mind you, he doesn't bother us much these days since Edward Bruce kicked him out of both his domains.'

'I left Ireland fifteen years ago and joined the Templars,' Savage rejoined. 'The only overlords I recognise are my grand master and the Pope. Set beside the greater struggle against the Saracens, the battles of Ireland are irrelevant; worse, a worthless distraction. Christians should not be fighting Christians.' He was doing his best to play the Templar zealot. It was not difficult as there was a time when it would not have required acting on his part.

'That's easy for you to say,' Breslin spat over the side. 'You are not being attacked in your own home by foreigners. ˙lands are not stolen, your laws overridden, your traditions destroyed. You were once a vassal of the Earl of Ulster. How do I not know you aren't still on his side?'

Savage stiffened, pushing back his shoulders and straightening his spine, playing the part of an offended pilgrim. 'I broke that bond of loyalty long ago when I joined the Templars. Also I can no longer serve de Burgh because he serves the English King Edward, who betrayed my Templar brethren to the Inquisition. If I return to English lands they will arrest me as a heretic.'

Captain Breslin nodded but did not relax his challenging gaze. 'It's well over ten years since your order was dissolved. Like I said, I carried many a Templar north from La Rochelle but the last one was over a year ago. You appear now? What have you been doing? All the Templars in France are long dead or converted to Hospitallers. Where did you come from?'

Savage was aware of the other four crew members hovering closer to catch his response.

'I was in the east, in Outremer,' he said, 'a prisoner of the Saracens. I was captured years ago on a Templar raid into Egypt. They held me in a terrible dungeon until I managed to escape. I spent another three years trying to get back to Europe. By the time I made my way back here to France I found that my order had long been persecuted and dissolved.'

Breslin looked at him for a long moment, clearly trying to decide if this was plausible or not. He shook his head, which Savage took as a bad sign. The other crew members edged closer and he saw that they now stood between him and his bag of belongings, which rested on the deck where he had been sitting. Strapped to it was his new sword, the

claidheamh mòr he had used in the tournament and which
Mortimer had given him as a weapon to use on his mission.
Savage cursed himself for being so stupid. He glanced
around to see if there was any other potential weapon
within reach, but the only thing near him was the heaped
mesh of a fishing net that lay on the deck close to his right
foot.

'What are your plans now?' the captain finally said. 'Why
are you going to Ireland?'

Savage knew his chance had come. Edward Bruce had
taken Galiene and he had to get to Ulster if he stood a
chance of saving her. To hell with Mortimer and his mission.
Galiene came first. He shrugged as nonchalantly as he could
manage. 'If I stay in France I will be arrested. If I go to
England the same thing will happen. I need to get away
from wherever the Pope's authority stretches or I will end
up back in a dungeon or tied to a stake waiting for them to
light the fire. I hear Edward Bruce needs trained men for his
fight in Ireland. I want to join his cause.'

Breslin spat over the side again as a general murmur of
discontent went around the other crew members.

'Last year that might have got you some credit here,
friend,' Breslin said. 'But times have changed. Edward Bruce
isn't an ally of Tír Chonaill. His bastard brother attacked
our cousins in the Western Isles and he's now as much an
enemy of ours as he is of the English. If you intend to join
Edward Bruce then your journey with us ends here. Even if
I wanted to take you to Bruce I couldn't. The borders into
Ulster are closed by our bastard cousins in Tyr Eoghan who
side with the Scots.'

He looked at Savage for another moment, his head

cocked to one side. Then he added, 'But something about you tells me you aren't being straight with me. What do you think, lads?' Breslin addressed his crew.

'I think he's full of shit,' the fisherman the captain had referred to as Niall replied.

Breslin nodded. 'I agree. Throw him over the side.'

24

Breslin turned away as his crew stalked towards Savage, malicious grins cracking their weathered faces. Niall held the fish-gutting knife before him. Two of his companions now also openly brandished the knives they had been concealing behind their backs, and the fourth man – a huge, bald brute with very few teeth – gleefully swung a heavy blackthorn club that looked more than capable of knocking Savage's brains out.

Savage assessed his chances. They were not great: it was four against one. He felt weak from not eating properly for days and unlike the fishermen, who advanced barefoot with the steady, practised gait of sailors, he lurched and swayed as the deck pitched and rolled with the waves.

The big man shouldered his way past his companions to get to Savage first.

'Come on, you English bastard!' he shouted as he swung his club up in a blow aimed at stoving in the side of Savage's head.

Savage ducked, crouching down on his thighs. He felt the wind from the head of the club as it swiped past, narrowly missing the top of his skull. He threw himself sideways, dipping under the big fisherman's right arm and grabbing a handful of the fishing net on the deck at his feet as he went. Directly ahead, the man's three companions were coming on, knives at the ready. Savage delivered a vicious sideways kick to the right knee of the big man who shrieked in pain as he dropped heavily to the deck.

Savage dashed forwards towards the other oncoming fishermen then swerved left towards the side of the ship, trailing the net with him.

The fishermen let out cries of surprise as they realised what he was doing. They raised their arms to try to stop him, hoping that the blades would slice through the web of the net before it engulfed them. They were too late and Savage half threw, half hauled the net up and over their heads, completely covering and entangling them in its rough, fish-smelling mesh. They shouted and struggled but their wild thrashing only succeeded in further ensnaring them.

Savage spat on the tangled heap. 'Don't call me English,' he said as he stepped away from the trapped fishermen. He had temporarily dealt with most of his assailants but this would not last long. The men in the net were already desperately sawing at the mesh with the knives and the big man was already clambering to his feet again. Alerted by the shouting, the captain had turned back towards Savage and was drawing the long dagger that hung from a scabbard on his belt.

Before he could get it clear, Savage charged into him, dipping his shoulder and crashing straight into the man's chest. Savage checked himself but Breslin staggered backwards and hit the side of the ship. His momentum carried him over and he toppled off the ship, tumbling head over heels. His cry of surprise was cut short by a loud splash as he hit the water below.

Savage ran to his bag and ripped his sword from its sheath strapped to the outside of it. The long blade of the claidheamh mòr slipped noiselessly from the lambswool-lined, mutton-greased scabbard. A sense of relief and satisfaction settled on Savage as he felt the weight of the weapon in his hands. He swung round to face his enemies but to his surprise he found no immediate danger. The men in the net had fallen over, their struggles having increased their entanglement to the point that they were now hopelessly caught – at least until they managed to saw through the mesh, but their pinioned arms meant that with restricted movement this would take some time. The big man with the club had run to the side of the ship and was staring down at Breslin, a look of helpless distress on his face as his captain struggled in the surging waves below. Swinging round to Savage, his toothless face a mask of panic and despair, he cried, 'He can't swim!' pointing at the captain, who plunged beneath the surface as he spoke.

'So what?' Savage said. 'He wanted me to drown.'

'He's my uncle,' the big man said, his voice pleading. His voice was high and cracked with an almost childlike terror.

Savage briefly considered the situation and came to a quick conclusion. 'Help him,' he ordered the big man as he went to the men still clogged in the net. He placed a foot on the bottom of it to pin them down. He pressed the point of his sword onto one of the men through the net and applied some downward pressure – enough to give them the message without causing injury.

'Lie still,' Savage ordered. The men in the net immediately obeyed.

The big man ran to the prow of the ship and grabbed a rope. Returning, he threw it over the side into the heaving green water. Breslin had resurfaced, at least temporarily, thanks to his desperate thrashing and kicking.

'Grab this, Uncle!' the big man shouted. Before long he was hauling Breslin with impressive strength up out of the water. Once over the side and back on board, the captain collapsed onto the deck and lay sprawled on his back gasping and coughing. Water streamed from his clothes while his impressive mane of white hair was now a sodden mass plastered over his face.

Realising that Breslin represented a hostage with a higher value than the men in the net, Savage strode across to where he lay spluttering and planted the point of his claidheamh mòr firmly on the man's chest. His heart was pounding now and he once more felt strong and in control. The exhilaration of the brief fight had banished his sickness and weakness.

'Get everyone's weapons and bring them to me,' he ordered the big man. 'Don't try anything or I'll skewer your uncle here to the deck.'

With a surly glance, the fisherman loped off to untangle his crew mates from the net and take their knives. Breslin appeared to have lost his knife during his time in the water. Before long all the weapons were deposited at Savage's feet while the crew stood warily by, looks of both hostility and trepidation on their faces. They were unarmed, but their eyes darted this way and that, clearly watching for any opportunity that would allow them to have another go at Savage.

'What are you going to do to us?' asked Breslin, who had regained his composure and now lay still under the point of Savage's blade, looking up at the knight who stood over him.

'If you do what I say, then you'll be all right,' Savage said. 'Your ship is now under my command. If you ever want it back – and you want to stay alive – then you will do what I say and take me where I want to go.'

Breslin sighed and nodded to his crew members. 'All right,' he said. 'Can I get up though? I can't take you very far if I'm lying on my back.'

'First swear you will not try to attack me,' Savage said. He doubted such an oath would hold much water, but it was worth the effort of extracting it, just in case it did.

'I swear by Jesus, Mary and Joseph and the blessed Saint Patrick,' Breslin said. He did not go further and Savage applied some more downward pressure on the sword point.

'That you will not attack me,' Savage prompted.

Breslin winced and gasped, 'That I will not attack you.'

Savage waited one more moment then lifted his sword from the captain's chest. 'Very well,' he said, moving quickly away from him and out of any form of striking distance. He kept his weapon raised and ready while Breslin struggled to his feet.

'Get back to the oar,' Savage ordered, indicating with the tip of his sword towards the long handle of the steering oar. Breslin nodded and staggered back to the stern of the ship.

As the crew began busying themselves with the tasks of setting the sails and getting the ship back on course, Savage took up a position near the rear of the boat where he stood, sword drawn and ready in case the crew tried anything further. He was within easy striking distance of Breslin, who steered the ship from there, and from this vantage point could see everything that was happening on the deck.

The ship, which while unattended had drifted to a halt, sails flapping, began to surge northward once again and the strip of dark land on the horizon grew larger as they got nearer. Keeping a close eye on the crew, Savage began to think about just what his next steps should be. He now had command of a ship. All he needed was some sort of plan for what to do with it.

25

Carrickfergus

MacHuylin had hidden in the surgeon's house until nightfall. The Scots army thronged outside the castle, launching ineffective attacks on the gatehouse, but like all their previous attempts, they had got nowhere. As the day darkened into night and the Scots began to leave the market square, MacHuylin simply walked out and joined them. With his axe hefted over his shoulder, his helmet dangling from its shaft by its straps and whistling like he had not a care in the world, MacHuylin sauntered out of the town like any other Scottish soldier.

Carefree as he looked, he kept a wary eye on the soldiers he moved among, in case he bumped into some of the survivors of the fight in the town square earlier. Around him were warriors of all kinds, the collection of different cultures that Robert Bruce had somehow managed to weld together into a nation. There were armoured knights on foot and on horseback, the nobles descended from Norman adventurers who, like their Irish counterparts, had left the borders of England and forsaken all former allegiances as they went. They were accompanied by men-at-arms in mail and leather armour, squat spearmen from the lowlands whose forefathers had been a mixture of the Old Welsh of the last northern British kingdoms and the Saxons who had conquered them.

Among them were barefooted warriors, kerns from the highlands and islands in long kilts and padded linen jerkins, indistinguishable from their Irish cousins on the north and west coasts. As MacHuylin walked among them he considered how easy it would be for him to switch sides. With his weapons and armour he did not look out of place, and though a big man there were plenty of other big men with blond hair, mixed Norse-Gaels from the north and west of Scotland. Edward Bruce would welcome a professional soldier like him on his side and right now it looked like the Scots were winning. Some of these men were probably cousins of his, he reflected; blood relations or kin through marriage. His own family's origins lay in Scotland after all, so why continue to fight against them?

As fast as the thought arose, he dismissed it. It was true his clan had come to Ireland a century before, but now this was their home. His forefathers had fought for the kings of Ulster, then when they were conquered, their new Anglo-Norman overlords. This was not the time to start jumping ship. His kin may come from the Western Islands of Scotland, but like many there they had supported the Dunkeld line of the Scottish Royal House, who tended to leave the wilder parts of their kingdom to their own ways. Preferring this freedom to subjugation, they had repeatedly opposed the Bruces on their relentless march to power and in the end had paid the price. Robert Bruce had marched west on several campaigns to subdue the people of Galloway and the isles and many had lost life or lands, been deposed and sent into exile, which usually meant a southward migration into Ireland.

Mercenary though he was, MacHuylin felt deep inside that joining an army led by one of the Bruce brothers was a step too far. Aside from that, there could be reasons that Bruce would not, in fact, welcome him. MacHuylin's father had taken part in the failed invasion of the north of Scotland by the Irish in 1298. Also, although the galloglaich was no saint, even he could see that the conduct of the Scottish army in Ireland so far had been brutal. Because of it they were losing friends and allies among the native Irish, the people who should be supporting them. Finally, and most importantly, what really made up his mind was the thought that although they were on the ropes at the moment, the one thing he could be sure of was that the English Exchequer held a lot of gold and they always paid their dues, even if it took a long time. He was not so sure about Edward Bruce. It was this final consideration that convinced him to continue with his present mission.

MacHuylin filed out of the town gates into the dusk with the rest of the Scottish army, which was based in a now semi-permanent encampment outside the ramparts of the burned town. In the gathering gloom of evening he ducked off the path into some undergrowth, making a show as if going for a piss. After a quick glance to see no one was watching him, he sloped off into the trees that lined the road and kept on going.

He needed to get to Dublin to the seneschal, Thomas de Mandeville and the Earl of Ulster, to tell them that the castle was desperately low on food. If they were not relieved soon then Henry de Thrapston would have no choice but to surrender it, and if it fell, then the last toehold of resistance against the Scots in the north would go with it.

Once he was sure he was reasonably far away from any Scots patrols, MacHuylin used the last moments of daylight to build himself a shelter in the woods from stones and branches hewn from the trees with his axe. Then as the chill of the early spring night settled around him, he crawled inside, wrapped himself in his cloak and fell asleep, his belly gurgling and rumbling with ever-present hunger. At dawn's light he awoke, breakfasted on water from a nearby stream then started on his long journey south.

As he walked, he passed through countryside that was familiar to him from before the war but now was hostile and occupied. The Scots army in its desperate need to feed itself had stripped the land bare. Fields were empty, cattle and other livestock gone; farmsteads and barns had been robbed and burned to the ground. What had once been the lush, fertile Ulster countryside around Carrickfergus now resembled a barren waste land. The constant rain conspired with the war to churn the abandoned fields to mud. The people who had once owned and tended the land were either dead, fled or laid too low and weak by hunger to do anything about it. MacHuylin was shocked at how desolate and ravaged the land was. Over the months he had watched from the battlements of Carrickfergus Castle and seen the smoke of countless fires all along the lough shore and inland but he had no idea of the extent of the ruin that had been visited on the surrounding country.

MacHuylin kept to the main road south. Now and again the thrumming of hooves on the ground alerted him to an approaching Scottish patrol and he ducked off the road to hide behind a stone wall or into some bushes. Here and there rotted human corpses, reduced to mere skeletons, held together by sinew and scraps of black flesh, dangled from the branches of roadside trees, the remnants of summary executions.

He passed very few people, but several miles south of Carrickfergus there was a small group of men and women sitting beside the road. All looked to be in a terrible state. Their clothes were little more than rags. They were emaciated beyond belief, gaunt-cheeked and staring at him from hollow, dark and hungry eyes as he passed. He noticed with a start that their mouths and teeth were stained dark green and realised they must have been reduced to eating grass and leaves to survive. They did not say anything, but just watched him go past. MacHuylin did not like the ravenous looks they gave him and glanced over his shoulder to make sure none of them followed. He had little doubt that the sight of his axe and his demeanour, which conveyed the fact that he could take care of himself in a fight, probably saved him from the gruesome fate that would befall a weaker and more defenceless traveller along that road. He shuddered to think what acts of depravity starvation might drive these people to.

He was not exactly in good shape himself. The months spent besieged had taken their toll and he was half the man he used to be. He could see his bones under the skin of his ribs and sometimes when he pushed his tongue against his teeth he was sure they were starting to move in his gums. His fitness had suffered too, though he had made sure that he and his men filled much of those hours of forced inaction within the castle with training and exercise. Nevertheless, he found the going hard, especially as he had his weapons and chain mail to carry. Walking in armour was too uncomfortable, so his chain mail coat now also hung from the shaft of his axe, and the weight of it combined with the reduced meat he had on his bones meant that the shaft dug an uncomfortable groove into his shoulder.

He needed a horse.

Eight miles south-west of Carrickfergus he came to the familiar environs of Syr Thomas de Mandeville's manor. MacHuylin knew the place well. De Mandeville, as Seneschal of Ulster, had been MacHuylin's commander and the galloglaich had been de Mandeville's right-hand man. In the chaos that followed the army of Ulster's defeat by the Scots, de Mandeville had retreated south with the earl, Richard de Burgh, and what was left of the army.

As he approached the gates of the estate, MacHuylin could see that the Scots had been busy there too. Edward Bruce had clearly paid special attention to the dwelling of one of his principal opponents. De Mandeville's large, modern mansion was now a gutted ruin, burned to the ground and the remnants of the walls pulled apart. The barns and all the outlying buildings had been destroyed as well. The vegetable patches before the manor house had been stripped and dug up. The pond that once had been home to a flock of ducks now was a black pool on which a few bedraggled feathers drifted. The motte, a defensive mound topped by a palisaded fence – the last place of refuge in desperate times – had been destroyed and pulled down.

MacHuylin sighed, reasoning to himself that it had been a forlorn hope that anything would remain at all, never mind that the stables might still contain any horses. As he surveyed the silent ruins the sound of raised voices came to his ears. He tensed, but then relaxed, realising that the sound was coming from some way off through the copse of trees that stood behind where the manor house had once been. He knew that a path led off a short way through the woods to the farm of one of the seneschal's tenants. Thinking that if there was a farmstead, there might be something useful there, he placed his axe over his shoulder and set off to have a look.

The path was edged by hawthorn hedges beginning to speckle with white blossom. Despite this welcome sign of spring, as he walked through trees he saw little sign of new green foliage yet. The weather was delaying the turn of the seasons, which did not bode well for the prospects of harvest later in the year. The track itself was muddy and to his excitement he could see the deep impressions of horse hooves in it. Given that it had been raining almost constantly for weeks, they must be reasonably fresh. As he rounded a corner, MacHuylin stopped dead, utterly astonished at the sight that lay before him.

Two hobynys, the light, manoeuvrable horses used by both the Irish and Scots, stood tethered a little way ahead. One grey and one black. He couldn't believe his luck. They were just standing there, unattended on the woodland path, waiting for him to take them. Not wanting to scare the creatures, he began to advance carefully towards them, taking light footsteps and trying not to make much noise.

As he got closer to the hobynys, he saw that it was a good thing he had been so stealthy.

26

A little further ahead, beyond the horses, the path ran out of the trees and into a wide, open area. Several houses stood in the clearing; round, daub-and-wattle dwellings with no windows and flat, thatched roofs. These were creats, the houses built by the Irish. They were the homes of a family of the seneschal's tenants, peasants who worked the land for the lord and paid their rent in livestock, crops and labour.

The family were on their knees outside their house, their hands clasped on their heads. Two sergeants in mail coats, one with a drawn sword and one with a mace, towered over the peasants, shouting in their faces and prodding them with their weapons. A little way off three bored-looking kerns squatted or lounged on the ground, their spears propped against their shoulders.

The sergeants wore surcoats that told MacHuylin they were soldiers of the Earl of Moray, one of the nobles in Edward Bruce's army. He surmised that the horses must belong to them and the kerns would have jogged alongside them. There were four captives, which included an older man of perhaps forty, the balding crown of his head only slightly covered by wisps of lank, greasy hair. His grey-haired wife cowered beside him, a look of desolation on her dark, skeletal face. Their two children – not quite children but not yet adults – a boy and a girl, hung their heads in submission, not daring to look up at the armed men who towered over them. All of them were dressed in the long tunics and hoods worn by the Irish, but their clothes hung on their skinny frames like flags on a standard pole.

MacHuylin lurked behind the horses, watching and listening to the scene before him.

'You've taken everything we have,' the bearded farmer wailed. 'You know we've nothing left.'

'Oh have we now?' one of the men-at-arms said, his voice high and holding a nasal quality common to some Scottish accents. 'Well our scouts said they saw you all down the beach earlier digging in the sand. We think you've got a nice wee pot of whelks or mussels somewhere.'

'That's all we have to eat,' the woman cried. 'We worked all day for them.'

'Hush, woman, now they know we have them!' the farmer said, glaring at his wife in disbelief.

'Shut your mouth,' the Scots sergeant said, cuffing the farmer backhanded with a mailed glove and sending him reeling to the ground. 'Where's the food, woman? You know well that your king, Lord Edward Bruce, has decreed all food must be shared with his army.'

The woman glanced at her husband, a look of shock and fear on her face as she saw the blood oozing from the cut opened across his left cheekbone by the blow. She pointed in the direction of a nearby house. 'We put them in the back when we saw you coming.'

MacHuylin turned his attention away from the scene and

back to the horses. The farmer and his family were causing a very welcome distraction and if he was to get away with stealing a mount then he was best not to waste this golden opportunity. Walking with light feet so as not to disturb the creatures, he closed the distance to them and laid a soothing hand on the neck of the grey. When he was satisfied it was not going to jib, he opened one of the saddle bags and pushed his chain mail coat into it. He put his helmet on, more for a means to carry it and free up a hand than for defence, so did not bother to lace it. Swiftly he unwrapped the reins that tethered the horse to a tree branch and, whispering calming noises and clicking his tongue, began to lead it back down the path away from the farmstead. To his further advantage the soft ground muffled the sound of the horse's hooves while the animal's owners were busy bullying the farmer and his family. For the second time, MacHuylin thanked his lucky stars, then judging himself far enough away, swung himself up into the saddle and began riding away.

'You'll leave us some?' the farmer's wife pleaded behind him. 'We're starving!'

As he rode, MacHuylin looked back over his shoulder to make sure he was getting away without being spotted.

'We might've, if you'd been honest in the first place and told us about them,' the nasal-voiced Scot said. 'But we'll be taking them all now. Eoghan, get your men in there and find that pot of whelks. With any luck she'll have cooked them for us too.' He gestured to the tallest kern who stood up and led the other two into the nearest house. The sounds of ransacking soon began inside.

MacHuylin reined the horse to a stop. He closed his eyes and sighed. He knew it was stupid but he just could not ride away. Consoling himself that what he was about to do was actually because he was starving and needed food himself and not because he was going soft, he turned the horse.

Axe in one hand, reins in the other, MacHuylin kicked his heels into the horse's flanks, goading it into a startled gallop. The drumming of hooves made the Scotsmen turn but he was already almost on top of them. The nearest was a veteran warrior, but MacHuylin judged that months with little to do but bully and rob peasants had dulled his instincts. He was still opening his mouth to ask MacHuylin's business when the galloglaich's axe scythed into his face. The wide, crescent-shaped blade drove through the man's head, taking the top half of it off like opening a boiled egg. A fountain of bright red blood erupted from the horrific wound as the Scotsman staggered backwards, already dead but still on his feet. The corpse collapsed to the ground and his companion yelled an inarticulate warning to the kerns in the house. He had no shield to defend himself but crouched in the path of the horse, sword point levelled at its breast.

Without mercy, MacHuylin wrenched the horse's head up so it could not see the man before it and kicked his heels into its flanks, charging it directly into him. The sergeant tried to move out of the way, but there was no time. He went down under the thrashing hooves with a cry of dismay. As he did so, he managed to stab his sword upwards and the blade went deep into the creature's flesh. The hobyny horse screamed. A combination of the wound and having the man tangled in its legs brought it down, falling forwards face first in a tangle of flailing legs and smashed Scotsman. As it fell, MacHuylin swung his right leg over the horse's back so he would not be trapped beneath the beast. He jumped clear of the carnage, landed in a crouch and rolled head over heels.

In an instant he was back on his feet and running back the way he had come. He swerved around the writhing horse, not even pausing as he chopped down with his axe on the man beneath it just to make sure he was dead, then he was away, back across the clearing. From the corner of his eye he saw the farmer and his family gaping open-mouthed as he passed and the startled kerns emerging from the doorway of the round house.

MacHuylin made it back to the second horse. Grabbing its mane he swung himself up onto its back. There was no time to untie the reins but a chop of his axe freed the creature from its tether. The galloglaich grabbed the remnants and steered the creature round to face the approaching kerns.

The men were coming forwards, cautious, spear points held out before them. MacHuylin reined the agitated horse to a prancing stop. He hefted his axe up in one hand and levelled his gaze at the approaching warriors. Seeing that he was not advancing, they also stopped.

'The way I see it, lads, it's like this,' he said, addressing the kerns in their own language. 'There are three of you against one of me but I have a horse. You could well kill me but I will kill at least one of you, maybe two. Let's face it; it didn't take much to kill your two sergeants.'

The kerns exchanged glances.

'Now, given that your officers are dead,' MacHuylin continued, 'how about you boys just walk away and leave these folks alone and we say no more about this? That way we all stay alive and with those two dead, when you get back to camp who's to say you weren't ambushed by a whole horde of screaming Irishmen and you were lucky to get away with your lives – after a hard, desperate fight of course? We all get to stay hale and hearty and you boys maybe even get to look like heroes.'

One of the kerns nodded. 'Sounds like a good idea, Cathal,' he commented to his larger companion who seemed to be the leader.

Cathal looked at MacHuylin, trying to assess how hard it would be to kill him. It did not take long to decide that it would be far from easy.

'Aye,' he said, lowering his spear. He spat in the direction of the dead sergeants. 'I never liked those bastards anyway.'

MacHuylin grinned, noting with some interest that all was clearly not well in the Scottish-Irish alliance. 'Good choice, lads. Off you go.'

The kerns took off at a jog down the woodland track. MacHuylin watched them go then when he was sure they were gone he dropped his axe to his side and walked the horse into the clearing, going first to the still-struggling hobyny pony to end its misery with a chop to the throat.

'Thank you, thank you.' The farmer was on his feet, his face brightened by a look of surprise and relief.

'Get those whelks,' MacHuylin replied. 'I'm starving.'

Dismay clouded the face of the farmer's wife. 'You mean to rob us too?'

MacHuylin pointed to the dead horse with his axe. 'There's enough meat there to keep you going for a month.'

The woman nodded, the expression of ravenous delight that lit her face made MacHuylin wonder if they would even wait to cook it. She went into the house and returned with the pot of boiled whelks, draining it and pouring the contents into a bag that she handed to MacHuylin.

With something to eat and a horse to carry him, it was a considerably happier Connor MacHuylin who recommenced his journey south towards Dublin.

27

At sea, off the south coast of Ireland

They sailed onward towards the shore for some time in sullen, resentful silence. The crew busied themselves with setting the sails and other chores but watched Savage the whole time. He knew they were waiting for him to drop his vigilance and present them with a chance to rush him.

Captain Breslin stood at the steering tiller, implacable in his task of keeping the boat on course. Finally he spoke. 'Sooner or later you're going to have to tell me what you plan to do with my ship,' he said. 'Otherwise we'll run aground on the rocks.'

Savage looked at him for a moment, trying to decide if he should just tell the man to shut his mouth or not, then concluded that he probably had a point. 'I've already told you. I need you to take me to Ulster,' he said.

Breslin grunted and spat over the side, a habit that was beginning to annoy Savage. 'So you do mean to try to join Bruce's Scottish army there? Well like I told you before, it's out of the question.'

Raising the point of his sword, Savage placed it against Breslin's throat. 'I think you're forgetting who is holding the weapon here,' he said. 'If I tell you that is where we are going then your only concern is how to get me there. You've no say in this matter.'

Cormac Breslin smiled. 'The problem is that there's no way to get to Ulster, whether I wanted to take you there or not.'

'You said the border between Tír Chonaill and Ulster was closed,' Savage said, a frown of irritation crossing his face. 'This is a ship. We can sail around the coast to get there. What do we care about land boundaries?'

'It's true that there is no way through Tír Chonaill by land into Ulster any more – unless you get permission and safe passage from our king that is – but have you heard of Tavish Dhu?' Breslin said.

Savage nodded. Black Tavish – known to the English as Thomas Dun – was a notorious pirate commissioned by Edward Bruce to supply a fleet of ships for his invasion of Ireland.

'Well clearly you aren't aware that Tavish rules the seas between Ireland and Scotland these days,' the captain said. 'His fleet of ships are like a navy for the Scots. They're just pirates really, but Robert Bruce pays him to keep the supply route for his troops in Ireland open and at the same time keep those of the English closed. Tavish attacks any ships that try to cross the Irish Sea or go into Ulster, unless they're Scottish. He seems to have eyes everywhere and appears like magic somehow anywhere from the northern coast of Ireland to south of Dublin. When the King of England sent the new governor to Ireland last year he was so scared of being attacked by Tavish Dhu that he travelled with a fleet. We are just a little fishing boat. If one of Tavish's ships spots us they'll attack, cut our throats and sink our boat. The sea routes into Ulster are closed. You need to rethink your plans, I'm afraid.'

Savage was quiet as he considered the implications of this information. How on earth was he to get to Ulster if this was the case?

'Not that it's important but no, I do not want to join Edward Bruce's army,' he finally said with a sigh of resignation. 'As a matter of fact the bastard has kidnapped my daughter. I want to get to Ulster so I can rescue her.'

Breslin looked at him for a long moment, his eyes narrowed, clearly trying to work out if Savage was telling the truth.

'In that case your best bet is to go by land, but even that will be difficult,' he said. 'As I told you, our king is no friend of Edward Bruce or his Irish lackey Ui Neill of Tyr Eoghan.'

'So why doesn't King Aed of Tír Chonaill attack Bruce in Ulster?' Savage asked.

Breslin shook his head and sighed heavily. 'We won't be fighting Bruce or Ui Neill either, to our eternal shame. No, we'll just be sitting idly by like a bunch of cowards while the war continues. Unless they attack us, we won't be attacking them.'

'Because to do so would help the English?'

'No. Because of the *Liopard*,' the captain grunted. 'He tells our king he is not to fight and so we don't fight.'

Savage's interest was pricked. *Liopard* was the Irish word for leopard. Breslin must be referring to the mysterious knight that Mortimer wanted dead. 'Who is this Liopard?' he asked. 'Aren't they wild beasts from Africa?'

'This is a wild beast from France,' Breslin said. 'A beast of a man. He's a knight, like you, and also on the run. He came to our kingdom about four years ago for the same reason you want to go there: neither English nor Papal authority holds sway there, though we swear allegiance to the Holy Father. He's a vicious fighter and fears neither man nor God. He took lands in the west of Tír Chonaill, made his home on an island in the middle of Lough Dou that has an ancient fort on it. Some monks had made it their home, but he chased them all away. They say he has made a pact with the Devil.'

'He must be very wise in the ways of war if your king listens to his counsel,' Savage commented.

At this Breslin laughed, but it was a harsh, bitter laugh that held no mirth. 'He listens to his counsel because he has no choice. Something you may understand if you are telling me the truth about your daughter. The Liopard took Aed's daughter Brianna and holds her hostage. If the king does not do what the Liopard wants he'll kill her.'

It was all starting to make sense to Savage. 'But he's just one man. Why doesn't the king just storm his island with an army and take his daughter back?'

Breslin shook his head. 'The Liopard is too strong. When he is in his armour none can defeat him. On top of that he keeps his own war band around him, men-at-arms who guard the island. He's a vicious bastard and the king loves his daughter – God help him – and if they saw him coming the girl would be dead long before their boats reached the shore. If anyone tries to sneak onto the island, well...'

he hesitated and looked away, avoiding Savage's eyes for a moment '…there's the dragon to contend with.'

'Dragon?' Savage glanced around at the captain, checking he was not having a laugh. 'What is this nonsense? There's no such thing as dragons.'

The captain returned his gaze with one of sudden burning conviction. 'Aye, you may laugh but it's true. The Liopard has a dragon that guards his island. We call it a paiste in Irish: a water demon. The beast has lived in the lough for a thousand years, but when Saint Columba brought the Christian faith he banished it to the bottom of the lough and it lost all its power. But now the Liopard has expelled the Christian priests from his lands and the devil has made it powerful again. It's a great, evil-looking thing covered in scales as hard as the iron armour a knight wears. Its teeth are like saws. I can see by the look on your face that you think this is peasant superstition, but you can ask the widows of the eight men it tore to shreds if it's true or not. Niall there's own brother was one of them.' He gestured at the little crewman who was busy hauling in rope attached to the mainsail. 'Ask him if you don't believe me. All they found of his brother was his foot.'

There were a few seconds of intense silence as Savage met the challenging glare of the captain who seemed to be daring him to continue his disbelief.

Savage could see he would get no further sense on this topic. 'Why do they call this knight "the Leopard"?' he asked, deciding to change the subject. The only man Savage had heard referred to as "the Leopard" before now was Edward Longshanks, King of England, and the current

King Edward's royal father. This certainly could not be him. The old king had been dead for ten years.

'He wears the spotted pelt of one of those beasts around his shoulders when he rides into battle,' Breslin said. 'And he has three of them painted on his shield as his coat of arms.'

Savage frowned. Again here was something strange. Three leopards or perhaps lions – lions passant as the heralds would call them – were on the coat of arms of the royal family of England. What was going on and why did Mortimer want this man dead? More importantly, why send him to do it? Perhaps Mortimer wanted there to be no connection between himself and the killing?

'Where are we?' Savage once again changed the subject.

'Off the south coast of Ireland,' the captain said.

Savage thought for a few moments. 'How far to Limerick?'

Breslin shook his head again. 'You're out of luck there too, my friend. The Red Earl of Ulster lost the Kingdom of Connacht to Felim O'Connor earlier this year. O'Connor is on Bruce's side. You'll be no more welcome there than we are as Tír Chonaill men.'

'I thought O'Connor was a vassal of de Burgh,' Savage said, eyebrows raised.

'He was,' Breslin said, 'but when Edward Bruce kicked the earl out of Ulster, Felim saw his chance to kick him out of Connacht too. I can't say I blame him.'

'Is Earl Richard dead?' Savage asked, astounded at the advances Edward Bruce and his Irish allies had made in the last year. Between them they must now control half of Ireland – the north-east and the south-west. Aed Ó Donaill controlled the far north-west while the Lordship of Ireland was reduced to the bottom south-east of the island.

'No,' Breslin said. 'He was sent packing with his tail between his legs and he's now holed up in Dublin with the rest of whatever's left of the English-backed government.'

Savage considered this for a moment. If Earl Richard de Burgh was in Dublin then Syr Thomas de Mandeville, his Seneschal of Ulster and military commander, would be there too. Along with him would be other people he knew he could trust from his former adventures: perhaps Guilleme le Poer or even Connor MacHuylin. Those men could help him get back to Ulster.

'Tell your crew to turn this ship around,' Savage announced. 'We have a new heading. We sail for Dublin.'

28

Carrickfergus

Galiene felt as if she had escaped from a boiling pot only to land in the fire. Since she had been snatched from her home her world had been turned upside down and life had been a series of trials that just seemed to keep coming. She worried terribly about what had happened to her mother. The last she had heard of Alys was her frantic screaming as the Scotsmen had carried Galiene off. She had been tied hands and feet and thrown over the back of a horse. As they rode away she had seen the black smoke rising behind them that could only be her home burning.

The ride to the border with French territory was frantic and, slung over the back of a horse as she was, almost unbearable. Distressed and worried, she had cried most of the way until one of her captors, the big, foul-breathed Scotsman called Harper, had finally declared he had heard enough of her wailing and tied a filthy piece of cloth around her mouth. Added to the discomfort of her position she had then to cope with the gagging sensation

156

this induced as she fought not to vomit with every jarring step of the galloping horse. Once over the border they were met by a conroi of French troops and thankfully the pace of their journey slowed.

Harper told her on the sea voyage back to Ireland that they had taken her to make her father return the Holy Grail. The Grail belonged to the Bruce brothers and they wanted it back. Galiene had laughed and told him the truth, that her father had thrown the Grail away. To her satisfaction she could tell that this unnerved the men around her. Harper had barked that she should be quiet. When instead she had continued to taunt him, he had punched her hard in the stomach, a blow that left her in agony on the deck of the ship. Seeing how easily the Scotsman was prepared to hit her, the girl did her best to stay out of his way for the rest of the journey. This was not easy, however, as Harper had treated her as his personal slave, making her get him food and drink, fetch things for him or wash his clothes – tasks all encouraged by a kick to her behind or a cuff round the ear.

'I'll teach you manners, you wee bitch,' he had said. 'By God and all the saints I will. I'm not allowed to kill you, but I've permission to chastise you if you misbehave, so it's time to start doing what you're told.'

By the time they reached Carrickfergus she had been black and blue with bruises. She was still trying to come to terms with her sudden, bloody rescue, where the seemingly harmless, lunatic preacher had unexpectedly dealt two swift, professional strokes that killed the men holding her. This had been followed by the mad dash through the carnage of the battle in the marketplace and into the castle, where she ought to have finally felt safe. However she felt far from it.

In France her mother had taken her to church every week. Her father had never come along: just one more part of family life that from her point of view he had refused to take part in. These thoughts, however, brought a pang of regret, as she had come to see something of what her mother saw in Richard Savage; the man whom Galiene now knew as her father. He toiled hard to try to make the farm in Gascony work, even though it was obvious he was not cut out for farming, and in his own clumsy way he was affectionate and kind to her.

At the church they had attended, the florid-faced priest had ranted about the new doctrine of Purgatory, the strange state that existed beyond death that was neither Heaven nor Hell. He had been obsessed by the topic and talked endlessly every Sunday about the ghosts that existed in that place, a misty region populated by those who were neither alive nor completely dead. Galiene now felt she had arrived in that very place. The men who defended the walls of Carrickfergus Castle were clad in plate armour, chain mail and padded leather, but when they stripped this off, their clothes hung limp over their scrawny frames, their bones protruding through their flesh. Their cheeks were gaunt and their eyes sunken into dark hollows by the starvation imposed by the siege. Wherever she went in the castle, all of the besieged watched her with those hollow eyes and she was painfully aware of their hostile glances. Part of her could understand their thoughts. She was a young girl. She could not fight on the walls; she could not take part in the defence of the castle. She was just another useless mouth that had to be fed from a store that was already empty.

Her main problem was occupying her time and finding

somewhere that she did not have to endure the endless, resentful glances. Her rescuer, Guilleme le Poer, was immediately pressed into military service defending the walls and she saw little more of him. Henry de Thrapston had been kind to her and let her sleep in the castle keep but he was busy running the castle and she could not just follow him around all day. He had tasked her with helping out in the kitchens, but in a besieged castle that had run out of food there was not much to do after the daily cauldron of thin gruel had been produced. So, aching with hunger, Galiene took to wandering about the ward and the walls of the castle, trying to keep out of everyone's way and be as inconspicuous as possible.

When she had brought up with de Thrapston the subject of her unpopularity he had been sympathetic but at a loss as to how he could help her. It was an unfortunate symptom of the brutal realities of life in a besieged castle. He had shrugged and pointed across the inner courtyard of the castle to a figure scurrying along close to a wall. She had seen this boy a few times since she arrived: a dirty-faced urchin who seemed to appear and disappear like magic from places all over the castle. Everywhere he went he had a small crossbow slung over one shoulder and a hemp sack over the other.

'It could be worse,' de Thrapston sighed. 'You could be the rat boy. Nobody likes him.'

It was clear just how desperate the position of the defenders was. There were barely enough warriors in the garrison to man the walls. Added to that were some servants and other castle denizens – armourers, a blacksmith, a cook and the like – the minimum required to keep the fortress operational. Supplies of arrows and other missiles were running very low. There were some refugees, survivors of the initial Scottish onslaught, who had made it to the safety of the castle only to become stuck there. Aside from starving people, rats were now the only living creatures in the castle and they were getting fewer by the day. Galiene found out to her horror that the rat boy's job was to hunt down these rodents, not for extermination but for the cooking pot.

The remains of the horses and other castle animals were now just a heap of bones that had been boiled and reboiled until white and brittle without a scrap of meat left or an ounce of flavour in them. The remnant hides of the horses still provided some taste to the daily potage, but it was becoming little more than flavoured water. Over the last few months the seagulls had learned to stay well clear of the castle walls. There was an ominous patch of ground in the inner ward where the cobbles had been dug up and freshly turned earth denoted the graves of those who had already succumbed to hunger and disease.

Galiene had been in the castle for a couple of days now and for once it was not raining; this was the first time she had seen the sun. As she made her way across the ward the sound of excited voices came from above, quickly followed by the urgent ringing of the alarm bell.

Henry de Thrapston came running out from the keep behind her. 'What's happening?' he shouted to the men on the battlements above the gate tower. 'Is it an attack?'

'No, sire,' a defender called back, 'it looks like a delegation is coming.'

The constable hurried across the outer courtyard and up the steps to the battlements. Curious, Galiene followed close behind him. They travelled quickly along the wall until they reached the double-turreted tower that guarded the entrance to the castle and the portcullis-barred gate. The warriors defending the top were all peering down at something below.

Galiene went to one of the crenellations in the wall and looked down. A cart had been pushed up the hill to the edge of the ditch that was spanned by the drawbridge when it was lowered. Galiene's eyes widened when she saw the cart was laden with food. Loaves of bread and salted fish filled the bed of it. All the defenders gazed down at it with longing and Galiene could actually hear their swollen, empty bellies rumbling around her.

A herald, easily identifiable in his brightly coloured clothing and the long white wand he bore, stood beside the cart.

'My lord the king wishes to parley,' the herald shouted up to the battlements. He spoke in French but with a cultured Scottish accent. 'He demands you return something that belongs to him.'

A group of Scottish noblemen, resplendent in their brightly coloured surcoats emblazoned with heraldic devices and coats of arms, were approaching cautiously up the hill behind the herald. In the lead was a stocky, bearded man with blond hair, his jerkin displaying a silver lion, rampant on an azure background.

'That's Edward Bruce himself,' de Thrapston commented to the men around him as he pointed at the tall figure in the lead. 'What does he want?'

Galiene had a sinking feeling that her situation was about to get a lot worse.

29

'His Majesty, Edward de Brus, Edubard a Briuis, King of Ireland and Earl of Carrick,' the herald announced, giving Bruce's name in both its French and Gaelic forms. He made a sweeping gesture with his hand then scurried off back down the hill out of missile range.

Bruce waited a moment, looking up at the defenders who were gathered on the battlements of the gate tower above.

'Is Henry de Thrapston there?' he finally asked.

'I am,' de Thrapston called back.

'Henry.' Bruce's face cracked into a smile that bore all the sincerity of a cat letting a captured mouse run away a short distance. 'When are you going to give me my castle?'

'It's not mine to give,' de Thrapston shouted back. 'It belongs to my lord, Richard de Burgh, the Earl of Ulster. If I were to surrender the keys of this castle, I am sure Earl Richard would only want me to give them to your brother, Robert. Robert Bruce is, after all, still your commander is he not?'

Bruce shook his head and looked at the ground, still grinning but promising himself that when the castle finally fell he would have its castellan hanged, drawn and quartered like the English had done to William Wallace.

'Henry,' Bruce called, looking up again, a hard edge entering his voice. 'You jest with me. You know I am now King of Ireland. This is my land and that is now my castle. But today I will talk no more of that. Sometimes I wonder about this nest of thieves I rule. You have another thing that belongs to me. A girl came into the harbour a few days ago and she is now inside your walls. She is the brat of Richard Savage, a knight of this country, and I want her back. To show you I am not an unreasonable man, I am willing to exchange her for this generous supply of food.' Bruce gestured to the cart with a flourish.

Galiene felt her stomach churn. Around her the men on the battlements began to mutter to each other, their ravenous gaze fixed on the cart of food below. She bit her lower lip as she looked to de Thrapston, waiting to see what his response would be. The keeper of the castle did not immediately reply; his face bore a look of dismay and worry and that made her feel even worse.

'You cannot tell me you're not hungry,' Bruce called up, a wicked grin on his face. 'I know that you've run out of food. What do you say? I'm a reasonable man. It's a reasonable offer. I can give you some time to think about it, but I want her back before Easter.'

'Take it,' one of the defenders urged. Galiene flinched at the words and saw that it was the same gap-toothed sergeant who had questioned her entry on her arrival. Others were nodding their agreement.

De Thrapston took a deep breath and straightened his back. 'No,' he said to those around him. 'I don't trust Bruce to give us that food even if we do hand the girl over. Remember the de Logans and Byssets who surrendered to him believing his promises of safe conduct? Their corpses are still hanging from the gibbets down there in the town. Besides,' he added, almost as an afterthought, 'it is unchivalrous. She is a defenceless girl and I am a knight sworn to protect widows and orphans.'

The faces of the defenders took on looks of dismay, disappointment and the first stirrings of anger.

Galiene felt something tugging at her sleeve and she turned around. To her surprise she saw the pinched features of the rat boy, who had somehow crept up alongside her without her even noticing. He stared earnestly into her eyes and flicked his head towards the castle. The meaning of the gesture was obvious to Galiene: it was time to go.

He pulled on the sleeve of her dress again. With a final glance around to see that the defenders were now occupied arguing with de Thrapston, she followed the boy as he led her away, quickly but carefully, so as not to attract attention. They hurried down the steps from the battlements and across the outer courtyard. Carrickfergus Castle was the shape of an oyster and built in three concentric circles. Off-centre, like a pearl at the heart of the fortress, was the tall, square keep that stood as a citadel, the point of final refuge if all the outer defences fell. Around it and the inner ward was wrapped the inner curtain wall. Outside that was another fortified wall, which created a narrow gap between it – the middle ward – and the inner ward. Circling all of this was the newer, much longer outer curtain wall that enclosed the courtyard, stables, banqueting hall, kitchens, garrison quarters and various other buildings and guard towers. The rat boy, still holding her sleeve, hurried Galiene across the outer courtyard, through the gate into the middle ward and on through the gate in the inner wall.

They dashed through the gate in the high wall, passing the former great hall to their right and headed for the big keep. The entrance was on the first floor and the rat boy led them up a flight of wooden steps and into the keep itself. Almost immediately they had passed through the door, he turned left to the spiral staircase in the corner of the keep and began to descend. Galiene ran her right hand along the wall and her stomach lurched as they went down into the gloom, hurrying at a pace that was almost dangerous. One slip and they would go tumbling down the narrow, twisting staircase, breaking bones on the way.

After four turns around the spiral they came to a wooden door and the bottom of the stairway. The rat boy opened the door and they entered the cool gloom of the castle cellars. The cellars were below ground and windowless, but a couple of waxen torches guttered in brackets in the walls so the vaulted rooms were not in complete darkness. The room was stacked with crates and barrels, once packed with smoked meats, grain and wine but now as empty as the bellies of the men defending the castle. The rat boy led Galiene further into the cellars, passing under the low vaulted ceiling to where two huge barrels, formerly filled with wine, sat on their sides against the wall. He squeezed into the gap between them. Galiene hesitated. The space between the barrels was dark and she wondered where this strange boy was really leading her. Realising she had stopped following, he turned and spoke for the first time.

'Come on, you'll be safer in here,' he said in Irish.

Galiene glanced around the gloomy cellar then decided

she had little choice but to trust the boy. The castellan owed her nothing and if it came to a choice between handing her over to the Scots or facing a mutiny from his soldiers, she had a good idea what he would do. Taking a deep breath, she squeezed herself into the gap between the barrels. The boy nodded and pressed on ahead.

Galiene blinked. It seemed as if the boy had simply vanished. She pushed forwards further between the barrels and, as she approached the wall, realised that where the wall of the cellar met the floor, behind the barrel on the right was a ragged gap in the stones, just big enough for a small person to crawl through. She wondered where it led. They were in the deepest part of the castle right beneath the keep. There could be nothing under this but the black rock the fortress was built on.

Behind her, the clattering of footsteps came from the staircase at the far end of the cellar, accompanied by the sound of voices echoing up the spiral. She had to get away somehow and at that moment this was the only escape route open to her.

Bottom lip clenched between her teeth, Galiene dropped to the ground and crawled through the hole in the wall into the blackness beyond.

30

Galiene heard the sound of a flint being struck. Sparks ignited in the darkness and a few strands of straw flared alight. The rat boy touched the flame to a torch stuck in a bracket low on the wall, seemingly heedless as the straw burnt his fingers. With a crackle and an acrid smell of tallow the torch blazed into life and Galiene saw that it was not a room they were in so much as a cave. It seemed to be a triangular-shaped gap in the rock on which the castle was built, sealed by the wall of the cellar on one side and the floor of the keep above. The walls were dark rock on two sides and the stone blocks of the keep formed the cellar wall side and the low ceiling.

There was barely enough room for them to stand up in but it was wide enough that two or three people could sit or lie down. Galiene wondered if it was perhaps an old blocked-up oubliette or other prison from the very early days of the castle. The floor was deep in rushes that were far from clean, though Galiene doubted that even the keeper of the castle had clean rushes on his floor after so long under siege. A harsh, fetid tang assaulted her nose, but it was surprisingly warm and more important, dry. There was also what looked like a cooking pot in one corner of the room sitting on a blackened hearth made of flat stones. The rat boy's crossbow was carefully propped against the wall near a bundle of rags that Galiene surmised were probably the rest of the clothes he possessed.

He stooped and dragged a heavy stone over the hole they had come in. 'No one will know we're in here now,' he said with a grin that was far from reassuring. 'No light gets out and the stone is so thick they can't hear anything either.'

Galiene nodded, a knot of anxiety gathering in her belly. What had she got herself into?

'Sit down,' the rat boy said, plonking himself down in the straw. 'May as well make yourself at home. You can stay here for a bit if you want. At least until they forget about you anyway.'

Galiene gingerly set herself down in the filthy straw, at the same time realising that this was actually the rat boy's home and then wondering just where he went to relieve himself.

'They hate me too,' the rat boy said. His eyes gleamed in the torchlight as he flicked a greasy lock of long, mouse-brown hair away from his forehead. 'They need me, but they don't like me. I think I remind them of the fact that they're reduced to eating vermin. I know where the rats live and the soldiers think I'm like the rats or something.'

Galiene peered at the boy through the gloom, getting a good look at him for the first time. She realised that he was probably a year or so younger than she – maybe eleven or twelve years old – though his small scrawny frame made him appear younger. He had the clear, piercing blue eyes some of the old Irish possessed. There was no doubt he was thin, but he lacked the gaunt, emaciated look that the others in the castle bore. Looking around she spotted a heap of tiny bones in the corner and tasted a surge of hot, sour gorge as it rose in her throat at the thought that the boy was keeping some of his catch – beyond what he handed over to the castle kitchen – for his own consumption. Hungry as she was, she could still not come to terms with the thought that these people were reduced to such desperation.

'What's your name?' Galiene asked.

'Everyone just calls me the rat boy. I used to be the dog boy for the castle. I looked after the earl's hunting dogs. But they've all been eaten, so now I'm the rat boy,' the boy said.

'You must have a name, though,' Galiene pressed.

The boy frowned, clearly trying hard to remember. 'It's been so long since anyone used it.' He shook his head. 'I've been here since I was a baby. My parents sold me to the earl so I could be a servant. I think it's Fergus.'

'So you've lived in the castle all your life?' Galiene said.

The boy nodded. 'I know the place like the back of my hand. I know all the ins and outs and places like this that no one knows about but me. Everyone thinks I'm nothing but dirt beneath their feet and here I am living in the keep like the earl himself!' He grinned, revealing bright red gums and gaps in his brown-stained teeth.

'Why did you help me?' Galiene asked.

'I've seen you working in the kitchen. Yesterday I heard you singing while you stirred the gruel. I thought it was the most beautiful sound I'd ever heard.' The boy reddened and looked down, avoiding her eyes. His voice reduced to little more than a mumble. 'I was hoping, perhaps, you might sing for me?'

Galiene stared at him, wondering just what sort of

miserable, love-starved life this boy had lived if he could be so impressed by her singing.

'Of course I will,' she said with a smile.

Fergus's eyes lit up. He leaned forward, excitement dancing across his face. 'Will you? Oh thank you!' He remained in that position, clearly expecting her to begin.

'Now?' Galiene frowned. 'Won't people outside hear? I want to stay out of their way.'

The boy slapped the stones of the cellar wall. 'Don't worry about that.' He grinned. 'Like I said, the stones are too thick. No sound gets out. Even if it does they'll think it's the ghost.'

'Ghost?'

'Aye,' the boy went on. 'The castle is haunted don't you know? They say a little boy fell down the well years ago and his ghost still haunts the keep. It's rubbish of course. I've never seen hide nor hair of a ghost anywhere in this castle.'

Galiene pondered that the boy's own sudden exits and entrances, combined with the sounds that occasionally travelled from his lair up through the walls to others in the castle, probably did a lot to fuel the impression that there was a ghost in the fortress. She gave a hesitant nod trying to think of something that she could sing to the boy. Finally she decided on a French carol she had learned while in Gascony. Keeping her voice soft, Galiene began to sing. At first she was self-conscious and embarrassed, given that there was no one there but her and the strange boy, but as the song continued she found herself being carried away by the music and she forgot her surroundings. The rat boy sat captivated throughout, staring at her with bright, adoring eyes. When the song ended there were a few moments of silence.

'Beautiful,' the rat boy said in a breathless voice. 'You're like an angel.'

Galiene blushed. 'I'm not that good…' she mumbled.

'No, but you are,' the boy gushed. 'I've never heard anyone sing like you.'

'Oh come now.' Galiene frowned. She looked around the room, hoping to see something to change the subject. Finally her eye alighted on the small crossbow that rested against the wall. 'Is that yours?' she asked.

The boy's face broke out in a beam of pride and he reached over to pat it. 'Aye,' he said. 'You're the best singer I've heard, but I'm by far the best shot in the whole of this castle. Do you know how hard it is to hit a rat on the run? Well I can do it. Every time.' He raised his arms and closed one eye, mimicking taking aim with the weapon. 'Pow! Crack! Dead. Another one for the pot. That's why they let me have it.' He gestured with a thumb in the direction of the cellar wall and Galiene surmised that he meant the denizens of the castle. 'All weapons and missiles are needed to defend the walls, but I'm allowed that one because with it I hunt the only meat they can get.'

A smile crossed Galiene's lips as an idea began to form in her head.

'If I keep singing to you,' she said, 'could you teach me how to use it?'

31

Bordeaux

For Alys, the days passed in a haze; she was unsure how many times the sun rose and set. Time slipped by as she either slept, her repose haunted by strange dreams and weird nightmares, or lay in a languid daze, feeling too tired and uninterested to get out of bed. Her brief moments of lucidity when she got up almost immediately prompted a visit from her nurse, who gave her something to eat then administered a new draught of medicine and Alys soon felt herself drifting off back to sleep once more. She was vaguely aware that there was something strange going on and that it appeared that Eloise seemed intent on keeping her sedated well beyond the time when it may have been medically necessary, but in a way she welcomed the torpefying effects of the drugs that numbed the pain of her physical wounds and the aching emptiness that yawned within her from the loss of the baby. The herbs also dulled the anxiety that gnawed at her belly when she thought of Galiene or Richard.

Perhaps it was her body getting used to the powers of the

herbs in the potions or perhaps it was just the resolute part of her mind finally asserting itself, but eventually Alys came to the conclusion that all was not well with her situation and it was time to do something about it. She had Galiene to think of. The poor girl was enduring who knew what hardships alone and then there was Richard on his mission to save her. She could not simply lie around in comfort while they were in danger.

Gingerly, she rolled out of bed. Her muscles were stiff and sore from inactivity but her wound had healed enough that she was able to stand up without it causing her too much pain. Her ribs ached, but it was with the dull pain of bruising rather than the sharp needlepoints of broken bones.

She was dressed in a simple linen smock. There was no sign of the clothes she had been wearing when she had been taken to the nunnery. They were probably too badly torn to have been kept. She hitched up the smock and examined the stab wound in her abdomen. To her surprise the stitches that she could recall the nuns sewing to close the wound were gone, leaving a ridged scar. To her dismay she realised that this could only mean she had been in this room for much longer than she had thought: days, possibly weeks. More?

The room was bright and she took the few steps to the window. Pulling aside the curtain she saw that it was a grey, overcast spring day, probably in the afternoon. She looked down onto the busy courtyard of a large town house. A stable covered the opposite wall and sleek, expensive Arabian horses looked out over the half-doors while stable boys and grooms went about their work combing the steeds, carrying water buckets or forking hay. Servants rushed around the courtyard on various tasks, some were fetching ale for the kitchens from a brew house, others were carrying in wood for fires in the house. A large, impressive-looking carriage was parked to one side of the yard. Its bright blue and red paints practically glowed in the weak sunlight. Alys frowned as she noticed the plaque on the back of the carriage, which would normally have borne the heraldic crest of whichever nobleman owned the vehicle, had been obscured by matte black paint.

At that moment the door of the room opened behind her. Turning away from the window she saw the smiling, pretty face of her nurse, Eloise, who had entered the room carrying her customary jug of herbal preparation and a goblet.

'Ah! You are up!' Eloise appeared surprised but continued to smile. 'It is time for your medicine, madame.'

Alys shook her head. 'I feel fine thank you. There is no need for me to take any more of that now.'

Eloise, still smiling, gave a little sigh. 'I am your nurse and I'm afraid it is me who will judge when you need medicine and when you are well enough to stop it. I must insist, madame. Please return to bed. You could burst your stitches. Your wound could reopen.'

'I've examined my wound and it's well healed,' Alys said, not moving from the window. 'The stitches have already been taken out... as you would know if you were really taking care of me.'

Eloise shook her head, a confused look on her face. 'I don't know what you mean, madame.'

Alys narrowed her eyes, deciding to grasp the bull by the horns. 'Why are you keeping me drugged?' she demanded.

The nurse stopped smiling and her eyes became hard orbs of malice for a moment. Then it passed and her customary pleasant grin returned. 'What is this foolish notion, madame? I am giving you medicine to make you better. You are not yet strong enough to stop taking it.'

'You are giving me medicine to keep me asleep,' Alys said. 'I know what is in that drink: poppy seeds, hops, valerian and other herbs. All with the power to induce sleep. There is something else as well, something very powerful, which makes them fast-acting.'

'Ah! I understand now.' Eloise said. 'Sometimes the herbs in the drink – the poppy seeds and such – when taken over a long time can make the patient imagine they are being persecuted. That is what is happening to you, madame. I can assure you that you are safe here. You must rest. Your mind is agitated.' She proffered the jug of herbal medicine once more to suggest that it was the answer to Alys's anxiety.

'All the more reason to stop taking that,' Alys said.

Eloise shook her head. This time as her smile faded Alys thought she detected a look that suggested fear. 'Madame, I must insist.'

'And I must insist also.' Alys folded her arms. 'No.'

Eloise sighed. 'Very well – have it your way,' she said and left the room.

As the door closed behind her Alys rushed over to it but before she reached it she heard the click of the key being turned in the lock. She rattled the latch uselessly a few times, then with an exasperated curse went back and sat down on the bed, thumping her clenched fists into the mattress. As she sat in frustrated silence she contemplated how she could get away. Her first problem was working out how they knew when she was awake. How did Eloise manage to arrive so swiftly virtually every time she opened her eyes?

As if in answer a soft click made her turn her head towards the door. She just had time to see a flurry of movement as a small peephole situated at eye level slid shut. That was one mystery solved: they were watching her.

There was another rattle of the key and the door opened once more. Eloise re-entered the room, still bearing the pewter jug full of medicine.

'I told you I'm not taking any more of that,' Alys said, her tone both angry and warning.

'I'm sorry, madame, but this is for your own good,' Eloise said and before Alys could reply a burly man-at-arms entered the room. He was dressed in a studded leather tunic and was tall and muscular. The scars on his bald head, his badly broken teeth and his flattened nose all testified to his familiarity with violence.

Alys rose from the bed but in two steps he was on her. She tried to duck around him but he spread his long arms wide, catching her around the waist and lifting her bodily off the ground so that her legs kicked uselessly in mid-air.

'Get off me! Help!' Alys screamed. The man-at-arms threw her roughly onto the bed again. Before she could spring back up the man was on her, pinning her down with his own weight. Alys became frantic, screaming and kicking, aches and pains forgotten, thrashing around as the man-at-arms placed his meaty hands on her shoulders and pressed downward, fixing her on her back and restraining her there.

She saw Eloise approaching the bed bearing a goblet of the herbal drink.

'No,' Alys said, her voice barely more than a feral growl. Defiantly she clenched her teeth and closed her mouth.

Calmly Eloise leaned over and grasped the end of Alys's nose, pinching it closed. In seconds Alys felt her lungs bursting for air and was forced to open her mouth. Instantly Eloise pushed the goblet up against her lips and tipped it up, the bitter-tasting liquid pouring into Alys's mouth, filling it and gushing over her face and chin.

'There, madame, that was not so bad,' Eloise said, withdrawing the cup when most of it was empty.

Some of the liquid went down her throat, but with supreme effort, Alys managed to spit most of it back out again. The herbal concoction jetted upwards, splashing across the man-at-arms' face and shoulders. Eloise sighed and began refilling the goblet from the jug.

'That was very foolish,' she said, shaking her head as the man-at-arms changed position, moving to pin Alys's left shoulder with his right elbow, while his right hand roughly closed around her jaw. On one side his thumb pressed into her jaw muscle and his fingers on the other as he forced her mouth open. Alys could feel the strength in his arm and realised if she did not comply he could break her jaw. There was nothing she could do but allow her mouth to be opened. Eloise poured more of the liquid into her mouth and this time the man-at-arms clamped his hand over her mouth to prevent her spitting it out. Unable to breathe, Alys had no choice but to swallow the liquid. The man-at-arms let go of her mouth and Alys sucked in desperate but welcome mouthfuls of air.

'You bitch,' she said and spat at Eloise. The nurse seemed as impassive as ever, though as she turned away Alys was sure she spotted a malicious smile creep over her lips.

'Keep her pinned down until she passes out,' Eloise said to the man-at-arms as she once more left the room.

32

It was dark when Alys awoke. Her sleep had been troubled by dreams of Galiene, who had somehow become trapped down a dry well shaft. When Alys looked down at her she saw that the girl was crying and in her arms she cradled the tiny cold, white, blood-covered body of Alys's dead baby.

When she woke she realised that her smock was stuck to her body with cold, drying sweat. Memories of what had happened earlier flooded back and she closed her eyes quickly again, recalling that she was being watched from the peephole in the door. She needed some time to think and the best way to buy it was to pretend to still be asleep, otherwise Nurse Eloise would be straight in with her jug of sleeping potion.

Anger swirled in Alys's breast as she considered her situation. First the Scots had come and taken her daughter and killed her unborn baby. Then Earl Mortimer, the man her husband was supposed to be helping by returning to Ireland, was holding her a prisoner, drugged and constantly watched. It was the thought of them watching her that made her most angry. This was the final indignity on top of everything else she would endure. They had been standing outside the door all the time, spying on her. Mostly she had been sleeping, but in her rare conscious moments she walked around fretting, worried about her kidnapped daughter and Richard on his mission to find her. They must have even watched her pissing in the chamber pot from under the bed. She closed her eyes, the thought flooding her with embarrassment and deepening her resentment.

At that point her eyes snapped open again. She had an idea.

33

'You'd better take a look.' Arnauld, the burly man-at-arms spying through the peephole in Alys's door, turned his head to address Eloise. 'She must be awake and wandering about. I can't see her.'

He stood aside as Eloise opened the door, a large candle in her hand to illuminate the room. A brief moment of panic gripped the nurse. She could not see Alys on the bed or anywhere within sight. Hurrying into the room, she looked to her left and her customary vacant smile returned to her face as she saw Alys was squatting in the gloom at the far side of the room, in a position that was not visible from the door. She was clearly relieving herself into the chamber pot that sat on the floor beneath her. As Eloise entered Alys stood up, smoothing down her smock.

'What are you doing?' Eloise asked. 'The chamber pot stays under your bed yet you take it all the way over there to use it?'

'I couldn't stand the smell of it,' Alys said, coming back to the bed. 'Besides, I have no desire to have you and your loutish friend watch me while I pee.'

Eloise shrugged and looked away as if to indicate whatever Alys wished was of no consequence to her.

'There is no need to be so coy,' she said with a malicious smile. 'While you are unconscious we have changed your clothes. We've seen you completely naked. We have cleaned you when you soiled yourself in your sleep. You have no secrets from us.'

Alys glared at her, her face reddening, but did not reply.

'Now, it's time for your medicine,' the nurse said, setting the big candle on the bedside table and holding up the jug of herbal concoction she bore in her other hand. Alys opened her mouth to speak, but before she could say anything Eloise cocked her head to one side like someone warning a small child. 'You don't want me to get my friend Arnauld to come and help me again do you?'

Alys sighed and looked down. Her long black hair fell around her face as she shook her head.

'No, I didn't think so.' Eloise's smile took on an aspect of triumph. 'Now take your medicine like a good girl.'

Alys took the proffered goblet. She hesitated slightly then drank it down in one gulp.

'Excellent!' Eloise positively beamed with delight. She took the goblet back and as Alys lay down on the bed once more turned and left the room, closing and locking the door behind her.

The nurse was about to walk off down the corridor outside the room when she paused. Eloise cocked her head back towards the door, alerted by choking, coughing sounds from behind the door. Frowning, she pushed her eye up to the peephole. Once more she could not see Alys on the bed but as she watched she heard the heaving noise yet again, accompanied by the sound of splattering liquid.

'She's making herself sick!' Eloise spat angrily, turning

the key once again. She flung open the door and pointed inside. 'Arnauld, get in there. Stop her!'

Arnauld rushed into the room, closely followed by Eloise. Looking to the left they saw Alys hunched over the chamber pot, facing away from them, head down and puking into it. Arnauld strode across the room towards her, one arm outstretched to grab her by the hair and wrench her head back out of the chamber pot.

At the very last moment he suddenly realised that Alys was not actually being sick. She was crouched on all fours and making vomiting noises but her head was down to allow her to look backwards under her left armpit and see him coming towards her. At the same time Eloise caught sight of a large brown pool of vomit beside the bed and realised that Alys had indeed been sick, but was now only pretending. The nurse gave an inarticulate cry of warning. It was too late.

Alys rose and spun around in a blur of motion. Gripping the chamber pot handle in both hands she smashed it across the side of Arnauld's head. The pottery vessel broke against his bald temple, shattering to a thousand pieces amid an explosion of still-warm piss that showered sideways across the room. The man-at-arms staggered to his right. A gash like a pair of livid lips opened across his forehead. Almost immediately the wound filled with blood that gushed down into his eyes, blinding him and adding to the stinging induced by the urine.

Alys dropped the remnants of the chamber pot – one surviving handle surrounded by jagged edges of pottery – and stepped in close to the man-at-arms. Without further thinking she grabbed the hilt of the long dagger that was sheathed at his waist and pulled it free, raising it above her head, point downward.

She was not a warrior and had never been trained where to strike the various parts of a man's body to cause most damage, but she had studied the healing arts for years and knew the places where the blood flowed and where the major organs were. Grasping the hilt in both hands she drove it down again with all her might into Arnauld's exposed neck. The long narrow blade plunged into his flesh, going behind the collarbone and down into his chest cavity. The dagger tore through the large veins in his neck and sliced into his heart, dark blood rose up and gushed out of the wound. The man-at-arms collapsed to the floor like a puppet whose strings had been cut, his body weight pulling away from the dagger still clutched in Alys's hand. His eyes rolled up as he uttered a terrible groan that turned into a rattling gurgle.

Left holding the bloody weapon, Alys looked up and saw Eloise, the supercilious smile finally gone from her face. The nurse was gaping open-mouthed at her from beside the bed. Then, realising her situation, she suddenly bolted for the door. Alys tore after her, aiming to intercept her.

Eloise made it there a fraction before her and was halfway through the door when Alys threw herself against it, her shoulder smashing all her weight into the back of the door. It slammed into Eloise, momentarily stunning her, knocking her sideways and pinning her between the door and the frame.

Still clutching the knife, Alys reached around the door and grabbed the nurse's dress by the neck.

'Get back in here,' she said, hauling the woman bodily

back into the room and slamming the door shut behind her. Eloise staggered backwards across the room, staring wide-eyed at Alys, who flattened her back against the closed door, the bloody knife pointed at the nurse's chest.

'Help! Help!' the nurse screamed.

Alys strode over to her and placed the point of the knife against her throat. It pressed Eloise's white skin in a little and marked her with a smear of Arnauld's blood.

'Your friends will think it's me screaming. No one will come,' Alys hissed through bared teeth. 'Now be silent.'

The nurse complied immediately. Her eyes were like full moons and her usually smiling face was now a terrified mask.

'Who are you working for?' Alys demanded.

Eloise just stared back, her bottom lip protruding and trembling like a blob of pig fat in a frying pan. Alys pushed the dagger a little. The razor-sharp point broke the nurse's skin and a small bead of blood trickled out to mingle with Arnauld's.

'Tell me or by God I swear you will never speak again,' Alys said. 'Why was I drugged?'

'It was the Lord Mortimer,' Eloise burst out. 'He said you were a valuable hostage who may be of use sometime. I was to keep you out of the way and asleep while his guest is here. He did not want you causing any trouble, nor did he want you running away.'

'Guest?' Alys said, her mind racing. Mortimer had promised Richard he would look after her while he was away. What had he asked Richard to do that may result in him needing to hold her as a potential hostage?

Eloise shook her head. 'He will kill me if I tell you.'

'And I'll kill you if you don't,' Alys replied.

A desperate look of fear flashed across Eloise's face but she shook her head again. 'I cannot, even if I wanted to,' she said, her voice catching in a sob. 'We're all sworn to secrecy – all the servants. Lord Mortimer is here to meet someone. She arrived in the night. We are all kept out of the rooms when she is in them. All we know is that she is a highborn lady. Please don't kill me.' Her bottom lips jutted out further, turned down, and big tears rolled down her cheeks.

Alys looked at her, trying to work out what to do. Killing the man-at-arms had been necessary and in the heat of the moment she had not given it a second thought. Looking Eloise in the eyes and seeing her pathetic terror was a different matter. Alys doubted if she really could coldly murder the girl. Then a smile flickered across her face as she caught sight of the pewter jug the nurse had set down on the bed.

'I think it's time you got a dose of your own medicine,' she said, bobbing her head in the direction of the jug. 'Drink that.'

Eloise's eyes widened further but she did what she was told, gagging a couple of times, to Alys's pleasure.

A short while later, as Eloise lay on the bed, knocked unconscious by the powerful soporific concoction in the jug, Alys slipped out of the room and locked the door behind her. She now wore Eloise's robe, wimple and hood, but she still kept her head down as she looked left and right along the ill-lit corridor she found outside. To her relief it was empty. She did not know where to go next, or even where she actually was, but at least she was out of the room; she had a knife and she was determined to escape.

34

Alys walked purposefully down the corridor. She knew that if she met anyone the quickest way to draw attention was to look as if she was creeping around, unsure of where she was going, which was guaranteed to attract questioning. There was no doubt that she was in a very grand house. The whitewashed walls were hung here and there with tapestries, holy pictures and jewelled crucifixes. The floor was dark, highly polished wood. There were no windows; instead the light came from flaming torches held in brackets on the walls. Arriving at the end of the corridor she came to a door. It opened onto a wide landing where a set of stairs went down to the ground floor.

Which way now? Her mind was quickly made up by the sound of heavy footsteps in the hall below. At least two sets of boots accompanied by the clink of mail rose from below. People – armed men – and they were coming closer.

'Make sure no one is near the hall,' a gruff male voice said in English. 'Lord Mortimer has ordered all the servants out of the house.'

Alys ducked to her right, opening a door as quietly as she could and pulling it closed behind her. She found herself in yet another corridor. What size was this house? It appeared to be bigger than most of the castles she had been inside in Ireland. She hurried down the gloomy corridor, aware of the clattering of boots on the wooden floor of the landing she had left. Her heart sank: she had chosen the wrong option. The men-at-arms were coming the same way.

Seeing another door on the right Alys dived through it. To her surprise she found herself in some sort of gallery. Seating benches were pushed up against the end wall. The room was open on one side and there was a low banister overlooking a much larger room with a very high ceiling. In fact it appeared to be the entire height of the house's two storeys. The narrow room in which she stood was level with the second storey and built into the wall of the bigger room, which was lined with dark wood panelling and hung with rich tapestries. Gazing down at them, Alys realised she was in the minstrels' gallery of the great hall – the grandest room in the house – and that the benches were for the musicians to sit on when they entertained the bishop and his noble guests feasting in the hall below.

As quietly as she could, Alys closed the door, hearing as she did so a cough beneath her. She froze. There was someone down there. At the same time she heard the tramping boots of the men-at-arms entering the corridor outside. She was trapped.

From where she stood she could see only the far side of the hall and there was no one in sight there. Whoever had coughed must be directly below her. She knew she had to do something fast so looked around for somewhere to hide. The minstrels' gallery was long and narrow, just wide enough for one person to pass another.

Keeping low, Alys crouched beneath the top of the banister

and shuffled along the gallery to the far end. Diving to the floor she rolled underneath the musicians' benches and lay in the dark, trying desperately to control her breathing and painfully aware of the pounding of her heart, which seemed so loud in her ears that it must surely be audible across the room.

The door of the gallery opened. Alys held her breath and tried to push herself as far under the benches as she could. Peering out she could see the door was now wide open and two pairs of heavy boots had entered the gallery. They stopped for a moment as their wearers looked around.

'What's going on up there?' a refined male voice, speaking in English from below in the hall, said. 'Osbert? Is that you?'

'Yes, my lord,' one of the men-at-arms in the gallery responded. 'We're going round the house making sure the servants have all left, as you ordered.'

"My lord?" Alys thought. He could only be referring to Mortimer.

'And?' the commanding voice from below demanded in a tone that bore more than a little tetchiness.

'It looks like they're all gone, sire,' the man-at-arms, presumably Osbert, replied.

'Then get out of here, man!' Mortimer thundered. 'I have important business to attend to.'

'Right away, my lord.' The boots almost fell over each other in their effort to get out of the gallery and Alys was alone once more. She crawled out from under the bench as carefully as she could and as she did so she heard an amused chuckle coming from the room below accompanied by an odd noise that sounded strangely like a splash.

Alys crawled on all fours over to the balcony and getting

onto her haunches, risked a cautious peek over the edge into the sumptuous room below. A roaring fire blazed in a huge iron grate at one end of the room and set before it was a very large wooden tub, the sort that could be found in a castle and was used for communal bathing. Indeed, it was full of water and steam rose from it into the air. It must have taken an army of servants running in and out with buckets of boiling water to fill it. Alys caught her breath as she caught sight of the man sitting in the water. He was naked.

Alys, who came from an obscure, impoverished family in a minor northern branch of the Anglo-Irish nobility, had never met Baron Roger de Mortimer, the Lord of Trim and one of the most powerful nobles in England, but she had little doubt that it was he who was relaxing in the hot water below. He was a young man and his body was lean and muscular, which was fitting for a frontier lord who spent most of his time in fighting harness. He lay in the water with his arms spread wide along the top of the wooden tub, his eyes closed and his fashionably long black hair hung, wet, behind him over the edge of the bath.

Alys froze at the sound of a door opening into the hall. Mortimer opened his eyes, but whoever stood in the doorway was clearly hesitating for there was no sound of the door closing. Sloshing water onto the floor, Mortimer stood up. Alys blinked, uncomfortable to be looking down at a naked man. Despite her anxiety, she smiled to herself in the half-darkness of the gallery, reflecting that though she was a married woman, the handsome, fit young man in the bath below was nevertheless not too unpleasant a sight.

'It's all right, there's no one here,' Mortimer said to the newcomer, speaking now in French. 'Come in and join me.'

Alys heard the door close and a woman came into view. She too was young, much younger than Mortimer, and her long blonde hair spilled around her shoulders and reached down to her waist. Her features were stunningly beautiful and she was simply dressed in a white linen shift. As Alys watched, the woman shrugged her shoulders out of the long shift, letting it fall to the floor so she too was completely naked. She stepped gingerly into the hot water and as she did so Mortimer rushed over to her, clasping her in an embrace and locking his lips to hers in a kiss of such obvious lust that it left no doubt of the manner of the relationship between the two of them.

A shocked thrill surged in Alys's breast. She had never seen Mortimer before, but she had seen his wife. Years before, Joan de Geneville had visited Ulster with her father, Syr Piers de Geneville of Trim Castle. Her grandfather, Syr Geoffrey de Geneville, was Justiciar of Ireland at the time. Alys had accompanied her own father to a grand tournament held in their honour at Carrickfergus. She had been impressed by the then young Joan's self-possession, her sumptuous dress and how she had deported herself among such vaunted company. She had made such an impression on Alys that she remembered her still.

One thing Alys could be sure of was that the woman in the bathtub below was not Mortimer's wife Joan. She grimaced, hoping fervently that she was not going to have to endure being stuck in the gallery listening to Mortimer swive some courtesan.

The woman pushed Mortimer away from her playfully,

ignoring his obvious arousal and sitting down in the warm water.

'Leave me alone, Lord Mortimer. You are insatiable,' she said. She spoke refined French with an accent that portrayed it was her native tongue. 'Was our time together earlier not enough for you?'

'How can any man leave you alone?' Mortimer said, smiling like a wolf and sliding into the water beside her. 'You are so beautiful.'

The woman frowned. 'My husband leaves me alone. He prefers to spend his days swimming or playing around in boats.' As she spoke her expression darkened and a look of genuine anger soured her fine features. 'He would rather spend time with stable boys than with me.'

'Your husband is a fool,' Mortimer grunted. 'Edward is not a real man. He prefers boys to a woman like you. How can such a man sit on the throne?'

Alys gasped and bit her lower lip. The woman below could be only one person. She too was married and Mortimer not her spouse. This had to be Queen Isabella, wife of King Edward Plantagenet of England. The impressive carriage in the courtyard must be hers and the reason the crest had been covered up was now obvious. The enormity of what she was seeing made Alys's head spin. No wonder there was so much secrecy in the house.

This was not mere adultery; this was treason.

35

Mortimer sat back in the water, his lust temporarily forgotten and a look of annoyance on his face. 'It drives me mad that the country is in the power of that idiot. Someday we shall both be rid of him. Then a true king, a real man, will sit upon the throne of England.'

'You refer, of course, to my young son, Edward, my lord,' Queen Isabella gently chided with a chilly smile.

Mortimer looked momentarily uncomfortable then his face took on a reconciliatory cast. 'Of course I do, my love,' he crooned, 'but young Edward is but a baby. He will need help; guidance and counselling if he is to be a good king.'

Isabella 'humphed' and looked away, suddenly seeming annoyed. Mortimer moved closer to her, putting an arm around her shoulders, clearly desperate to wheedle his way back into her affections. Alys marvelled at the way the woman so skilfully manipulated Mortimer. It reminded her of a cat playing with a mouse.

'I begin to think we will never be rid of the awful man,' the queen sighed.

'Our plans go well, my lady,' Mortimer cooed. 'Take heart. The barons of England despise the king. He has lost most of his power to the Duke of Lancaster and I. The Scots openly defy him. Now the war in Ireland goes badly for him too. It's only a matter of time before we can make our move. We just have to make sure all our pawns and rooks are positioned correctly so that when Edward moves his king, he moves directly into the checkmate we have set up for him.'

'And how do our current plans proceed?' Isabella asked, her smile returning. 'What of that awful Gaveston? When I heard your news I could not believe it. Will we ever be rid of him?'

Up in the gallery, so engrossed in what she was witnessing that she forgot her own predicament, Alys listened with renewed interest. Piers Gaveston had been a Gascon knight who had become King Edward's favourite companion. King Edward had lavished gifts on Gaveston, elevated him from a lowly knight to Earl of Cornwall and by all accounts held him in higher regard than his own wife. Many said that in fact the two men were lovers. The closeness of the two had scandalised England and almost led to civil war.

Gaveston had not helped things by his arrogance and haughty attitude to the nobility. He had particularly infuriated some of the most powerful men in England by first inventing then freely using insulting nicknames for them. He had called the Earl of Warwick 'The Dog' and the corpulent Earl of Lincoln 'Burst Belly'. His most dangerous move was to habitually refer to the Earl of Lancaster – the second most powerful lord in the realm – as 'The Churl'. This had sealed his fate. The Churl and The Dog, tired of the disrespect and jealous of the power Gaveston had gained, had hunted him down about five years before and killed him.

Alys frowned. The fact that the man was long dead made

her wonder what the queen was talking about. As far as anyone knew, she had been "rid of him" for years.

'Don't worry, my love.' Mortimer smiled. 'Soon he will trouble us no more. I finally found the right man – an ex-Templar – who has both the right profile to get into that wretched country Gaveston is hiding in and the skills to dispose of him. By luck his daughter has been kidnapped by Bruce so he will be so desperate to get to Ulster he won't think too much about what I've asked him to do. I concocted a story about the man's identity – well, I told him a half-truth. Those are the lies most likely to be believed. Don't worry, he doesn't know the man I've sent him to kill is Piers Gaveston.'

Alys gasped again, biting her lip so hard she broke the skin and tasted the iron flavour of her own blood. This Templar Knight could only be her husband, Richard. How could this be? How could Gaveston still be alive and why would these two want him dead?

Queen Isabella looked happy for a moment then the clouds fell across her face once more. 'What if this assassin of yours finds out what is going on?' She frowned. 'Our enemies would pay dearly for that information. If he finds out the truth about who Gaveston really is, then my son may never sit on the throne. And if that does not happen, my Lord Mortimer, he will not require any help, guidance or counsel from you on how to be a good king.'

Alys narrowed her eyes. Who Gaveston really is? What could that mean? Why would Gaveston's true identity be a danger to Isabella or her son, Prince Edward? None of it made any sense.

Mortimer shook his head. 'How can he find out? Besides,

I have taken precautions. I will be sending von Mahlberg to tie up any loose ends when the job is done. Savage will never return from Ireland alive.'

Alys gasped. Simultaneously shouting erupted from somewhere behind the door of the minstrels' gallery and she froze. Her eyes swivelled to look over her right shoulder. The commotion could only mean that her absence had been discovered. Her ears strained, listening as cries of alarm came from beyond the corridor outside, followed by the clatter of heavily shod feet along the floor and the slamming of doors. At the sound of boots thumping down the stairs Alys finally took a breath. They were not coming her way – yet – but she knew she had little time.

A fist began an urgent hammering on the door of the hall below. Alys glanced back through the banister and saw the angry look on Mortimer's face. Queen Isabella grimaced, her concern evident in her expression.

'I ordered that I was not to be disturbed,' Mortimer yelled.

'Sire, I'm sorry, but the prisoner has escaped,' the voice of the same man-at-arms who had spoken earlier came from below. 'Arnauld is dead. Killed. The nurse is unconscious on the bed.'

Mortimer was on his feet now, heedless of his nakedness. 'What? Find her. Now!'

He leapt out of the bath and disappeared from the range of Alys's vision. She stood up and backed away to the door. She had to get away and somehow find a way to warn Richard. She pulled open the door and slipped out as quietly as she could.

Just then, Isabella glanced upwards.

'There is someone up in the gallery!' the queen shouted.

36

Alys turned and ran down the corridor, stealth and caution now redundant. She crashed through the door and out onto the landing. Grabbing the post at the top of the main stairway she swung herself around and began to patter down the stairs.

She stopped dead.

Below her, two men-at-arms in mail were clattering across the hallway towards the bottom of the stairs. Alys spun round and ran back up the stairs onto the landing. She looked left and right. The door to the corridor where she had been held prisoner was open so she sprinted through it, slamming it behind her, anything to slow down her pursuers even for a moment. She pounded down the corridor back to the room. Skidding on the wooden floor she ran into the bedroom, praying fervently that there was no one in there.

She was lucky. The only people in the room were Eloise, dead to the world, sleeping soundly on the bed, and the man-at-arms, who actually was dead. He lay in a wide, dark pool of blood, his eyes fixed and staring at nothing, his final expression of shock and pain forever fixed on his face. Alys's nose wrinkled at the metallic stench of the blood and felt a brief stab of remorse at what she had done.

She had no time to stand and wring her hands in regret, however. She had to get out of there and she had very little time. Heavy booted footsteps were already thumping up the stairs and onto the landing behind her. Alys stepped over the corpse on the floor and went to the window. The courtyard outside was lit with torches, but thankfully there did not seem to be too many people about, except for one guard at the gate and he was looking out through the peephole into the street.

It was too far to the ground to jump, but the window was the only other way out. She wrenched it open and looked around, trying to assess her options. Straight away she saw the only one. The queen's carriage was a little way off, but if she jumped far enough out she could land on the top of it. It was quite a distance though.

Muttering a swift prayer that she would not break her neck, Alys pulled herself up onto the sill. She paused for a moment, legs hunched beneath her, knees drawn up to her chin. She took a deep breath then leaned out of the window, letting herself first fall forwards then springing with all her might from her thighs. For a few moments she was plummeting through thin air, both dropping and moving forwards at the same time.

She made it, just. Alys thumped down onto the roof of the carriage, sprawling face first onto it, the fall driving her breath from her lungs and making the carriage rattle and rock forwards on its wheels.

Pain exploded from her bruised ribs and it was all she could do not to gasp out loud. For a couple of moments she lay, breath held, heart pounding in her chest so hard it felt as if it was about to leap from her panting mouth. She lay there for a moment, assessing if she had hurt herself in the fall and waiting to see if anyone had been alerted by her descent.

No shouts came to her ears. It seemed that the man-at-arms at the gates was still too preoccupied to have noticed her. She let out a sigh, judging that she had got away with it, for a few moments at least. Her ribs felt sore and bruised, but there were no sharp pains when she inhaled, so nothing was broken or cracked.

She had to get away from this place fast. Focusing her gaze on the man at the gate and praying that he would not turn around, she pushed herself backwards so her legs went off the top of the carriage and dangled down the back, then lowered herself as far as she could go until she was hanging, the still-bloody knife clenched between her teeth, her feet still a little way off the ground. Now, even if the guard at the gate did turn around, she was hidden from his view. If someone came out of the front door, however, they would spot her straight away. Holding her breath she let herself drop, landing lightly on her feet on the cobblestones of the courtyard.

Gripping the knife in one hand, Alys folded her arms into the wide sleeves of her gown to hide it, hoping it would look as though she was merely keeping her hands protected from the night's chill. Head down, her features shadowed by Eloise's wimple, she strode across the torchlit courtyard towards the gate. The guard heard her footsteps on the cobbles and turned.

'The prisoner has escaped,' Alys said, taking a chance

and speaking in English. She reasoned that all the armed men in the house would be Mortimer's. 'Lord Mortimer wants everyone inside to help search for her.'

Frowning, the guard – a tall thug with a badly broken nose – looked confused. 'I have strict orders not to leave the gate while the lord's guest is here. No one is to be allowed in or out.'

Alys hesitated. She had no alternative plan – had had no time to think of one – now that her first rouse had failed. Almost at the same time a shout came from the house behind her.

'The prisoner has escaped! Stop that woman!'

Both Alys and the guard turned to see two men-at-arms leaning out of the bedroom window from which Alys had escaped. One of them was pointing at her.

The blade of her knife flashed in the torchlight as she pulled it from her sleeve and pointed it at the guard.

'Open the gate. Now!' she ordered.

The guard looked down at her; Alys was a full head and shoulders shorter than he was. His lip curled in a sardonic sneer as he reached for his own dagger at his belt.

'Listen, woman, you're not really going to—'

He never finished. Alys's right arm shot out. Her knife entered the guard's neck, point first, just above the collar of his chain mail shirt and to the right of his Adam's apple. His eyes widened in shock and he gave an odd choking cough as the blade opened his windpipe and severed the large vein in his neck, unleashing a gush of blood that spurted over his chest.

Still looking at her in shock, the dying guard dropped to his knees, hands moving to his throat. The thought crossed

Alys's mind that she had spent her life trying to save people's lives and now in one night she had ended two. She was surprised at how little it seemed to disturb her, but all she could think of at that moment was that she needed to get to Galiene and Richard. She bore the dead men no malice, but both had been in her way.

Alys slid the bolt on the door in the gate, as the guard fell face first onto the cobblestones. She pulled open the door and ran out into the street. The unlit blackness outside hit her like a slap in the face, gold and multi-coloured stars swimming through her blindness as she felt her feet sink into soft, hideous-smelling ordure, the stench making her gag.

Behind her in the courtyard armed men were spilling out of the doors of the archbishop's house. With her arms held out before her in the dark she stumbled forwards, down into an equally foul-smelling ditch and back up the other side, her hands making contact with the rough daub and wattle of a house wall. She crabbed sideways, feeling her way along the front of the dwelling. A few steps along and her right hand fell into open space. She lurched forward, realising that this must be the gap between two houses or an alleyway.

An idea came to her mind and she followed the corner with her hands, moving into the alley. She stumbled forwards but kept moving, worried that she had no idea where she was going, but also desperate to get further away. When she had gone a little way into the gap between the houses her legs bumped against something and she crouched down into the dark, her feet sinking once again into something unpleasantly soft and foul-smelling, no doubt the usual household rubbish discarded to rot in a pile in the town's alleyways.

As her eyes became accustomed to the darkness she could discern the walls that made up the sides of the alley and, beyond, the street at the end of it. Opposite, the high wall surrounding the archbishop's palace was jet-black, but a halo of light radiated above it from the blazing torchlights in the courtyard on the other side. As Alys watched, the gates of the courtyard swung open with a rattling creek of hinges, spilling more light out onto the dark street. A slight gag of disgust rose in her throat as she saw the filth in the ditch she had waded through to get across the road.

Armoured men, burning torches clasped in one hand and weapons in the other, poured out into the street. They divided into two groups, one going one way up the street and the other going in the opposite direction. As she had gambled, they clearly assumed any fugitive would want to get as far away as fast as possible, so none of them lingered to search nearby.

As the last of the men-at-arms disappeared from view, Alys breathed a sigh of relief and began to rise from her crouched position. She froze once again as she caught sight of a figure striding across the courtyard towards the gate. It was Mortimer. He was now wrapped in a robe, but steam rose from his still-wet hair and face into the chilly night air. He reached the gate and looked left and right up and down the street. His chest heaved and it was clear he was having trouble controlling his anger.

'Von Mahlberg!' Mortimer shouted over his shoulder. Watching from the darkness of the alley, Alys saw a tall man clad in plate armour, one hand resting on the hilt of his sheathed sword, march from the inner door of the bishop's house. His hair was blond and with the orange glow of the torchlight behind him Alys could see his head move from side to side as he scanned the darkness of the street outside.

'Yes, my lord?' the swordsman said, his voice holding a distinct German accent.

Mortimer turned to face him. 'Von Mahlberg, you remember our talk about how I need you to get rid of Richard Savage when he completes his mission for me?'

The German nodded, a slightly amused smile on his face.

'I was not joking, Sire, when I told you I have never been beaten in a straight fight,' he said. 'Savage cheated me out of winning that tournament. I yearn for the day of our rematch. Then there will be no rules, no judges to save him.'

'Good,' Mortimer said. 'And it looks like circumstances have changed. Syr Savage's wife has just become a problem as well. I want you to go now. Find them both, von Mahlberg. Find them and their child. Kill them all.'

37

North Ireland

MacHuylin rode south for two days. He headed along the lough shore from the devastated de Mandeville manor through the town founded by Robert de Jordan and on to the small village of Béal Feirste that sat in the wide, sandy mouth of the River Lagan. From there he followed the Lagan's valley inland and south towards the dark mountains that rose from the sea and marked the southern border of Ulster.

As he rode he passed the burned ruins of several manor houses and the occasional band of scared peasants. He avoided the mottes and forts, once garrisoned by his own galloglaich troops and the soldiers of the earl, but now occupied by Scottish warriors. As he approached the mountains the landscape became countless little rolling hills that resembled a frozen green sea covered with hedges, gorse and stone-built field walls. The land rose higher, the vegetation more sparse, trees thinned out and the ground became covered by heather as he entered the mountains proper.

There was one pass, Innermalane, that ran between the mountains. It was long and narrow and lined on both sides by high, dark granite mountains that soared up into the clouds. The Gap of the North, as it was also known, was the only place an army could march through without having to go over the top of the mountains. For that reason it was heavily fortified by the clans who lived there. Edward Bruce on his march south had had to fight his way through the elaborate system of hurdles, fences and ditches built along its length. They had made it through, but after the Scots had turned back following the Battle of Ardscull, they had been forced to fight their way back through the pass again on their retreat north. The mountain clans were far from beaten.

The folk who lived there were a strange crowd, MacHuylin knew. Isolated, inbred – MacHuylin suspected – and wedded to strange customs and beliefs that went back to the days before Ireland had heard about Jesus Christ. They were a law unto themselves and loyal to no one, neither the English nor the Scots. To them, everyone from outside their clan was a foreigner and therefore fair game. The high uplands they inhabited were no good for farming, but they made a good living by extracting taxes from anyone wanting to travel north into Ulster or south from it – or, if travellers couldn't pay the price, by robbing them of whatever they had.

MacHuylin had no desire to tangle with them, nor did he want to lose time going the long way round and avoiding the pass by climbing the mountains. Instead he waited until nightfall then dismounted and carefully led his horse through the pass by the light of the moon. There were a couple of moments when his heart stopped as he thought he had been spotted or when he saw shadowy figures on the cliffs above. At those times he froze, white knuckles gripping his axe handle, readying himself for attack, but in the end none came. Twice he saw the low silver shadows that he knew were wolves loping along the hillside above. His luck held, however, and as the orange fire of dawn spread over the horizon he was through the pass and the wide, central plain of Ireland spread out before him. The sea was to the east and miles of flat country to the south and west, ending only in the far distant mountains that were south of Dublin. MacHuylin swung himself up onto his horse again and set off at a trot.

He was heading for the town of Dundalk, which lay a few miles away between a bend in the River Fane and a wide, deep bay of the sea. The last time MacHuylin had been there it had been a thriving port with a new castle, a market and a renowned school in the Franciscan friary that some were saying may even become the first of the new universities to be founded in Ireland. However, while besieged in Carrickfergus Castle they had received intelligence from le Poer that the Scots had sacked the town, and the ominous black stain MacHuylin could see on the landscape ahead did not bode well. As he rode closer his worst fears were confirmed. He passed the remnants of the manor of the de Verdun family, now little more than a pile of ashes, and rode on to the town.

MacHuylin stopped his horse at the bridge that crossed the river into Dundalk. The bridge was intact but the gates on the far side were smashed and lay in pieces on the ground. The houses and shops had been destroyed, their walls now mere blackened stumps around charred rafters, which were all that remained of the upper floors and roofs. The streets between them were littered with debris, stones and burnt wood. There was no sign of life anywhere.

His plan had been to ride to Dundalk then catch a ship to Dublin. His horse was exhausted; he was barely halfway to Dublin and a boat could get him to Dublin in a day. Despite le Poer's news, he had not expected this utter desolation. He was sitting on the horse trying to decide what to do, when he spotted that there were indeed a few ships in the harbour. Normally he would not have been able to see them, but now the town had been levelled the masts of the ships could be seen through the ruins. It was strange that there would be ships in the harbour of a destroyed town, but perhaps their crews had just needed to find a port. Maybe there was a chance one of them could take him to Dublin. At least this far south – and through the Gap of the North – he doubted they would be Scottish.

Pulling his chain mail on over his head first, MacHuylin then put his helmet on and strapped it under his chin. With his axe in one hand and the reins in the other, he coaxed his tired horse across the bridge and into the town. Not sure what he was riding into, he rode at a walking pace through the deserted streets, his mount picking its way through rubble, debris and the odd sun-bleached bone; whether human or animal, MacHuylin could not tell. As he neared the centre of the town he was shocked to see that even the Franciscan friary had not been spared the ravages of the Scottish army. It too had been destroyed by fire.

A mangy, emaciated dog skittered across the street. It cast a worried glance in MacHuylin's direction before disappearing into the remains of a shop. He rode on through the ruined town towards the harbour, passing no signs of life apart from the dog. As he arrived at the docks he entered a wide, open square with a stone quay at the waterside. MacHuylin reined to a stop and looked around, ready at any moment to spur the horse into movement again. The three docked ships showed signs of battle. Sails were torn, some strakes were smashed and two showed the blackened marks of fire. Briefly MacHuylin considered that perhaps the ships had been there when the Scots had attacked and they had been damaged when the town was burned. Then he saw seven corpses stretched out on the stones of the quay. They were wrapped in dirty white sheets but their shape was unmistakably human and the bloodstains on them were red and new. These could not be casualties of the Scottish attack, as it had happened months before.

MacHuylin turned the horse's head but as he did so he caught a flicker of movement from the corner of his eye. Grabbing his axe by the handle he looked right and left only to see men emerging from the rubble of the houses and burned-out dockside warehouses all around him. They slunk out from hiding places behind half-ruined walls and piles of debris. As the horse turned the galloglaich saw that there were already four men blocking the street behind him – his only exit. Two of them held loaded, cocked crossbows that were aimed in his direction. More men came onto the street and within moments he was surrounded by a ring of armed men. They all had the dark, tanned skin of sailors. Their faces bore the scars of fighting, and they wore a motley collection of leather and chain mail armour.

Unless he was very wrong this was a crew of pirates: the scum of the sea.

MacHuylin swore under his breath, cursing himself for riding straight into an ambush. He reined the horse to a halt again. As he did so, a tall black-haired man of wiry build swaggered out from behind a wall. He walked with the splayed stance and rolling gait of one used to standing on the heaving deck of a ship. His very long hair was plaited and hung down his back. His beard, similarly plaited, was long enough to tuck into his belt. He wore a chain mail vest over the top of a black leather tunic and in one hand he bore a large, single-edged sword: a cleaving falchion. For several long moments he regarded MacHuylin then finally he spoke.

'Who might you be?'

To MacHuylin's dismay he spoke with a Scottish accent. He did not reply.

'This port is now under the command of Tavish Dhu,' the pirate continued, bobbing his torso in a mocking bow. 'That's me. I'm captain of these ships and lord of these waters. So you better have a good reason for coming into my port.'

MacHuylin's mind raced as he looked at the corsairs who surrounded him. He had no way out. If he tried to run, the crossbowmen would take him down before he got far. His gaze roved across the sheeted, bloody corpses lying on the dock and the damaged ships as he tried to think of something to say.

'Greetings,' he finally said, trying his best to raise a smile. 'I bring news from King Edward Bruce.'

38

Tavish Dhu narrowed his eyes. He raised a hairy, heavily tanned forearm and pointed his falchion at MacHuylin. 'Who are you?' he said. 'You wear the armour of an Irish galloglaich yet you say you come from Edward Bruce?'

MacHuylin thought fast, trying to construct a plausible story. He knew well who Tavish Dhu was. This was the infamous killer recruited by Robert Bruce to make use of the pirates' ships as a navy for the fledgling Scottish nation, ferrying troops across the Irish Sea and harassing English vessels in turn. Before the war Tavish had been a nuisance. MacHuylin recalled him taking three of the Earl of Ulster's ships off the north coast a few years before. With the freedom to operate opened up by the conflict between Scotland and England, the notorious renegade and his fleet had become a positive menace. In the last year alone he had sunk countless ships, sending many men to their deaths and many others – so it was rumoured – he had sold into slavery among the Moors of Andalusia. All the while Tavish had grown richer from the booty he had taken and stronger from the extra ships and crew his successes had enticed to join his fleet.

'I am Connor MacLean of the Clan MacLean of the

Western Isles,' MacHuylin said, being careful to choose the name of a clan he knew fought with Robert Bruce at Bannockburn. 'I wear the armour of a warrior of the isles. Some of my cousins fight against us here as galloglaich it is true—' he turned and spat to indicate his opinion of them '—but like the rest of the MacLeans I am with the army of King Edward Bruce. I see you've had some problems?' He nodded towards the sheeted corpses.

The pirate lowered the falchion but his gaze was no less suspicious. 'No problems. That's the aftermath of an encounter with some war cogs of the Lordship of Ireland. We caught them sneaking up the coast from Dublin. Just the everyday rough and tumble of life on the sea.' He gave a nonchalant shrug. 'The cogs are now at the bottom and her crew are dining with the fishes. What do you make of this man, Pol?' he said, turning to a veritable giant of a man with curly brown hair and a wild, bushy beard, who stalked over to join his captain. He was clad in what looked like a black sheepskin jerkin and carried a huge quarterstaff in one meaty paw. The giant cocked his head to one side and squinted at MacHuylin. After a few moments he shook his head.

'I don't know, Boss,' his voice boomed.

To MacHuylin's surprise he spoke with a northern English accent. Tavish must have crew from all over.

'He might be telling the truth. He might not.'

MacHuylin looked down from his horse at the big man, noticing the expression of strained concentration on his face, the dull eyes and the huge, tombstone-like teeth in his mouth. He appeared to be Tavish Dhu's second in command but by the look of him was definitely not the brains of the pirate crew.

'What does Bruce want?' Tavish Dhu asked, turning his attention back towards MacHuylin.

'He sends a warning,' MacHuylin lied. His main aim was to escape from this unexpected encounter alive, but if he could do any good to help the cause in the process it would be a bonus. Perhaps it was possible to distract the pirate ships and send them scurrying home out of the way. 'His spies tell him the English have mustered a fleet of ships and are sailing for Ireland with orders to capture or kill you.'

Tavish Dhu raised a pair of black, bristling eyebrows. 'A fleet? What nonsense is this? The English have no ships to spare for the Irish Sea. All their warships are engaged in the war in France. I don't believe it.'

The big man called Pol frowned. 'Boss, what if it is true? Our ships are damaged already from that last fight. If we come up against serious warships we could be in bother. Maybe we should run and lay low for a while.'

Tavish looked down and shook his head. 'We've plenty more ships. Pol, Pol, Pol. How many times must I tell you we need to start changing the way we operate? You're stuck in your old outlaw thinking. We don't need to hit and run any more. We're no longer just a small band of pirates. We're a navy in the employ of the nation of Scotland and we need to start thinking and acting like one. If the English are really mustering a fleet against us – which I doubt – then we should think about how to deal with them.'

Pol's eyes widened. 'You mean to stand and fight? That's not the way we do our business.'

'Up 'til now, no,' Tavish said. 'But we have to change that. We have the strength to do it now. Tell me something –

if someone wanted your job as my right-hand man, what would you do?'

The big man grinned. 'I'd kill him.'

'Of course you would.' Tavish nodded. 'And if you didn't I'd kill you for being weak. It's the same with the English. We rule this sea now and anyone who challenges us should be treated the same way you would treat someone who thought he could take your job.'

MacHuylin had to admit he was impressed. Tavish was no mere freebooter. He had leadership and could think well beyond just the next robbery. Pol nodded, realisation dawning, but MacHuylin thought he could still see some doubt in his eyes.

'What about those warships you just fought against?' MacHuylin decided to try to fan the embers of Pol's misgivings. 'Is there a chance that they were the scouts for a larger force?'

Tavish glared at MacHuylin but did not immediately reply. Pol started as if the thought had occurred to him too. 'He could be right, Boss! If we're caught in the open sea with these damaged ships we'll all be dead men. We should make a run for it back to the Isle of Man and get reinforcements. The Saracen slaver is due there soon anyway and we need to meet him.'

Tavish's lip curled in a snarl of fury. He reached out with his left hand and grasped a fistful of Pol's sheepskin at chest level. With his right he brandished the falchion again. The sight of the smaller pirate chief glaring up at his giant second in command, and the big man's evident terror, was faintly comical. Despite the situation, MacHuylin found it hard not to smile.

'Shut your big mouth, you dozy ox!' Tavish hissed. 'I ought to gut you like a fish.'

'Sorry, Boss,' the big man whined, though he adjusted the grip of his right hand on his quarterstaff so it now was in a ready position.

MacHuylin glanced round. All the other pirates were distracted by the confrontation between their leaders. Several were moving forward, anticipating a fight and preparing to either try to step between Tavish and Pol or perhaps take sides. Judging that this may be an excellent opportunity to leave, he wheeled his horse's head and turned around in the devastated street.

'I must go. My mission is done and I have to get back to Carrickfergus,' he said over his shoulder. Behind him he could hear the raised voices of the arguing pirates.

The horse had taken a couple of steps when he heard Tavish's raised voice behind him.

'You! Where in Hell's name do you think you're off to?'

MacHuylin did not reply. Instead he dug his heels into the flanks of his beleaguered mount, hunching himself forward behind the beast's head. The horse surged forward, hooves sliding and clattering on the cobblestones of the street. In moments he covered most of the way towards the pirates who were blocking the street behind him while they were still reacting to the sudden change in situation.

'Stop him, you fools!' Tavish roared.

MacHuylin rode straight at one of the crossbowmen. He gripped the reins in one hand and swung his axe with the other. As it rotated he loosened his grip, letting the long shaft slide through his hand then grasping it once more almost at the base, extending the reach of the weapon to its maximum. The axe continued its circular path, coming up over his head and crashing down onto the crossbowman as he was still fumbling with the catch to loose the quarrel. Holding it at such an extent MacHuylin's blow did not have its full impact, but it was enough to smash the crossbow from the man's arms.

At the same time something whizzed past MacHuylin's head, buzzing like an angry wasp. From the corner of his eye he could see that the second crossbowman had loosed at him. The quarrel had just missed. The galloglaich slipped his left foot from the stirrup and lashed out with his boot at another pirate who was slashing his sword at him. MacHuylin's foot caught the man in the teeth, dislodging the few remaining ones and sending him spinning sideways out of the way of the horse.

Yelling at the top of his voice, MacHuylin spurred his mount onward. As he crouched close to the horse's neck it galloped up the street and away from the pirates. A quick glance over his shoulder told him that they were running after him but without horses they did not stand a chance of catching him. The second crossbowman was reloading, however.

MacHuylin shouted and kicked the horse on. He was almost at the end of the street and once round the corner would be home free.

Just as he reached the corner, he felt a stunning blow on the back of his right shoulder. It knocked him forwards in the saddle as blazing pain erupted from the site. It was all he could do to stop from falling off the horse. His right arm went limp, his hand loosening and his axe dropped, rattling onto the cobblestones of the street. Gasping, he reached round with his left hand and felt the stub of a feathered shaft that now protruded from the back of his shoulder. Where it met his body, his fingers felt the smashed rings of his chain mail and the warmth of the blood that now coursed from the wound.

The crossbowman had hit him.

39

At sea

On Savage's orders, Captain Breslin sailed his ship around the southern coast of Ireland. They stayed someway offshore with the land on the larboard side and the open sea to starboard. As they sailed, a steady rain began to fall. It had the crew donning sealskin jerkins and Savage pulling up the hood of his long, black woollen cloak. The rest of the crew were well to the fore of the ship, warned to keep clear if they wanted their captain to remain alive. They complied, for which Savage was glad. They sailed all day and he was dog-tired, exhausted from the constant vigilance required in holding the whole crew prisoner.

Despite the circumstances he was in, Breslin remained implacable, almost cheery. He talked a lot, asking Savage about his life in France and where he had grown up in Ulster, then regaling him with tales of his native Tír Chonaill, a land so beautiful, he said, that God himself liked to wander through the mountains there on his days off. Savage listened with half an ear, maintaining his focus on the sullen crew.

As the day darkened, one of the crew brought shares of fresh fish, cooked on a pan over a cooking stone in the centre of the boat. Savage and Breslin devoured the meal then Breslin shouted an order and the anchor was thrown over the side.

'What do you think you're doing?' Savage demanded.

'Well I for one am going to get some sleep,' Breslin said. 'Unless you expect us to sail through the night?'

'I give the orders here, remember?' Savage said, raising the blade of his sword.

Breslin sighed. 'Look, friend, I'm wet, I'm cold and I'm tired. It's getting dark and if we go on we'll probably run aground on some of those rocks along the shore. We gain nothing by travelling on tonight except putting my ship in danger. And it is still my ship. You can threaten all you want but I'm going no further tonight.'

Savage narrowed his eyes. Frustration at Breslin's sheer facetiousness boiled within him. The man simply acted as if he wasn't a prisoner at all, but Savage could see there was little he could do about it and Breslin knew it. The rest of the crew were already crawling under spare canvas sails in the bow and lying down to sleep. He sighed and nodded his agreement. Breslin walked down his boat and found another sail, which he brought back to the stern and wrapped himself in before settling down beside the handle of the steering oar. In a few moments the sound of snoring came from under the sheet.

Exhausted, Savage sat down on the deck. Lying down would probably be suicide; he would just have to try to stay awake and keep vigilant. As the dark hours drifted on and no one moved, however, he found it impossible to keep his eyes open any more and fell into sleep.

He did not know how long he slept but he woke up with a start and saw that the colour of the sky had lightened considerably. Realising what had happened he was extremely surprised to find himself still alive. He could only assume that everyone else had stayed asleep and thanked God he hadn't snored.

At dawn he gave Breslin a kick to wake him. The rest of the crew woke and the voyage resumed. They reached the rocky peninsula of Duáin, which protruded out into the sea like a flat, green-covered finger. They were reaching the south-west corner of Ireland. As they sailed by, Savage watched the dark rocky shores, their tops shrouded in mist, and felt a strange mixture of longing and dread. Ireland: his homeland. He had tried to escape it twice now, but the damnable place had dragged him back again. And could he really call it his home? The Gaelic Irish certainly wouldn't say so. On his mother's side he was descended from Gaelic nobility, but his father was from a Norman family whose forefather had landed almost one hundred and fifty years before on the very headland they were sailing past.

In the eleven hundred and sixty-ninth year after the birth of Christ, the first Norman knights, a band of mercenaries under the command of Raymond le Gros, had come ashore in Ireland. Considering that now, Savage thought it ironic that his own lineage was almost exactly the same as that of Edward Bruce and yet here they were fighting on opposite sides of the war. They were both half-Gaelic, half-Norman, both descended from Norman knights in the army of

Duke William who had conquered England and crowned himself King William I. The differentiating factor was that a century later, Bruce's ancestors had invaded and taken lands in Scotland, while Savage's had done the same in Ireland. They had been fighting ever since. Fighting to hold on to the land; fighting each other. Would it ever end?

Once around the headland and past the port of Wexford, they swung north. Leaving behind the sea between Ireland and Spain, they entered the Irish Sea proper between Britain and Ireland. The crew became noticeably more jumpy and the smallest one, the young lad called Niall, was sent up the mast and told to keep a lookout for other ships.

'What are they frightened of?' Savage wondered aloud.

'Tavish Dhu,' Breslin said.

'The pirate?'

The captain nodded. 'These are his waters now. His hunting ground.'

'Who is this man? Why is everyone so afraid of him?'

'He's an evil bastard, worse than Eustace the Monk,' Breslin replied. 'Some say Tavish was a Scottish nobleman from the far north who lost his lands in a blood feud. He was also excommunicated from the Church for some terrible deeds. He took to the seas and made a living by preying on the shipping between England and Ireland and grew rich by it. The war between Scotland and England has given him free rein and he's been terrorising these seas for the last few years. Robert Bruce saw the advantage of having him on his side and pays him to attack English ships. Tavish has built up a fleet for himself, recruiting every piece of scum and every lowlife north of Spain with a ship and a desire to make money without caring how. God alone knows how many ships he's taken or sunk. And when he takes a ship there is no mercy for whoever is on board, even if they surrender without a fight. The men are killed. Any children or women are sold to the Moorish slave traders. It's a crying shame. The man is worse than the Devil himself.'

Hugging the coast, they sailed north, the rugged coastline of Ireland on their left and the wide, green open sea on their right. The rain returned and the mist greyed out the horizon. Later in the day it cleared up a little and they caught glimpses of high, dark mountains rising up away from the sea.

'Wicklow,' Breslin commented. 'Home of the O'Briens. A fierce bunch of lads. They'll sort you and your lot out if they get the chance.'

Shortly after that the rain cleared up and they rounded a headland into what looked like a huge bay.

'We're nearly there,' Breslin said. 'This is Dublin Bay.'

An excited shout went up from the boy on the mast. Everyone turned to look in the direction he pointed and a gasp went up from the crew at the sight of a group of masts that lay ahead. About the middle of the bay, near the wide mouth where a river met the sea, a flotilla of ships was resting at anchor in the deep water a little way offshore.

'Calm down, lads,' Captain Breslin raised his voice. 'Tavish may be bold but he's not that strong that he can anchor just outside Dublin. Those are not pirate ships.'

Savage felt a surge of excitement at the sight of the vessels. They were clearly gathered there for a reason and he hoped it was for an expedition north to attack Bruce. This could be his passage into Ulster and his way to Galiene.

As they got closer they could see there were five large ships, merchant cogs riding at anchor. The sounds of hammering and sawing drifted across the water. Men were working on the boats, building fighting platforms, crenellated castle-like defences and reinforcements to the decks. They were making preparations for war. On the shore beyond the flotilla of ships Savage could make out the buildings and stark walls and towers of Dublin. Rising from it into the sky drifted the hazy smoke from thousands of chimneys.

The captain steered the ship towards the mouth of the river and the town beyond. As they passed the fleet of ships, a couple of sleek, light patrol boats were rowed out from the largest ship to intercept them. The boats were filled with soldiers in chain mail with kettle helmets. Seeing Savage beside Breslin with a drawn sword in hand immediately prompted four loaded crossbows to be raised and aimed directly at him.

'Who are you and what is your business?' a soldier standing in the prow of one of the boats demanded. Over his chain mail he wore a tabard which was half yellow, half red.

'I am Syr Richard Savage,' Savage shouted back as the boat drew alongside. 'I am travelling on orders from Lord Mortimer. Is the Earl of Ulster still in Dublin?'

'He is, but first tell me why you hold that man hostage,' the soldier shouted back.

'These sailors are from Tír Chonaill, trading with our enemies in France. He and his crew tried to get in the way of my mission. I persuaded them otherwise,' Savage rejoined. 'Is Syr Thomas de Mandeville with the earl?'

The soldier cast his gaze over Breslin's crew and took note of their wild Irish dress. Years of ingrained prejudice prompted a sardonic smile of approval at Savage's actions. 'Lord de Mandeville is here as well,' he replied. 'He is at the castle.'

'Can you take me there?' Savage asked.

The soldier looked unsure at first, but then nodded. 'What about them?' He waved his sword at Savage's hostages.

Looking at Breslin, Savage remembered the night before when he had fallen into an exhausted sleep and not awoken to find himself dead.

'Let them go on their way,' he said.

'What?' The soldier's eyebrows rose into his helmet. 'These men are enemies, hostile to the Lordship of Ireland.'

'They just made a mistake; one we probably all would have made,' Savage said. 'They can go back to Tír Chonaill.'

'Out of the question, I'm afraid,' the soldier shouted. He nodded his head in the direction of the gathered fleet. 'They've seen that. We don't want them telling their friends about it. They can't leave until after the fleet sails. We have orders to stop all shipping leaving the city.'

Savage looked at Breslin again. 'What do you say to a few days' stopover in Dublin?'

The captain laughed, his blue eyes twinkling. 'I'll have a hard time keeping the lads out of trouble, but it looks like we don't have much choice in the matter.'

'Very well,' Savage said, 'then here we shall part. I am sorry I took you so far out of your way.'

Breslin just grunted. Savage turned and walked to the side of the ship. As he began to clamber over the wale, preparing to climb down into the smaller patrol boat, the Irishman spoke again.

'Syr Richard?'

Savage turned his head back, his right eyebrow raised.

'I hope you find your daughter,' Breslin said, his face serious. 'We may be proud of our sons, but losing a daughter is enough to break any father's heart.'

Savage nodded then turned and carefully lowered himself into the other boat.

'Now take me to Dublin,' he said to the soldiers.

40

The rowing boat had three sets of oars and a narrow draught that allowed it to skim over the surface of the water. Propelled by the arms of the burly soldiers, they entered the wide river mouth and began to head upstream. Savage's nose wrinkled as the smell of the city began to reach him: the cloying aroma of smoke from fires mixed with the malty fragrance of brewing ale and the stench of human and animal dung. The River Liffey was wide, dark and filthy. At the point where it met the sea it had become the main drain and sewer for the city. Detritus, rubbish and sewage began drifting past the boat. Savage grimaced as the bloated corpse of a dog, pale and hairless, bobbed by.

A little way past the mouth of the river the Liffey diverged and to the south widened into a pond. This was the original "black pool" – in Irish, *dubh linn* – which had given the city its name. Where the pool met the main river a huge defensive tower dominated the approach to the city from the sea. Isolde's Tower, as it was known, was the largest of the many that punctuated the one and a half miles of high stone walls encircling the city. As the first line of defence against attack from the sea it was the first building to greet travellers arriving by boat. A catapult sat on top of the tower and, as the boat approached beneath it, Savage spotted at least three crossbows lining them up from above.

Ahead, along the edge of the river and underneath the walls, stretched the wooden merchant quays of Dublin. These were cluttered with docked ships, boats and other vessels, the dock sides piled high with crates, barrels and other packages. Cranes, pulleys and slings for unloading and loading cargo stood on the quayside like bizarre giant wooden birds. Savage noticed that none of them were moving. In fact there was surprisingly little activity going on for the port of a major city and he surmised that this must be due to the shipping embargo imposed by the pirates.

The ground rose from the riverbank, which allowed Savage a little view of what was behind the city walls and he counted the spires of at least six churches. The massive stone bulk of Christ Church Cathedral with its square central tower dominated the city like a manmade mountain. Behind the walls that stretched to the south away from the Liffey, along the banks of the black pool, the round towers of Dublin Castle squatted.

Looking further upstream past the quays, Savage was astonished to see that the stone and wood bridge, which spanned the Liffey from north to south and ran to the main gate of the city, had been destroyed. He had visited Dublin years before, entering via that bridge. On that occasion he had marvelled that the ancient structure could support the mass of houses and shops crammed on top of it so precariously it seemed they were in danger of toppling into the water. Now the bridge was gone completely, except for a few stout wooden supports that still jutted from the water.

This was not all. Looking north of the river Savage

surveyed a scene of devastation he could scarcely believe. From his previous visits to the city over the years he remembered the crowded, busy streets that had lined the River Liffey on the north bank opposite the walls on the south. A vibrant town-outside-the-town had evolved on the north bank over the century or so since the English had arrived and kicked the Norse-Irish out of the city that had been theirs for three hundred years. The Anglo-Norman lord, Strongbow, had taken the city, beheaded Hasculf MacTorcall, the King of Dublin, and expelled all the inhabitants of the town.

The townsfolk had not gone far, migrating north of the river and creating their own settlement outside the walls of what was now a Norman city. They had called their new town "Ostmenstown", after the name of those of Viking descent, who still called themselves the Ostmen – men from the east. From what Savage could see, Ostmenstown was now just a ruin. Everything had been flattened, destroyed and burned. There was not a single building left standing aside from a few stone churches. All was blackened desolation.

'It looks like the Scots came very close to taking the city,' Savage commented, mostly to himself as he looked at the ruins.

The soldier in the yellow and red tabard, who had since introduced himself as Meiler of Braganstown, shook his head. 'Edward Bruce did not do this. The people of Dublin did this themselves.'

Savage turned to him, eyebrows raised, but before he could comment, Meiler continued: 'When the Scots were on the march last year it looked like no one would be able to stop them. The Dubliners panicked. They pulled everyone back into the walled city south of the river then destroyed everything north of the river to deny the Scots army cover as they approached. All the buildings outside the walls were destroyed. Houses, halls, warehouses and shops were pulled down and set on fire. Anything made of stone was dismantled and carried back across the river to shore up the defences of the city. That included the bridge.'

'But not those churches?' Savage pointed out.

'No. That would be sacrilege.'

'Did it work?' Savage asked.

'In the end it wasn't needed,' the soldier said with a bitter laugh. 'The Scots never made it this far. Mortimer managed to stop their advance north of here at Skerries. Sooner or later they'll be back though, so it may prove very prudent.'

Savage nodded, taking another look at the ruins. Dublin seemed to be crouched in defence, its already battle-scarred face staring north, waiting for the inevitable onslaught.

'You're not a Dubliner,' Savage said, remarking on Meiler's accent and second name, both of which spoke of origins to the north. Braganstown was in Louth, between Dublin and the southern border of Ulster. 'Did you come here with Earl Richard?'

Meiler grunted and grinned, revealing an array of yellowed teeth. 'I did not. I'm a captain in John de Bermingham's company. Earl Richard is yesterday's man. He lost Ulster to the Scots, and Connacht to Felim O'Connor. Now he has no lands, no army and no home. He still has his money, though. Between you and me—' he leaned closer to Savage and lowered his voice '—there are many who see his lack of success against the Scots and the fact that his daughter is married to Robert the Bruce as not entirely unconnected.'

Savage nodded, remembering his previous adventure in Ulster. Earl Richard Óg de Burgh had proved to be at best ambivalent on whose side he was actually on.

'Now Mortimer has gone back to England, the only man capable of stopping the Scots is Lord Bermingham,' Meiler said as the boat pulled alongside the quays. 'Thank the Lord the king saw that too and made him justiciar.'

'What happened to Edmund le Bottelier?' Savage asked, remembering the balding, careworn man he had met in Carrickfergus the year before. 'He was justiciar when I left Ireland.'

Meiler shook his head. 'Kicked out of office. He lost too many times to the Scots. The defeat at Ardskull before Christmas was the final straw. Mortimer and King Edward moved him aside. My Lord Bermingham is now in charge.'

Savage did not reply. He had never met John de Bermingham, but the family – an Anglo-Norman clan with lands in the north and the west – had a reputation for ruthlessness and brutality. Perhaps in desperate situations like these he was the sort of person who was required to lead.

On landing, they were immediately surrounded by soldiers wanting to know their business, but the presence of Meiler, who appeared to carry some authority and respect, meant that they were allowed onshore. Meiler led Savage through a big, double-towered gate in the walls, large enough to be a castle tower house by itself. They passed under the iron-clad teeth of a raised portcullis and Savage glanced up at the murder holes in the ceiling above them from where, if the gate fell to an enemy and the portcullis was breached, the defenders in the tower could unleash boiling oil, scorching sand and rocks on the attackers below. Savage had once seen that happen on a Templar raid into Egypt and the smell of incinerated flesh and the screams of the men boiled alive in their armour still haunted him. Today all that came from above were wary glances from pairs of suspicious, watchful eyes.

They were now inside the city proper. The place was filthy, crowded and noisy. Houses and shops were crammed on top of each other in chaotic disorder. The street leading away from the gate was barely fourteen feet across, overhung and oppressed by timber-framed houses. Large piles of human and animal dung were everywhere and a sort of culvert drain full of slow-moving filth slithered its way down the middle of the street. Throngs of children, merchants and other townsfolk struggled to make their way; almost everyone seemed to be going in a different direction.

They walked uphill until the street opened into a small square space where the church of Saint Michael nestled. Built by Norsemen over three hundred and fifty years before, the church had survived despite the intermittent wars and invasions that had engulfed Ireland in the intervening years. Beyond the square they entered Winetavern Street. Like most medieval streets, Winetavern Street was named after the trade of the majority of people who lived there. There were wine distributors, wine merchants, wine importers and, of course, wine taverns. There seemed to be an air of heightened jollity about the area, with the sound of singing and raucous banter coming from the taverns. As Savage and Meiler passed by one of these, a drunken brawl spilt out onto the street and they carefully skirted their way around it.

At the end of Winetavern Street they went by the towering Gothic majesty of Christ Church Cathedral and through another, older set of walls, the remains of the Norse defences of the city. Here they entered another crowded, busy street where the walls and towers of Dublin Castle glowered down on them from above the houses and shops. Savage and Meiler followed the street until they turned a corner and came to the imposing gates.

Dublin Castle was a large fortress set in the south-west of the city, making one corner of the defences. A fortification within a fortification, it stood defiant like a symbol of the beleaguered Lordship of Ireland. On the way into the main, double-towered gate, human heads – black and rotten – were impaled on spikes. They were traitors, rebels or defeated enemies – ordinary thieves and other criminals did not warrant post-mortem display at the castle – but it was a forlorn, almost petty display of attempted domination. The way the war was going the Lordship of Ireland was no longer a power to be frightened of.

Meiler gave the day's password to the sentries and he and Savage walked through the gates unchallenged. Savage had never been inside Dublin Castle before and was surprised to see that it was an old-fashioned fortress with no central keep. Instead, the rectangular walls enclosed a confused jumble of wooden and stone buildings: barracks, smithies, stables and a very tall, very long great hall.

'Thomas de Mandeville should be in there,' Meiler said, pointing to the hall. 'I can't say where the Earl of Ulster is, but I know his seneschal is in there working on plans for our expedition.'

'Where is your expedition headed?' Savage asked.

Meiler tapped the side of his nose and shook his head. 'That would be telling, now. Come with me.'

With that he led Savage to the doors of the great hall.

One of the huge double doors stood open, both to allow entry and to let light in. Years before, as a new recruit to the Order of Knights Templar, Savage had travelled through London for initiation in the Templar headquarters there. He had seen there the great hall of the king at Westminster, the largest building in the world, so they said. This hall was not quite as big, but it was certainly the largest he had seen in Ireland. Inside, the walls were painted white and hung with tapestries. Clean rushes lined the floor. There was a large dais or stage at the far end and tall windows, which reached to the ceiling high overhead, let lots of daylight in.

As they entered the hall, Savage and Meiler were immersed in a hubbub of chattering and raised voices. They were in the administrative seat of the Lordship of Ireland and the centre of government activity. Around the hall, seated at benches or tables, were various groups of men engaged in discussion, reading documents and generally occupied in the business of running the country, aided by a small army of clerics who documented proceedings as they happened. Spread across a table on the dais Savage saw the large chequered cloth that was used to tot up the country's accounts. Despite the war, regardless of the famine, bureaucracy continued.

Beside a bench on one side of the hall, not far from the door, there stood a tall man with close-cropped grey hair. He was in his late forties, but lean and fit and showing no sign of his mature years. He was talking to a group of men in chain mail. Spread out on the bench were a variety of documents, maps and other scrolls. A young cleric with ink-stained fingers was seated at the bench watching them, his quill poised over a piece of parchment, waiting for material to write.

Savage smiled, recognising the grey-haired man as Syr Thomas de Mandeville, the seneschal and military commander of Ulster. Despite his exalted rank, de Mandeville wore an old leather jerkin stained with oil and rust, a sure sign that he spent a lot of time wearing chain mail over it. He was a frontier lord who had spent his whole adult life in the saddle and on campaign, fighting wherever the earl sent him, from Ireland to Scotland to Gascony.

As Savage and Meiler approached, the seneschal caught sight of them out of the corner of his eye and turned to face them, a look of startled confusion on his face showing he was unsure about what he was seeing. Then he grinned.

'Richard Savage! Is that you?' he said. 'I thought you'd got yourself killed.'

Savage saluted de Mandeville and the seneschal returned the gesture.

'Syr Thomas.' Savage smiled. 'I was afraid you would not remember me.'

'This man says he comes here on the orders of the Lord Mortimer, sire,' Meiler said. 'I thought I should accompany him in case he was up to something. However, it looks like you do indeed know him.'

De Mandeville's face became serious. He gave Savage a look that seemed to hold a sudden hint of concern, perhaps even suspicion. He nodded to Meiler. 'I know this man all right. You should get back to the ships.'

'Yes, my lord.' Meiler saluted, turned on his heel and marched away.

When he had gone, de Mandeville beckoned Savage closer. 'What are you doing here in Ireland? Didn't you go off to France or something?'

Savage told him the whole story, surprised at how relieved he felt to finally unburden himself of the tale. 'I have to get to Ulster, Syr Thomas,' he finished. 'If Bruce is there then Galiene is being held there too.'

The seneschal looked him in the eye. 'Well, I just might be able to help you out there. Come with me.' De Mandeville laid a hand on Savage's shoulder and steered him over to the bench.

'My friends, this is Syr Richard Savage,' the seneschal informed the three men clad in chain mail to whom he had been talking when Savage arrived. 'A knight of Ulster, formerly a knight of the Temple of Solomon, one of the best jousters I have ever seen in action and the man who stole the Holy Grail from Robert Bruce – though what he did with it I can't say.' He glanced sideways at Savage. 'Savage, these three are Syr John d'Athy, Syr Patrick FitzWarin and Syr Paschall. We are all here to discuss the same problem you face: how to get into Ulster. This studious young man here—' he laid his hand on the bony, painfully thin shoulder of the tonsured cleric '—is the Earl of Ulster's personal scribe; de Burgh generously donated him to our efforts to handle documentation.'

The cleric nodded but did not smile, regarding Savage with hollow, dark-rimmed eyes. Savage surveyed the young knights, unable to keep a look of slight disapproval from his face at what appeared to him to be a collection of beardless boys. Syr Paschall looked to be in his early twenties. His chain mail was immaculate and shone like polished silver. His leggings were rich wool and his long boots were of the supplest leather. Syr Paschall's bobbed black hair was curled at the ends, not naturally, Savage suspected, but by the application of hot irons. He was clearly foreign. No self-respecting Irish knight – at least none Savage knew – would take such time over his appearance. The young man returned his gaze with equal disdain as he eyed Savage's scruffy appearance.

FitzWarin was perhaps mid-twenties and his broken nose meant at least he might have been in a fight sometime. D'Athy had long blond hair and eager blue eyes but looked as fresh-faced as his companions.

'John d'Athy?' Savage turned to de Mandeville, remembering the fat, outrageously dressed Constable of Carrickfergus. 'Any relation to the fool who tried to arrest Alys?'

D'Athy's lip curled into a snarl. He surged forward, left hand reaching for Savage's throat while his right bunched into a fist. The seneschal stepped between the two of them while d'Athy's two companions stepped in to restrain him. Savage was genuinely surprised by the vehemence of the young man's reaction.

'John here is his son,' de Mandeville said over his shoulder. He turned back to look the young man in the eyes.

'Calm yourself, Syr John. Savage had no idea your father was hanged by Edward Bruce last year.'

'He was?' Savage raised his eyebrows.

'After he took Carrickfergus, Bruce hanged anyone he captured who had been in a position of authority in the earldom,' de Mandeville explained.

'I had no idea,' Savage said, looking over the seneschal's shoulder to meet d'Athy's gaze. 'In that case I apologise.'

The younger man grunted, nodded his assent and relaxed. His companions let him go.

He was still an idiot though, Savage thought to himself.

The seneschal stepped away from between them. 'Let's not fall out this early. We all have a common purpose here.' He pointed to a large piece of parchment unrolled on the bench. On it pictures and symbols had been drawn. Realising what it was, Savage raised his eyebrows.

'Is this a map?' Savage asked, looking at the ragged-edged, elongated oval shape outlined on the parchment.

'It is,' de Mandeville replied.

Savage was impressed. 'When I was in the Templars we saw Saracen maps in Outremer but I never thought I'd see one here. It must have cost a fortune. Is that Ireland?'

The seneschal nodded. 'Ulster is at the top. You can see where Carrickfergus is by the drawing of the castle here.' He laid a leather-gauntleted forefinger at a position in the top right corner of the map. 'No doubt you saw the ships on your way in?'

Savage nodded. 'That's quite a little navy you have gathered. Are you planning an invasion by sea?'

'A relief mission,' de Mandeville said. 'The Scots

have taken the north of Ireland but Carrickfergus Castle has still not fallen. God alone knows how, but the garrison has managed to hold out. They've been besieged for nearly a year now, but de Thrapston refuses to give in. MacHuylin's up there too.'

The seneschal's voice was edged with concern but there was a slight hoarseness to it that betrayed his pride and admiration for the men formerly under his command.

John d'Athy coughed. 'Sire, should we really be discussing our plans so openly?' He glanced at Savage.

'I appreciate your concern, John,' de Mandeville replied, 'but if there is one person I know we can trust it's this man.'

Turning down the corners of his mouth in a gesture that showed he both accepted the fact and was impressed by the seneschal's confidence, d'Athy shot Savage another look, this time with new appreciation. Savage wondered to himself how bad the situation was if even here, right at the heart of the English-backed administration of Ireland, these men felt the need to be suspicious of others.

'While that castle resists we still have a toehold in the north,' de Mandeville continued. 'We don't have the strength for a full-scale re-invasion right now, but we will do later in the year. Carrickfergus has a harbour that can serve as a landing point for that expedition, so at all costs it must not fall. We plan to sail up the coast, land at Carrickfergus and either break the siege or at least deliver supplies to the castle so they can continue to hold out. They must be growing desperate by now. Our main problem will be that damned pirate.'

'Tavish Dhu? I've heard a lot about him lately,' Savage said.

'We could lose half our ships to that bastard before we get as far as Carrickfergus,' d'Athy said. 'He appears like magic every time a ship sails north up the channel between Wales and Ireland. He is able to attack, slip away then come back and attack again.'

'Not just that, the whole enterprise depends on the element of surprise,' de Mandeville said. 'If Tavish spots us he'll alert Bruce straight away. If the Scots know we're coming then we won't get as far as the shore, never mind the castle. That's our biggest problem right now. The justiciar won't give us permission to launch the expedition unless we can present a plausible strategy for how we deal with that pirate.'

'So the way is dangerous, perhaps impossible,' Paschall said with a grin that was infectious. His accent confirmed Savage's deduction that the young man was a foreigner, probably Italian. 'All the better! More chance for glory, eh?'

They all laughed. Savage felt a thrill of excitement. This was beyond what he had hoped. Those ships could take him right to where Edward Bruce was camped and most probably where Galiene was being held.

'A hazardous expedition with small chance of success,' he said, looking around at the other men and meeting each of their gazes in turn. He gave a slow grin then added, 'Count me in!'

42

Bordeaux

Even though it was not long after sunrise the harbour of Bordeaux was a swarm of activity. Ships of all shapes and sizes lined the quays, loading or unloading cargoes. It was mostly wine that was leaving – the full effects of the terrible weather had not yet been felt by the wine merchants who were still exporting barrels of their produce that had been laid down over a year before. Lean years were ahead, but being businessmen, they were adjusting their prices for future compensation. Others doing well amid the misery were the fishermen, who being the one source of reliable food had found their profits rise dramatically. Masters of fishing vessels, formerly barefoot and barely clad in rags, now strutted around the docks and quays dressed in the latest, two-coloured hoods over brightly dyed tunics, ostentatiously better fed than everyone else. The fact that they still walked barefoot and with a lolling gate to counter a ship on the waves, betrayed their somewhat humbler past.

Coming into port were weapons, armour and soldiers,

barrels of newly made arrows; sheaves of staves for axes, coats of mail and lean, hungry men: veterans of many conflicts, who knew that the best place to survive in times of hardship were lands of war where they could take what they needed. They came streaming off recently docked boats. Regardless of the famine and the weather, the affairs of men continued. King Louis of France waited just over the border, slavering like a hungry wolf to regain this part of his kingdom, and English-held Gascony needed every single one of them.

The harbour master in Bordeaux was an important man, and another of those who found no hardship from the continuing famine. As comptroller of customs, Guymer de Bertenac oversaw the importation and taxing of goods arriving at the harbour and the collection of mooring fees. This included the many fishing vessels that unloaded their wares on the quays. Berths were at a premium and in these straitened times he was more than happy to accept backhanders in terms of fish or wine. Guymer had been a very corpulent man before the famine and incredibly he had retained much of his bulk, though he was heartily sick of eating dried fish.

He had been up since just before dawn and now, with the early morning sunshine streaming through the window, the harbour master stood at the tall writing desk in his office at the entrance to the harbour, munching his way through a bowl of fish potage, a sour scowl of displeasure on his face that deepened with every mouthful. The sound of the door opening made him look up. A woman entered his office. He raised an eyebrow at the sight of her. She was not a young girl in the first flush of youth, but she was still undoubtedly good-looking, although her white skin was tinged with a grey pallor and her eyes were rimmed with red. She looked exhausted. Her long dress was ill-fitting and the hem was clotted with muck from the town streets.

'I wish to find a boat sailing to Ireland,' she said. She spoke in French but the accent was strange. It had a harsh tone to it, Norman in dialect but not Norman, nor quite the French they spoke in England.

'You wish to book a passage to Ireland?' Guymer said. 'That might be difficult in these times.'

The woman shook her head. 'I cannot pay. I have no money. I need to get to Ireland. I'm looking for a ship that perhaps I could work on...'

Guymer grunted, a look of amusement chasing the scowl from his face. It was obvious to him now that her accent was Irish. 'Have you... ahem... worked on any boats before?'

From the withering look the woman cast in his direction, the harbour master surmised that the answer was no.

'In Ireland I owned a castle,' the woman responded. 'However, I can cook. I have medical skills—'

Guymer blushed and held up a hand, palm towards the woman. 'I am sorry, my lady; I have misunderstood your intentions slightly. You see, women are not allowed on the crew of a ship. It's the law. Having a female on board inevitably leads to conflict and trouble among the male crew members, you see. Even so, some ships do bring women along to... shall we say, "service" the crew members. It's against the law, but nevertheless some captains see this as a way to keep their sailors happy.'

'You mean they bring prostitutes on voyages?' The Irish woman frowned.

'Regrettably, madam, they do. I imagine that is not the sort of work you were looking for?' Guymer responded. At the same time he thought that with her looks and figure, if this woman was inclined to enter that particular profession, she could probably make a good living from it.

'It certainly was not,' she said, glaring at him from under lowered eyebrows. 'What am I to do? I must get to Ireland.'

Guymer gave an unhelpful shrug. 'No money. No passage. I'm sorry, madam...'

The woman bit her lip and was about to say something else when the door of the office opened again. Both turned to see a young lad of about fourteen winters enter the room. He was simply dressed in a brown woollen tunic and hose and a Breton cap. A large, full canvas bag was slung over his shoulder by a strap. He directed his gaze at Guymer, his face pale. It seemed he was about to say something then he hesitated.

'Are you lost?' the harbour master guessed. 'Can I help you?'

The boy's shoulders fell and a grateful smile spread across his face. 'Please... I need to find *La Trinite*, the ship of Bertrand de Grissome. I am the new ship's boy. It's due to sail soon. I had trouble getting here and I'm late. I just hope it hasn't left already.'

Guymer glanced briefly at the Irishwoman. 'I'm sorry, madam,' he said. 'Now if you were a boy like this one, then you would have a better chance of getting to your destination. As it happens, Bertrand's ship is one of the few that is due to sail for Ireland. And your luck is in, lad.' He smiled broadly at the boy. 'The ship has not yet left the harbour. Make your way to the south quay – that's the first one you will come to. *La Trinite* is the third cog along.'

'Thank you, sir,' the boy said. 'My mother worked hard to get me this job. I thought I had let her down and missed the ship.' He turned to go, but as he did so, the harbour master grabbed his forearm. Looking back, the boy raised his eyebrows at the serious expression that had settled over Guymer's previously jolly face.

'Do you know much about Captain Bertrand, lad?' he asked in a low voice.

The boy, colour draining from his face, shook his head.

'Well you just be careful of him, all right?' Guymer said, fixing the lad with an earnest stare. 'He goes through ship's boys at a terrible rate. Not many stay on his crew. Most don't stay past their first voyage.'

Seeing only a blank look on the boy's face Guymer let go of his arm and turned away. 'Don't worry about it,' he said. 'Off you go. Don't miss your ship.'

Guymer shook his head as he watched him go, a twinge of guilt making the fish in his belly suddenly lie uneasily. He had tried to warn him, but how to explain the lecherous predations of Captain Bertrand to a young lad who did not understand such things? Oh well. What could he do? The boy would find out soon enough.

The harbour master turned to address the Irishwoman again, but raised his eyes when he saw that she too had gone and he was once again alone in his office. He picked up a writing quill with a heavy sigh. He had a lot of work to do updating the shipping ledger. Paperwork was something he particularly despised, but he needed to complete it while the morning sunlight was still strong. He worked patiently for some time until boredom once again took over and he found his mind wandering from the task in hand.

Resolving that he needed a break, Guymer decided to take a walk around the harbour. He pushed open the door of his office and stepped out into the morning sunshine. The smell of the sea air tugged his nostrils as the cacophony of noise generated by the busy docks filled his ears.

He frowned. The noise was slightly different than usual. Above the cries of gulls, the general conversation and the clatter of a working harbour he heard shouted orders and the clanking of arms. A troop of men-at-arms marched onto the quay, chain mail clinking. They were led by a tall, well-built officer with close-cropped blond hair, who walked with his right hand on the pommel of his sheathed sword. Guymer just had time to notice the large bruise on the man's chin when his attention was further distracted by the sound of raucous laughter, hoots and catcalls from further down the quay.

Stumbling towards him, a piece of sacking grasped around his waist to preserve what was left of his modesty, came the ship's boy who had been in his office earlier. If he had looked worried before, the lad now looked terrified. His eyes rolled wildly and he staggered as if he had drunk a quart of wine. One hand was held against the side of his head and the other clutched the piece of sack. Apart from this meagre covering he was now totally naked and the sight of his pale, skinny body was causing much hilarity among the denizens of the docks, who pointed and laughed as he passed by.

Guymer strode towards the lad and clapped a steadying arm around his shoulder. 'Good Lord, boy! I knew Bertrand was a terrible man but I thought he would at least wait until he was out of port!'

The look of confusion on the boy's face told Guymer he no more comprehended him than he had earlier.

'I don't know what you mean, sir,' the boy replied. 'It was the Irishwoman, the one who was in your office earlier. She knocked me out and took all my clothes.'

As he said this, the blond-haired captain of the men-at-arms approached and fixed the boy with cold eyes the colour of steel. 'Did you say Irishwoman?' he demanded in a clipped German accent. 'Where is she?'

'I don't know, sir.' The boy flinched at the forcefulness of both the German's words and his stare. 'She tricked me into going into a warehouse on the quay then knocked me out. When I woke up my clothes were gone and all my belongings. Worst of all, the ship I was supposed to go on has sailed. My mother will kill me.'

Ignoring him, the German turned to the harbour master. 'Do you know where this ship was headed?'

'Ireland,' Guymer replied.

'That bitch!' the German roared in anger and kicked a nearby barrel. 'Find me another ship heading that way. Now!'

43

At sea

Alys felt the timbers roll beneath her feet as the ship surged out of the harbour and into the open sea. Like the rest of the crew, she was now barefoot as it enabled her to get a better grip on wet decks. Her current attire she owed to the hapless ship's boy she had followed out of the harbour master's office. It was with relative ease that she had persuaded him to enter an empty warehouse a little further down the quay. Whether the boy thought it was his lucky day or he was just a gullible fool she had no idea, but she thanked her lucky stars that he'd complied.

Once inside Alys had exclaimed, 'What's that?' in mock surprise, one hand flying up to her mouth, the other extending towards a dark corner of the warehouse. As the lad turned to follow her pointing finger she had quickly stooped and grabbed a pulley that lay nearby. Before the boy turned back to her she had whacked him around the head with it. His eyes rolled upwards and he crumpled, unconscious to the floor. With no time to feel guilty, she had stripped him and scrambled into his clothes. The breeches were a bit big but she was able to find a piece of rope on the warehouse floor to keep them up. She tore a strip of cloth from the hem of her undergarments and wrapped it around her chest, binding her breasts flat against her body, wincing as she did so, for they were still tender from her recent pregnancy. Then she pulled on the boy's tunic. Thankfully it was loose enough to cover any remaining hint of femininity in her body shape. After that she had pulled her hair up and pushed it under the boy's cap then bundled her dress into his bag, shouldered it and with a glance at the boy to reassure herself he was still breathing, left the warehouse.

Alys was exhausted. She had been up all night. After getting away from the archbishop's mansion she had lurked in the alleyway until she was sure no one would spot her. Finally, she had sneaked away, feeling her way through the dark, empty streets of the town, always tracking downward and heading towards the sea and the harbour. She had no clear plan, but she knew that her daughter was in mortal danger, her husband was on a wild goose chase and Mortimer had ordered a German killer to assassinate all of them. Galiene and Richard were both in Ireland so now she had to get back there too.

Getting aboard the ship had been relatively easy. They had been on the verge of departure and the captain was desperate to get away on the rising tide. She just had time to run aboard before the gangplank was kicked away and the ship's voyage began. Captain Bertrand's greeting had been puzzling. He seemed angry that his new ship's boy was late, but at the same time the look he gave her was not what she would have expected. The man had actually licked his lips and at first Alys had been worried that he saw through her disguise. Perhaps he could tell that she was a woman?

Any doubts, however, were temporarily lost in the blur of activity that marked the start of the voyage. Ropes were stored, top sails unfurled, anything that might get in the way taken below decks. The crew scurried around the deck like ants as the ship leaned into the wind; the mast creaked as it took the strain, the sails whipped taut and the ship slid away from the harbour and into the open sea.

As the voyage progressed, Alys soon found that the role of ship's boy was one of general dogsbody: she was expected to work on the sails, make repairs, sweep the decks, help the cook and generally do all the menial tasks the rest of the crew felt were beneath them. The sailors treated her like a servant, sending her to fetch, hold, clean or mend things as their needs arose. Even when she ran out of work she was denied rest and ordered to fish over the side to get fresh food. After a few days spent in the starved port the crew were ravenous and demanded a lot of fish.

The first two days of the voyage went by in a blur of activity and hard work and it was not until late each night that she could finally swing, exhausted, into her hammock beneath the decks, only to be roused at dawn by rough shaking as her crew mates demanded she fetch breakfast. The scene beneath the decks was horrible and despite her tiredness she was glad to get out of it. The crew slept in hammocks suspended above the floor. Bottles and pots served as chamber pots for during the night when darkness, cold or stormy weather kept everyone beneath decks. Over the years many spillages had occurred as feet had accidentally kicked them over in the dark or the lurching ship had spilt their brimming contents. Hence the crew quarters reeked of the urine, excrement and vomit that had soaked into the wood. The stench was choking and Alys struggled not to retch.

Her main fear was being discovered as a woman. However she found that keeping that particular secret proved surprisingly easy. No one ever undressed. Quite the opposite, they all wrapped themselves up in as much clothing as possible. Most of the men pissed freely off the edge of the ship but the latrines were at the bow and no one paid much attention to whoever was hanging over the side, grasping onto the rope for dear life while they emptied their bowels. Fortunately, the boy's long tunic covered Alys to mid-thigh, but in any event, most of the crew studiously ignored what was going on and seemed too busy to notice her careful modesty when need drove her to relieve herself at the bows.

Her chief problem was the captain. It was impossible to ignore the way he leered at her. He frequently asked her to do little jobs for him and as she carried them out he would stand very close to her, usually at her back. She could feel his hot breath on her neck and smell its rancid onion-soaked stench. It became clear that he had no idea she was a woman, something that was confirmed the second evening into the voyage. The weather deteriorated, the swell of the seas rose and rain pelted down from the sky. Alys was thankful that she did not share her husband's fear of ships or his proneness for seasickness. Instead, her worst difficulty lay in negotiating the lurching deck, which tilted this way and that, threatening to send her sprawling onto her face or sliding towards the sides of the ship and certain death in the waves below.

The bad weather had sent most of the crew into the cabin at the fore end of the ship and the captain had retired to his own private cabin. The crew were playing dice and drinking wine and Alys was carrying bowls of stewed fish to them.

'Here's the captain's new favourite,' said Ernault, a gangly, bald crewman with only three remaining teeth. The other men all laughed.

'What do you mean?' Alys demanded, trying to keep her voice as deep as possible.

'Haven't you noticed, lad?' Ernault gloated. 'He moons over you like a love-sick youth, but his thoughts won't be half so innocent I'll assure you. You watch yourself. Old Bertrand is fond of fresh-faced boys like you. You could do well for yourself if you let him have his way.'

'I'm not interested in that sort of thing,' Alys said, not having to put too much pretence into her outraged tone.

Ernault caught her forearm in a vice-like grip. He stared hard into her eyes. 'If the captain gets you on your own, boy, you won't have any say in the matter. Don't let him catch you below decks. He's not the most restrained of men when it comes to his lust.'

The other crewmen apparently found this hilarious and fell about laughing. Frowning, Alys pulled her arm away, turned and left the cabin. She returned below decks to where the ship's cook was boiling fish in a huge cauldron set over a stone hearth that allowed cooking fires to burn without setting fire to the ship. To her dismay, the cook handed her another bowl of steaming fish. She knew it was not for her.

'The captain wants his supper in his cabin,' the cook said. 'Take it up to him quick.'

With some trepidation, Alys climbed up the ladder and crossed the swaying deck, trying to keep from spilling the broth as she struggled along. By the time she got to the captain's cabin at the back of the ship the supper bowl was half full of rainwater. She knocked on the door of the cabin, then when she heard a muffled response, pushed open the door.

The interior of the cabin was warm and Alys felt some relief to be out of the storm. Captain Bertrand sat at a table set up next to his bunk, but he sprang to his feet when she entered. He was not a fat man but bore a paunch well out of proportion to the rest of his body. His shirt was unbuttoned to his midriff, revealing his bulging belly and the thick coarse hair that matted his chest. Alys noted the empty wineskin that lay flaccid on the table and the glazed expression in the captain's eyes. She surmised that he was very drunk. At the sight of her, his face broke out into its usual unpleasant leer.

'Now here is a sight for sore eyes,' the captain slurred. 'Come my boy, entertain me.'

'I've brought your supper,' Alys said, moving quickly to the table and putting the bowl down on it. Her movement was so rushed that half the contents sloshed out of it. She immediately turned to go but the captain staggered forward and stood swaying, now between her and the door.

'Who's a careless boy then?' he said. 'You've spilt my dinner. Now you'll have to make it up to me.'

He lurched forward, the awful leer on his face as he leaned against her. He was now so close that Alys could feel his member straining stiffly against his breeches. Repulsed, she realised that the man was very drunk indeed. If he was as bad as the crew said he was normally, what would he be like when drink had removed the last of his basic decency? If indeed he had any. Cold fear churned in her guts as the man towered over her, one eye half closed and the other trying hard to focus on her.

'I have to go,' Alys said, her voice trembling. 'I have more work to do.'

'Work? Never mind about that. It's time to play. Isn't it nice and warm here?' The captain swayed, his head rolling with the up and down motion of the ship. 'You don't need to go back to those stinking quarters the crew have. Stay here with me.' He belched and Alys was almost overwhelmed by the odour of wine and onions, so strong it made her eyes water.

At that moment the ship, battered by a high wave, took an unusually violent lurch. The deck heaved and the drunken captain toppled sideways with a surprised cry. He crashed into the table, upending it and sending everything on it clattering to the floor. The captain himself hit the deck in the middle of it all and rolled through what was left of the fish broth.

Alys saw her chance and dashed for the door. She got there and turned to see the captain try to rise, grunt and then collapse in a drunken stupor back onto the floor. She opened the cabin door and rushed out into the wind and rain of the storm, praying silently that the journey to Ireland would not take much longer.

The next time she could not hope to be so lucky.

44

Carrickfergus

Henry de Thrapston strode across the inner courtyard of Carrickfergus Castle. His step was purposeful but his heart was heavy with the dilemma that faced him.

Richard Savage was a friend, but as keeper of the castle he had a duty and that was to do whatever it took to ensure that the fortress did not fall into the hands of the enemy. Until he received orders to the contrary from the seneschal, the Earl of Ulster or the king, that obligation had to supersede all others. Right now, the presence of Savage's daughter within the walls of the besieged castle could jeopardise the chances of the garrison continuing to resist the Scots. On the other hand, by accepting Edward Bruce's offer to exchange Galiene for food, he could potentially lengthen the time they could hold out. When considered in the cold light of day, the correct course of action was obvious and he had to prepare for it.

The starkness of the choice did not make him feel any better about it, however. As a damp mizzle began descending from the grey sky, he sighed at how miserable his life had become. Before the war he had been a wealthy man in a position of authority, a fact demonstrated by the size of his paunch. Now his once-fashionable, once brightly coloured clothes hung in faded, filthy rags around his starved frame. The bundle of huge iron keys, the symbol of his position as keeper of the castle, now weighed down his belt like the burden of the fortress itself. What had been the thriving bastion of power at the heart of the economy of the Earldom of Ulster was now surrounded on all sides by enemies; the last remaining few yards of land in Ulster still in the possession of the Lordship of Ireland, its garrison starving and almost at the end of their tether.

The one person whose presence could have made it more bearable, his wife Edith, was far away and unreachable. He had sent her south with the rest of the refugees from Carrickfergus just before he had closed the gates of the castle and the siege had commenced. He prayed that she was safe and longed for the day when he would see her smiling face again. He knew she worried incessantly and would be beside herself wondering what had become of him.

His only beacon of hope was that MacHuylin had made it to the seneschal and told him how desperate the castle was for relief. He hoped beyond all else that de Mandeville would listen and would not let them down.

In the meantime he had the problem of Galiene to deal with.

As he entered the inner ward de Thrapston saw the man he was looking for. 'Le Poer!' he called. 'A word if I may?'

Guilleme le Poer was talking to a soldier at the entrance to the inner gate. At the sound of Henry's voice he turned and walked over to join him. He was a different man from the mad, shaggy-haired preacher who had come into the fortress several days before with Galiene. His hair was combed straight and tied behind his head. His outlandish beard had been trimmed to chin level and instead of the rags of an itinerant priest he was now clad in a leather jerkin and trousers, over which he wore a coat of chain mail. A sheathed sword was buckled around his waist and he looked alert and every inch a warrior.

'Walk with me,' de Thrapston said, laying a hand on le Poer's shoulder and guiding him towards the castle keep. 'We must talk about the girl you brought here.'

'Galiene?' le Poer replied, concern tinging his tone of voice. 'That look of tired resignation on your face does not bode well, de Thrapston.'

'Yes.' De Thrapston stopped, straightened his back and looked le Poer in the eye. 'I'm afraid I will have to accept Edward Bruce's offer and exchange her for food.'

'What?!' Anger flashed across le Poer's face. 'She's a child. We can't throw her to the wolves like that! It's... unchivalrous.'

'It's my only choice,' de Thrapston responded. 'The garrison are angry that they have another useless mouth to feed. They don't mind you because you can fight. I can't risk a rebellion that could threaten our ability to hold on to the castle.'

'It's that damned sergeant from the gate isn't it?' le Poer snarled. 'What's his name? MacKillen? He's a troublemaker if ever I saw one.'

'Calm down,' de Thrapston soothed, laying a hand on each of le Poer's shoulders. 'It's not just him, though admittedly he's the ringleader. It helps that she seems to be keeping herself out of the way, but they haven't forgotten about her. A delegation of them came to me this morning, demanding that we comply with Bruce's offer and hand Galiene over in exchange for food. They were respectful but they made it clear enough they weren't asking for my opinion in the matter. I can't afford to be in conflict with my own troops, Guilleme. There's also the contrary scenario to consider. The food Bruce offers could help us hold out a bit longer, at least until relief arrives.'

'And what do we tell Savage next time we meet him?' le Poer said. 'Sorry but we swapped your daughter for a few loaves of bread? I risked my life to bring her in here, Henry.'

'I know, I know,' de Thrapston said. 'I'm sorry, but it has to be done. The garrison simply can't hold out much longer. They are almost too weak to fight. Some of them are starting to see things.'

'Eh?' Le Poer's lip curled in barely disguised contempt.

'Haven't you heard? The story's going round that the keep is haunted. People have heard strange unearthly wailing in the cellars. Things have gone missing. Several people swear they've seen ghosts in the night. It's nonsense of course, but a symptom of how far gone with hunger some of the garrison are.'

Both men were silent for a moment. Le Poer looked around at the imposing grey bulk of the keep that towered above them, a square mountain of stone. As he did so he caught sight of a pinched white face peeking out of the first-floor entrance door. It quickly disappeared back into the shadows. He sighed, realising the brutal logic of de Thrapston's argument.

'Perhaps if the rat boy had more harvests like he did today we wouldn't need Edward Bruce's bribes,' he said bitterly. 'He brought in a bumper crop of rodents this morning.'

De Thrapston shook his head, his stomach lurching at this reminder of what he would be faced with later when the time came to eat. 'We can't rely on rats and mice to survive, Guilleme. We need bread. Good meat. Otherwise we may as well just surrender now.'

Le Poer shook his head again but he knew if it came down to it he would have to accept the decision or fight the garrison himself.

'I'm telling you, so perhaps you can prepare her for what is coming,' de Thrapston said.

Le Poer grunted. 'That would be a good trick. I haven't seen her since Bruce made his offer. I've no idea where she's gone.'

45

Dublin

Savage awoke. His eyes were raw and his head foggy. He knew he could do with a few more hours' rest but the noise going on around him meant that was impossible.

He sighed and looked at the thatch of the roof above. A mouse poked its face out through a gap directly above him then scuttled upside down across the ceiling to disappear into another hole at the top of the wall. Savage gave a little involuntary shudder at the thought that during the night while he was dead to the world, vermin like that had probably been crawling all over him.

The man in the next bed to him grunted in his sleep and let out a loud fart that made Savage wince. The air in the room was bad enough already, thick with the stench of unwashed bodies, sweat, sour beer and stale vomit. With one more sigh he realised it was probably time to get up.

He was staying at an inn near the river that de Mandeville had recommended to him. For some reason the seneschal had been reluctant to give him quarters in the castle, which had made Savage wonder what was going on. De Mandeville had promised to tell him everything, but not in the castle, which had made Savage even more suspicious. He did what he was asked, however, and dog-tired from a night without proper sleep, had sought out the tavern according to de Mandeville's directions.

The inn stood near the city walls, close to the river and right beside the main gates to the north, guarding the entrance to the city by the old bridge that had been torn down to prevent access to the Scots. The sign for the tavern was what looked like a human head cast in a metal that shone like gold, but which Savage reasoned was more likely to be copper. Like the sign, the inn looked good from the outside, but once through the doors was less than salubrious. The sleeping quarters on the upper floor comprised a large open room that was shared by all the guests, who also had to share wooden boxes filled with far from fresh straw – furniture that the landlord had euphemistically described as "beds". The other clientele were the usual collection of scum, lowlifes and nervous travelling merchants who were found in city taverns. Savage was glad he'd had the foresight to deposit most of the money Mortimer had given him with de Mandeville at the castle before he left. He had kept just about enough to cover bed and board, and looking around at his fellow guests, he was sure that anything extra would have been pilfered while he slept.

Exhaustion had overcome his misgivings about the sleeping arrangements and he fell fast asleep, fully clothed, soon after he lay down, his cloak the only barrier between him, the filthy straw and whatever crawled about inside it.

'Savage?' a familiar voice called up from the ground floor. 'Are you up yet?'

Recognising the seneschal's commanding tones Savage crawled out of the straw and clambered down the rickety wooden ladder to the ground floor of the inn.

'I thought I'd buy you your breakfast,' de Mandeville said. 'We can talk while you eat.' He gestured to the burly innkeeper who, delighted to have such a prestigious client as the seneschal, hurried over with a pot of ale and a steaming bowl of gruel. He laid it on a rickety table and Savage and de Mandeville took seats on the benches either side of it.

Savage took a swig of the ale and immediately grimaced. Seeing his expression the seneschal chuckled. 'What's the matter? Lost your taste for Dublin ale?' de Mandeville commented.

Setting down his pot, Savage looked at it with a mixture of suspicion and disgust. 'That's not like any ale I've ever tasted before.'

'The famine's hit us hard in Ireland.' The seneschal's face took on a serious expression. 'Combined with the war it's a real disaster. There's a shortage of barley so they have to make up the ale with other stuff: herbs and the like.'

'It's the same all over,' Savage said. 'France is as bad, but at least there's still plenty of wine to drink there. Next year it might be a different matter. The last grape harvest was very poor.'

The seneschal shook his head. 'It's a disaster. I've heard men say that the end of the world is coming and I'm starting to wonder if they have a point. We've no idea how many here in Ireland have died. With the famine, the war, and now disease is spreading. It's as though the Four Horsemen of the Apocalypse have been unleashed.'

Savage took another swig of ale and grimaced again at the sour taste. 'Christ's blood this is dire. It tastes like they've put wormwood in it.'

'They probably did,' the seneschal said. 'A crannock of wheat fetches twenty-three shillings these days in Dublin. Christ alone knows how the peasants are surviving.'

Savage's jaw dropped open. He did not reply, contemplating that the answer to that question was probably that they were not. Twenty-three shillings was more than half a year's income for a labourer; well beyond the means of the average peasant. Looking around the tavern he could see that the effects of the famine were obvious even here. There were few customers breaking their fast and the board that would normally have displayed drawings of the food they could buy was blank. Both men were quiet for a moment as they mused on the current circumstances. Being men of action, neither felt any compulsion to bewail the gravity of the situation beyond anything more than grim nods.

'So what's with all this cloak-and-dagger stuff?' Savage finally broke the silence. 'Why can't we talk at the castle and why did you send me to this godforsaken tavern?'

'This is the "Brazen Head", Savage – one of the oldest taverns in the city,' the seneschal said with a glance that was both reproachful and playful at the same time. 'It's been here for over a century.'

Savage cast a cold eye around the soot-blackened and cobweb-clogged beams of the ceiling, the rank straw that covered the floor, the battered tables and benches and the chipped drinking cup he held in his hand. 'Well it's about time they thought about refurbishment,' he commented with a wry grin.

The seneschal's face became serious. For the first time since he had met him at the castle, Savage thought de Mandeville looked his age. A man of infinite vigour and unbounded energy, the seneschal had always seemed a lot younger than his forty-six years. Now, however, he looked tired and drawn. The lines around his eyes seemed deeper and some of the bright light had faded from his gaze.

'I wanted to talk to you away from the castle because I'm not completely sure I can trust everyone there,' he said.

Savage frowned. 'Why?'

'You said you were here on Mortimer's orders?' de Mandeville asked.

'I am,' Savage confirmed.

De Mandeville shook his head. 'Mortimer. There's another snake in the grass.'

Savage raised his eyebrows. 'Another?'

The seneschal looked around the tavern then rolled his eyes, as if trying to make up his mind about something. He sighed and took a reluctant slurp of bitter ale. Finally he leaned forward across the table and fixed Savage with his brown eyes. 'I'm talking to you about this only because you and I were with the earl on the battlements of Carrickfergus Castle last year. No one else was.'

Savage's mind raced as the seneschal spoke. De Mandeville must be talking about Richard de Burgh, Earl of Ulster: the man to whom they both owed loyalty as their feudal lord. There could be only one incident the seneschal was talking about. The year before, he and de Mandeville had met the earl in Carrickfergus Castle. Savage had just been instrumental in uncovering a plot by the devious Templar-turned-Hospitaller, Montmorency, to undermine the defences of Ulster, allowing the Scots army to land virtually unopposed. De Burgh was a vassal of the King of England, but he had married his daughter to King Robert Bruce of Scotland. At that moment he had admitted that he had been playing both sides in the war, not taking any position until he was sure who was most likely to win. De Burgh had then said he had seen the error of his ways and rejected Bruce's cause.

'I suspect the earl is back at his old games,' de Mandeville continued. 'The war goes badly for the Lordship of Ireland. England is on its knees. I fear that all de Burgh cares about is holding on to his lands and his money.'

'I heard he's not had much success with his lands,' Savage said.

De Mandeville nodded. 'He's lost both Ulster and Connacht.'

'You think he lost his lands deliberately?'

The seneschal shook his head. 'There's no doubt they were lost in battle but I fear he's turned his tail again. He's desperate to regain his realms and I suspect he may be thinking of doing a deal with our enemies to get them back. On top of that, his cousin William was captured by the Scots at Connor last year and he's now held hostage.'

Savage nodded. Allegiances in Ireland were often like sand dunes whose profile could change with a switch in the direction of the prevailing wind. 'Is he acting alone or do you think there is a wider conspiracy?' he wondered aloud.

De Mandeville shrugged. 'Who knows? This is Ireland, remember? Half the nobility are related to the Scottish upper classes by blood or marriage. The earl still has many friends. I'm just suspicious about how hard it has proved to kick the Scots out. We've marched to battle many times yet always something goes wrong. A baron with his battalion of troops turns up a little too late, supplies are diverted or the Scots seem to know our battle plan. The last battle at Ardscull is a perfect example. We actually won. The Scots were finished. They'd suffered far more casualties than us, but then our leadership fell to arguing, everyone either wanting to take the field and get the glory and refusing to let anyone else get it first, or cautioning that we hang back in case of a trap. In the end the Scots were declared victors simply by dint of holding the field. It was a disgrace.'

His frown deepening, Savage thought about it for a moment, but made no comment.

'Because of this I'm reluctant to talk at the castle,' de Mandeville continued. 'This expedition to Carrickfergus is vital to the whole war and I want nothing to jeopardise it. I trust my lieutenants completely, but beyond them I can't be sure who is in the employ of the earl or a spy of Ui Neill or Bruce.'

'You said Mortimer was another snake in the grass,' Savage said. 'Do you suspect he is secretly on the Scottish side?'

De Mandeville leaned forward, planting his elbows on the table and fixing Savage with a steady gaze. 'I suspect he's on his own side. Mortimer is Lord of Trim through marriage and a capable general, but I think he has ambitions beyond being the premier baron of England.' The seneschal stopped for a moment, took a hasty glance around the room then continued in a lower voice. 'I hardly need to remind you that King Edward of England is far from popular. Since the defeat at Bannockburn his reputation and favour among the barons of England has fallen further and every defeat in Ireland makes it worse. I believe if Mortimer put his mind to it he could easily defeat the Scots here, but he doesn't. We have enough supplies and troops to stave off total defeat but not enough to drive Bruce out. I think it suits Mortimer to let the situation get worse here for a while, because with it the reputation of the king goes down and when Mortimer eventually rides in, the conquering hero, well...'

He did not finish the sentence. The door of the tavern burst open and Savage and de Mandeville turned their heads to see a tall, broad-shouldered man in chain mail outlined in the threshold. After a moment he stumbled in, staggered his way up to the bar, and leaned on it with both forearms. He was breathing heavily and his head hung like someone who had taken too much drink.

'Someone get me an ale,' he growled in a hoarse voice.

Savage saw a large patch of black, dried blood amid broken chain mail rings on the back of the big man's right shoulder. The newcomer first unstrapped, and then pulled off the conical helmet from his head, unleashing a torrent of long blond hair that cascaded around his shoulders. His face was grey, slick with sweat and drawn with pain, but both Savage and the seneschal recognised him instantly.

'MacHuylin!' Savage and de Mandeville said in unison.

46

'I saw your daughter,' MacHuylin said. His eyes were glazed and his hair was stuck to his forehead with sweat. The galloglaich lay on snow-white, clean sheets. His hair was washed, his wounds dressed, but his pallor was still a ghastly shade, his red-rimmed eyes sunk in dark shadowed rings above his gaunt cheeks.

Savage and de Mandeville had rushed MacHuylin out of the city walls into the southern suburbs of Dublin. De Mandeville had led the way to a large hospital run by the Knights Hospitaller at Kilmainham. Savage had almost balked at entering – the castle and surrounding buildings had once been the property of the Knights Templar, but on the order's suppression for heresy, their possessions had passed into the hands of their greatest rivals, the Order of Knights Hospitaller. Now instead of the red and white Templar banner that had flown above the gates the last time he had been there, the black and white cross of the Hospitallers floated in the wind. However, MacHuylin needed their help and beggars could not be choosers.

While providing hospitality for pilgrims and other travellers was the main purpose of the hospital, the brothers of the Order of Saint John also specialised in medical care.

It was a strange dichotomy of the order that Savage had never understood. The Templars' purpose was clear: they fought for God. They killed the enemies of the Church. The Hospitallers also fought, but so too did they help the sick and the wounded, making no discrimination between friend or enemy. It was a common joke that a Hospitaller would cut you down, then patch you back up again.

The monks at Kilmainham had stripped off MacHuylin's shattered chain mail, carefully washed the site of his wound then cut the head of the crossbow quarrel out of his shoulder. Savage had been impressed at how little the man had cried or flinched. They had given him a draught of poppy liquor to help kill the pain, but it still must have been an agonising procedure. When they had finished they sewed the wound closed, smeared it with honey, then left him to rest. He lay on a comfortable bed in a long, brightly lit room that had about twenty similar beds in it, each occupied by another patient.

Savage and de Mandeville sat on stools beside the bed. When MacHuylin mentioned Galiene, Savage started. For a moment an odd expression coming to his face as if he was having trouble swallowing something. 'Was she all right?' he asked hesitantly, fearful of what the answer would be.

Despite the pain and the drowsiness imposed by the poppy draught, MacHuylin smiled. 'Yes. She's in the castle… We had a plan that went badly wrong, but…' With some effort he told the tale of what had happened in Carrickfergus and how le Poer had managed to grab Galiene from the Scots and escape with her into the castle.

Savage's face relaxed and he sighed; his tense posture

straightening as if an enormous weight had been lifted off his back. 'So she's safe,' he said. 'Thank the stars.'

'For now,' MacHuylin grew serious. 'That's why I'm here. She's away from the Scots for the meantime, but the castle can't hold out much longer.' He turned his attention to the seneschal. 'Sire, all the food is gone. The garrison are starving. If a relief force is not sent soon Henry de Thrapston will be forced to surrender. Edward Bruce won't be merciful. We've been a thorn in his side from the first day he landed in Ireland. You must do something or Carrickfergus will fall.'

The seneschal frowned. He took a cautious look around the room then leaned over and laid a hand on MacHuylin's uninjured shoulder. 'Have no fear, old friend,' he breathed. 'We are in the process of taking action. Carrickfergus must not fall.'

The dullness in the eyes of the galloglaich disappeared and he struggled to sit up. 'You are planning a rescue mission...?' he began, then winced, his left hand moving towards his injured shoulder. He gasped and fell back against his pillows once more, eyes closed against the pain.

De Mandeville looked around again then held up his hands, palms first towards MacHuylin. 'Easy now,' he said. 'I can't say too much here but you're on the right track.'

MacHuylin opened his eyes again and fixed them on the seneschal. 'Count me in,' he said.

De Mandeville and Savage smiled at the man's courage but the seneschal shook his head, an apologetic look on his face. 'I doubt you will be going too far with that wound, old friend,' he said. 'You're in no condition to fight and won't be for a long time – certainly not in time for us leaving.'

Between gritted teeth MacHuylin swore quietly. 'Damned pirates,' he said. 'I should've killed them all.'

A slight cough made them all turn and they saw a brother of the Order of Saint John standing behind them. Unlike the warrior monks from the order whom Savage was accustomed to seeing, this man, whose main job was attending to the sick and injured, wore a simple red and white robe. He was small and thin, bearing none of the scars or physique of a brother whose main occupation was fighting.

'Your friend needs some rest,' the monk said. 'Can I suggest you leave him alone for a while so he can sleep?' The way he said it conveyed the message that this was more an order than a suggestion. He showed deference to the rank of the seneschal, but still spoke with the calm firmness of someone who was confident of his authority in this place of the sick.

Sleep was probably what MacHuylin needed most, thought Savage as he and de Mandeville stood up to leave. 'We have work to do anyway,' murmured the seneschal. 'You stay here, MacHuylin, and look after yourself. Get well.'

'Can I get you anything?' Savage said as he turned to go.

MacHuylin grunted. 'Some Water of Life would be good, though I don't know where you would get it these days. I haven't tasted *uisce beatha* for so long.'

Savage nodded and left.

47

At sea

A lys crawled uneasily into her hammock and lay awake for some time, expecting the captain to follow her. When he did not, she reasoned that the odious creature had probably passed out on the floor where she had left him. With that thought she fell into a fitful sleep for what was left of the night.

The next day the weather kept the crew under cover unless it was otherwise strictly necessary and Alys was for once happy to be kept busy with chores and away from the captain.

Eventually the storm cleared and the violent swaying of the ship subsided as the sea calmed. Glad to be out of the cloying stench of the cabins, the crew spilt out onto the deck and began the tasks of checking sails and lines and exploring the ship to see how it had fared in the bad weather. The cook put Alys to work fishing yet again.

As the sun began to peek through the grey clouds, the door of the captain's cabin banged open and Bertrand stepped out. His face was as grey as the sky, his eyes bloodshot, and the glowering look on his face was enough to ensure no one met his gaze. Most of the crew hurried past him making sure they looked as busy as possible. Alys noted with some satisfaction that the captain had acquired a large purple bruise on his left cheek, most probably during his fall the night before. As the sunlight hit his eyes he winced and rubbed his temples.

'Where is Ernault?' he shouted. 'Ernault!'

Ernault, who seemed to play the role of second in command of the ship, scurried over. 'Master?'

'Any damage in the storm?' the captain demanded.

'None, master,' Ernault said. His back stiffened with evident pride in his vessel. 'We're just finishing checking, but everything seems to be in order.'

'Are you sure?' The captain narrowed his eyes. 'She seems to be listing a bit to me. She is making heavy weather of turns. Have you checked below decks?'

'Yes, master,' Ernault responded. 'All except the bilges.'

'Well they need checking, man. We might be letting in water down there,' the captain responded.

'I'll get someone down there straight away, master,' Ernault turned to go.

'Don't worry. I'll do it myself.' The captain's tone was both peeved and desultory.

'Very good,' Ernault grovelled.

'I'll need someone to help me.' The captain shaded his eyes and looked around, licking his lips. 'Where's the boy?'

Alys flinched. She had heard the crew talk and knew they were afraid of going down to the bilges. They were the deepest, darkest part of the boat, where only a skim of planking separated you from the infinitely deep, dark sea outside. They were beneath the waterline and most men spoke with fear of the stench of stagnant sea water and the oppressive feeling that at any moment the sides of the boat would give way, the sea would rush in bringing an inescapable cold, choking death. It would be bad enough to go down there at all, but to be with the captain in the very bowels of the ship, where any cries for help would be inaudible was the stuff of nightmares.

'Boy! The captain wants you.'

Ernault was looking over at her with an unpleasant smile on his face. Resentment burned in Alys's chest. There was no need for the man to take pleasure in her misery. She set down the fishing pole and stood up.

'Come with me,' the captain said brusquely as he strode past. Alys followed behind him, dragging her feet.

They went to the hatch in the deck and climbed down the ladder. The next deck below was the cargo deck. The captain stopped to light a horn lantern so they could see around them in the darkness. The flame lit up the rows of crates, boxes and the inevitable barrels of wine from Bordeaux.

'You first,' Bertrand said, pointing ahead. Alys turned and walked on until they came to another hatch in the floor. She strode with the heavy, reluctant step of the condemned. A deep dread about what was about to happen weighed heavily in her chest.

'Open it,' the captain said, pointing at the hatch. His voice was thick and his eyes gleamed.

Alys pulled the bolt from the hatch and raised it. Another rickety ladder descended into total darkness. Like the stale breath of the ship the stink of foul water rose from the hole. The captain did not say anything but simply pointed downward. Avoiding his leering gaze, Alys clambered down the ladder into the dark below. The floor beneath her feet was sloped, following the hull of the boat. She stood in the pool of light that came down through the hatch from the captain's lantern above her head. Beyond it was complete darkness in which tiny rodent claws skittered over wood. The planks of the ship groaned and creaked as they ground together while the waves made a rhythmical thump against the hull. Alys looked up. At first the captain made no movement to follow her, simply staring down with an odd glitter in his eyes. A bolt of fear shot through Alys's chest at the thought that he might simply close the hatch, leaving her down there in the dark, alone apart from the rats, then he seemed to snap out of his strange reverie and began climbing down the ladder.

When he reached the bottom he turned around, holding the lantern up high to illuminate the dark.

'It looks fine,' Alys said, not seeing any sign of leakage. The only water was a dark green, slimy pool that had settled in the centre of the hull, washing back and forth to the movement of the ship. From its thickness, colour and smell it had obviously been there a long time.

'Of course it is, boy,' the captain said, his tone dismissive. 'This is the best ship I've ever owned. She doesn't leak a drop.'

'So why are we down here?' Alys said. She tried to sound angry but there was a tremor in her voice.

The captain's leer returned, somehow made more hideous by the flickering yellow light of the lantern. 'You know why, boy. Get your clothes off.'

Alys froze; horror and indecision rooting her to the spot.

The captain's free hand lashed out, catching her backhanded across her right cheek. The force of the blow sent her sprawling to her knees in the filthy water.

'Don't piss about,' the captain said, his leer turning to an angry glare of urgency. He set the lantern down and began fumbling to untie his breeches. Alys, face stinging, rose to her feet again. Her head was down, her hands trembling. Some strands of her hair escaped her cap and dangled around her face. Instinctively she turned away from him, her fingers numb and awkward as they struggled to unlace her tunic. She felt as if she was in a trance as she mindlessly complied with his will, dread weighing heavy in her chest as she contemplated what was about to happen. It was bad enough that he thought she was a boy, but what would he do when he found out she was a woman?

She stopped for a moment, an idea springing into her mind.

'What are you waiting for, boy?' the captain breathed behind her. She heard the sound of his breeches hitting the floor.

Alys recommenced unlacing her tunic. When it was open she reached in and pulled down the cloth she had used to bind her chest. Without hesitation she spun around, holding open the tunic.

The captain looked as though he had been struck by lightning. His mouth dropped open in stunned amazement, staring at the sight of Alys's naked breasts as if his eyes were about to pop out of his head.

As he stood, thunderstruck, Alys swiftly reached down and grabbed the lantern off the floor. The captain came to his senses and reached for her but he was too late. She came up from a crouch, smashing the lantern across the side of his face. The lantern shattered, blazing oil exploded out, engulfing Captain Bertrand's head and shoulders in a cloud of flame. He shrieked, flailing his arms as he tried to extinguish the agonising fire.

Alys shoved him out of the way and hurried up the ladder. She got to the top and scrambled out onto the cargo deck. Spinning round she grasped the hatch. To her horror the captain was coming up after her, howling, the top half of his body now completely engulfed in flames. Alys slammed the hatch closed and slid the bolt home just as the captain reached the top of the ladder. As his head hit the underside of the hatch he screamed and sobbed, his fists banging frenziedly on the wood. Then the banging stopped. There was another scream followed by a clattering sound and a loud thump. There was no repeat of the impact on the hatch. It seemed to Alys that the captain's screams were further away and she surmised that the captain had fallen off the ladder.

'What's going on?'

Alys turned to see that Ernault and several more of the crew had come down to the cargo deck. The anger already ignited in her chest flared further at the thought that they had probably come to witness her misery. At the sight of her exposed breasts they all stared, mouths agape, and Alys quickly pulled her tunic closed, pulling and tying the laces to keep it in place.

'You're a woman...' Ernault said. There was such incredulity in his voice he might have been looking at a mermaid.

After a moment the spell of amazement seemed to break and Ernault strode forward. He shoved Alys roughly aside and knelt to unbolt the hatch.

'Seize her!' he shouted to his companions as he lifted the hatch. Alys was grabbed by two other crewmen. One stood on either side of her, each holding an arm, grim expressions on their faces. Alys did not struggle nor try to run – after all, there was nowhere to run to. She needed to think of some way out of this.

Unlike the last time the hatch had been opened, this time a blaze of light illuminated the gloom of the cargo hold. The flickering of flames was evident, but no cries or any other human sounds came from the hatch. Ernault gave a little cry then rushed down the ladder.

'Get sand, canvas, water!' he shouted to his companions. 'Hurry! There's a fire!'

Apart from the two men holding Alys, the others sprang into action. From the look of near panic on their faces she guessed this was a sailor's worst nightmare. A fire at sea could be the end of them all. If the ship burned they could not just run away. Thankfully, this also meant that they were well prepared for it. The sailors grabbed buckets of sand, kept for this very purpose, and carried them down the hatch. One seized a spare sail and descended the ladder to smother the blaze. From where she was held, Alys could not see what was going on, but the firelight coming up through the hatch quickly diminished, then went out completely.

Ernault's face appeared at the hatch opening again. It was slick with sweat and smeared with soot. He glared at Alys.

'The captain's dead,' he snarled. 'And you nearly sunk the ship. You'll hang for this, you bitch.'

48

'He was going to rape me,' Alys said. She spoke quietly, having little hope that it would hold much sway with the crew.

'Bind her. Take her up to the deck,' Ernault said to the men holding Alys. Her hands were pinioned together behind her back and tied with rope then they hauled her up the ladder onto the top deck.

When she emerged into the sunlight she immediately noticed that something was not right. A sailor came running up to Ernault, his face pale and his eyes wide.

'Where's the captain?' he said.

'The captain's dead,' Ernault snarled. 'This bitch killed him.' He turned and smacked Alys across the face, managing to strike her in almost the exact same place as the captain had hit her. Her head snapped sideways, her vision dissolved into stars and her knees gave way, but the two men holding her by the arms stopped her from falling to the deck. As her vision returned to normal she could see that the other sailor looked as if his whole world had just collapsed before him.

'Ernault, we're in trouble,' he panted. 'Ships are coming towards us. They're on a course to intercept us.'

Both men looked at one another for a moment, a common dread establishing itself in the silence.

'Pirates?' Ernault said.

The other man nodded. 'Looks like it. They're built for war but they fly no flag.' He pointed over the bows.

Ernault and Alys followed the direction of his finger. Not far ahead, three ships surged through the waves directly towards them. Sleek and fast with high fighting platforms built fore and aft, they bristled with men. The weak sunlight reflected on iron helmets, chain mail and weapons.

'Turn around!' Ernault shouted.

'We can't outrun them,' the second sailor whined. 'We must surrender. Throw ourselves on their mercy.'

'Mercy?' The expression on Ernault's face somehow portrayed both terror and incredulity at the same time. 'Men like that don't know the meaning of the word.'

Enough of his fellows agreed with him to spring into action. Men leapt to the steering oar and threw it hard to one side. The sails flapped as they swept around, the mast groaning in protest at the strain as the cog lurched into a turn. They began to pick up speed, but the pirate ships also changed direction, dispelling any idea that their former course had been an accident. As Alys watched, the lead ship appeared to sprout a forest of new masts. Then these poles went over the side and she realised that they were oars. Like wings on either side of the pirate galley, the oars began to beat rhythmically. The ship surged forward faster, getting closer and closer with every wave. The gap between them narrowed and any lingering doubts about the pirates' intentions disappeared as a flurry of black streaks rose from the deck of their ship.

'Arrows!' a sailor shouted a warning. Everyone looked around for cover as the missiles arched through the air above. Her two guards let Alys go and ran to find somewhere to hide. In the moments she had available, it was all Alys could do to crouch down onto the deck, huddling herself into a ball, trying to make herself as small a target as possible.

Her heart pounded in her chest. Every nerve felt stretched to breaking point as she waited, knowing that her death could right now be hurtling down from above.

Then like a hundred hammer blows, the arrows thudded into the cog. Some fell in the sea but most crashed onto the deck, turning it into a pincushion of shafts. Two unlucky crew members screeched with pain. Alys saw one pinned through his calf, the other burbling bloody froth from his mouth, the end of an arrow shaft protruding from his upper chest. The rest of the crew fled into the cabins, down the hatch to the cargo deck or cowered behind what meagre cover the various barrels and trunks on the upper deck could give.

Alys was not hit. She got up awkwardly, her hands still behind her, then staggered across the deck. She threw herself through the door of the captain's cabin just as another hail of arrows rattled down. She stumbled once more and fell face first onto the floor. Looking up, Alys saw that Ernault and another crewman were also taking cover in the cabin.

'Have you nothing to shoot back at them?' Alys said. The look of annoyance on Ernault's face told her the answer was no. 'Well we can't stay in here,' she said. 'Can't you see they're just keeping us inside so they can board without a fight?'

'Shut up!' Ernault said. 'You want to go outside and end up riddled with arrows, then go.'

As if in response, another wave of arrows thudded into the deck outside, one landing right in the middle of the open doorway. A new sound came after that: a rattling crash from the back of the ship.

'Grappling irons!' someone shouted from further down the deck. The pirates had cast long, multi-headed iron hooks on ropes from their own vessel to snag the fleeing ship and bind the two vessels together.

'Cut those ropes,' Ernault shouted. Two of the crew left the shelter of the other cabin, short swords gripped in their hands. They ran to cut the ropes of the grappling irons but before they got there one man was swatted backwards, as if by a giant, invisible hand. He crashed onto the deck, blood spouting from the end of a crossbow bolt protruding from his chest. His companion stopped and sank to his knees, also felled by a pirate crossbow, then pitched forward face first, dead.

After that, none of the crew dared show his face. Alys knew that the battle was lost before it had even begun.

Before long the cog was held tight by grappling irons and squashed between two pirate galleys; a third lurked astern. The pirates swarmed over the sides and in no time the merchant cog's crew and Alys were all hauled out from their hiding places and lined up on their knees on the deck, hands on their heads.

The pirates were one of the most dangerous-looking collections of motley individuals Alys had ever seen. They wore no standard uniform. Instead they all had a variety of different arms, chain mail or leather armour. All were deeply tanned by life on the sea and most bore the scars of combat: missing teeth, badly broken noses and deep facial scars from former blade slices.

When it was obvious that the fight was over, another man swung himself on a rope over from the pirate ship. He was tall and wiry, bearded and with very long, plaited black hair. He carried a big, square-bladed sword that reminded Alys of a huge butcher's cleaver. He walked along the deck regarding his prisoners with a cruel glitter in his eye. From the confident swagger of his gait and the deference the other pirates gave him, Alys surmised that this was their leader. She wondered bleakly what sort of a man this must be if such dangerous men were scared of him.

'Who is the master of this ship?' the pirate leader said, speaking in a gravelly Scottish accent.

No one responded.

Without warning, he lashed out. His wicked blade swooped through the air, embedding itself in the cleft between the nearest kneeling sailor's left shoulder and his neck. It bit deep, separating the meat and bone, slicing through veins and arteries. The man cried out, eyes wide, hands reaching to grasp the terrible wound as blood erupted and gushed down his front. He tried to rise but collapsed immediately onto the deck. In moments he was dead, a pool of hot, iron-smelling blood spreading out across the deck around him. The pirate gingerly stepped away from the blood, pulling his falchion from the corpse with a wet, sucking sound.

'I repeat,' the pirate said, 'who is the master?'

'The captain is dead,' Ernault spoke up. 'That woman killed him. We were about to hang her.' He nodded his head in the direction of Alys.

The pirate looked down at Alys with raised eyebrows, noting her hands bound behind her back and the swelling bruise on her cheek.

'Did she now?' he said. Alys felt he was appraising her like a man thinking of buying a horse. She glared back at him as defiantly as she could manage. 'A woman, eh? This is an unexpected prize.' He looked up and down the line of prisoners again. 'Where are you sailing from? What's your course?'

'We're taking cargo from Bordeaux to Dublin,' Ernault said. 'We are simple traders, sire.'

The pirate chuckled and shook his head. 'You perhaps know of me? I am known as Tomas le Noir in France; "Black Thomas" to the English and Tavish Dhu in Scotland and Ireland. We are a naval force in the employ of the free and sovereign nation of Scotland. This is a Gascon ship, and Gascony is an English province. For the time being Dublin is an English city. Therefore you are not simple traders. You are providing supplies to the enemies of Scotland.'

'Take what you want,' Ernault said, a note of desperation entering his voice. 'What do we care if our masters lose their goods? Take it all.'

'Oh we will, don't worry about that.' Tavish grinned. He turned back to Alys, running another cursory glance over her that again made her feel she was being assessed.

'Pol!' the pirate called over his shoulder. 'What do you think of her?'

A huge, hulking giant of a man clambered over the side of the pirate ship onto the merchant cog and strode across the deck to where Alys knelt. He looked down his nose at her, eyebrows raised as if trying to come to some conclusion. Finally he turned down the corners of his mouth and nodded.

'She's pretty enough. Maybe a bit old though?' he said in a booming voice.

'Mmmm.' Tavish rubbed his beard, nodding also. 'You're right: she won't command top price. But she'll get enough to cover the bother of looking after her 'til the Moor arrives and still make a tidy profit.'

'Aye,' Pol agreed.

'Right, take her on board our galley.' Tavish jerked his head. The big giant reached down and hauled Alys to her feet then shoved her in the direction of the side of the ship.

'Where are you taking me?' Alys demanded.

'Back to our base on the Isle of Man,' Tavish said. 'We are due a visit from Ibn Al Bakri, an old friend from Spain. Old Ibn is a slave trader and not too fussy. I reckon you'll fetch a pretty penny in the markets of Andalusia,' he said with a grin.

'No!' Alys shouted as she struggled against the giant who held her, but his grip was like iron. As she was pushed over the side of the cog and into the pirate ship she caught a glimpse of Ernault and the look of sly triumph on his face.

'Take the cargo,' Tavish ordered his men then swept his bloody falchion around in the direction of Ernault and the cog's crew. 'Kill the rest of them. Sink the ship.'

49

Dublin

For Savage the waiting was like torture. Several days passed and throughout them he found himself embroiled in an agony of anxious worry about Galiene. At first there had been some comfort in the knowledge that she was at least away from immediate danger, but would the seneschal's expedition arrive in time before the castle fell to the Scots? Would Galiene's very presence there provoke Edward Bruce to attack the fortress with renewed intent?

Then there was Alys, in France with Mortimer and his henchman – the brutish German, von Mahlberg. Should he really have left her alone in their care?

It was Holy Week already and Bruce's deadline was set to expire. Savage was taking a gamble by relying on de Mandeville's expedition to get him to Ulster. Time was running short.

Thankfully, there was plenty to keep him busy. De Mandeville included him in the planning of the relief expedition and he spent the days with the others in the great hall of Dublin Castle, poring over lists of supplies that the ships would transport north. The other young men in command of the expedition, Paschall – who, it turned out, was from Lombardy – d'Athy and FitzWarin, proved enthusiastic help if a little inexperienced.

Late in the afternoon, Savage rubbed his eyes and set down the inventory he was reviewing. Among weapons and soldiers, one of the ships was to carry supplies to re-provision Carrickfergus Castle's depleted stores, and in the current famine conditions the cost of the food was frighteningly expensive. He wondered who was paying for this.

The sound of purposeful footsteps made him turn around to see de Mandeville striding across the hall towards them, a broad grin and a look of obvious excitement on his face. 'Men!' he said. 'I believe we are almost ready to go. I've asked the justiciar to come for final review of our plans and to give us his approval.'

As if on cue, a group of men entered the hall. Two men in the middle of the group walked with the assurance of command and wore the expensive clothing of nobility. They were surrounded by a band of armed men, all clad in mail and kettle helmets and carrying spears. Over their mail they wore surcoats coloured the same yellow and red as Meiler had worn. Just behind them scuttled the serious young cleric whom Savage had met when he first arrived in Dublin.

Savage recognised one of the nobles straight away. He was Richard Óg de Burgh, the Red Earl of Ulster. Savage was surprised at the change in the man. It was only a year since they had last met, but the earl, who was in his fifties, seemed to have aged ten years in that time. Savage remembered him as having retained most of his chestnut-coloured hair, but the long braid that now hung down his back was completely iron-grey. The earl still wore his Irish saffron kilt that hung down to his knees; it was wrapped over his left shoulder where it was fastened with a large, gold Celtic brooch, but his expensive English-wool cloak showed signs of wear at the hems. His normally upright stance had the hint of a stoop and his eyes bore a tired, almost haggard look as they peered around the great hall from amid a tangle of wrinkles.

The other man was half the Earl of Ulster's age and Savage thought he must be Irish, either a king or a prestigious nobleman, as his clothes and hairstyle were all native Irish in form. His hair was long, black and braided and a drooping moustache hung over his mouth. His beard was forked into two braids and a thin band of silver circled his head at forehead height to keep his hair away from his face. He wore a white linen tunic and tight-fitting leggings or *truis*. A short, heavily embroidered jacket with tight sleeves, and a long, red woollen cloak covered the top half of his body. All his clothes were of the utmost quality and his bearing exuded wealth and high rank.

The group approached and the younger man smiled at Savage and the rest of the men gathered around the benches. While broad and revealing a set of very good teeth, his smile lacked any warmth and the gaze from his flint-hard eyes spoke of a deadly ruthlessness.

'Syr Thomas, what have you got for us?' He spoke in French with an upper-class accent and Savage realised with a start that the man he had thought was an Irish king was actually John de Bermingham, the new Justiciar of Ireland –

the man appointed to run Ireland in the name of the English Crown.

De Mandeville hesitated slightly. He and de Burgh exchanged glances and in their look of mutual suspicion Savage saw how far the relationship between the two had degenerated. Last time he had been in Ireland de Mandeville had followed the earl's orders without question. As de Burgh's seneschal he had kept the borders of the Earldom of Ulster peaceful by constant raiding, but now Ulster was lost and it was clear to Savage that much had changed between the two men as a result.

'My liege,' de Mandeville said eventually, bending his head then turning to d'Athy and beckoning for him to speak. The young man came forward and outlined the plans to send five ships north, loaded with food and soldiers. They would storm into Carrickfergus harbour with the aim of either completely breaking the siege or at least getting supplies to the castle so it could continue to hold out.

'And what will the Scots be doing while you are disembarking?' de Bermingham said, one eyebrow raised. 'There is a whole army of them up there. Are you counting on them just letting you land and walk into the town?'

De Mandeville's face cracked into a knowing smile. 'Sire, it is almost Easter, when the Peace of God is in effect. Christians are not supposed to fight Christians during this period. Spies have told us that Edward Bruce means to undergo the pilgrimage to the graves of Saint Patrick, Saint Bridget and Saint Colmcille at Dun Patrick and is taking most of the army with him. We intend to take advantage of the situation.'

The Earl of Ulster raised his eyebrows. 'You intend to

break the truce? Won't that be inviting the wrath of God down on the expedition?'

'The Pope has declared the peace and Bruce will assume there will be no fighting during Easter, but we have no formal agreement with the Scots, sire,' de Mandeville answered.

John de Bermingham nodded as he rubbed a forefinger along his moustache, pondering what had been outlined to him. 'Edward Bruce is doing exactly what de Courcy did when he first invaded Ulster: appropriating the local saints, styling himself as the new king in the Gaelic way.'

'What about the pirate?' de Bermingham said. 'Tavish Dhu acts at will on the seas from here to Scotland. How are you going to get to Carrickfergus without him either attacking you or warning Bruce you are coming? Or both?'

The expedition planners all exchanged glances. At first no one responded then de Mandeville gave an embarrassed cough. 'We will just have to take that chance and fight our way through, sire,' he said. 'We've fortified the ships in anticipation of battle.'

De Bermingham returned his gaze for a moment, a frown creasing his brow, but the Earl of Ulster tutted and shook his head. 'Tavish Dhu has as many ships as you do, Syr Thomas. Even if you beat him you'll probably lose half your vessels and men in the fight. More likely he will hit you, run away and keep hitting you all the way to Ulster. By the time you get there you'll have nothing left.' He turned to de Bermingham. 'This will never work,' he said.

De Mandeville's face flushed red, his look of embarrassment replaced by one of frustration. 'Sire, we just have to take the chance. The Easter truce allows us the perfect opportunity that may not come again until who knows when. MacHuylin—'

'The mercenary? Is he still alive?' de Burgh interrupted.

'He is,' de Mandeville confirmed.

'I am,' said a new voice.

All the men swung round to see Connor MacHuylin entering the great hall. He wore a long tunic of black wool, belted at the waist. His right shoulder was raised by the padding and bandages that swathed it. He was deathly pale, his eyes were hollow and Savage was sure he was thinner than the last time he had seen him, but at least he was on his feet and he looked steady enough on them.

'Connor, what are you doing here? You should still be in the Hospitallers' infirmary,' de Mandeville said in a half-scolding tone.

'I got bored hanging around with those monks.' MacHuylin shrugged.

'Richard Savage is here too, my lord,' de Mandeville said, clapping a hand on Savage's shoulder and nudging him forward.

'Savage?' The earl narrowed his eyes as he noticed him for the first time. Savage thought he detected a distinct look of either hostility or suspicion in de Burgh's gaze. It disappeared in an instant, leaving Savage wondering if he had really seen it. Then the earl's face broke out in a sunny grin. 'It seems all the old cohort from Ulster is here. Syr Richard, it is good to see you again. I look forward to catching up with you sometime...' His tone of voice did not suggest any enthusiasm, however.

'MacHuylin narrowly escaped Carrickfergus with his life to bring us de Thrapston's message,' de Mandeville broke in. 'He sends word to tell us that the castle cannot hold out much longer. Without supplies he will be forced to surrender.'

'They are at the end of their tether,' MacHuylin added, approaching the group of men clustered around the map-strewn table. 'All the stores are gone. They're down to eating rats and mice and there's not that many of them left.'

'We have to go now, sire!' de Mandeville urged, his flush of anger deepening.

'It's too risky,' de Burgh said, his voice rising and edged by an anger that matched de Mandeville's. 'The supplies on those ships cost an absolute fortune and there is no guarantee of success. May I remind you that we are at war right across this island? There are other places where they could do more good.' His gaze flicked to the justiciar. 'John, we discussed the other matter these supplies could help with…'

De Bermingham nodded.

'What "other matter" is more important than stopping Carrickfergus from falling?' said de Mandeville, his eyes glinting with suspicion as he stared at the justiciar.

'It is a matter of politics,' de Bermingham said, as if that was all that was needed to bring the subject to a close.

'Couldn't you get us more ships?' de Mandeville said, clearly exasperated.

Savage felt despair and anger rising in his own chest, echoing the tone of desperation that had entered the seneschal's voice.

De Burgh and the justiciar exchanged glances, the latter brandishing a roll of parchment. 'Maybe a couple,' he said, with an apologetic shake of his head. 'But I wrote to the king asking for ships to help fight the pirate. His reply arrived today. He cannot spare any. All ships are required for the war in France. In fact—' he sighed and rolled his eyes '—His Royal Majesty asks if we have any we could spare to send to him.'

A collective, despairing groan rose from the gathered men.

'John.' De Burgh laid a hand on de Bermingham's shoulder. 'As we discussed, the provisions are needed elsewhere and at least we can be sure of the result there.'

De Mandeville's control slipped, his anger boiling over. 'Where can possibly be in greater need than Carrickfergus? We cannot risk losing the castle!' he exclaimed.

Savage's feeling of dread intensified. His chance of getting to Carrickfergus and Galiene with an army at his back was disappearing before his eyes. 'No, we can't,' he blurted out.

The earl and the justiciar turned, twin looks of irritation on their faces at this unasked-for intervention by an irrelevant outsider. Ignoring Savage, de Bermingham turned away and addressed de Mandeville. 'Syr Thomas, I appreciate your courage and admire your chivalry and the fact that you are prepared to take this risk.' He looked away then looked back. 'But with regret, I cannot allow this expedition to go ahead.'

De Mandeville looked up at the ceiling. D'Athy slammed a fist on the table.

'No!' Savage shouted. 'We have to go north!'

The justiciar shook his head. 'I am sorry. I really am. It's a hard decision but we are in desperate straits here. The earl is right…' He turned back to de Burgh, who folded his arms and smiled, but made no comment.

After a pause, de Bermingham continued, 'There are other causes for which the supplies on those ships can be used and we have to use what little we have in the most prudent way we can. Besides—' the serious expression left his face and he broke into a grin '—how can I refuse the requests of my future father-in-law?'

'Syr John and I have signed a contract that he will marry my daughter Aveline,' de Burgh said, responding to the puzzled looks from the others. Both men were now grinning, a display of mirth that was shared by no one else in the discussion.

De Mandeville's jaw tightened as he gritted his teeth. 'I see. May I offer my congratulations, sire.'

'Thank you.' De Bermingham smiled, before repeating, 'I am sorry, truly, but I cannot authorise this expedition.'

Savage swore and stormed out of the hall.

50

At sea

Captain Breslin sat contented at the steering oar of his ship. He was finally on his way home. He loved the life on the open sea, the travel to foreign lands and the adventure it brought, but he was always glad to get home to Tír Chonaill, to his wife and his family, the clan and all that was familiar and comfortable. This trip in particular, there had been far too much adventure for his liking and he made a mental note that when they made it back to God's own country, he would make a point of refusing to carry any future passengers claiming to be Templars. The old Templar masters at Ballymote paid handsomely to have their fugitive brethren ferried to safety, but every year there were fewer and fewer of them and the risks of being caught with heretics on board were starting to outweigh the financial benefits. As the last escapade had demonstrated, Templars were now more trouble than they were worth.

The few days Breslin and his crew spent in Dublin had been enjoyable, but it had been time to go. Several days of drinking and whoring had expended all their money and it was only a matter of time before they got themselves into serious bother. They were in an enemy city after all, and the chances of a fight breaking out were always high. The lordship's fleet had not yet left, but some pleading on his behalf by the knight, Savage, had resulted in the justiciar granting them leave to go. All the same, he had sent a couple of patrol boats to shadow them and make sure they went south rather than north. Breslin chuckled to himself at the thought of that. They did not have to tell him now where those ships moored outside Dublin were headed.

Eventually, south of Wicklow, the patrol boats had turned back, leaving Breslin's ship to go on its way. They had a long journey ahead, almost right around Ireland, but at least they were finally on their way home. Breslin spat over the side and began whistling a song as he watched a seagull wheeling in the sky above the mast. They had a fair wind behind them, the sea was brisk but not rough, for once it wasn't raining and generally everything was right with the world.

'Ship!' Niall's shout came from the top of the mast. The wiry crewman was once more on lookout.

Peering up at him, Captain Breslin did not like the look of concern on the young man's face. 'Coming our way?' he asked.

'Aye. Right for us,' Niall responded. The other three crewmen gathered at the base of the mast.

'Where?'

Niall pointed outward and Breslin squinted, trying to make out what lay beyond the heaving, green undulations of the waves. Eventually he spotted a sail and it was indeed headed directly for them.

'Pirates?' said Rurui, the bald-headed giant, who was still walking with a pronounced limp from the kick Savage had delivered to his knee. His face, like the others, had visibly paled despite his heavy tan.

'It's coming from the south,' Breslin said with a shake of his head. 'Tavish Dhu would be striking from the north. That ship is coming from the direction of France.'

'They're heading straight for us though,' Niall argued.

'Well, let's see if it's us they want or not,' Breslin said. 'Prepare to turn.'

The captain went back to the oar and soon the curragh was heaving through a turn and off on a new heading.

After running hard for a while the captain looked aloft again. 'Well?'

Niall shook his head. 'They're still after us. And they're catching us up.'

Captain Breslin made several more evasive moves, but all to no avail. The other ship, which had the look of a sleek new Genoese galley, was fast. It followed remorselessly, getting closer and closer all the while.

'They're flying a white flag,' Niall shouted eventually. 'There's someone on the prow waving.'

Breslin sighed. They could not outrun this ship so there was little more he could do than hope this was not more trouble. 'Ask him what he wants,' he commanded.

Niall hailed the other boat in French, Irish and finally English. The boats were now close enough that Breslin could see the tall, blond-haired man standing on the prow, arm raised to attract their attention. He wore chain mail and had a sword strapped to his side.

'Can you let me come aboard?' the man shouted. Breslin noted that he spoke with a distinct German accent. 'I'm a business partner of Gaston of La Rochelle. I need to talk to you.'

Breslin knew Gaston, the weasel-faced merchant in the French port with whom they sometimes did business. He nodded and shouted back, 'Very well. I'll send the boat over. Niall, get down here and row over to get that man.'

As he turned away, from the corner of his mouth he added to Rurui, 'Tell the lads to get their weapons; best to be prepared, just in case.'

The fishermen quickly armed themselves then lowered a coracle over the side. The little, lightweight boat, of similar construction to the curragh, but tiny in comparison and barely more than a wicker frame with animal skins stretched over it, bobbled violently on the top of the water. Niall shinned down the mast and leapt into it with impressive agility, landing in a half-crouch and pausing only momentarily to steady himself before sitting down and grabbing the paddle. Soon the unwieldy little boat had covered the short distance of sea to the galley. The German swung himself over the edge and lowered himself gingerly into the coracle. Breslin could see that other armed men had gathered on the deck of the galley and were watching proceedings.

Shortly the coracle returned and the blond German was standing on Breslin's deck. 'Good day.' He smiled. 'I cannot believe my luck to have run into you like this. I am Syr

Heinrich von Mahlberg. As I said, I've business dealings with Gaston in France. I am trying to find a man who Gaston says you ferried to Ireland.'

Breslin remained impassive. He stared at the tall, heavily muscled swordsman, noticing the fading bruise on his clean-shaven chin, his close-cropped blond hair and the white-toothed smile, whose warmth did not make it as far as his pale blue eyes. The man looked dangerous.

'And who might that be?' he asked.

'Richard Savage,' von Mahlberg said, the unconvincing smile not leaving his face. 'He claimed to be a Knight Templar.'

'Never heard of him,' Breslin said. Even as he spoke he saw the confused look flash across Niall's face. Breslin himself was unsure why he had said it. He certainly owed no loyalty to the haunted-looking Templar who had taken over his boat days before. However there was something in the German's arrogant insincerity that made Breslin disinclined to do the man any favours. Out of the corner of his eye he saw that Rurui, his blackthorn club concealed behind his leg, had shuffled his way to almost within striking distance of Heinrich von Mahlberg.

The German's smile disappeared and a hard look came to his face. 'We have only this instant met and you choose to lie to me. You know very well who that man was.'

Von Mahlberg moved with a sudden speed that amazed everyone. In one flowing movement he had drawn his sword, spun in a circle and come up behind Rurui, who was still trying to raise his club as the cold steel of the German's blade came to rest across his throat.

'Drop it, you oaf, or I'll slit your gizzard,' von Mahlberg spat in the big man's ear. Rurui complied and the blackthorn clattered onto the deck.

The other fishermen had drawn their knives, but von Mahlberg stood sheltered behind Rurui, peeking round the bald man's ear, his sword clamped across Rurui's neck. The big man gave a little whimper, looking at the captain, his uncle, with pleading eyes.

'Easy on, friend,' Breslin said, reassuring hands held out, trying to look into his big nephew's eyes and convey some sort of comfort. 'No need to get rough. Can't we just discuss this like sensible men?'

'Your man started it,' von Mahlberg said. 'But let's try again, shall we? And this time no lies. Where is Savage?'

Breslin sighed, 'We left him in Dublin, all right?'

'Dublin? He was supposed to go to Tír Chonaill,' the German said.

'There was a change of plan...' Breslin said. 'Something about his daughter being kidnapped. He took over our ship – held me at swordpoint and made us take him where he wanted to go. We had no say in the matter.'

The German did not reply. For several moments they stood looking at each other across the rocking deck then he seemed to make up his mind. 'This is good,' he said, as if talking to himself. 'Savage and his woman will be in the same place. Very well.'

'Let him go,' Breslin said, nodding at his nephew. 'He's just a big dumb ox. We'll take you back to your ship.'

Von Mahlberg held Breslin's gaze for a moment then his right arm drew downward in a swift motion. Rurui's eyes widened as the German's blade opened his throat from ear to ear. He coughed as blood erupted from the wound and poured down his front.

'No!' the captain shouted in dismay.

The German shoved the already dying Rurui away from him. The big man collapsed forwards, face first onto the deck.

Falling to his knees beside his nephew, Breslin and one of his crew tried desperately to staunch the blood gushing from his nephew's neck. Niall let out an incoherent screech. He charged, knife drawn, but von Mahlberg lunged forward, his blade flashing in the sunlight. The point slid easily into the fisherman's flesh, deep into the right side of his belly. Niall's shout of rage changed into a scream of agony. He dropped to the deck and, drawing up his knees, huddled whimpering in a ball.

His diversion successfully achieved, von Mahlberg stepped away and made for the side of the curragh. He swung himself over into the coracle and began paddling quickly towards his ship. As he did so, his chest swelled with triumph. It was sheer good luck that he had recognised the fishing vessel Gaston had described. Had he not done so, he would now be on his way to Tír Chonaill. Instead, with Savage and his woman likely both in Dublin, he would more easily accomplish the task Lord Mortimer had set him. Having them both in the one place would make it easier to kill them.

51

Dublin

'Where are you going?' Connor MacHuylin called.

'North,' Savage said over his shoulder as he kept walking across the castle courtyard. 'I've got to get to Carrickfergus.' He heard running footsteps and turned around to see MacHuylin jogging towards him, a wince of pain creasing his face with every footfall of his right foot.

'Don't be stupid,' MacHuylin said as he caught up. 'It's going to be dark soon. You can't go tonight.'

'Don't try and stop me,' Savage said, continuing to walk and now going backwards. 'I've wasted enough time here already. I've got to get to Carrickfergus and help my daughter. Time is running out.'

'Think about it,' MacHuylin said. 'She's in the castle. So far as we know, she's safe from the Scots for the time being. She's probably hungry, but she's not going anywhere. You running off into the dark tonight isn't going to do her much good. It might get you killed by bandits on the road, though.'

Savage shook his head and turned forwards again. Instantly he collided with the wall of the castle gate tower. His chest, right leg and left cheek whacked hard into the cold stone. His head snapped back and the impact propelled him backwards to land on his backside on the cobblestones.

Rubbing his sore cheek, Savage looked up to see MacHuylin chuckling above him.

'You saw me walking towards that, you bastard,' Savage said, a sheepish grin on his face.

'I thought maybe it'd knock some sense into your head,' MacHuylin said. 'I'd help you up but I'm injured.'

Savage nodded and scrambled back to his feet.

'We can leave in the morning and there'll be no harm done,' MacHuylin said. 'Tonight I've a terrible thirst on me. Why don't you come with me for some of that Water of Life – uisce beatha – I was talking about?'

'We can leave?'

'You don't think I'd let you go to Carrickfergus on your own, do you?' MacHuylin said.

Savage tutted. 'Great. So instead of going to Carrick with an army I'll be going on my own with a cripple.'

'Here now,' MacHuylin said, a look of mock reproach on his face. 'I'm injured. I'm not a cripple.'

'All right,' Savage said with a sigh. His initial anger and panicked reaction to the cancellation of the expedition were fading now to a deep sense of disappointment that bordered on despair. A drink would probably do him good.

'Come on,' MacHuylin said. 'I've heard there's alchemists on Winetavern Street who boil the Water of Life better than anything you've ever tasted.'

They left the castle and headed downhill through the

mizzling rain and the busy, filthy streets of the city, avoiding the mounds of rubbish, bones and excrement that were piled in mounds on every thoroughfare, occasionally sending a kick in the direction of a wild dog or pig that rooted in the garbage and refused to move out of the way. Despite the gathering gloom of evening, hawkers and merchants still barked out their wares and the streets were clogged with people going hither and thither.

They passed the massive stone edifice of Christ Church and turned downhill onto Winetavern Street. With the onset of evening, the usual jolly atmosphere of the street was intensifying, the raucous noise-level heightened and along with it a simmering threat of potential violence. Clearly there was a shortage of food, but no sign of shortage of wine – yet. The denizens of Dublin were guzzling drink at the same rate they always had done, perhaps even more as they tried to replace the hunger that gnawed at their guts with the forgetfulness brought by wine and ale.

MacHuylin led the way into the first tavern they came to. Inside it was loud, warm and stinking. The air was a foul mix of sweat, sour ale, dirty straw and the fug of rain-soaked woollen clothes steaming dry in the heat from the smouldering peat fire. Men were jammed onto benches, talking loudly in the manner of the inebriated. Some sang and some argued. There was a lot of hearty laughter and in the corner a band of Irish musicians tried to make themselves heard over the din.

They found places on benches and sat facing each other across the long ale table. A serving woman approached.

'Uisce beatha,' MacHuylin ordered. 'Two, please.'

Savage detested uisce beatha. He found neither the taste,

the aroma nor the effect in any way enjoyable. As the serving woman set down two wooden cups before them, he eyed the clear, evil-smelling liquid they contained with a degree of trepidation. The fumes rising from it made his eyes water. God knew what drinking it would do.

The 'Water of Life' – *aqua vitae* in Latin, *uisce beatha* in Irish – was becoming ever more popular, Savage reflected. Alchemists had discovered the process of distillation during their search for the purification process to create the ellusive elixir of life and the practice had spread to monasteries. While most of the rest of Europe produced aqua vitae for use in medicines, the Scots and Irish had perfected the production of the drink for entertainment purposes.

'What do you think the earl wants those supplies for?' he wondered aloud, trying to delay the ordeal of having to swallow the uisce.

'Politics. To your good health!' MacHuylin said. He knocked back the cup of burning liquid in one gulp. After an appreciative sigh he wiped the back of his hand across his mouth and fixed Savage with eyes that were more watery than before. 'The nobles decide what's best and we just have to accept it. It's not the business of the likes of us.'

Savage instinctively wanted to respond that he was a knight, but stopped himself as he ruminated that he had no manor, no lands, and no castle. He had no stake in this game. Nothing but the life of his daughter, that was; but to the magnates and nobles like de Burgh and de Bermingham such sentimentality had no place.

'The earl,' MacHuylin said, rubbing his beard in reflection. 'Now there's a man with a complicated family life. One daughter married to Robert the Bruce and now another to be married to the English Justiciar of Ireland. Talk about a foot in both camps!'

'What do you make of de Burgh?' Savage asked, wondering if he should repeat de Mandeville's concerns. 'You were his bodyguard. What do you think he's up to?'

'Yes, I was his bodyguard,' MacHuylin said, raising a forefinger to the serving wench for more uisce, 'but we were always commanded by the seneschal. The earl is the canniest man I ever met – maybe too smart for his own good sometimes. Are you going to drink that or look at it all night?'

Savage blew out his cheeks then raised his cup, attempting to imitate MacHuylin's bravado. The liquid poured past his teeth and tongue, setting his mouth then throat on fire. He screwed his eyes shut as his chest began to heave and he desperately fought to keep the uisce down. He bent double over the table, a spasm of uncontrollable coughing erupting from his mouth. MacHuylin laughed and began slapping him on the back.

Savage realised with growing panic that he had no hope of keeping the liquid in his stomach. All of a sudden the heat and the smell of the inn were too much to bear. Brushing aside MacHuylin's hand, he lurched to his feet then stumbled towards the door, desperate for fresh air and the cool of the rainy evening.

Throwing open the tavern door, Savage barged out into the street but it was too late. He felt his stomach heave and he doubled over, spewing the rotten liquid and the remains of the potage he had eaten for lunch into the detritus in the street. There was not much in his stomach and after several more retches he found himself once more in control and able to straighten up again. He coughed and drew the back of his hand across his face to wipe away the trails of drool and the embarrassing tears that streamed from his eyes, aware suddenly of the chortles and mocking comments of passers-by in the street.

Doing his best to regain some self-respect, he swept a glance around the street, trying to look as threatening as possible. As he did so his gaze landed on a small group of men walking up the hill on the other side of the road. There were five of them and they wore long cloaks, most with the hoods pulled up against the rain. The tall, bulky man in their midst, however, had his hood down.

Savage froze.

The big man had a blunt face and greying hair cut down to mere stubble. With an arrogant glare he looked around at the people he passed in the street, as if almost daring them to challenge him. Savage had only met him once before but he knew this was typical of the man.

It was Gib Harper, the leader of the crew who had kidnapped his daughter.

52

Savage's first instinct was to charge across the street and grab the Scotsman by the throat. Something deep inside him caused him to hesitate, however. He dropped his gaze, his mind in turmoil. The brazen arrogance of the man to walk blatantly through the heart of his enemies' capital city made Savage's anger boil further. Also, he was more than a little intrigued. What was Harper doing here? Maybe it would be better to try to find out rather than kill him straight away.

Savage glanced up again and saw that Harper and his crew of men had passed on up the street without noticing him. They were dressed like any other men-at-arms in a city at war and bore no insignia to denote they were Scottish. They blended in with the locals just the same as they had in France. This was clearly the sort of thing Harper was good at. Before they got too far away, Savage slipped back into the tavern.

Inside, MacHuylin had finished his second uisce and was gesturing for a third. His grin of mockery froze when he saw the expression on Savage's face. 'Who walked on your grave?' he asked.

Savage quickly outlined what had just happened.

'Let's go and get him,' MacHuylin said, rising to his feet.

Savage shook his head. 'There are five of them and with that shoulder you won't be much use in a fight. Besides, I want to see what they're up to.'

'What if it's to kill the justiciar?' MacHuylin said.

Savage just shrugged. He didn't exactly have much of a plan in mind. 'We'll follow them and see what they're doing. If it starts to get dangerous then run and get de Mandeville and his soldiers. We can't let them get away.'

'Why don't we just do that now?' MacHuylin said.

'We don't know where they are going,' Savage said, frustration and anxiety in his tone. 'This is a big city. By the time we get back they'll have disappeared who knows where. I'm going. Come on.'

Savage turned and hurried back out into the street just as the serving woman returned with a new cup. MacHuylin looked at it with regret. He threw some coins onto her tray and stood up to leave, then picked up the cup and drained it before following Savage.

Outside, the dreary early April day was dissolving into a miserable evening. The earlier mizzle had turned to heavy, constant rain. Braziers were being fired in the streets to bring some illumination to the gloom. Passers-by trudged through heavy mud and the conduit that ran down the middle of Winetavern Street had become a torrent of filth. Savage was glad to have an excuse to pull up his hood and keep his head down as it made it easier to follow the Scots as anonymously as possible.

By now, Harper and his contingent were much further up the street. Savage and MacHuylin followed, not close enough to get their attention but not so far away to risk losing them. MacHuylin hobbled along beside Savage but was audibly out of breath and occasionally gasped in pain, to the point where Savage began to worry that the injured man would not be able to keep up.

At the top of Winetavern Street, Harper and his group turned left and headed into the open square around Christ Church Cathedral. Despite the rain, the square was a busy place; the very heart of city life.

As it was Holy Week, many people had been to the church. The evening services were over and the square was filling with people, most on their way home, Savage surmised, but a group of young men had taken advantage of the open area to mark out a handball court. Their boisterous antics provoked scowls from the church leavers, who clearly thought such frivolity out of place during the most solemn week of the Christian year. Some of the surrounding shops had expensive glazing and their merchant owners appeared to be similarly disapproving, but presumably, thought Savage with a wry grin, this was due more to concern about stray balls coming their way than concern for the young men's souls.

On the opposite side of the square two lines of children, holding hands and facing each other, were about to start a round of the prisoner's base game, and at the centre of the square, before a large, carved stone Celtic cross, a desultory felon half-stood, half-hung in the stocks. His head and arms were clamped in the punishment device. His head hung down and his long hair, rain-soaked and clogged with mire, dangled in rats' tails obscuring his face. Normally he would have been pelted with rotting vegetables, but due to the scarcity and price of food these had been substituted by stones, mud and clumps of shit. The poor man looked half unconscious from the onslaught, though as Savage briefly contemplated, he probably deserved it.

The Scots skirted around the stocks and continued along the side of the cathedral to the far end, where they stopped. All of them began to look around them to ensure they were not being followed.

On the other side of the square, Savage flattened himself against a doorway and pulling MacHuylin alongside him pointedly looked away, so they would not see he was watching them. MacHuylin sucked in a sharp breath through his teeth at the jarring his body endured coming against the door. He raised a comforting hand to his injured shoulder. After a moment, Savage leaned forward and peeked carefully towards the cathedral door, just in time to see the Scots disappear inside. He was about to set off across the square when he stopped again, holding MacHuylin back with his left hand.

'What now?' MacHuylin said.

'God's blood and bones!' Savage exclaimed, pointing across the square at another figure scurrying towards the cathedral door. MacHuylin squinted at the scrawny, hollow-eyed young cleric who hurried through the rain, his tonsured head dipped against the weather.

MacHuylin scowled. 'Who is he?'

'That's the Earl of Ulster's personal cleric,' Savage hissed, whispering though not sure why. The cleric was much too far away to hear him. 'He's been helping us draw up the plans for the relief of Carrickfergus! He could mean to betray the whole plan.'

'Could be a coincidence,' MacHuylin said.

Savage shook his head as the cleric glanced over his shoulder then he too entered the cathedral. 'I'm not taking the risk. Go. Get the seneschal. Get the justiciar and soldiers. I'll keep an eye on them while you're gone.'

'Maybe it would be better if you go?' MacHuylin said. 'I'm not exactly fast in my condition.'

'No,' Savage said, patting the hilt of the sword sheathed at his waist. 'If they try to get away, someone will have to stop them and you won't be much use in that respect.'

'You won't be much use on your own,' MacHuylin countered. 'There's five of them.'

'I'll just have to do my best,' Savage said. 'At least I might be able to delay them. No, you go. But hurry up for God's sake.'

MacHuylin lurched off in the direction of the castle while Savage crossed the square, pushing through the traffic of people and horses to the door of the cathedral.

Inside the atmosphere changed from the rainy evening to the cool stillness of the air captured within the vast stone walls that now surrounded him. Beyond a short entrance porch and antechamber, Savage entered the body of the cathedral proper. For a moment he was awed by the dizzying height to which the roof soared above him. His stomach churned slightly as he looked up at the arched ceiling, ridged like the ribcage of some vast skeleton or the inside of an enormous, upturned boat. The nave stretched forward before him in a straight line towards the stone rood screen and the altar, which seemed very far away and provoked in him a habit, old and half-forgotten, and his hand crept to his chest to cross himself. Two rows of stone pillars rose to the Gothic arches in the roof, and enormously tall windows allowed in plenty of the fading early evening light to illuminate the interior. In addition, torches and candles lined the walls so that the whole interior was ablaze with light. The walls themselves were covered floor to ceiling in brightly coloured paintings depicting Jesus, John the Baptist and a variety of Christian scenes. To the right was a particularly fearsome painting of Satan, twenty feet tall and covered in black hair. Flames belched from his mouth and a myriad of faces emerged from his chest, stomach and buttocks.

The cathedral proved to be no less busy or quiet than the streets outside. Like a lot of churches, the space and shelter afforded by the nave provided a place where commerce was conducted. Deals were made, business ventures launched and plans hatched. Savage knew of the long-held tradition that had arisen in Dublin that the place where many deals were to be struck was at the tomb of Strongbow, the first Norman lord to conquer Ireland. Looking down the nave he saw the tomb about halfway along between two sets of pillars, and the adjacent area was crowded with merchants and others all going about their business.

Savage, his hand moving to rest on the hilt of his sword, stepped cautiously forward, scanning left and right for a sight of either the Scotsmen or the cleric. A little way ahead a rat scuttled around one of the pillars. It was quickly followed by a tall, mangy and very skinny cat. It was, thought Savage, a bit like him and the Scots – only who was really chasing whom, he wondered.

Finally he spotted Harper. He and the other men of his group were kneeling, facing the altar as if in prayer, but he could see their heads moving, looking up and around to check who was around them. They were positioned about halfway down the nave near Strongbow's tomb. Savage walked closer and realised they were part of what looked like a queue of people that snaked across the nave, all awaiting their turn at the tomb in the hope of striking a deal.

Savage studied the tomb. It consisted of a stone plinth that rose from the flagstones of the floor to about waist height. On top of it was the carved effigy of the old knight, resplendent in full armour and mail. He lay on his back, one leg crossed over the other, hands clasped above his chest as if in prayer, shield still strapped to his left arm. His face had a smooth and slightly worn appearance. It was the custom for parties to a deal to each place a hand on Strongbow's face to seal their agreement. Over the years the effect of those countless thousands of caressing hands had begun to show.

Savage stiffened, noticing to his surprise that the group of men currently conducting their deals at the tomb included a tall, dark-skinned Moor. The man's head was swathed in a turban and he was dressed in long, flowing white robes beneath a chain mail tunic. He was armed with a huge scimitar, its curved blade sheathed at his waist. All in all he cut an impressive figure. His arms were folded, his features moulded into a sceptical expression and it was clear to Savage that he was driving a hard bargain with the local merchants. With his exotic dress, the Moor was like a splash of colour amid the dismal surroundings of the city. Savage's instant reaction was one of suspicion and hostility. He had spent years fighting Saracens who looked very like this one.

Drawing a deep breath, Savage forced himself to relax, contemplating that despite the war, Dublin was still a centre of commerce and the Moor had as much right to be there as everyone else. The tradition of dealing at Strongbow's tomb was known across Europe, so there was no reason that someone from Muslim Andalusia or even further afield would not know of it too. Besides, Savage had much more pressing things to worry about.

Savage moved to a pillar adjacent to the tomb, trying his best to look like he was casually leaning on it. He became aware that his hood was still up which, while it hid his features, would look strange now he was indoors. He pulled it down and waited for what seemed an age as the businessmen at the tomb completed their dealings. Finally, the Moorish merchant broke into a broad grin and his hearty laugh echoed around the stone vaults above. All the men in the group were also smiling; clearly whatever deal had just been struck was to everyone's advantage. Laying his left palm on Strongbow's face the Moor held out his right hand. One of the Irishmen he had been talking to spat into the palm of his own right hand and followed suit. They grasped hands with enthusiasm then, their deal done, the immediate crowd of merchants dispersed.

With a clinking of chain mail, Harper's group rose almost as one and approached the tomb. Savage frowned, puzzled at what they were up to. Were they here to make some sort of secret deal or was this just a convenient meeting place? As they gathered around the effigy of the long-dead knight, Savage spotted the Earl of Ulster's cleric once more, and he was making straight for them.

One thing was for sure, thought Savage: he was going

to have to take action. He looked around in the vain hope of seeing MacHuylin, accompanied by the seneschal and a troop of soldiers, coming in through the cathedral door. Instead, all he saw was the Moorish merchant and his companions leaving.

Whatever he was going to do, he would have to do it alone.

53

Ahead, he saw the earl's cleric speaking to Harper. The man was facing his way, while Harper and his men had their backs to Savage. The cleric's expression was serious and he was talking rapidly, though Savage was too far away to hear what he said.

Savage approached as quickly as he could, trying to look nonchalant and unobtrusive while at the same time keeping a rapid pace. His right hand was on the pommel of the longsword sheathed at his waist.

He was almost behind Harper when the cleric's expression changed to a frown. With a spark of recognition his eyes locked with Savage's and he knew the time for stealth was gone. He ripped the blade from its scabbard. Harper and his men all turned as one. There was a brief moment of confused consternation on their faces. Savage had no idea what would happen next. It was five to one – six if he counted the cleric, but he had few worries about dealing with him. The others were a different matter.

To his surprise, none of the Scots went for their weapons then. Instead their initial shock melted quickly into cool gazes and a few sardonic smiles. Savage was thrown by this and for a moment simply stood, sword in hand, point levelled at Harper's chest.

'Richard Savage,' Harper said, a grin breaking out on his face that was all malice and no mirth. 'Should you not be on your way to Ulster with the Holy Grail? My Lord Edward is expecting you there.'

'Stay where you are,' was all that Savage could think to say, feeling more than a little foolish. 'Your master's plot has been discovered—' he shot a glance at the cleric '—and the justiciar is on his way with a troop of soldiers.'

Harper folded his arms. 'Oh is he now? And why would that bother us? We're here with his and the Earl of Ulster's permission. Do I not have every right to come here when I have both an invitation and a guarantee of safe conduct from the highest powers in this city? I see you've drawn your sword. Surely you don't mean to break those guarantees? Surely you wouldn't spill blood in a holy place?'

'It wouldn't be the first time I've done that,' Savage replied. 'No more of your lies, Harper. You must think I was born yesterday. Safe conduct? For a Scottish dog like you? The justiciar is outside as we speak,' he said, fervently hoping it was true. Surely MacHuylin, even injured, had been gone long enough to get to the castle and back by now? 'And he'll have you hanged, drawn and quartered like that other bastard Scotsman, William Wallace.'

Harper's face darkened and Savage could see the man was barely restraining his anger and desire to attack him.

'Careful now, laddie,' Harper said. 'Don't speak ill of the dead like that.'

'It's true, I'm afraid, Syr Richard,' the cleric interjected, looking at Savage with a distinctly apologetic expression.

'I'm meeting these men on the direct orders of the Earl of Ulster. Their safe conduct in the city of Dublin is guaranteed by the justiciar while we make these arrangements.'

Savage felt confusion dissolving his resolve. 'What "arrangements"?' he asked, his lips curling into a snarl that was more suspicious than angry.

Behind him, the doors of the cathedral banged open.

Everyone turned to see what was going on. Through the doors came MacHuylin accompanied by the three most important men in Dublin: the justiciar, John de Bermingham; the Earl of Ulster, Richard de Burgh; and the Seneschal of Ulster, Thomas de Mandeville. Behind them, in close order, came a troop of heavily armed spearmen, including Meiler.

Savage sighed with relief, but it was short-lived when he saw the expression on MacHuylin's face. The galloglaich shot him a look that warned him he was not going to like what he was about to hear.

'What's going on here?' de Burgh demanded, his wet cloak swirling around him as he came to a halt at Strongbow's tomb. His stance was straight-backed, his expression confrontational and to Savage's growing dismay his question seemed to be aimed in his direction rather than Harper's.

'These are Scottish rebels, sire,' Savage said, pointing at Harper with the hilt of his sword.

'I know that, Savage, but what, in God's holy name, do you think you are doing?' The earl's eyes blazed with anger. 'These men are here under my protection to complete an important agreement. How dare you stick your nose in and try to ruin everything!'

Savage glared back at the earl, his own anger boiling in

his chest. 'What do you mean, "under your protection"?' he said.

The justiciar stepped forward and laid a hand on Savage's shoulder. His expression was one of embarrassed conciliation. 'Strictly speaking, Savage, they are here under my protection,' de Bermingham said. 'As the man who represents the King in Ireland I am the only one who can allow them into the city.'

The tip of Savage's sword dipped, disbelief raging in his mind. 'But why?' was all he could manage to say.

'We need to make a deal with Edward Bruce,' the justiciar said. 'And Harper represents him.'

'A deal?' Savage said, contempt dripping from the word like the caustic piss that tanners used to tan leather.

'A deal,' de Bermingham repeated. 'War and statecraft is not all about charging into battle, Syr Richard. Sometimes, even when we don't like it, we must employ politics. The earl's cleric was empowered to confirm with Harper here that we will keep the Easter peace. The Pope himself has requested it and I concur that there will be no fighting between us during Holy Week. Secondly—'

The earl's face fell into a scowl. 'I don't see why you are bothering to explain this to him. This is none of his business,' he complained.

'Syr Richard is entitled to an explanation,' the justiciar replied. 'I understand he has a very personal interest in these dealings.'

De Burgh raised his eyebrows and crossed his arms but said nothing more.

'Secondly,' de Bermingham resumed, 'we need to confirm ransom terms for the release of William Laith de Burgh, currently being held hostage in Scotland by Robert Bruce. He is the earl's cousin and soon, through my impending marriage, will be mine also.'

Savage's mind went back to earlier in the day and the "other business" de Burgh had talked about to de Bermingham. He felt the fight go out of him and he lowered his sword. 'Is that where the relief supplies in those ships will be sent?' he asked, bitterly. 'Instead of sending them to Carrickfergus Castle we'll be handing them over to the Scots? Instead of relieving the garrison and saving the last castle still holding out in Ulster we're going to ransom one nobleman?'

'In a word, yes,' de Burgh said.

Savage shoved his sword back into its sheath. He looked balefully at the men who stood around him. Harper smiled at him. Savage did not respond to the expression. Instead he spat on the floor and walked off in disgust.

'Damned insolence!' the earl blustered. 'He has no respect for his betters.'

'Let him go,' the justiciar said. Turning back to the Scots delegation he addressed Gib Harper. 'Now, sir, what are the exact terms of this deal?'

Savage walked over to where MacHuylin and the seneschal stood, arms folded, disapproving looks on their faces that matched Savage's feelings.

'Politics,' MacHuylin said with a shrug.

Savage just grunted.

'There's no honour in this,' de Mandeville commented, shaking his head, his expression turning to one of sadness.

'So be it,' Savage said. 'Like I said earlier, I'll go north on my own. All that matters to me now is getting Galiene back safely. I don't care about this war any more.'

'I'll go with you,' MacHuylin said.

Savage, his mouth twisting into a bitter smile, looked up at the tall galloglaich. 'Thank you, Connor, but I'm afraid you're just not fit for it.'

The nobles, the cleric and the Scots concluded their business quickly. There was no ritual caressing of Strongbow's tomb, but each side saluted the other and then the gathering broke up. Harper's contingent strutted down the nave of the cathedral with the arrogance of men walking with ensured safety right through the middle of their enemy's city. As he passed Savage, MacHuylin and de Mandeville, Harper stopped.

'Syr Richard,' he said to Savage, 'perhaps you should be spending more energy on the task you were set? My Lord Edward is not a patient man and he wants the Grail back. I wouldn't let him down if I were you, not when he has that awfully pretty daughter of yours,' he smirked.

Savage, his rage bubbling to the surface, but not thinking it prudent to let Harper know that he was aware Bruce no longer had Galiene, just glared at him. Harper, still smiling, winked then continued out of the cathedral and into the night. Hard on his heels came the Earl of Ulster.

'I don't appreciate your meddling in the affairs of state, Savage,' he said. 'From now on keep your nose out of the business of your betters and leave politics and statecraft to those of us who were born for the job.'

The justiciar joined him, a warm, slightly apologetic smile on his lips.

'The man's a blunt instrument, John.' De Burgh waved a

gloved hand in Savage's direction. 'That's all he's good for. You should remember that.'

De Bermingham's smile became fixed. He looked down at the flagstones beneath his feet, hands clasped behind his back as he rocked backwards and forwards on his heels. 'Sometimes, Richard, blunt instruments are required,' he said.

The earl grunted in derision, turned on his heel and with an impatient flick of his wrist to indicate to his cleric that he should follow, left the cathedral. The cleric shuffled after him, his head hung low, his face a red blush.

'At least the cleric has enough integrity to be embarrassed in his role in this,' de Mandeville commented.

The door closed behind the earl and his cleric, leaving Savage, MacHuylin and de Mandeville alone with the justiciar and his troop of guards. For a few moments no one spoke. Savage did not even want to speak to de Bermingham. His disgust was so great it choked the words in his throat.

'Well, now that's concluded you men should get some rest,' the justiciar finally broke the silence. 'You've a busy day tomorrow.'

'We do?' De Mandeville's face wore a puzzled frown. 'What do we have to do now the relief expedition is cancelled? If we're now at peace with the Scots for the duration of Easter what do you expect us to do? Go to church?'

'If you can do that before you leave, I'm sure that would be an excellent start,' de Bermingham said. Savage noticed a mischievous smile playing across the justiciar's lips. 'Though I will make sure the bishop blesses your ships on departure regardless.'

Seeing the looks of barely held tolerance on their faces, the justiciar held up his hands. 'All right, no more jokes. The expedition to relieve Carrickfergus is back on. I suggest you leave at first light.'

Savage, de Mandeville and MacHuylin looked at each other then looked at the justiciar, mouths open.

'You said it was cancelled,' de Mandeville said. 'What about the deal you just made with the Scots? What happened to your concerns about the pirate? What about the element of surprise?'

De Bermingham shrugged. 'I think I've just about guaranteed that now, haven't I?' Savage noted how very pleased he seemed to be with himself. 'The Scots think the peace of Easter is assured and that the flotilla of ships leaving Dublin will be headed for Scotland to pay the ransom for the Earl of Ulster's cousin. You don't think I'd really sacrifice the last stronghold we have in the north to save one nobleman foolish enough to get himself captured, do you?'

Savage shook his head, grinning at the duplicity of the justiciar. For one so young he was quite a politician.

'This won't go down well with your new father-in-law,' he said.

'Let me deal with that,' de Bermingham said. 'If I'm honest, I'm not sure how much I trust him. I do still worry about that pirate though. Tavish Dhu is the one element that could throw the whole plan awry.'

'Tavish Dhu?' MacHuylin said. 'He's holed up on the Isle of Man. It was his crew that shot me in Dundalk. They were talking about heading back to their base on Man to meet a Saracen slave trader.'

They all exchanged glances, looks of excitement lightening their faces. 'Perhaps we could kill two birds with one stone here,' de Mandeville wondered, rubbing his chin with one hand.

'I leave it up to you,' the justiciar said. 'Just get the job done. Now I must take my leave. I'll see you in the morning.'

They all began trooping out of the cathedral.

As they approached the door, Savage suddenly stopped and grasped the sleeve of MacHuylin's jerkin.

'What did you say about a Saracen?' he asked.

54

At sea

Alys found she was not mistreated on the pirate ship. If anything, the pirates were cautious of damaging her. When she kicked or spat at them they moved out of her range. When she was told to go below decks and she refused to move, instead of hitting her, the big man – Pol – had simply lifted her bodily from behind, pinioning her arms. He had hoisted her over his shoulder and carried her down the ladder to the dark deck beneath, where spare sails, equipment and looted booty were stored. She was painfully aware, however, that all this care was from fear of affecting the price she would fetch from the slave trader rather than concern for her wellbeing.

'Old Ibn won't pay top price for damaged goods,' Tavish Dhu said. 'Any man who leaves a mark on her will answer to me.'

His threat was enough to make sure the pirates did what he asked. As if that was not enough to remind her of her fate, once below decks among stolen chests of money, clothes and barrels of merchandise, Pol had fastened an iron slave collar around her neck. It was a circular band of metal that was not tight enough to choke, but still tight enough to be uncomfortable. A chain came from the front and connected to two sets of shackles, one around her wrists and the other around her ankles. The weight of metal was enough to stop her moving too far and the shackles meant it was impossible anyway. There was little for her to do but to sit with her back to the rocking hull of the ship and mull over her predicament.

There seemed no way out of this. Even if she could escape her bonds what would be the point? The ship was in the middle of the wide, cold sea, miles from land. A deep despair descended on her that weighed heavier than the chains. Galiene was in dreadful danger. Richard was who knew where? Even if he had managed to rescue Galiene, the German assassin, von Mahlberg, was on his way to kill both of them. What fate awaited her, sold into bondage among the Saracens? Was she destined to be the handmaiden to some heathen lady? She grunted bitterly to herself. *Only if I'm lucky*, she thought, knowing that she could as easily end up sold to a brothel, a silver mine or some other unthinkable outcome.

She squeezed her eyes shut and looked up at the ceiling, throwing back her head so it thumped against the wood behind her.

She cursed Mortimer and his whore, Queen Isabella. This was their doing, the conniving, conspiring pair of traitors. The thought brought anger and with it the resolve not to give in. She would bide her time. Wait for her moment and if the chance arose, she would escape.

In the gloom beneath the deck it was hard to tell how much time had passed, but she judged it was at least a day. Her captors had brought her bread to eat and some watered wine that was little more than vinegar. When she asked about relieving herself the pirates had simply shrugged and climbed back up the ladder. Musing that at least they had not stayed to watch, she found a place at the far end of the deck and pissed against a wall. After she had dragged her heavy chains back to her original position, exhausted by the effort she had dozed off lying on a sail. Later she awoke but with no idea how long she had slept.

Finally, the hatch in the upper deck was opened and the black-bearded face of Tavish Dhu appeared above. 'We've arrived.' He grinned down at her. 'And to prove it we're here.'

Big Pol descended the ladder, put Alys over his shoulder again and carried her back up. He set her down on the deck as a cold wind caught her hair. It was an overcast day but she squinted slightly in the daylight after the gloom beneath the decks. The ship still surged and fell on heavy swell but there was land ahead and they were close to the calmer waters of a natural harbour. On either side, the encircling arms of a wide bay reached out to fill the gap between the sea and the sky. The land was dark green above black, rugged rocks and evoked in Alys memories of her lost home in the north of Ireland at Vikingsford. A settlement was at the top of the harbour and the squat, rectangular stone tower of a castle glowered over it. Behind the castle and settlement rose the slopes of a large, dark mountain that disappeared into the misty clouds above.

'And where is "here"?' Alys asked.

'This, my dear, is Balley Castle on the Island of Mannan MacLyr,' said Tavish Dhu. 'It's where we now call home.'

Alys knew of the Isle of Man, named after the ancient Gaelic sea god. It lay a few hours' sail away from the coast of Ulster, right in the middle of the sea that divided Ireland from England. A similar distance to the north was the southern coast of Scotland. Robert Bruce had taken the island from the English a few years before and Alys reasoned that it now was a perfect base for these pirates. Within easy reach of the shores of the three nations and the sea between them, they could hit ships at will then run back to their harbour and disappear again.

At the edge of the Earldom of Ulster was a huge lake, Lough Neagh, which divided it from the Kingdom of Tyr Eoghan to the west. The lough was vast, more an inland sea than a lake. When Alys was a child her mother had told her the old legend of how the giant Finn MacCool had created the lough by scooping up a massive lump of rock and mud to sling at a rival giant in Scotland. His throw did not quite make it and instead it landed in the sea, creating the Isle of Man.

'We're safe here,' Tavish said. 'I've lookouts at either end of the bay who send the word soon as a ship is sighted. We're ready and waiting for them before they even get to the harbour. Then when they do... you see that?' He waved a hand at a wooden construction that sat on the quay on one side of the harbour entrance. It looked like a short tower with a very long arm set on a pivot on top of it. At first Alys thought it was a crane, then she saw the sling attached to one end of the arm and the counterweight at the other and realised it was a war machine, the kind of giant catapult used to hurl massive rocks at castle walls.

Assuming her to be ignorant of such things, Tavish continued, 'That there's a trebuchet; a siege engine if you like. It can fire a rock as big as a cow halfway to Ireland. Lords and kings use it to smash down castle walls, but I use it to sink ships, unwanted ships coming into my harbour. This is our home and it's now your home too.' He grinned at her, but the smile was unpleasant and full of malice. 'For a day or so, at least until Ibn Al Bakri gets here.'

He looked at her appraisingly, head to one side, and reached out to run a hand through her long black hair. Alys flinched as the pirate stroked her cheek with his callused palm. 'There's me thinking you were a bit old,' he mused, half to himself. 'In the light of day you're a good-looking woman. You'll fetch a fine price, my lovely.'

'You sell Christians into slavery with heathen Saracens?' Alys said, her voice laden with bitter accusation. 'I hope there is an especially deep, burning and excruciatingly painful corner of Hell set aside just for you.'

The pirate's smile faded and she could tell he was struggling not to strike her. Instead he dropped his hand to the chain connecting the iron collar around her neck to the shackles on her wrists. He gave it a tug, jerking Alys's head painfully forward.

'I'm just carrying on an old, dishonourable tradition, my lovely,' Tavish sneered, 'one you should know all about, you being Irish. That slave collar round your neck was made a couple of hundred years ago in Ireland. It took the English to invade Ireland to stop your lot making a living in the slave-trading business. That castle there—' he pointed at the fortress on the shore '—was built by the Danes. They used it as a staging place for slaves going to and from the slave markets of Dublin, so don't you get all high and mighty with me, girl.' He released the chain and glared at her. 'I don't see old Ibn's ship in the harbour so we'll get to keep you a day or two.' Again he gave her a mocking smile. 'Don't worry though. We expect him any day now, so you won't have long to wait.'

With that he walked away.

55

Isle of Man

The pirate ships sailed into the harbour and tied up at the stone quay. The stolen loot was unloaded, and then Alys was pushed and prodded up the quayside and into the settlement. As she shuffled along as best she could, she noticed how the locals – mostly peasants and fishermen – seemed cowed, afraid even to look at the pirates as they walked by. Instead, they studiously minded their own business, going to great effort to look in any direction but that of Tavish, lest they caught his eye.

A short walk across a street brought them to the castle. It was far from the largest fortress Alys had ever seen. It had one tall, square central keep with a high surrounding wall and a second, smaller gate tower. The sea had been diverted to form a moat around the castle and Alys and the pirates had to cross a short drawbridge to access the gate in the entrance tower. As she passed through the portal Alys looked up and saw the teeth of a portcullis and a murder hole. Her chances of escape looked about as slim as when she was on the ship.

'Put her in the dungeon, Pol,' Tavish ordered. He left in the direction of the door in the main tower while Pol pushed Alys towards a set of steps that led downward at the base of the gate tower. As they descended the twisting stairway to below ground level, water from culverts and drains above their heads dribbled down around them and the steps became slippery with green moss. Eventually they came to a heavy iron-bound door. Pol shoved Alys to one side and thumped on the door with a huge fist.

A peephole in the door opened and a bloodshot eye peered out. 'Who is it?' called a weedy voice from within.

'It's me, you fool,' Pol said. 'I've another one for you.'

There was the sound of heavy bolts being drawn back, then the door creaked open, its hinges complaining like a badly tuned hurdy-gurdy. A short man with a fearsome squint looked out, shading his eyes with one hand against the sunlight filtering down the steps. The jailer looked as if he got out into the air about as much as his prisoners did. His skin was deathly pale, apart from dots of angry red pockmarks on his face, and his shoulder-length brown hair was lank and greasy. He was perhaps middle-aged and had a crook in his back that bent him almost double. A large bunch of keys hung at his belt. When he saw Alys his eyes lit up.

'She's to be sold to the slave trader,' Pol warned, reading the jailer's mind. 'Don't get any of your ideas. You're not to touch her, understand?'

With a scowl the jailer nodded then pulled Alys inside by her sleeve. Pol left, climbing back up the stairs again.

Alys found herself in a small room. It was below ground so there were no windows. The walls were stone and glistened with damp. An oil lamp guttered on a table, casting feeble yellow light on the rest of the furniture, which consisted of a rickety chair and rancid-looking bed that she could smell from across the room. A rat scuttled under the table then turned beady, defiant eyes in her direction.

'Is this to be my prison?' Alys said, her voice thick with dread.

The jailer laughed, his strange, high cackle more like an old woman's than a man's. 'This place? No such luxury for you, my dear,' he wheezed. 'This is my room. You'll be going with the rest of them in there.'

With a look of distinct pleasure he pointed towards another door in the opposite wall. It too was stout and bound with iron. The jailer prodded Alys over to it then fumbled in his bunch of keys until he found a large black one and inserted it into the keyhole. The door clanked open and he pushed it wide. Inside was pitch-black. A breath of cold air that reeked of decay, damp and human waste came out of the opening. From somewhere in the darkness beyond came a terrible, low moaning sound. Alys felt as if she had arrived at the mouth of Hell.

'In you go,' the jailer said, putting both hands to the small of her back and shoving her over the threshold. As she stumbled into the darkness he slammed the door shut and Alys heard the lock clank behind her.

56

As her eyes adjusted Alys became aware that the dungeon was not totally dark. The ceiling of the room was very high, probably at ground level, and there seemed to be a small, narrow opening up there. The daylight that came through it fell on the top of the wall directly opposite where she stood, leaving everything below in complete shadow. Tentatively she reached out a hand, the chain tugging at her neck as she did so. Her fingers touched the nearest wall, feeling stone that was wet with damp and slippery with cold slime. The sound of water dripping from on high echoed from several places and the foul stench was overpowering, prompting her to gag.

As she began to shuffle carefully forwards she was glad it was too dark to see the floor and thanked God for the sailor's boots she wore as she felt her feet sinking into something soft that coated the stone floor. There was a wailing sound from somewhere ahead in the dark and Alys recognised the despairing sound of inconsolable human misery. It was a woman weeping bitterly. Carefully she made her way towards it.

When she felt she was almost upon the woman, Alys spoke. 'Hello. Who is there? I can't see you. Are you all right?'

The crying ceased for a moment then began again, louder than before. From its direction Alys judged the woman to be below her, possibly kneeling or sitting on the floor. She lowered herself down to a squat, reaching forward with a cautious hand into the dark, careful this time not to jerk her slave collar. Her fingers touched cloth and flesh beneath. In an instant the wailing turned to a momentary screech and the weeping woman flinched away from her touch as if burnt by it.

'I mean you no harm,' Alys said in as reassuring a tone as she could muster. 'I'm a prisoner here like you.'

The woman just kept on howling, her cries now mixed with hysterical sobs.

'I'm afraid you're wasting your time, my dear.'

Alys nearly jumped out of her skin as the sound of a cultured, English, male voice came out of the dark from somewhere nearby.

'Who's there?' she hissed, her squat turning to a defensive crouch in one reflexive movement, taking up the slack on the chains at her ankles.

'I'm sorry I didn't mean to startle you,' the voice said. 'Allow me to introduce myself. I am Syr Henry de Bellomonte. I'm afraid our friend here is quite inconsolable. She has been weeping like that on and off for days now, in fact since she arrived. I fear she may have lost her mind a little. Unfortunately, despair and grief can do that. I've seen it many times. Too many I'm afraid.'

'You're a prisoner, too?' Alys asked.

'Indeed I am.' The voice was pleasant but had the cracked weakness of age in it and she surmised that Syr Henry was quite an old man. 'You surely don't think I stay here out of choice? Indeed, I sometimes like to refer to myself as the prisoner.' A little chuckle came from the darkness.

Alys was about to ask him what was so funny when she sensed movement before her. Fingers grasped at her and caught hold of her shirt then she felt the weight of the other woman as she stumbled into Alys then dropped down to the ground once more.

'Who are you? Do you bring news? How long 'til the slaver gets here?' the woman shrieked, her voice now strident, demanding and filled with terror. Alys could not make out her face, but the stench of her breath betrayed her close proximity. Fighting the urge to pull away, Alys spread out her arms to the extent of her chain and enfolded the woman in a clumsy embrace. Her hands encountered slightly built, bony shoulders and long, unbound hair, tangled and matted with filth. The woman seemed to dissolve in her arms, sagging against her, returning her hug and clinging on desperately with worryingly strong fingers.

'They killed my Roger,' she sobbed, 'my husband. They cut his throat and laughed as they threw his corpse into the sea. They're going to sell me to a Saracen slave trader. Oh what a fate! We were supposed to be travelling to Ireland to start a new life. Roger took a manor rent from the Earl of Kildare. We were going to resettle there and start our family. We took passage on a merchant ship and were on our way, but the pirates attacked us. They killed everyone else on board and brought me here. I'm young and pretty. They said I'll end up a whore in the harem of a Saracen. Oh cruel, heartless fortune!'

Her words were delivered in a distracted staccato as if reciting something she had learnt by heart and Alys began to suspect that Syr Henry was correct and grief had disturbed this woman's mind. Despite her own sense of despair, Alys patted the woman's matted hair in what she hoped was a reassuring gesture. 'Have courage,' she said, trying to convey a confidence she did not feel. 'I won't accept this. We just need to wait for the right moment then make our escape.'

A low chuckle came from Syr Henry. 'Good luck with that,' he said. 'I've heard that before. Never seen anyone manage to do it, though.'

'Well maybe you just haven't been here long enough,' Alys retorted. 'There is no way I intend to stay here.'

Syr Henry chuckled again, the sound infuriating Alys further. 'Oh I've been here long enough, my dear. I've been here longer than anyone. Even before the pirates.'

Intrigue replaced some of Alys's anger. 'You mean you weren't captured by Tavish Dhu?'

'Oh no,' Syr Henry replied. 'I was already in here when Robert Bruce granted them the Isle of Man as a base. I was in here before the Scots invaded the island. I've been a prisoner in this dungeon for years.' At the last words the kindly good humour in his voice cracked and something close to a despairing sob burst from his lips. 'Years and years,' he said, much more quietly.

Alys did not know what to say so she kept her mouth closed.

'Would you believe I once was keeper of this castle? I was in charge of the whole island,' he said. 'Oh the irony of it! Now I'm a prisoner in my own dungeon.'

'What happened?' Alys asked.

A heavy sigh came out of the darkness. 'It was my own

stupidity. I was sent here in the year of Our Lord, thirteen hundred and ten—'

'That's six years ago!' Alys interrupted, shuddering at the thought of how long this man had been shut away in this dark hellhole.

'Is it? I suppose it must be now.' Syr Henry sighed again. 'I came to be governor here in the name of King Edward of England.'

'So you're a prisoner of war?' Alys said, surmising that he had ended up in this dungeon after the Scots took the Isle of Man.

'No,' the old knight said. 'If only I was they might have ransomed me. No, I got a bit greedy. I thought no one would know what I was up to out in this godforsaken island. I thought I'd line my pockets and set myself up for a wealthy retirement. I diverted a portion of the taxes I raised into my own coffers and thought, well, what King Edward doesn't know won't hurt him. And why not? Then the king sent a new seneschal to the island, Piers Gaveston.'

'Gaveston?' Alys echoed. It was the second time she had heard the name of the king's former favourite in the last ten days. 'King Edward's lover.' She heard a chuckle in the darkness. Despite his horrific plight, Syr Henry seemed remarkably jovial. Maybe his mind had gone too.

'Lover, eh? Is that what they say these days?' he said.

'Many do. They also say King Edward loved Gaveston like a brother,' Alys said.

'Like a brother, eh?' Syr Henry's old voice took on a bitter edge. 'I remember Piers Gaveston. He was a haughty young shit who thought himself better than everyone else. He had the skills to back it up, mind you. He was a superb horseman and one of the best jousters I've ever seen. The problem was he knew it and wanted to make sure everyone else did too. There wasn't an ounce of humility in that man's whole body. He dressed in the finest fashions, wore armour that was pretentious and showy beyond anything needed for personal protection. Polished to gleam like silver in the sun it was. He used to prance about with the pelt of a leopard worn over it, and we all knew what he was trying to say there, don't we?'

Alys didn't, and said so.

'Who else called himself "The Leopard", my dear?' Syr Henry said. 'Surely you're not so young that you don't remember King Edward's royal father, the first King of England to bear the name Edward? He liked to refer to himself as "the Leopard". It was a term of abuse at first. A troubadour wrote a song about the Battle of Lewes and in it compared the old king to a leopard: powerful and unpredictable. He liked that and kept the title, though everyone else called him Longshanks on account of his great height.

'Anyway, Gaveston caught me fiddling the books and put me in here. He then moved on to somewhere else. That was when the Scots took the island. They weren't sure what to do with me. I'm of noble birth, but also a criminal, so who would pay a ransom for me? So they just left me here. I think I was forgotten about for a time after that. The pirates keep me in case I have potential as a hostage. Perhaps they think one of my noble relatives might someday remember about me and pay a ransom. Whatever; I suppose I should be grateful someone still sees use in me, otherwise I'd be dead.'

Alys was still trying to work out what the old man had said about the first King Edward and Gaveston. 'Why would the king's lover want to adopt the same nickname as the king's father?' she wondered aloud.

'What was it you said earlier, my dear?' Syr Henry lowered his voice to a conspiratorial whisper. 'King Edward loved Gaveston like a brother?'

'Well yes, but...' Alys gasped and her jaw dropped open as it dawned on her what the old man was implying. 'By God's blood,' she breathed, 'Gaveston was Edward's brother, not his lover.'

'I think we are finally getting to the point,' the voice in the darkness responded. 'Oh dear. They always said I talked too much and here I am running off my mouth again to someone I've hardly met. I can't help myself. But I've had no one to talk to in the last year except that howling madwoman you just managed to calm down. Yes, that's the conclusion I came to, my dear: Gaveston was the illegitimate son of Edward Longshanks. Imagine the scandal that would have caused if it became known? King Edward and his Queen Eleanor were renowned throughout the world as the epitome of courtly love. She even went on crusade with him so they wouldn't be parted. That chivalric facade would have been ruined had people found out he'd got a bastard son on another woman. Old Longshanks couldn't have that. His legitimate son and heir knew the truth, though.'

'And the barons of England killed Gaveston,' Alys said, her astonishment at the scale of the conspiracy making her voice sound vague. 'But they said it was because of his influence over the young Edward.'

'They killed a Prince of England – illegitimate, maybe, but

still the son of a king,' Syr Henry said. 'All the more reason to concoct a story to cover the truth, don't you think?'

In the darkness, Alys suddenly remembered what she had heard Mortimer and Isabella discussing in the bath. "If he finds out the truth about who Gaveston really is then my son may never sit on the throne," Isabella had said. Had Gaveston somehow survived the assassination? If so, it would be an incredible feat. Everyone knew Gaveston had been beheaded. Could it be true? And if it was, and Mortimer and Isabella were plotting against King Edward, then the existence of a rival claimant, albeit illegitimate, would cause all sorts of issues for them if they tried to replace her husband on the throne, either with themselves or with Isabella's son.

'Oh well. It hardly matters now.' The old knight sighed in the darkness. 'I doubt I'll ever see the light of day again, and where you are going no one will be interested in old tales of King Edward Longshanks and his sainted Spanish Queen.'

'I mean to escape,' Alys said, a gritty element of determination in her voice.

The old knight chuckled softly. If she could see him, Alys was sure he would be shaking his head. 'I admire your determination, my dear,' he said. 'But I've been here a long time and seen a lot of other prisoners come through here. In all those years not one person has managed to escape. I'm sorry, but you'd best resign yourself to the fact that you don't have a hope in Hell.'

57

Carrickfergus Castle

As he walked towards the gatehouse of Carrickfergus Castle, Guilleme le Poer could guess the reason for his summons. Edward Bruce's deadline to hand over Galiene was upon them. This could only be about that.

The castle was quiet. There had been little activity since the raid, apart from a few arrows shot over the curtain wall, and the Scots had stopped that when they realised they were just giving the defenders missiles to throw back at them. After that, life in the castle had settled back into the quotidian routine of siege warfare, while Death, deprived of taking more victims by violence, resumed his stealthy, drawn-out strategy of stealing lives through starvation and disease.

Le Poer rapped on the wooden door of the castellan's chamber. Hearing a curt 'Come in', he rattled the latch and entered. Henry de Thrapston stood at a wooden writing table – its top scratched, gouged and stained with ink, witness to the many years it had served him. It was the workbench from which de Thrapston administered the central fortress of the Earldom of Ulster. Le Poer mused wryly that now Carrickfergus Castle was all that remained of the earldom not in Scottish hands, the castellan was essentially running the whole country from that scarred desk.

The chamber was circular and several chests sat against the wall. There was also a huge, open-fronted cabinet that was absolutely stuffed with parchment scrolls, the administrative documentation of the earldom. As le Poer entered, de Thrapston set down a wooden bowl that was half full of steaming broth. A gamey, meaty aroma filled the room that immediately provoked a gurgling rumble from le Poer's starved guts.

Beside the keeper of the castle there stood a foot soldier of the garrison. Le Poer narrowed his eyes when he saw that it was MacKillen, the sergeant who had made such a fuss when Galiene and he had arrived at the gate. The sergeant's presence dispelled any lingering doubts about the purpose of this meeting.

'Ah, Guilleme,' de Thrapston said, his attempt at a smile failing miserably. 'Thank you for coming so promptly.'

'Henry,' said le Poer and made a casual salute to the castellan. 'I imagine this is about the girl, right?' He shot a glance in the direction of the sergeant.

'Yes, I'm afraid it is.' De Thrapston lowered his gaze, his cheeks flushing red behind his beard. 'Edward Bruce's time limit to hand her over is approaching and Sergeant MacKillen here came to inform me that it is the opinion of the men that we should hand her over.'

'Oh he did, did he?' Le Poer, his voice laden with scorn, looked again at the gaunt soldier in the dirty surcoat bearing the red cross on a yellow background over his chain mail. The man had removed his kettle-shaped helmet, revealing lank strands of greasy black hair that were stuck to his forehead. He had a large frame and would have been well built had the famine and starvation of the siege not taken its toll.

'I thought you were in charge here, Henry. Since when do we take orders from the common soldiery?'

A look of anger flashed in the sergeant's hollow eyes but he remained silent. He was in the presence of two members of the nobility, after all.

Looking up at le Poer, de Thrapston sighed and tilted his head to one side. 'The garrison of this castle, Guilleme, are also a fine bunch of men who have sacrificed everything to keep this fortress out of Scottish hands. And I do mean everything. Homes, family; half of them have lost their lives.' His voice bore a tone of reproach. 'If we want them to continue to defend the castle in the king's name then we have to take their wishes into account.'

'And your wish is to throw an innocent little girl to the Scottish wolves outside, is it?' le Poer said, turning his full, disdainful gaze on MacKillen.

'Food is scarce enough, sire,' MacKillen said, his voice heavy with apology, whether real or feigned it was hard to tell. 'And she's an extra person who uses up our supplies but contributes nothing, which makes her a useless mouth. Useless mouths are one of the main dangers to any besieged garrison.'

De Thrapston nodded. Le Poer did not respond but in terms of military strategy, he had to admit the sergeant was correct.

'On the other hand,' MacKillen continued, 'if we hand her over, she could be of some use. We all heard Edward Bruce's offer, sire, and we need that food. We could maybe hold out 'til the summer if we got it.'

Le Poer shook his head in disgust.

'I'm just the messenger, sire,' MacKillen added. 'It's the collective opinion of the lads.'

'Yes, I'm sure it is,' le Poer said, in a way that suggested the exact opposite. He knew MacKillen's type: a jumped-up nobody taking advantage of the situation to raise his own importance. Le Poer was certain that the opinion of the garrison had been well moulded by a few choice words and strongly stated opinions from Sergeant MacKillen. The man was far from the mere spokesman he claimed to be. He was an upstart and a troublemaker, typical of a rising class of professional soldiers raised by the war to a status where they felt they could push the boundaries of the position society and God had put them in. Men like MacKillen thought they could challenge – influence, even – the commands of their betters. Le Poer's blood boiled at the thought that times had changed so much that nobles like himself could now be beholden to men such as this common soldier. In the old days, le Poer's father would have strung MacKillen up for his insolence, yet now de Thrapston had little choice but to acquiesce to the man's demands. Such upheavals of the natural order – an order ordained by God – could lead to no good. What would be next? le Poer wondered, barely able to contain his anger. A revolt of the peasants?

De Thrapston noticed le Poer's mood and shook his head in warning. 'I'm sorry, Guilleme,' he said, his tone suddenly stern, 'but this is the course we have to take. We're in a desperate situation and cannot afford to be sentimental. The girl has to go. MacKillen is correct. We need the food Bruce is offering. Without it we'll have no choice but to surrender or starve to death. We cannot hold out much longer.'

'The rat boy has been bringing in bumper crops for the last few days,' le Poer began to appeal. 'The rats breed so quickly there is no sign of them running out.'

De Thrapston held up a hand to stop him talking any more but did not respond straight away. He glanced at the bowl of broth on the table, a look of disgust coming to his face at being reminded what type of meat it was made from. His Adam's apple bobbed several times as he swallowed, trying to keep the contents of his stomach down. After a moment he regained control of himself and was able to speak again.

'That's true,' he agreed. 'Lately, somehow, he's been able to catch twice as many as usual, but we can't live on rat meat, Guilleme. We won't have a tooth left in our heads and our bodies are erupting in sores already. We need proper food. Bruce says he will supply it if we hand the girl over. In the grand scheme of things it is a small price to pay. We will just have to trust that she will come to no harm.'

'And what will we tell Savage?' le Poer snapped. 'Will you look him in the eye and say that you swapped his daughter for a few sacks of grain?'

'Not sacks of grain, Guilleme, but the lives of all the people in this castle for whom I am responsible.' De Thrapston straightened his back, returning le Poer's glare with one every bit as indignant. 'I will tell him the truth. I have a duty, Guilleme, and that is to keep this castle out of

Scottish hands until I am told otherwise. And by God I will do whatever it takes to fulfil that duty.'

The two men stared at each other across the room for a few seconds in angry silence.

'I suppose you want me to tell her?' le Poer said eventually, with a heavy sigh as he accepted defeat.

De Thrapston nodded, his face softening. 'I think it would be best coming from you. Will you go and fetch her back here, please?'

Le Poer glanced sideways at MacKillen, sure he had spotted a smirk of triumph on the sergeant's face.

'I don't know where she is,' le Poer said. 'I told you that.'

'Well find her. She must be somewhere in the castle,' de Thrapston retorted. 'Unless she's grown wings and flown away. MacKillen here will help you search. I suggest you start in the keep.'

'Me, sire?' The sergeant looked suddenly uncomfortable. The smirk had disappeared.

'Yes, you.' De Thrapston turned his confrontational stare in the sergeant's direction. 'You demanded this. What's wrong? Are you not man enough to carry it through yourself?'

'N-no, sire, I m-mean yes...' MacKillen stammered. 'That is... it's just they say the keep is haunted. It's not just me, sire. None of the garrison will go in there these days.'

'Oh, for God's sake – get out of my sight, the pair of you!' de Thrapston said with an exasperated sweep of his arm. 'And don't come back 'til you find that girl.'

Le Poer opened the door. He held a hand out, a sardonic expression on his face, indicating that the sergeant should precede him. MacKillen, looking worried, left the room.

With one more look at the castellan, le Poer followed. As he left he caught a final sight of Henry de Thrapston as he turned a queasy eye on the remainder of the rat broth in his bowl.

58

As the two men marched across the castle courtyard in ill-disposed silence, le Poer, glancing at MacKillen's face, noticed how pale it had become and how the man's gaze darted to and fro in evident nervous distraction. Le Poer was astonished to realise that the sergeant was genuinely afraid of going to the keep.

'Pull yourself together, man,' le Poer said gruffly. 'Don't tell me you believe all this ghost nonsense. You're a soldier. Surely you aren't superstitious?'

Even as he said it, le Poer realised how silly that statement was. Soldiers spent their days surrounded by death. If they weren't dealing it out, they were watching their friends and comrades being taken by it, and all the while anticipating the final sword blow, the speeding arrow or the spear thrust that would bring their own. For that reason, the merest detail took on an almost religious significance. Good omens were fervently watched for. Armour was always laced up a certain way, boots put on in a specific order, swords always sheathed to a certain place on the waist – all little rituals repeated in exactly the same way every time because that was what had been done on the occasions before when death had been confronted and avoided, and were therefore deemed "lucky". If anything, there were few people in the world who were less superstitious than soldiers.

The sergeant blushed, much to le Poer's amusement.

'It's been heard by many,' MacKillen said, trying to cover his embarrassment with aggression. 'Horrible wails and strange shrieks when there's no one there. They say it's a ghost that lives in the well; the spirit of a wee boy who fell down it and drowned, but the chaplain says it's the Devil himself calling up the well from Hell.'

Thinking that the chaplain should know better, le Poer tutted, raising his hand to brush a strand of long hair away from his eyes.

At the centre of the keep on the ground floor was a well, sunk deep into the rock to tap into a freshwater spring that bubbled up from far beneath the surface. Although the castle was surrounded on all sides by the sea, the water that flowed into the well was drinkable. It was what made the Rock of Fergus, on which the castle had been built, the perfect defensive position. To le Poer, the idea that there was a ghost down the well was simply laughable, but it was clear the sergeant was scared witless.

'I've yet to meet anything that cold steel can't deal with, MacKillen,' he said, patting the hilt of his sword. 'Come on.'

They went through the inner gate and mounted the steps to the door of the keep. Le Poer's contempt of the man intensified as he noted with the light sheen of sweat glistening on the sergeant's pale face that had nothing to do with the effort of walking around in his armour. Irritated, le Poer opened the door and strode into the keep. MacKillen hastily crossed himself, took a deep breath then followed.

The immensely thick, cold stone walls blotted out the wind and noise of outside and surrounded them like a tomb. At this level there were no windows and the room they entered was lit by torches. From one corner a spiral staircase gave access both to the upper reaches of the tower and the cellars below. The room served as a general storage area for the garrison and around the walls, glittering in the yellow light, were stacks of helmets and sheaves of spears. Chain mail coats hung on racks like severed human torsos. In the middle of the floor was the castle well. It was sealed shut with a round wooden cover and above it, dangling from a wooden pulley attached to a ceiling joist, was a rope and hook.

There was no one around; the keep was silent as the grave.

'Galiene?' le Poer called, his voice bouncing off the walls. There was no reply.

'Listen!' the sergeant breathed, one hand held up, right ear cocked, eyes wide.

'What?' Staring at him in annoyance, le Poer noted with increasing contempt that the man's bottom lip was trembling slightly.

'I can hear something,' MacKillen said in a half-strangled voice. 'It's coming from the well.'

The sergeant seemed so convinced that le Poer stopped tutting and fell silent, just in case there was really something there. As he strained to listen, his eyebrows knitted. Sure enough, he could hear something. Distant and barely audible, an ethereal sound that rose and fell as if coming from a long way away. There was a faint echo to it and it did indeed seem to be coming from the well. He looked at

MacKillen and flicked his head in that direction to indicate silently that they should take a closer look.

Both men approached, MacKillen more reluctantly than le Poer, though even Guilleme, despite himself, felt the hairs on his arms raise. He bent forward and raised the wooden lid. Beneath it the well shaft plunged into blackness. There was nothing to be seen, but the strange sound intensified, echoing up the stone-lined walls of the well.

'It's coming from below,' le Poer commented somewhat unnecessarily, looking up at MacKillen. The man's face had blanched even further; his mouth turned down on both sides as if he was about to cry. 'But listen – it doesn't sound like the howls of Satan to me.'

Stung by le Poer's mockery, MacKillen frowned and listened more intently. The sound drifting up from below was pleasant and changed tone, rising and falling to make a tune.

'It's singing,' le Poer said. 'Someone is singing down there and if I'm not mistaken, they have an incredible voice. I once had to impersonate a troubadour and spent some time working with a bard so I know what I'm talking about.'

'The Devil has the power to appear in a pleasing shape or make a beautiful sound,' MacKillen responded. 'He does it to entice sinners into his clutches. I've heard of water spirits whose singing lures ships' crews to sail onto rocks to their death. Others lure people into lakes to drown them. Maybe that's happening here.'

Le Poer shook his head, his face displaying an annoyed expression that betrayed the fact he had come to the end of his patience with the sergeant. 'I think I know what's going on here. Come with me,' he ordered. Dropping the lid of the well with a bang he strode away.

With the sergeant trailing along reluctantly behind him, le Poer grabbed a torch from a wall bracket and crossed to the staircase. Much to MacKillen's apparent dismay they began to descend rather than climb, completing four turns around the spiral steps until they came to the wooden door at the bottom of the stairway. Le Poer opened it and they entered the cool gloominess of the castle cellars.

The torch sent long shadows across the floor, its illumination enhanced by a couple more torches that guttered in brackets on the walls. The shadows danced and flickered around the empty crates and barrels stacked around the vaulted room with its very low ceiling. Down here the strange sound was louder and more distinct. Not strange at all, in fact, thought le Poer, but the sound of a young woman singing.

He pointed at a cylindrical tower, the walls constructed of stone, which rose from floor to ceiling about midway along the room. 'The well shaft,' he whispered. 'It goes from the floor above through this vault into the bedrock below. There must be an opening in here and the sound travels up into the keep above. The echoes in the shaft give the sound its unearthly quality. This is the truth behind your ghost, MacKillen. Listen to that voice. It's exquisite!'

The sound in the cellars was enchanting, echoing around the vault and delighting the ears. It was beautiful; crystal clear, pitch-perfect and haunting. The sergeant looked confused, his eyes sparkling in the torchlight and his mouth dropping open to reveal his stained, broken and chipped teeth.

To le Poer's surprise he realised that the sudden glistening in MacKillen's eyes was caused by unshed tears. After months of starvation, hardship, violence and death, the effect on the hardened warrior of something so beautiful, coming so unexpectedly, was devastating. His walls of reserve and gruff cynicism dissolved in the purity of the singing.

'It's the voice of an angel,' MacKillen sobbed.

'Not quite.' Le Poer smiled and took a step forward. As he did so, a rat, disturbed by his presence scurried across the floor from somewhere near the door. Claws clicking on stone it scuttled for the safety of a nearby barrel, moving so fast as to be barely discernible in the torchlight, a mere blur of grey-brown fur.

There was a click from further along the cellar. Something else shot across le Poer's vision and when he looked again the rat had stopped short of the barrel and now lay on its back, twitching and squirming, transfixed through the body by a small arrow. Simultaneously, the beautiful singing stopped.

A young girl emerged from the shadows between two very large barrels at the far end of the cellar. Her curly blonde hair cascaded around her shoulders and even in the gloom they could see the flash of her bright green eyes. In one hand she carried a small crossbow and the grin on her face showed how pleased she was at completing such a difficult shot.

'Got it!' She spoke to no one in particular and in a delighted voice.

'Galiene?' le Poer said.

Noticing the two men for the first time Galiene froze, her smile replaced by a look of fearful uncertainty.

'Don't worry.' Smiling broadly le Poer turned back to slap a hand on MacKillen's shoulder, laughing at the amazement that lingered on the man's face. 'I think the sergeant here has just realised you are far from the "useless mouth" he thought you were. Eh, MacKillen?'

Mouth open, the dumbfounded sergeant simply nodded.

59

Dublin

The Earl of Ulster, Richard de Burgh, was far from happy. In fact he was downright furious. He took another angry swig of brandywine, relishing the fiery taste that blazed its way down to his gut. He had drunk a lot, he knew, much more than was seemly for a man in his position, but he welcomed the way the drink relaxed him and blunted the edge of the emotions raging inside him. His doctor had told him that his humours were out of balance. Too much black and yellow bile were causing his temperament to be too choleric and too melancholy. Perhaps that was true, but if so the brandywine seemed to go some way to counteracting the bile.

But did he not have every reason to feel this way? His anger blazed again and he took another gulp from his silver goblet.

The earl was slouched in a chair in the solar room of his town house in Dublin. The house was spacious, modern and expensive, near the city centre and all in all a dwelling suitable for a magnate like him. It had two storeys, seven bedrooms, a feasting hall, kitchens, cellars, servants' quarters and this room, the solar, which was de Burgh's favourite. It ran the full length of the back of the house and its ceiling reached right up to the roof. Along the back wall were tall windows glazed with terribly expensive glass that allowed in the maximum amount of sunlight, giving the room its name. In happier times his wife had used the extra light in here to work on her embroideries and he had spent many pleasant hours talking with her as she sewed. Now Margaret was dead and he was alone in the house, his solitary existence yet another reminder of just how much he had lost.

A mere year and a half ago, he had been the most powerful man in Ireland. As both Earl of Ulster and Baron of Connaught, his wealth had been enormous; he commanded two armies and was lord of seven castles. How times had changed. Now Edward Bruce ruled Ulster and the rebel O'Connor had stolen de Burgh's lands in Connaught. Margaret had died, his armies had been defeated and scattered to the four provinces and all but one of his fortresses had fallen, and that one – Carrickfergus – was besieged with little hope of recovery. Now all he had was this house. It was one of the biggest in Dublin, but what did that matter? Its very size was a taunting reminder of how far he had fallen. Fortune had spun her wheel and now he, once at the apex, was plunged down to the nadir.

A short time before his word had been law, but now even his prospective son-in-law mocked him. The thought caused another surge of bile in his belly and he sucked down more brandywine, his features falling into a sneer of impotent rage. The little shit. This time two years ago John de Bermingham had been no one of consequence, the second son of a family who were de Burgh's own vassals. A few easy victories and now the jumped-up nobody was the man of the moment, his star risen higher than the earl's, which had fallen so far that he'd been pushed into arranging a marriage between his daughter and de Bermingham in an attempt to retain some influence and standing. De Burgh gave a bitter snort. Such were the fortunes of war. To add insult to injury he now found that the arrogant bastard had duped him. He, the Earl of Ulster, had been played like a pawn in a game of chess.

He had learnt of de Bermingham's deception earlier through Brian MacJordan, his cleric. Outraged, he had stormed into the justiciar's chamber at the castle demanding to know why his cousin's ransom would not be paid as agreed and why he had not been privy to the alternative plan. The supercilious wee shit had stated blithely that the information had been restricted to those who "absolutely needed to know, in order to ensure the success of the mission". The response had been delivered with deadly seriousness, but de Burgh couldn't help but discern an insolent half-smile playing on de Bermingham's young face.

If he was completely honest with himself, it was the secrecy that worried de Burgh rather more than the change of plan. Despite his misfortunes, he had thought himself as still right at the heart of government, still a player in the games of power; but this told him he had been deluding himself. Now he had to decide on his future. Those who had been within the inner circle of power were never safe for long once outside it. To put it simply, they knew too much, too many secrets, the truth behind too many clandestine agreements to be allowed to just walk away. For de Burgh the game had now shifted to one gone beyond who held power in Ireland. It was now about his very survival.

The earl went to take another sup of brandywine; however, he saw his cup was empty. He stood up, the room swaying around him slightly. He intended to call for a servant, but noticed that his butler was hovering near the door. The old man, his eyes downcast, coughed apologetically. It was his job to run the earl's household and govern his wine cellar, but he was clearly nervous at interrupting his master in his current mood.

'Begging your pardon, sire,' he said, 'but there is someone here requesting an audience with you.'

De Burgh frowned, wondering how long the servant had been standing there and fervently hoping that in his drunken bitterness he had not descended as far as muttering to himself. 'Who is it?'

'A German knight, my lord. He says his name is Syr Heinrich von Mahlberg and he is here on the business of the Lord Mortimer.'

The earl narrowed his eyes. Mortimer was another of de Bermingham's breed of two-faced politicians. What did he want with him? 'Very well, send him in,' he said with a wave of his hand. 'And bring me more brandywine.'

De Burgh settled back into his chair. Before long a tall, heavily built man with blond hair was ushered into the room. He wore a leather jerkin and thigh-length hunting boots. A sword was buckled at his waist and, as he regarded the earl with cold blue eyes, de Burgh was reminded of a young wolf looking at a field of new-born lambs.

'Where's that drink?' de Burgh barked at his butler. The servant, now bearing a clay jug, scurried forward and refilled the proffered silver goblet.

'Brandywine?' the earl offered the knight.

As von Mahlberg shook his head, de Burgh was sure he saw the flicker of a smirk cross the German's face, but told himself he was getting paranoid. Not everyone could be laughing at him, could they?

'Thank you, no,' the German replied, his French accented but perfectly understandable. 'I cannot stay long.'

The earl shrugged and took a swig of the dark amber liquid. 'So what does Mortimer want of me?'

'My Lord Mortimer has sent me to Ireland to track down a former vassal of yours, one Richard Savage,' the German said, pulling off his embroidered gauntlets. 'I am informed he came to Dublin.'

'What does Mortimer want with Savage?' the earl said, puzzled. Why would one of the most powerful men in England even know who a landless nobody like Savage was, never mind have business with him?

'His lordship engaged him on a special mission – one that Savage has reneged on,' von Mahlberg said, hands behind his back, as he nonchalantly strolled closer to where de Burgh sat. 'Lord Mortimer has sent me to rectify that situation.'

De Burgh frowned. 'You're too late. He's part of an expedition force that sailed north this morning.'

Von Mahlberg nodded. 'I am also aware of that,' he said, looking down at the floor then up again to meet the earl's gaze. 'That is why I have come to you.'

'What do you think I can do?' the earl said bitterly. 'If

Mortimer thinks I'm still relevant then he's sadly mistaken. I've lost everything: my lands, my armies, my influence. I'm no longer in the game of power, sir. Tell Mortimer to talk to my future son-in-law, de Bermingham. He's the justiciar, not me.' It was all de Burgh could do to stop from spitting with disgust into the rushes on the floor.

The German was smirking – it was definite this time – and de Burgh felt a surge of anger. He rose to his feet, glowering at the insolent knight. Before he could say anything, von Mahlberg held up a conciliatory hand.

'Calm yourself, sire, I mean no offence,' he said. 'I doubt my lord de Bermingham would be able to help in this situation. Unfortunately he has proven himself rather short-sighted. I'm afraid he seems incapable of seeing beyond this little regional conflict to appreciate the bigger picture. He cannot understand that sometimes one must forfeit some battles in order to win the war. You, however—' von Mahlberg nodded in de Burgh's direction '—are more like Lord Mortimer. The games you play go beyond who rules a few bogs and mountains. You appreciate that this conflict is part of a wider one and the winner will end up the most powerful man in Europe. You and my Lord Mortimer play games for thrones.'

Disconcerted, de Burgh continued staring at the man for a moment, then nodded. He sat down with a bump and took a desultory gulp of brandywine. When he finally spoke his voice was hoarse. 'This time last year, von Mahlberg, I was as rich and powerful as a king. If I had wanted to, I could have called myself "King of Ireland", which is how Edward Bruce now crows about himself. Now? Now I have nothing.' He paused then speaking slowly in a vain attempt not to slur his words, he banged his fist on his knee and said, 'But I will be back, sir. By God's blood and balls, I swear I'll get back every inch of my territory, every castle, every manor and—'

'My Lord Mortimer understands that,' the German interrupted, his voice edged with impatience. 'He knows of your qualities and your skills in statecraft. This is why he instructed me to make contact with you, sire. I am given to understand that you had an arrangement with Bruce to gain the release of your cousin William, but that it has since been thwarted?'

The earl nodded. It seemed there was little that escaped the ears of Mortimer and his agents, even when he was not in the country.

'I will speak frankly with you. Lord Mortimer wants Savage dead,' the German said. 'And whilst he does not want the Scots to achieve ultimate victory in Ireland, neither does he want his English rivals to be successful in defeating them: not before he can do so himself. My lord is confident he can deal with Edward Bruce, but only when the time is right. In the meantime, his victory will be enhanced greatly, and his subsequent status as the greatest lord in Ireland, England or Scotland will be much more secure if other great men have failed in the attempt before him. He has the full support of the queen in this endeavour, of course.' Von Mahlberg's eyes slid sideways and he hastily added, 'And the king.'

De Burgh raised a sceptical eyebrow. This smacked of treason. He looked up, realising the full extent of Mortimer's ruthless ambition and his mouth moved into a bitter smile. Baron Mortimer was in so many ways like a younger version of himself; in the days when he let no one stand in his way.

'Perhaps,' von Mahlberg continued, 'from our mutual point of view the best outcome would be if this expedition to relieve Carrickfergus were to fail? You would then be free to continue with your original plan and secure the release of your cousin with the supplies; Syr John de Bermingham would appear as a rash, impetuous young fool, and the people would clamour for a greater man to save the day – someone with a proven track record of victory. Someone like Lord Roger Mortimer, who once successful will of course be very generous in rewarding those who helped him in his struggle.' He smiled down at the earl.

There were a few moments of silence as de Burgh contemplated what von Mahlberg had just said. Was this some sort of trap? Was this German swordsman really sent by Mortimer or was he sent by de Bermingham with the intention of probing his prospective father-in-law's loyalty? If true, what von Mahlberg said had some appeal. If the expedition to Carrickfergus failed then de Bermingham would certainly look foolish; every inch the rash young man lacking in experience, which de Burgh knew him to be. How long then would he be able to hold on to the office of justiciar? Once de Bermingham's star fell then the opportunity would exist for his own to rise again, and with his cousin William by his side – and even more important, the clan of Irish troops from the west that he would bring with him – he could start to rebuild his power.

'And where do I fit into this plan?' he said, eventually. His throat was still dry, his voice gravelly. He reached for his goblet.

'I just need your help to get north into Ulster fast so that I can warn the Scots that de Mandeville is coming,' the

German said. 'I understand that through your negotiations you may have contacts within the Scottish army? All I ask is that you connect me with them and vouch for me. If you do, I will ensure that the right people – on both sides – know the part you have played in the eventual downfall of Carrickfergus Castle.'

'You intend to go north yourself?' de Burgh asked. 'Would it not be safer to send a messenger?'

Von Mahlberg smiled but the expression was unpleasant. 'You are forgetting the other part of the deal. I need to get close to Savage so I can deal with him.'

His mind in turmoil, de Burgh raised the goblet and swallowed a deep draught. After a few more moments of silent contemplation he finally nodded.

'There is a man called Harper...' he began.

60

Isle of Man

Alys was woken by a commotion outside. The dungeon was completely dark but from the tiny window high above there came the noise of excited shouting and the clatter of running feet. Outside the door she heard the rattling of the key in the lock and the metallic scraping of bolts being withdrawn.

The prisoners groaned together. It was not the first time they had been disturbed by a commotion. Yesterday there had been a similar alarm in the castle outside the window. The sound of people shouting and running around, bells ringing and whistles blowing had all disturbed the scant rest the prisoners were able to get in the dank, vermin-infested, foul-smelling cell. After a time it had all died away, but Alys, hearing voices outside the door, had crawled across the cell and pressed her ear to the keyhole. Someone was telling the jailer that a flotilla of ships had been spotted sailing to the south of the island. It seemed there were too many of them to attack without heavy losses and so, once it was observed that the ships were on a heading to pass by and were not coming to the island, they were allowed to go on their way unmolested.

Quiet had returned after that and the prisoners had once more taken solace in whatever sleep they could get in their brutal surroundings.

This time, however, the heavy door squeaked open and the darkness was illuminated by torchlight spilling in from the jailer's quarters outside. The hunchback stood silhouetted in the doorway and towering beside him like a giant was the pirate named Pol.

'Your boat is here,' Pol said, leering at the prisoners as they struggled to their feet. 'The slaver has arrived.'

Alys squinted in the light and for the first time was able to make out her companions. The woman, whose name she had learnt was Eleanor (*named after the late Queen*, she had said with a rare smile), was gaunt, her skin blotched red with flea bites and sores; her hair a tangled, filth-clogged mess and her eyes wide, vacant and staring, confirming Alys's suspicion that the experience of incarceration had pushed the young woman beyond reason. Her dress had once been expensive and made of fine green material, but was now torn and smeared with muck from the dungeon floor.

While Eleanor was in a disturbing state, the sight of Syr Henry shocked Alys even more. He looked ancient, an emaciated bag of skin and bones. His hair and beard were white and flowed down around his shoulders and chest in tangled, mucky strands. What was left of his clothing was little more than rags and his skin was so pale it was almost translucent, stretched tight across his skeletal frame. He howled with pain as the light struck his eyes, so long used to the darkness.

'Get the women,' Pol ordered from the doorway.

'Goodbye, my dears,' the old knight said, crumpling to sit back on the floor, his voice laden with sadness. 'I wish you the best of luck.'

As the jailer advanced into the room Eleanor made a little whimpering sound. The hunchback grabbed her and Alys by their elbows and with eager, questing fingers began shoving them towards the door.

'Careful with them,' Pol said in warning. 'Tavish doesn't want any bruises on them giving Ibn the excuse to drop the price.'

The jailer shook his head in disappointment, but he loosened his grip, allowing Alys and Eleanor to shuffle out at their own pace. Once through the door the jailer prodded them in the direction of the stairs. As she tried to mount the first step, the shackles round her ankles stopped Eleanor from lifting her leg high enough and she tripped, falling heavily onto the slimy stone. She let out a howl of dismay and Pol rushed over to pull her to her feet again. His concern that she may have bruised or scraped her face was as palpable as his relief when he saw that this was not so.

'We can't climb the stairs with these shackles on,' Alys pointed out. 'Can't you take them off?'

Pol frowned for a moment then nodded at the hunchback and pointed at the women's shackles. 'Take them off. Just the leg irons mind, not the rest.'

Alys grimaced, disappointed that all her bonds had not been removed. At least it was something, she thought, still fervently hoping for an opportunity to escape. Having her legs freed improved her chances of running, if only slightly.

Once the shackles were off they made their way up the steps to the castle courtyard. A group of four armed pirates were waiting for them and fell into line around the two women, Pol and the jailer. This further dismayed Alys, as now she was completely surrounded by her captors. As they marched her and Eleanor out of the gate and across the drawbridge, she drew into her lungs a deep, appreciative breath of cool sea air, relishing its clean, briny taste and fresh aroma after the cloying stench of the dungeon. Above her head sea birds wheeled, their plaintive cries echoing the growing despair in her own heart.

After the short walk to the quay they found Tavish Dhu standing, hands behind his back, waiting for them. Through the mouth of the harbour, beyond the three docked pirate ships, a tall ship was approaching. It was wide-bodied and sailed low in the water. The deck was stacked high with crates and barrels and it sported two masts. From each one billowed long, triangular sails, hung on a long yardarm mounted at an angle to the mast, driven taut by the wind and curved like Saracen scimitar. There were several crew members on the deck, their heads wrapped in the long, winding headdresses that obscured their faces, as worn in Outremer and the deserts of the east, which she had heard Richard talk of from his days there. She did not need to see the dark-skinned man dressed in flowing white robes standing at the steering oar to know that this ship was what some called a dhow. It was undoubtedly a Moorish ship from Andalusia and the slave trader who had come to bear her into bondage.

As the dhow pulled alongside the quay and ropes were thrown to draw it closer, Tavish Dhu cast his appraising gaze over the two hapless women to check their condition for the upcoming sales negotiations. He shot a look of disgust at Eleanor, who stood head bowed, sobbing uncontrollably, mire-clogged hair hanging down to obscure her features. Pushing her forehead back with one hand, he peered into her face then motioned to Pol who stood behind them.

'Hold her hair so she keeps her head up,' he commanded. 'Make sure Ibn can see her pretty face.'

As Tavish turned his attention to Alys, she stood with her head up, back straight, glaring in defiance directly into his eyes.

The pirate gave a derisive little snort. 'Oh you're a haughty one all right,' he said. 'But your new master will break your spirit. I doubt even as bright a fire as that which burns in your belly will last long once you're in a sultan's harem in Andalusia.'

Alys did not reply, unsure if she could keep her voice from cracking. She knew he must see that her bottom lip was trembling and it was all she could do to stop her surge of despair from totally crushing her. She realised now that her hoped-for chance to escape would never come. She would be sold to the slave trader and shipped off to God knows what pagan land, never to return. She would never see Galiene again. She would never be enfolded in Richard's arms again. There was nothing ahead but years of servitude and an early death in foreign lands, worked to exhaustion by some pitiless master. She wanted to break down like Eleanor, to weep with despair, but she would not give the pirate the satisfaction of seeing that.

'Go and bring Ibn here so we can complete this business,' Tavish ordered the jailer, who loped off down the quay towards the Moor's ship.

A sudden crash from somewhere behind them, loud but distant, made them all turn their heads. Seeing a puzzled frown crease Tavish's brow Alys followed his gaze and saw a rising column of black smoke. It was some way beyond the town and the castle – and it was not the only one either. Farther off, up the slope of the mountain, they could now see orange flames and black smoke billowing from what looked like a substantial stone building. The distant sounds of raised voices began to reach their ears. 'That looks like Rushen Abbey,' Tavish said to Pol, his voice indignant. 'It's on fire! What the hell is going on?'

As he spoke, several armed men – some recognisable by their dress as members of the pirate crews and other local warriors – came running from the town to the harbour. All had weapons drawn. Two of them bore bloody wounds to the arms and chest and had clearly been fighting. One of them, seeing Tavish, dashed across the quay to meet him, his boots clattering on the cobblestones.

'Tavish,' he gasped, panting for breath and pulling an arm across his forehead to wipe away the stinging sweat that dripped into his eyes. 'We're under attack.'

'What?' Tavish roared, looking around wildly. 'Who by? Where from?'

The wounded man shook his head, sucking in great gulps of air. 'They took us by surprise. They just seemed to come from nowhere. Hundreds of them. Soldiers. Knights too. They've already burned Rushen Abbey, killed nearly all the men we had up there. Me and a few others just managed to get away. Now they're attacking the town.'

'They can't have jumped out of thin air,' Tavish shouted, spittle flying from his mouth to shower the unfortunate man's face. 'Are they English? Irish?' he demanded, then shook his head, already knowing the answer. Who else would be attacking him? His face fell in dismay. 'Of course they are. How come nobody saw them? Damn it, I had forty men in the garrison up there!'

Another burst of shouting, this time closer to them, made them all turn once more. As Alys looked for its source, she saw the jailer falling like a rag doll to the quayside, bright red blood gushing from a horrific wound where his head met his deformed shoulder. Above him on the deck of the ship stood the Moor slave trader, his long curved scimitar, drawn from its sheath and grasped by its hilt in both his hands. His formerly pristine white robes were now splattered with crimson. Around him his crew were unwrapping their head scarves to reveal white-skinned faces which were far from the expected dusky complexions of Saracens and Moors. They also now bore weapons – spears and swords – and they swarmed off the ship onto the quay, attacking any pirates near enough to engage.

The slave trader had jumped down off the ship after his men and as he landed on the quay he unbuckled his belt and pulled off the blood-soaked white robe. Beneath it he wore a chain mail jerkin and leggings and over the chain mail a dirty white surcoat emblazoned with the red, equal-armed cross of a Templar Knight. He too removed his foreign headdress to reveal close-cropped black hair and beard. Although his face and hands seemed to be stained a darker colour than when she had seen him before, she immediately recognised the man striding towards her and for a moment her vision swam as she almost fainted with relief.

Pol's eyes bulged as he stared in astonishment at the Saracen, curved sword in hand, stalking up the quay, advancing on them as if they were his enemies.

'What does the Saracen think he's doing?' he said.

'That's no Saracen,' Alys said. 'That's my husband!'

61

Tavish Dhu looked left and right. There were enemies advancing from the sea and from the land and he was caught right in the middle. His men were scattered all over and divided, trying to meet both threats. His guts boiled with rage that he had been so obviously duped. This was the very situation – an enemy landing – that he had always sought to avoid. The trebuchet at the mouth of the harbour was now useless, as was the wooden fighting platform he had built along the harbour wall. There was still another course of action open, however. The one reserved for this very eventuality.

'Back to the castle!' the pirate shouted to his men, pushing Pol with the back of his hand. 'We'll fight them from there.'

Pol began to move when Tavish grabbed his sleeve again. 'Take the women,' he ordered. 'We might be able to use them as hostages.'

Pol nodded and grabbed Alys and Eleanor by the upper arms, shoving them forwards with a violence that showed he was no longer concerned about the price they might fetch from the slave trader.

'Richard!' Alys called over her shoulder as she was pushed along, 'Richard, it's me – Alys!'

As they began running towards the castle, Tavish spotted more armed men pouring into the town square beyond the harbour. Some were clad in chain mail with yellow and red tabards over it. Others looked like Irish kerns in long, padded linen jerkins with plaid kilts beneath. Whoever they were, they were not his own men and it looked like the enemy was already in the town. His men were all over the place and he doubted there would be enough of them able to get to the fortress to make defence viable.

Carefully, he slowed down, allowing Pol, oblivious to what he was doing, to push the women on ahead towards the castle.

Then he ducked quickly towards some barrels nearby.

Back on the quay, Savage advanced at a measured jog, careful not to get too far ahead of the others from his ship. He was both amazed and delighted by the Saracen scimitar he bore in his right hand. The curve-bladed sword was heavy but so perfectly balanced that wielding it was almost effortless. A pirate ran at him, axe held high, screaming a war cry and revealing his rotten-toothed mouth. Savage checked his pace and struck with the scimitar. The blade slashed down, its metal flashing like a lightning strike, and his attacker fell backwards, his torso opened from left shoulder to right hip, his scream of rage switching to a screech of pain and horror.

When MacHuylin had mentioned back in Dublin that the pirates were waiting for a Moorish slave trader the plan had become obvious to him. The chances of the Moor who Savage saw doing business in Christ Church Cathedral not being the same man were slim. How many Saracen traders could there be doing business around the Irish Sea? It had not taken long for de Bermingham's men to find him in Dublin and his crescent-sailed ship was just as conspicuous in the docks. The merchant, Ibn Al Bakri, had quickly proved that there was no honour among thieves and told de Bermingham and de Mandeville everything about his current business voyage, which included dealings with both legitimate merchants in Dublin, Bristol and the new town of Liverpool and with lowlife like Tavish Dhu's pirate fleet. Al Bakri also told them everything about the pirate's lair on the Isle of Man and from there it had been simply a matter of plotting their attack.

The opportunity was there to remove the threat of the pirates as well as relieving the siege of Carrickfergus Castle with one expedition, a double blow that could potentially turn the tide of the whole war. It was too good to miss.

MacHuylin, much to his chagrin, had had to stay behind. His wound meant he could not fight and there were no room for passengers on this expedition. A group of the justiciar's soldiers, Meiler among them, took the clothes of Al Bakri's crew. Savage stained his face and hands with burnt umber paint pigment and pulled on the Saracen's flowing robes, then they had added the Moorish ship to the other five ships of the expedition. They sailed south of the Isle of Man, on a heading that suggested they were going to Wales. They had spotted the pirate lookout ships and steadily kept on course. When the patrol ships turned back they had sailed on for a few miles then changed course, swinging around the side of the island on a course to land at Ronaldsway. De Mandeville was familiar with the Isle of Man – his cousin had been an official there before the Scots invaded it – and he knew that the rise of the headland between Ronaldsway and Balley Castle would hide their approach until it was nearly too late.

Meanwhile, Savage and the Moorish ship had sailed back around the coast. Savage was no captain so it was Meiler who had actually steered the ship. All Savage had to do, as the tallest and therefore the most convincing Moor, was stand beside the tiller, pretend to be in charge and try to control the nerves that told him the boat was going to sink.

The firing of the abbey on the hillside had been a signal that they should approach the harbour and thus distract the pirates in the town. There had been a few moments of trepidation as he realised that the large trebuchet that guarded the mouth of the harbour was cocked, a massive stone loaded into its sling and it was pointing in the direction of the ship. A pirate stood at the very end of the harbour wall, left hand to his brow to shade his eyes, right hand raised high above his head, peering hard towards them. Savage realised that if the pirate was not happy with what he saw on board, he would drop his hand as a signal to the crew manning the war engine and the stone would be loosed, smashing through rigging, masts, deck and hull and sending them straight to the bottom of the sea.

Quickly he had jogged to the prow of the boat, resplendent in the Moor's white robes and waved enthusiastically with his dark-stained hand, trying his best to grin and hoping fervently the pirate on lookout was not familiar enough with Ibn Al Bakri that he would see through Savage's disguise.

The ruse had worked and the lookout had waved them into the harbour. At that point Savage felt a surge of new confidence. Luck was clearly on their side today.

Another pirate ran at him, thrusting a spear directly towards his guts. Savage sucked in his stomach, half turned and the point went past him, stabbing air instead of his belly. He brought the scimitar down in an arc, severing the front half of the spear as well as the pirate's left hand that still gripped the front of the shaft. The man shouted, more in anger than pain, and tossed the useless end of the spear shaft at Savage's head. Then pain and realisation of what had just happened hit him and the pirate collapsed to his knees, grasping the bleeding stump of his left arm.

Savage ducked to avoid the thrown shaft and ran forward again. His heart was thudding in his chest and he was out of breath already. It was over a year since he had been in actual battle and the time spent attempting to farm the famine-ridden soil of Gascony had taken its toll. He paused, deliberately trying to force a sense of calm on his spirit and get control of his breathing.

He frowned. Someone had called his name.

Looking around he saw that all the men off the ship were engaged in fighting. Above the clang of metal on metal and the shouts and screams of the wounded he heard it again. It was definitely his name and it was a woman's voice crying out. A familiar woman's voice.

His first reaction was that he was hearing things. Then he spotted a giant of a man at the far end of the harbour shoving what looked like two prisoners in the direction of the castle. One had wild bedraggled hair and a tattered, filthy dress. She was definitely a woman. The other seemed to be wearing the tunic and leggings of a boy but had long, black unbound hair. As she turned to look over her shoulder to shout again their eyes met and he knew immediately who it was.

'Alys!' Savage shouted. He saw from her expression that she knew he had seen her.

Disbelief and a thousand questions began to swim in his mind but he caught sight of movement from the corner of his eye and all thought vanished. The endless hours of training on the Templar training square took over and he instinctively raised the scimitar. With a crash it halted the downward sweep of a longsword inches from his brow. Turning he saw that another pirate, taking advantage of his momentary distraction, had attacked him from the side. An instant later and he would have been dead.

Savage raised his left leg and shoved his boot into the pirate's gut, pushing him backwards. The man staggered away, his sword scraping free along that of the scimitar. Savage advanced, pressing home his advantage, and struck towards the pirate's head. To his surprise the man managed to parry his blow then lunged forward in a stabbing attack aimed at Savage's chest. Savage blocked the sword with the base of the scimitar blade then lunged forward himself, propelling his weapon across the pirate's blade and into his neck. The man's eyes widened as bright red blood burst from his throat and gushed down his front. With a choking gargle he dropped to his knees then fell face first onto the cobblestones.

Savage turned again but to his dismay saw that Alys was now even further away and closer to the gate of the castle. He ran forward, heedless of whether he outran the warriors who could support him or not.

A row of three pirates ran forward to meet him. Savage

swung left and right, the great curved blade making whooping noises as it cut through the air, gouging into one attacker's shoulder and clattering off another's sword. The third man stabbed at him but Savage jumped backwards, away from the point of the blade.

Raised voices, cries of alarm and the thumping of running boots came from the direction of the town and Savage saw more armed men pouring into the harbour. They wore the colours of de Bermingham and Savage was delighted to see de Mandeville leading them. The seneschal was clad in plate armour but the visor of his helmet was raised, allowing him to shout orders to the warriors who surrounded him.

Confused panic overtook the two remaining pirates as they saw they were now heavily outnumbered both by Savage and the rest of the men from the ship and also the mass of warriors flooding the harbour from the town. Savage took advantage and surged forward, his blade coming up in a vicious blow that ripped open the belly of one of the men while he was still looking over his shoulder at de Mandeville. As the thick, luridly coloured loops of his guts unwound out onto the quay his companion turned tail and fled as fast as he could back towards the castle.

Savage pursued him but he could see he was already too late. Alys was being shoved through the gate of the castle. A moment later the heavy portcullis crashed down, sealing the entrance.

62

Savage swore and hurled the scimitar at the last fleeing pirate. The sword tumbled end over end through the air. With a soft thump it sank deep into the running man's back. The pirate gave a startled cry, staggered to a halt then collapsed to his knees, hands grasping over his shoulders in a vain attempt to reach the sword that now impaled him. Savage caught up with him, grabbed the handle of the scimitar and, enraged, shoved it forwards with all his might. The point of the sword burst from the pirate's chest and with a final cry he collapsed, dead as he hit the ground.

'Nice throw,' de Mandeville commented from behind him. Savage withdrew the blade and turned to see the seneschal approaching.

The battle in the harbour was over. All the defenders were dead, wounded or had surrendered. The town and quays were flooded by warriors wearing the colours of de Bermingham and de Mandeville or Irish plaids. The remainder of the pirates were now all inside the castle with the gates shut.

Savage squinted as a dazzling vision appeared beside de Mandeville in the gleaming figure of Syr Paschall. The Lombard was dressed head to foot in full plate armour, burnished to such an extent that every inch shone like a silver mirror. The weak sunlight sparkled and shone from the metal and Savage was startled to see his own distorted face reflected on the young man's breastplate. He noted with approval that the armour was sullied in places by blood splashes and the odd dent, so it was not just for show. Behind Paschall came d'Athy and FitzWarin, also both showing signs of battle. The young men all pulled helmets off to reveal wide grins. Around the harbour the other warriors were doing likewise, thumping each other on the back or embracing, delighted in their victory and glad to have survived the fighting.

'The plan worked like a dream!' de Mandeville said, his helmet now tucked under his arm, his close-cropped grey hair plastered to his head with sweat. A puzzled look came over his face at the scowl on Savage's. 'We won, Savage. Don't you realise that?'

'We haven't won yet,' Savage said, pointing at the castle. 'The rest of them are holed up behind those walls.'

'It won't take long to flush them out,' de Mandeville said. 'There's barely enough of them left to man one wall.'

'My wife is in there,' Savage said, realising as he spoke that he could still scarcely believe it himself.

'What?'

Savage shook his head. 'I don't know how. I don't know why. She's supposed to be in France! But I assure you that I just saw her being pulled into that castle by a giant of a man.'

De Mandeville nodded, accepting Savage's word immediately. 'Then we'd better get her out, eh? Men!' The seneschal raised his voice to be heard above the jubilant warriors around him. 'It's not over yet. We're going to take that castle.'

The shouts of joy disappeared as the warriors began putting their helmets back on and once more prepared for battle. Some grumbled in disappointment, but Savage was relieved to see that no one objected or refused.

'Thank you,' he said to the seneschal, who nodded his acknowledgement.

'We have to do this anyway.' De Mandeville shrugged. 'We must assault the walls.' He scanned the men around him. 'Go into the town. Search those ships. We need ladders, ropes, anything that we can use to get in.'

Men began to disperse in different directions to carry out the task as de Mandeville turned back to his captains and Savage. 'Pity we didn't bring any siege equipment,' he commented. 'De Thrapston will open the gates of Carrickfergus Castle for us so I never thought to bring any.'

'The trebuchet!' Savage exclaimed, remembering the war engine at the mouth of the harbour. 'What about that?'

The captains followed Savage's pointing finger to see the abandoned trebuchet, a stone still resting in its sling, aiming out towards the now empty sea.

'Does anyone know how to work one of those things?' de Mandeville asked, shielding his eyes to get a better look at the siege engine.

'I do,' the glittering Syr Paschall said, to everyone's surprise. 'My father commanded several of them in the war against the Papal States.'

'Excellent!' Savage said. 'Take some men and turn it on the castle, will you?'

The Lombard's face fell, offence obvious in his expression.

'No!' he said. 'All the glory and honour will be won in the attack on the walls, not lurking away from the fighting working a war machine!'

De Mandeville laid a gauntleted hand on the young man's shoulder. 'Syr Paschall, I promise you that you will have opportunity enough for glory when we reach Carrickfergus. That's our chief objective, remember? Please. This will shorten the fight and save the lives of many of our men and give us a better chance when we reach our real goal.'

The Lombard sighed and rolled his eyes, but nodded his assent.

'Good man,' Savage said with a smile. 'Concentrate on hitting the gate tower at the front of the castle, will you?'

'I will,' Syr Paschall said, and took off at a clanking run in the direction of the trebuchet.

'D'Athy – send six men to go with him,' de Mandeville ordered.

'Meiler,' Savage said to the man-at-arms who stood nearby. 'Get eight men and come with me.' Seeing the questioning look on the seneschal's face, Savage quickly outlined his plan. De Mandeville gave his agreement and they parted, the seneschal turning towards the castle while Savage, with Meiler and the eight men he had gathered, trotted back down to the harbour and along the quay to where three of Tavish Dhu's ships rested at anchor. Savage stopped at the first one they came to and indicated that the men should climb aboard.

'Look for grappling irons and ropes,' he said. 'Pirates use the hooks to ensnare the ships they attack and pull their victims close enough to board. If you don't find any on this one, search the other two. I know there's one on the Saracen's ship so I'll get that one.'

He ran off towards Al Bakri's dhow and clambered aboard, crossing the deck to the tiller where he had earlier seen the grappling iron.

As he bent to pick up the three-pronged metal hook with its long, stout rope attached, Savage paused. He had a strange prickling feeling that he was not alone. Turning full circle he scanned the deck, but there was no one else to be seen. Shaking his head, he chided himself and gathered the rope into a coil, slung the grappling hook over his shoulder then scrambled back over the wale and down onto the quay. Across the harbour he could hear the creaking of wood as Syr Paschall and his men manoeuvred the big war machine into a new position to face the castle instead of out to sea. The contraption was on huge wooden wheels, which eased the operation, but the lack of turning space on the end of the quay meant a lot of forward and backwards movement.

Savage met up with Meiler and the others, now all armed with grappling hooks, and led them at a steady run to where the seneschal's soldiers were gathering across the moat at the front of the castle. Several pirates peered over the top of the battlements and Savage was heartened to see how few of them there appeared to be, perhaps twenty or less. Certainly nowhere near enough to defend all the walls of the fortress. The attackers had already begun to throw planks and wooden poles across the moat as a means to cross the water and get at the base of the walls.

There was a loud clanking, clattering sound from the harbour followed by a bang and something hummed through the air above their heads. They all looked up to see a huge rock tumbling across the sky. Paschall had loosed his first stone from the trebuchet. The rock went high, however, sailing harmlessly over the castle and disappearing beyond it into the town. A moment after it disappeared from view the crash of splintering wood and brick signalled that it had landed. Savage looked around and saw Syr Paschall shaking his head at the far end of the harbour as the men with him went back to work, cranking the great arm of the war machine back into the launching position.

'Come with me,' Savage beckoned Meiler and his men and began to lead them around the side of the moat. As they moved, Savage, his eyes on the battlements above, saw a pirate had spotted them and was pointing down at them and shouting over his shoulder. Savage signalled his men to halt. At that moment another crack from the harbour heralded that Paschall had unleashed another stone. It hurtled overhead, humming like an enormous bee. This time the missile was better aimed. There was a loud crunch as it struck the crenellations above the gate, smashing the top of the wall into rubble and obliterating at least one defender in a pink splatter. The attackers cheered.

Seeing the defenders were distracted, Savage motioned to the men around him to start moving again. They made their way around to the back of the castle where, to Savage's satisfaction, there were no defenders on the walls. As he had hoped, all of the pirates were huddled above the gate, waiting to repel the seneschal's frontal assault. Dangling his grappling hook by the rope, he swung it back and forth a few times to gain momentum then tossed it to the top of the castle wall, letting the rope play through his hands as it flew. The hook fell short, hitting the wall well below the battlements and tumbling down to land with a splash in the moat. Hand over hand Savage began pulling it back by the rope, the hook trailing through slimy strings of green weed that clogged in the stagnant water.

Following Savage's lead, Meiler threw his own hook at the wall. He was more successful, one of the three prongs catching on a crenellation at the top. Meiler pulled in the rope until it was taut, then grasped it in both hands and swung across the moat, landing on the narrow rocky ledge at the bottom of the wall.

Savage tried again and this time he was successful. Unlike Meiler, however, his swing was more through, rather than over, the moat, his legs trailing in the foul-smelling, algae-clogged water. Cursing, he hauled himself, dripping, out on the other side and scrambled up onto the rocky ledge to join Meiler at the base of the castle wall. The rest of the men were now casting their hooks, most of which caught and held, and soon they were following over the moat.

Savage looked up, tugging at his rope to test that the grappling iron held firm. He knew it would not be an easy climb weighed down with chain mail, but thankfully the wall was barely three maybe four times the height of a man and mercifully there was still no sign of any defenders at the top. He wound the rope around his waist, once more grabbed it in both hands and, bracing both feet against the wall, he began to climb.

A very loud bang came from the far side of the castle as another of Paschall's stones struck home. The impact was almost immediately followed by the loud roaring of crumbling stone and further crashes of falling masonry and Savage deduced that this one had done serious damage to the front of the castle. It sounded like a wall had come down.

There were cries of fear, surprise and pain and to his horror, the sound of a woman screaming in agony.

63

Carrickfergus Castle

Henry de Thrapston stood on the top of the keep of Carrickfergus Castle. A light breeze tugged at his hair as he took in the magnificent view. The keep was the tallest building in the whole of Ulster. Its huge, square, stone tower and imposing curtain wall dominated the now destroyed town and the whole lough that stretched before it. The ominous facade of the stern fortress stood out immediately from anywhere on the lough shore. To the north, dark mountains rose and the late afternoon sun was beginning to cast shadows into the glens and valleys. To the south and around the castle, the wind whipped white-tops across the choppy green sea water in the lough. Across the water lay the distant misty hills of Holy Wood on the far shore.

From the dizzying heights of the keep, de Thrapston could see all of the devastated town of Carrickfergus, the Scottish army camp beyond the town's half-destroyed turf ramparts and the harbour that nestled directly in the shadow of the castle. This was the reason he was up there. The harbour and town were a hive of activity. From morning, boats had been arriving at the harbour. They ranged from small Irish curraghs to square rigged galleys. The camp was emptying and the town thronged with soldiers of the Scottish army. Some, mostly the nobility by the look of it, were filing down towards the harbour to board the ships. Once full, the boats set sail and headed off across the lough towards the far shore. The same ships then returned empty to refill with men. The rest of the men were forming into groups and heading out of the town, marching south-west along the lough shore towards the little village of Béal Feirste. As more and more Scots left, the besieged garrison of the castle watched proceedings with a puzzled, wary eye.

The door to the rooftop opened and Guilleme le Poer joined him.

'You wanted to see me?' le Poer said, saluting the keeper of the castle.

'What do you think they're up to, Guilleme?' de Thrapston asked. 'You were out there among them until a few days ago. Did you hear anything? Do you know what's going on?'

Le Poer shook his head. 'I heard nothing.'

'Do you think they're leaving?' De Thrapston's voice had a slight tremor, not even daring to hope that the long siege might be over. The disappointment if it was not true would be too much to bear.

'They're certainly going somewhere,' le Poer said, looking over the battlements, 'but I doubt very much they're leaving us for good. We're on our knees and they know it. To abandon the siege now would be ridiculous.'

The castellan nodded his agreement. 'Unless there is

something more important to them. I'd be thinking that perhaps the justiciar is finally marching north to attack, except it's obvious by the look of them that the Scots are not going to war.'

Le Poer grunted. 'Agreed. If anything they look like they are celebrating a holy day.'

By and large, the Scots wore no armour. Instead they looked like they were dressed in the best clothes they owned. The nobles wore brightly coloured heraldic surcoats over tunics that sparkled with gold and silver thread. The foot soldiers wore their clan plaids. They marched in squads and battles but there was mostly no sign of weapons beyond personal side arms. There were men ready for war amid the throngs but their capacity seemed to be as lookouts, rear-guards or other security positions to provide protection for their unarmed comrades.

A great number of priests and monks moved among the warriors, bestowing blessings on those who marched past, their singing of psalms and other hymns drifting up on the wind to de Thrapston and le Poer's vantage point high above. Various banners were carried among the throng, some showing the coats of arms of the earls and barons but most showing Christ on the cross, his holy mother or crosses of the Saints Patrick and Bridget. Most of the highland kerns normally marched barefoot but a significant number of men, even among the nobles, were not wearing any shoes or boots either.

'You're right,' de Thrapston said. 'This is a religious journey.'

Le Poer's mouth opened as realisation dawned on him. 'Of course!' he said. 'That's what he's up to. Bruce styles himself as King of Ireland but he has two faces to show. What has every Earl of Ulster and Gaelic King before him done at Easter?'

'Taken the pilgrimage to Dun Patrick.' De Thrapston nodded. Suddenly everything became clear to him. Dun Patrick lay to the south, an ancient town that held the grave of Saint Patrick and other holy sites. It was an Easter tradition going back to time immemorial to make a devotional journey there. Just over a century before, after Syr John de Courcy had conquered Ulster and made himself the first earl, the new ruler had miraculously discovered not just the bones of Saint Patrick there, but also the remains of Saints Bridget and Colmcille, though how they had got there from Kildare and Iona where those saints were buried was nothing short of a miracle. After that the annual pilgrimage to Dun Patrick had become an institution expected of the current ruler and his entourage to demonstrate devotion to the local saints. Bruce was obviously staking his claim to that title and taking most of his army with him.

'I'm sure Edward Bruce doesn't intend to leave us completely on our own while he is away,' le Poer said, nodding in the direction of the newly constructed siege works around the castle gates. Following the raid that had brought le Poer and Galiene into the castle, the Scots had invested a lot of effort in building new entrenchments and a berm to seal the fortress off once more from the land. The fortifications still bristled with armed and armoured men who watched and guarded the only possible way in or out of the castle that did not involve getting very wet.

De Thrapston sighed and looked around at le Poer, meeting his eyes for the first time. 'You know this would be the perfect time for the seneschal to launch an attack to break the siege. If only there was not the damn Peace of Easter!'

Le Poer smiled but his voice was bitter. 'It is the Peace of God, Henry, declared by the Pope himself. We cannot have Christians killing Christians at Easter. That's why Bruce feels safe enough to go on this pilgrimage.'

'Yes,' de Thrapston conceded, fighting back the urge to spit in disgust. The evening before, Edward Bruce had sent a herald to the castle informing him of the agreement the Justiciar of Ireland had made, guaranteeing that the peace would be kept. Bruce had also sent the message that he expected the denizens of the castle to abide by the same agreement.

From the distance, though still audible over the noise of the army embarking on pilgrimage below, came the sound of a bell ringing in the friary outside the town. It marked the hour of vespers.

'Come, Henry,' le Poer said, gesturing towards the door. 'We must see to our own souls; never mind theirs. It's time for Mass.'

Like every other evening in Holy Week, Mass was celebrated in the castle chapel at vespers. As it was Maundy Thursday, there was a special service, the Tenebrae.

'You know I really look forward to Mass these days,' de Thrapston said as they left the rooftop. 'If nothing else we're at least guaranteed something to eat.'

64

Isle of Man

Pol the giant had pushed both Alys and Eleanor through
the castle gate just before the portcullis came crashing
down to seal the entrance. They went from the chaos of the
battle outside to the relative quiet of the castle where
the meagre number of remaining pirates gathered around the
gate, trying to catch their breath. Eleanor seemed to
have retreated into herself. Her head was down, her face
covered by her straggling, matted hair. The constant changes
in fortune had perhaps been too much and she now seemed
insensible to what was going on, simply accepting whatever
fate sent. Unlike Alys, she had offered no resistance as they
were pushed up and into the castle.

Looking around, Alys realised that the fight was almost
over. The men gathered in the courtyard were a motley
collection of murderers, thieves and vagabonds. Some wore
chain mail, some leather but most were dressed in little
more than rags. These men were pirates, not warriors. They
were used to hit-and-run attacks, taking opportunities,

preying on the weak and vulnerable then making their escape. It was obvious that defending a castle against a greater number of disciplined professional fighters was beyond them and the expressions on their faces suggested that few had the stomach for it.

'Where's Tavish?' Pol said, turning left and right, looking for his commander. The other men just returned his questioning glare with blank faces.

Alys noticed the look of confusion on Pol's face. He seemed lost as he realised for the first time that his leader was not there. Seeing the same expressions of doubt on the faces of the men around him spurred him to action.

'What are you lot doing standing around here for? Get up on those walls, you lazy dogs!' he roared. Some of the pirates around him actually flinched at the intensity of his rage. 'Do you want to let those scum just walk in here? If you do I can tell you they'll hang us all from our own ship masts before sunset. If you want to see tomorrow then get up there and start fighting.'

His words had some effect and the men began scurrying for the steps to the battlements.

'He's left you, you know,' Alys taunted. 'He's saved his own skin and run away.'

'Shut your mouth, bitch,' Pol said in a dismissive tone. Then, almost as an afterthought, he spun around and smacked her backhanded across the face. Alys went sprawling sideways, a thousand stars exploding before her eyes, a high-pitched whistling blotting out her hearing. Her vision was only just starting to clear when something zoomed overhead. Moving fast and too big to be a bird, it flashed by, casting a brief shadow across the castle courtyard. As it disappeared from view there came the sound of smashing wood, bricks and stone from somewhere in the town beyond.

'Pol! Get up here!' the panicked voice of a pirate came from the walls above. Pol grabbed Alys and Eleanor by their upper arms, one in each mighty hand and half-pushed, half-hauled them up the steps onto the battlements at the top of the gate tower. Alys shook her head to try to clear her vision. She saw the swarms of men in armour outside, preparing to attack the castle gate. She searched for Richard among them but could see no sign. She saw the green sea stretching into the distance and the harbour between it and the castle. Something had changed.

'The bastards have turned our own trebuchet on us, Pol,' one of the pirates said, his voice shrill with panic. Alys looked and indeed the war machine was now pointing in the direction of the castle rather than the sea. A crew of men, one who seemed to be in armour that shone like the sun, were currently engaged in reloading the device for another shot.

This was not the only thing that was amiss. The Saracen ship Richard had arrived on had loosed its ropes, its sails were filled and it was heading for the harbour mouth. He was somewhat distant but it was still possible to make out the figure in black at the tiller with his long hair tied in a plait that hung down his back. Some of the trebuchet crew seemed agitated and were waving and pointing at the ship. Some threw spears at it. The man piloting the ship simply raised his right hand and waved in a gesture that even from the distance of the castle could be seen was mocking.

'It's Tavish,' Pol said, dismayed disbelief in his voice.

All the pirates recognised their leader immediately and an angry roar echoed around the battlements.

'I told you he'd save himself,' Alys said.

Pol's head whipped around and for a moment she thought he would strike her again. He did not and when she saw the look on his face she almost felt sorry for the big oaf. He was on the verge of crying.

'They're going to loose another rock,' a pirate on the battlements shouted.

The crew manning the trebuchet pulled its rope, releasing a long wooden lever. The big, rock-filled counterweight of the device dropped, pulling forward the great long throwing arm. At the end of it was the sling that held a rock about the size of a cow's body. As the arm rotated to its apex, the rock came out and hurtled towards the castle.

'It's coming this way,' the same man commented. He seemed to be mesmerised by the sight of the oncoming stone, somehow unable to move even while all his comrades desperately scrambled in panic to get out of the way. Alys saw one man jump off the battlements in desperation. She winced at the sound of cracking bones as he landed on the cobblestones of the courtyard below. The next moment the stone struck the castle. Alys flinched and it was all she could do to crouch into a ball and try to make herself as small as possible.

There was a tremendous crash. The stone floor of the battlement jumped beneath her feet. Her stomach lurched as she felt the gate tower they stood on actually rock. A hail of stone splinters showered over her, raising painful welts. A choking cloud of dust swirled around her, provoking a coughing spasm.

As the dust cleared she looked around, spitting out tiny stone fragments. A large chunk of the battlement wall at the front of the tower was gone and the rubble from it was strewn in an arc across the top of the tower. The man who had watched the stone come was gone too but there were horrible-looking chunks of pink and red meat smeared through the piles of smashed stone. Pol was on the ground also but he was already rising to his feet. Incredibly, Eleanor had remained standing throughout. Her hair was now swept away from her face, which the flying splinters had turned to a criss-crossed mosaic of tiny cuts. She continued to stare out at the sea as if unconcerned.

'It's hopeless,' Alys, still crouched on the ground, called to Pol. 'You can't hold out. You don't have enough men and they can pound this place to bits with that trebuchet. Surrender.'

Pol, now on his feet again, lurched over to her. 'I told you to shut your mouth,' he said, swinging a vicious kick into her stomach. Alys gasped, the wind completely driven from her. She collapsed sideways onto the floor, both hands at her belly, mouth working like a fish landed on a dock as she tried desperately to breathe in.

Eleanor spoke for the first time. 'Don't worry.' Her voice was flat and almost without emotion, though the eyes with which she looked down at Alys brimmed with the tears of sorrow. 'Perhaps your Richard will come. Perhaps he will save you. My Roger is dead. They killed him and he will not come for me. But maybe your Richard will.'

Pol looked down at Alys with narrowed eyes.

'Yes, just who was that you were shouting to down in

the harbour?' he said, bending over her and glaring into her face. 'Who is this Richard?'

'My husband,' Alys wheezed. 'He's outside and when he gets in he'll make you pay for what you've done.'

'Oh will he?' Pol said, his face breaking into a grin. 'Well this is some good news. Looks like old Tavish might have been right after all and you'll have some value as a hostage. I doubt lover boy will do much if I have my knife at your throat.'

He grabbed her upper arm again and hauled her to her feet.

'There's men climbing the back wall!' someone shouted from further down the battlement. Pol looked around, his face angry once more.

'Get back there and stop them,' he roared.

Realising he was momentarily distracted, Alys stamped her heel down hard on his left foot. As the big pirate yelped in surprise and pain, Alys swung her other foot, connecting hard with his groin. Pol shouted and released her arm. Alys pulled away and started to run as best she could. Behind her she heard Pol letting out an incoherent roar of anger.

Then the next stone from the trebuchet struck. Alys screamed as the world was obliterated in a welter of stone shards and dust.

65

Savage reached the top of the wall. He extended a gloved hand up, grasped the top of the battlement and scrambled over into the castle. Rolling over, he dropped onto the walkway at the top of the wall. Meiler was already over and had his sword drawn. There were no defenders on the battlements but a group of men were running along the walkway on the wall to the right to intercept them.

Savage made a frantic survey of the castle interior, trying to see where Alys was.

The front gate tower had taken a severe battering from the trebuchet. There was a hole in the battlements at the front. A second stone had come over the battlements, landing just behind the wall and causing the back wall of the gate tower to collapse into the courtyard below. The cobblestones were a mess of shattered rock, stone and masonry shards. There were several human bodies scattered around. Among them he spotted the big pirate he had seen in the harbour, now obviously dead, looking like every bone in his body was smashed and was thankful that he did not have to fight him at least. He could still hear the woman's frantic screaming. Heavy clouds of stone dust swirled around in the wind.

He couldn't see where she was but it sounded like she was somewhere down below.

Two more of Meiler's men came over the top of the wall. Savage drew the scimitar and pointed it in the direction of the pirates approaching along the battlements.

'Can you hold them?' he called to Meiler.

Meiler looked offended by the question. 'Hold them? I think we'll kill them.'

Savage nodded and ran in the opposite direction. He followed the walkway on the battlements to the corner where a set of steps led down into the castle below. Taking the stairs two at a time, he descended into the courtyard. Dust billowed and eddied in the wind and the cobblestones were littered with a million stone fragments from the collapsed wall. He crunched across the debris towards several bodies that lay on the ground. The howling was coming from one of them. He felt a deep sense of dread as he approached the figure. From her screaming it was obvious the woman was in profound agony. She was covered in black stone dust and to his consternation he saw there was a pool of bright crimson spreading around her. It was already large and growing at a rate that meant she could not survive much longer.

A yell cut short by the thump of a body landing nearby made Savage turn momentarily. A dying pirate lay at the base of the wall from which he had fallen: Meiler was being as good as his word already.

He turned his attention back to the injured woman and realised with horror that she had lost one of her legs. Whether it was when the rock from the trebuchet struck or in the fall of the tower, something had ripped away everything from her mid-thigh down. A few scraps of tattered flesh trailed across the ground and a jagged, broken stump of bone protruded from bright red raw flesh where the limb now prematurely ended. A frightening amount of blood was pumping out of the destroyed leg from severed veins and arteries to increase the rapidly spreading, copper-smelling pool. Already the woman's cries were fading to a weak mewling.

Savage felt the resolution drain from him like the blood that was emptying from her body. He could not move any closer but only looked down in despair.

'Alys?' he managed to croak, falling to his knees, heedless of the sharp pain that erupted when his kneecaps settled onto the sharp stone shards.

'I'm up here, you idiot.'

A familiar voice came from above. Savage looked up and through the swirling dust saw the outline of his wife, standing on what remained of the front half of the gate tower overhead. A wave of relief surged over him as he realised that the poor woman breathing her last before him must be the other woman he had seen at the harbour. A moment later, a figure with a bloody sword wearing a red and yellow surcoat over his chain mail, appeared at Alys's side.

'It's all right, Syr Richard. I'm with her,' Meiler called from above. He and his men had fought their way along the side wall and now were on the half-ruined gate tower as well.

The battle for the castle was over. Perhaps nine pirates survived on the battlements and they could see that further resistance was pointless. They were already dropping their weapons, deciding to take whatever slim chance an ensuing legal process might give them over the now certain death that continued fighting would bring.

Savage returned to the stair and bounded up the steps to the battlements. He followed the path of Meiler's fight, stepping over two corpses on the way. Cheers of victory were already starting to erupt from outside. Meiler was shouting down to de Mandeville's warriors below and runners were sent to the harbour with orders for Syr Paschall to halt the trebuchet assault.

Alys met Savage halfway along the battlements at the front of the castle. He took her in a fierce embrace, almost crushing the air from her in his eagerness and desperation to hold her.

'Easy on,' she gasped.

Savage pulled back, his hands on her shoulders, looking intently at her, his face suddenly a mask of dismay. He saw her bruised face, her black eye, the myriad cuts on her skin, the raw chafe marks the shackles were cutting into her wrists and neck. 'You're hurt,' he said. 'How bad is it?'

Alys shook her head, thinking of all the things that had happened to her since she'd last saw him. 'It really could be a lot worse,' she said, her face breaking into a smile of relief as she realised just how lucky she was to be alive, never mind in one piece. Tears welled in both their eyes then Savage grasped the back of her head and pulled her towards him, their lips meeting in a ferocious kiss. He felt light-headed, drunk and awash with love for her. To see her of all people amid the death and chaos that swirled around was unbelievable.

'What are you doing here?' he asked when they finally parted.

'I was about to ask you the same question.' Alys laughed, then her face fell. 'What about Galiene? Shouldn't you be in Ireland?'

'I'm on my way. Shouldn't you be in France with Mortimer?' Savage returned.

Alys's face darkened at the memory. 'Richard, Mortimer betrayed you – betrayed us all.' Quickly she recounted the tale of her stay and escape from Mortimer's clutches, the pirates and how she had ended up in the castle. 'Mortimer has sent his bodyguard, a German swordsman, on a mission to kill all of us and hide the truth.'

'The truth?' Savage frowned. 'About what?'

Alys shook her head. There was not enough time to go into everything. 'He's trying to cover up a secret about the king and Piers Gaveston,' she said. 'I'll tell you more later but what can we do now? What about poor Galiene? What if the German reaches her before we do?'

'He'll have to break into Carrickfergus Castle to get her,' Savage replied. 'Because that's where she is now. And that's where we're headed next.'

Savage put an arm around Alys's shoulder and led her towards the stairs.

'Come on,' he said. 'Let's go and get our daughter.'

66

Carrickfergus Castle

Syr Neil Fleming was finally satisfied enough to go to his bed. The young nobleman took enormous pride in the responsibility his king had bestowed on him while he was off on pilgrimage. Despite his young years, Edward Bruce had left Fleming in charge of making sure the siege continued while he was away. The young Scot had personally overseen the rebuilding of the siege works and created the duty rosters to make sure they were manned day and night, and not just with watchmen, with enough warriors to hold any attempts by the castle garrison to sally out again. There would be no repeat of the debacle of the week before. Not while he was in charge. He was determined that when his lord returned, the conditions of the siege would be exactly as when he left, preferably even worse for the defenders. There may have been a truce in force but Fleming had no desire to leave anything to chance.

For that reason he had once more inspected the siege works after darkness fell. He had one hundred men under his command. The barricades were manned by his own company of men-at-arms. The trenches were filled with spearmen ready for any attack. Four large wooden screens set at an angle on wheeled trolleys faced the castle, providing cover for warriors from arrows and missiles thrown by the defenders. Among those crouching behind them were a squad of twelve Genoese crossbowmen, expensive mercenaries in the pay of Syr Thomas Randolph. They huddled, ready to crank their bows and shoot at the first sign of trouble.

Happy that it was all right for him to retire, Fleming called to his manservant to bring his horse so he could ride back to camp. He had just swung his leg over the creature's back when a troop of riders trotted into the burned-out marketplace, hooves clattering on the cobblestones. Spotting Fleming's blue and red surcoat, the lead rider spurred his horse towards him.

In the light from the braziers and torches lit around the siege works, Fleming recognised the large frame and blunt face of Gib Harper. The other men were all spearmen from his troop but there was also a sixth rider who Fleming did not know. A rider who sat tall in the saddle and wore expensive, well-made chain mail with plate armour over it. His blond hair was close cropped and his clean-shaven chin showed signs of a fading bruise.

'Fleming,' Harper called. Syr Neil frowned at Harper's lack of deference. Ever since William Wallace had risen to fame Scotland had been plagued by professional fighting men like Harper who believed that being good with a sword somehow excused them from having to show proper respect for their social betters.

'Harper,' Fleming responded, touching his forehead in salute. 'What are you doing here? Lord Edward has gone to Dun Patrick.'

'This is Syr Heinrich von Mahlberg,' Harper said, gesturing to the blond-haired man. 'He is a knight from the German states. He brings grave news.'

Fleming saluted the German who returned the gesture. 'Your trust is going to be betrayed,' he said. 'The justiciar de Bermingham plans a surprise attack to relieve the castle. He will use the Peace of Easter as cover. The attack will come from the sea. The ships you think are sailing for Scotland with the ransom for William de Burgh are actually coming here instead.'

Appalled, Syr Neil looked at Harper. 'The Pope himself declared this peace!' he said.

Harper returned his look with one that betrayed his annoyance at Fleming's naivety. 'We're at war, Fleming. Sometimes men ignore the Papal edicts and ask for forgiveness after they have won what they want. Need I remind you that our own King Robert is currently excommunicated?'

'How do you know this?' Fleming demanded of von Mahlberg.

'I come here at the behest of Earl Richard de Burgh of Ulster,' von Mahlberg said. 'The earl is not happy with his cousin William's life being played with in this way. He raised that ransom at great personal expense. Also he is unhappy with the idea that a holy peace be used as a stratagem for war. Harper here can vouch for me.'

At the mention of the earl, Fleming and Harper exchanged knowing glances. Harper gave an imperceptible nod.

'They even made me part of the deception,' Harper said, anger turning his voice to gravel. 'It was me who did the deal with the earl in Dublin.'

'And why should we believe you?' Fleming said, turning his attention back to von Mahlberg.

The German straightened in his saddle. His eyes flashed with a cold light that left Fleming in no doubt the man was a killer.

'I am a brother member of the Order of the German House of Saint Mary in Jerusalem,' he said, his clipped tone hard as steel. 'To me, my word of honour is more important than my life.'

'A Teutonic Knight, eh?' Fleming said, frowning. 'Just what we need. More fighting fanatics. Harper, most of the army is on the pilgrimage. We don't have enough men to repel an invasion force of any size as well as contain the castle garrison.'

'Well we'll just have to go and get the army back,' Harper said.

'Lord Edward will not be pleased,' Fleming said. 'This trip to Dun Patrick seemed important to our Irish allies.'

'He'll be more annoyed if he comes back and finds the siege lifted and Carrickfergus back in the hands of the English Lordship of Ireland,' Harper said.

Fleming wrestled with his thoughts. There was real danger here but if it turned out to be untrue he would look like an immature fool frightened by false fire. Edward Bruce would never trust him with command again.

Harper sensed his indecision. 'I'll take responsibility,' he said. 'I'll go and get the king and the army back. I'm leaving now.'

Fleming hesitated a few more moments, then nodded his agreement.

'All you have to do is hold the town until we get back,' Harper continued. 'Can you do that?'

Fleming straightened his back. His chest puffed. 'I can,' he stated. 'We'll defend this position to the last man.'

'Good man,' Harper said, a broad smile betraying his gladness that he would not have to be part of that particular sacrifice. He turned to the German. 'Come on. We need to get going if we're to be back in time to save young Fleming here's skin.'

Von Mahlberg shook his head and, to the surprise of both Fleming and Harper, dismounted his horse.

'If you don't mind I will stay here,' he said. 'I have some unfinished business with one Syr Richard Savage.'

67

At sea

Savage felt a surge of exhilaration as the sea hissed by beneath the prow. On board a ship, he was used to anxiety and dread, but this feeling of anticipation and excitement was new. Perhaps it was because he was sailing to war.

There were five ships in their expedition carrying almost five hundred men. Savage had command of one and all the men on board. Syr Paschall commanded the lead ship. He had been promised the first chance at glory as reward for his work on manning the trebuchet in the Isle of Man. Savage had not argued. The first chance for glory usually also meant the first chance to die. De Mandeville was in charge of the second and d'Athy and FitzWarin had the remaining two. FitzWarin's ship was the one that held the supplies so it travelled at the rear of the fleet.

They had sailed from the Isle of Man that morning and made the short crossing to the Irish coast without incident. Now that the pirates who made up the Scots navy had been dealt with and dispersed, there was nothing to hinder them in their voyage north to Carrickfergus Lough.

At the insistence of Alys, Syr Henry de Bellomonte had been freed from the dungeons of the castle. As the decrepit old man had emerged from the darkness of his prison he had looked as if the shock of seeing sunlight after so long might kill him. De Mandeville had been far from happy at the thought of freeing a man who had been legally imprisoned under English law, regardless of ensuing circumstances. Alys had pleaded his case and eventually de Mandeville had conceded that he had probably served a long enough sentence by now to atone for his original crime. What would happen to him now – alone, frail and penniless as he was – was anyone's guess. The expedition force could not take him along; however, at least whatever was in store for him was now at his own behest and not that of his jailers.

Despite battling to regain it, they had to abandon the Isle of Man again. It was not the main aim of the expedition and they did not have enough men or resources to garrison the island. Every man was needed for the assault on Carrickfergus.

They did not simply abandon the island, however, not before more blood was shed. De Mandeville, as seneschal, set up an impromptu court in the courtyard of the half-destroyed castle. After cursory hearings for the pirates who had surrendered, sentence was pronounced and they were hanged from the walls. The cowed islanders turned on the small band of Scotsmen who had been appointed as overlords of the island in the name of Robert Bruce. The mob stripped them, beat them through the town and then demanded de Mandeville string them up with the pirates.

The seneschal was reluctant to carry out such summary justice but he was equally loath to leave Scotsmen on the island to potentially retake power when they left. Consoling himself that the mob would have killed them anyway, he first let the churchmen among them go, then ordered his men to hang the rest too.

To prevent disease, all the dead were collected together on a huge pyre for burning. The people of so many nations who had fought over the castle now all lay together in a pile amid its ruins. The one exception was Eleanor, whose corpse Alys had requested be buried nearby with Christian rites.

After that, de Mandeville's soldiers set fire to the bodies and the battered castle to prevent it falling into the hands of enemies. As the dark pall of smoke rose into the sky they boarded their ships and sailed away from the island.

Savage stood at the very front of the ship. Ahead was the coast of Ireland – not just Ireland but the black rocks of Ulster, growing darker as the sun sank towards the horizon.

He wore a leather jerkin and over it a chain mail hauberk covering his upper body and arms. His legs were wrapped in tight-fitting chain mail stockings over which he had a long pair of heavy leather boots. He still wore the faded old Templar Knight tunic over his chest. Savage was not entirely sure why. It was part of the ritual of battle for him. He supposed it had always brought him luck in the past so why tempt fate now? The other knights and the seneschal were protected by iron sheets of modern plate armour but Savage had eschewed this. His reasons were twofold. First, he preferred the agility and mobility allowed by the lighter, close-fitting mail. For this expedition he would have to move fast and hit hard. Secondly – and more decisively – he simply did not possess any plate armour. His meagre income in France had prohibited the purchase of such expensive items.

The green sea smashed itself against the rocks, throwing up white foam into the air. A brisk, fresh wind beat upon his face, drawing water from his eyes and pulling at his cloak, making it flap behind him like wings. With the waves crashing by below he felt like this must be what the gulls felt like as they swooped over the ocean.

His thoughts were interrupted by the feeling that someone was watching him. He looked around and saw Alys was there, regarding him with a half-smile on her face. She was still dressed in the clothes of the cabin boy she had stolen but Savage had commandeered a dark blue cloak for her and she wore the hood up to cover her hair, which in the absence of a wimple was the sort of modesty expected of a married woman.

'What's so funny?' he asked, putting an arm around her and drawing her to him.

'Oh I don't know,' Alys said. 'You, mainly. When we were sailing to France for you to become a farmer you looked like you were being taken to your execution. Now we're sailing into a fight you can't wait to get there. Same old Richard. You haven't really changed since we were children, have you?'

Savage didn't know what to say but had to nod his agreement. She knew him so well. Her expression changed suddenly to one of concern. He could not help notice in the fading light of day the lines that crept around her eyes.

She was still beautiful but she was also starting to show her age. They both were.

'We'll be able to get her, won't we?' Alys said, her eyes locking on his, searching for certainty and some form of reassurance.

'I'll be doing the getting, I think,' Savage said with gentle admonishment. 'I think you've had more than enough adventures. This requires fighting and that's what I do. I don't want you leaving this ship until I come back with Galiene.'

'I hope she's all right. If anything has happened to her I won't be able to forgive myself,' Alys said.

'It wasn't your fault,' Savage said, looking back out to sea. The coast was beginning to turn inland as they neared the wide mouth of Carrickfergus Lough. 'It was those bastards who dragged us back into their war who are to blame.'

Alys nodded, regarding the coast and realising just where they were. 'Dragged us right back,' she commented. 'We're home again.' Her eyes flickered to the north and the distant coast where she knew her castle at Vikingsford, now in the hands of the Scots, lay.

'Home? Is it still home?' Savage murmured. The question was asked as much of himself as her. There was no immediate answer.

'You'll be careful, won't you,' she said, grasping the edge of his cloak. 'I don't want to end up losing both of you.'

Savage smiled, grimly. 'It's not me you have to worry about. Pray for the soul of anyone who gets between me and that castle gate.'

'Did you hear Mass?' Alys asked.

'I did,' Savage admitted. Before they set sail Alan of

Galloway, the man appointed by Robert Bruce to be Bishop of the Isle of Man, had been reluctantly pressed into service to say Mass for the departing soldiers and bless them in their upcoming fight. As a Scotsman expected to bless men going to fight his own countrymen, he had been far from enthusiastic; however, having seen his fellow Scotsmen hanged by their necks from the castle walls, he was canny enough to decide that this was neither the time nor the cause for which he was prepared to suffer martyrdom. It was Good Friday and, besides, he knew they would be gone soon so if this helped them on their way all the better.

Alys raised her eyebrows. 'Well there's new light from old windows. Have you found your faith again?'

Savage sighed. 'I did it as much for Syr Thomas de Mandeville as for myself,' he said. 'I thought he needed some moral support. It was important to him that we confessed and heard Mass before we left.'

Alys nodded. 'I thought I sensed a real turmoil within him. He's really wrestling with his conscience isn't he?' she said.

'He is.' Savage nodded. 'It was his idea to use the Peace of Easter as cover for the attack. Now we're underway he worries that this might bring God's judgement against us. He worries that he has condemned the souls of the men who will die tonight to Hell.'

'Look how easy it was to beat the pirates,' Alys said. 'If God was against you there's no way you would have won.'

Savage shrugged. 'Perhaps God was asleep or looking elsewhere at the time?' He smiled. 'Well we've woken him up now, that's for sure.'

'This is all nonsense,' Alys said quietly. She squeezed the

bicep of Savage's right arm. 'This is what decides battles. That, the steel it holds and the heart behind it.'

There were a few moments silence. In the distance, on the north shore of the lough the last light of the sun caught an ominous square bulk jutting out from the land into the sea. It was dark and its outline symmetrical in a way nothing natural could ever form.

'Well we'll know soon enough,' Savage said. 'There's Carrickfergus Castle.'

68

Carrickfergus Castle

As darkness fell, Guilleme le Poer stood once more on the top of Carrickfergus Castle keep. The Scots were keeping him intrigued. Following the mass exodus on Maundy Thursday he had expected the activity of the contingent left behind to carry on the siege to settle down to the quotidian routine of blockading the castle. Instead, starting in the middle of the previous night, the Scots appeared to be engaged in frantic activity to secure the harbour. They left enough men guarding the siege works to deter the castle garrison from deciding to sally out while the rest of the men moved down the hill to the harbour.

The harbour of Carrickfergus was a natural bay that huddled in the lee of the castle. The black Rock of Fergus, the promontory that the castle was built on, provided one side of the sheltered bay with another further down the coast forming the other side. The shore was a mixture of sand and shingle, allowing smaller vessels and highland galleys to beach straight onto the land while there were also two long, wide wooden piers that jutted into the deeper water and allowed larger ships to dock. One of these ran straight out from the land parallel to the castle while the other came out from halfway along the Rock of Fergus at a right angle to it, running parallel to the shore. Together with the rock they made the sides of a smaller, man-made harbour within the wider bay. Along the beach were scattered a collection of little boats, pulled up beyond the high tide mark and upturned to keep the rain out of them. These were rowing boats, curraghs and coracles, once the possession of local fishermen but now commandeered by the Scots for patrols, transport and fishing expeditions on the lough.

The Scots had pulled two of their portable siege screens down to the harbour and placed one at the end of each pier. Armed men crouched behind the screens and among them le Poer could see crossbowmen and spearmen in chain mail. They had also pulled some of the small boats onto the pier and begun using them to form parts of makeshift barricades along the piers to fortify them. Le Poer was able to watch all this despite the fall of night because the Scots had lit bonfires, braziers and torches all around the harbour and the marketplace of the town so everywhere was illuminated almost like it was day.

Among it all he could see Syr Neil Fleming, the young Scottish nobleman left behind by Bruce to oversee the continuance of the siege. Fleming was in full, brightly polished plate armour that glittered in the firelight and le Poer recognised him by the blue surcoat with a red chevron emblazoned on it – the Fleming coat of arms – that he wore over his armour.

'What are you up to, Fleming?' le Poer said to the dark sky.

'I don't think he can hear you from up here.'

A new voice made him spin around and to his surprise he saw Galiene standing behind him. She had entered the rooftop so quietly he had been completely unaware of her coming.

'You shouldn't sneak up on people like that,' le Poer said, a half-amused, half-impressed smile on his face. 'Though you're good at it, I admit.'

'The rat boy's been teaching me how to move quietly,' Galiene said, her smile showing how pleased she was with herself. 'It helps to be quiet when hunting rats. He says I'm a great shot with the crossbow too.'

Le Poer nodded. 'I'm sure you are. Are you hunting now?'

The girl shook her head, her blonde curls bouncing from side to side. 'I couldn't sleep. Sometimes I come up here in the dark to watch what's going on. There's so much noise from the Scots tonight. What do you think they're doing?'

Le Poer sighed. 'I wish I knew. It looks very much like they're fortifying the harbour. I don't know why. It's almost as if they are expecting an attack from the sea.'

Galiene's eyes widened. 'Perhaps someone is coming to rescue us?'

Le Poer shrugged. 'Perhaps,' he said, though his voice lacked conviction.

'That's why I cannot sleep,' Galiene said. 'Edward Bruce had me kidnapped to force my father to return the Holy Grail. He gave him until Easter and that's the day after tomorrow.'

'You think your father is coming here?' le Poer asked, frowning.

'I don't know.' The girl hung her head. 'I hope he will but he doesn't have the Grail. He threw it away. He has nothing to offer Edward Bruce in exchange for me. Perhaps he won't come.'

Le Poer felt awkward. The girl's shoulders were shaking and it looked like she was sobbing. He held out a hand and gingerly laid it on her shoulder.

'Come now,' he said, his voice thick. 'The Richard Savage I know won't leave his daughter here stuck with us lot. He'll be here, don't you worry.'

'You really think so?' Galiene looked up, her eyes bright with tears. The look of desperate hope on her face hit le Poer like a stab to the heart. 'He left Mother before. He went to the crusades and left her behind, pregnant with me.'

'That was a long time ago,' le Poer said. 'Your father is a different man today.'

He looked away into the dark sky, hoping fervently that it was true. A seagull, disturbed by the activity below, sailed overhead, its white belly and wings like a ghost in the night.

'What's that?' Galiene said quite suddenly. Le Poer looked down and saw that her expression had changed to one of puzzlement. She was pointing out into the darkness. Le Poer squinted, following where she was pointing. Beyond the blaze of light in the harbour below was the black darkness of the lough shore and the waters that it edged. Somewhere in the darkness, way beyond the ramparts of the town, what looked like a river of fire was snaking its way through the night. As he looked harder, he saw that it was not one continuous body of fire, but was made up of hundreds, perhaps thousands, of individual pinpricks of light. The ones at the head of the column seemed to be approaching at a greater speed than the ones behind.

'Those look like torches,' le Poer said. 'And they're coming this way along the coast.'

He took a deep breath and stiffened his shoulders.

'If I'm not mistaken,' he said, 'it looks like Edward Bruce is bringing his army back. And they're in a hurry.'

69

Finding Carrickfergus in the dark of the lough had been simple as it was ablaze with light. There was a waning moon and starlight but all those on board the ships were concerned about sailing towards land in the darkness. The ships could blunder onto rocks, reefs or other unseen hazards, spilling the armoured men on board into the water and almost certain death. The Scots seemed to have lit Carrickfergus up like a bonfire, however, and the captains were able to steer their crafts up the middle of the wide lough, keeping to the deep water and well away from either shore, but still make a heading for the harbour and castle that stood out like a beacon in the night.

Savage was in the third ship in the convoy. The plan was for Syr Paschall to sail into the harbour first and secure one of the piers. Syr Thomas de Mandeville's ship would take the second pier. By then the harbour would be secure and Savage would sail his ship in followed by d'Athy and FitzWarin to dock ships alongside the others. For that reason the rearward three ships hung back a little, taking a wider arc in their turn into the lough and allowing the lead two ships to get ahead. All lamps and torches on the ships were extinguished and the only light was the glint of moonlight on helmets and spear points. They approached the harbour from behind the castle so the bulk of the fortress hid them from the town and harbour. There were a few lights in the castle but the blaze of fires burning in the harbour and town made it stand out like a black monolith.

Savage still stood at the prow and ahead he saw Syr Paschall's ship turning around the end of the promontory the castle was built on towards the harbour on the other side. The seneschal's ship quickly followed and they both disappeared from view. He turned away from the prow to survey the men behind him. At his request, Alys had gone to the stern of the ship and taken refuge in a cabin there. Savage turned around to survey his men. The deck was lined side to side with warriors, armed and ready for the fight. They were a mixture of crop-haired Anglo-Irish warriors in chain mail, kettle helmets and surcoats bearing the arms of de Bermingham, de Mandeville and other nobles, and long-haired Irish kerns in padded linen jerkins and long cloaks, warriors of Gaelic kings who had not joined the cause of Edward Bruce. Some were praying, others passed around flasks and took grateful swigs from them. Even with the sea breeze Savage caught the strong whiff of uisce in the air. As they noticed he had turned around, eighty pairs of expectant eyes fixed on him.

'We are almost there.' Savage raised his voice to be heard across the ship. 'I'm not one for speeches...'

He trailed off, suddenly realising that the ranks of men standing before him were expecting something more than a few mumbled words of encouragement. They were going to war. They would have to kill men, push their own courage to the very limit. Some of them would die. They required –

they deserved – something inspirational. He paused and took a deep breath, noticing Alys had appeared at the door of the cabin and now was also looking at him.

'Men,' he began again, 'we are going to war. Tonight we will attack the very heart of the enemy. The garrison of the castle have been holding out for more than a year. They've endured untold hardship, starvation and death. Despite everything, they did not give in. They did not surrender. We cannot let them down. We've already won a great victory in the Isle of Man. If we win again tonight it will be the first blow that turns the tide of this war. While Carrickfergus holds out against Edward Bruce, he cannot call himself king in the north. Bruce thinks he is invincible. And he has a right to think that. He has yet to be beaten in the field but tonight we will change that. Tonight we will beat him. We'll take back Carrickfergus. We will take back what was stolen from us and we will keep going until we send Edward Bruce and his army back across the sea to their own country where they belong. Our victory will be famous. The poets of Ireland will sing of your exploits tonight for centuries!'

Savage had surprised himself. He had no idea where those words had come from but to his delight he saw excitement and elation reflected in the eyes of the men before him. They raised a cheer that he hoped did not carry as far as the ears of whatever Scottish sentries waited on the land. Alys nodded her approval from the back of the ship.

'Now prepare for battle,' he concluded. 'Let me tell you this, you're a dangerous-looking bunch of men. Edward Bruce should be pissing in his armour knowing you are coming for him. Remember your training, get to the castle and kill anyone who tries to stop you.'

They cheered again and Savage turned back to the prow.

He realised he should not have been concerned about the cheering. The sound of battle had already arisen from the other side of the castle. He could hear shouting, the metallic clash of arms, the sounds of wood smashing, the roaring of war cries and orders and screams of pain. Clearly the first two ships had arrived in the harbour. He was slightly surprised by the level of the noise, which suggested a considerable level of fighting.

The ship rounded the end of the Rock of Fergus. Savage dropped his right hand, signalling to the captain at the stern that he should begin turning. The captain pushed the tiller to the side and the galley began to turn. Crewmen ran to reset the sails as they turned away from the wind to head towards the harbour.

As it came into view, Savage saw immediately that already the battle was not going to plan. Syr Paschall's ship was alongside one pier but the Scots had barricaded the length of it. The defenders were holding firm and the men on the ship were unable to get off. They had thrown grappling hooks onto the pier to pull their ship close but the Scots had cut the ropes. There was desperate fighting as they tried to get off the ship but the Scots were holding them. The men on the ship had to climb up to try to get onto the pier and the Scots were above them, stabbing down with spears and throwing rocks and other missiles onto their heads. It looked like it was turning into a massacre. As he watched two men tried to jump onto the jetty but the defenders easily pushed them off with their spear points and they went tumbling into the sea below.

De Mandeville's ship was having even less success.

It was struggling to come alongside the other quay but the Scots were using long poles to keep it from docking. With the wind gone from the sails the ship wallowed helplessly, tantalisingly close to the quay but too far away for anyone to jump across. Crossbowmen were wreaking havoc on the warriors in the ship. There were not many of them but at such short range it was like shooting a crossbow into a barrel filled to the brim with fish.

Savage raised his arm again. It was a disaster. He could save the lives of all on board and those in the two ships who followed by ordering the captain to turn around and sail away, back into the black night and safety.

His arm remained raised. There were still three more ships and enough men to overwhelm those on the jetties, despite the defenders' efforts. In a moment of revelation everything seemed clear to him.

Savage ran to the back of the ship to where the captain stood, guiding the ship by its steering oar.

'Listen to me,' he shouted above the din of battle, 'there's a change to the plan.'

70

The ship's captain looked at Savage, his eyebrows raised in consternation.

'Are you mad?' he said. 'We'll run aground.'

Savage nodded. 'It's the only way. We beach the ship between the quays and attack the defenders from behind.'

The captain looked confused, pained almost. This was against his very nature, the creed by which he lived his life. He had spent years steering ships away from rocks and trying to avoid this very thing and now Savage was asking him to deliberately ground his vessel.

Savage laid a hand on his shoulder. 'I'll answer to the seneschal and the justiciar,' he said. 'I'm in command here, remember? Please do as I say.'

'What if we need to get away?' the captain argued. 'The ship could be destroyed. If not it won't be easy to float her again. If we have to leave in a hurry—'

Savage held up a hand to silence him. 'We'll just have to hope there's enough room for us all on the other ships,' he said. 'I know this goes against your grain but we have to do it. Otherwise the battle will be lost before it's even started.'

The captain looked dubious but he reluctantly nodded.

'I'll guide you in from the prow,' Savage said.

He ran to the cabin where Alys was. She met him at the door and he quickly explained what was happening. 'Stay under cover but hold on to something,' he said. 'You'll have to get off the ship when we've gone...' He trailed off, clearly suddenly realising the implications of what was happening.

She saw the sudden concern in his eyes and quickly kissed him to break the moment. 'Don't worry about me,' she said, meeting his gaze. 'I think I can look after myself, don't you?'

Savage sighed, kissed her again then turned to go.

'Be careful, for God's sake,' he called back to her. 'Stay out of harm's way and get onto one of the other ships when the fighting is done.'

He rushed back to the prow.

'Men!' he shouted to the warriors on the deck. 'We're going to beach between the quays. Brace yourselves for the impact then get off the ship as fast as you can.'

He turned to look forward and saw that they were almost upon the ship of the seneschal as it wallowed beside the jetty that came out from the Rock of Fergus, parallel to the shore. Savage held up his left hand and the captain steered the ship past it towards the gap between the two jetties that marked the mouth of the harbour. The mast creaked as the wind took the sails once more and pushed the ship forward. When they reached the point to turn, Savage held up his right hand. The captain swung the tiller hard to the left and the ship lurched in a turn that took it between the piers and into the harbour between them. The men on the deck lurched to the left as the ship swung around. The crossbeam on the mast turned with the wind and the sail billowed taut again, driving the ship forwards with greater speed.

Savage lay down along the prow post and held on as best

he could. The ship surged forward into the harbour. As they sailed between the piers he caught sight of agitated defenders, realisation dawning on their faces as they gesticulated wildly in his direction. The ship travelled on, sailing at a diagonal to the piers and towards the gently sloping beach. Savage knew from years gone by that the harbour was sand and shingle, so they did not need to worry about rocks bringing their progress to an unexpected halt. They were forty paces from the shore. A crossbow bolt thumped into the side of the ship. The men on the deck scrambled to hold on to the sides or simply crouched down, laying their weapons beside them. The ship was thirty paces, then twenty.

There was a deep rumbling sound and the boat began to shudder violently. The flat bottom of the cog was grounding. Their speed rapidly decelerated and it was all Savage could do to stop himself from being thrown forwards off the prow. He felt as if his teeth would be shaken from his head as the ship shuddered to a halt.

There was a moment of silence, then a thump as a spear thrown from one of the piers embedded itself in the deck. Two men suddenly screamed in unison as a crossbow quarrel tore through one of them and embedded itself in the second man's chest. Crammed together on the deck the soldiers had no chance to get out of the way or dodge the missiles that were beginning to rain down on them. They had to get off the ship and fast.

Savage pulled his helm onto his head and quickly fastened its strap beneath his chin.

'Ropes! Ropes!' he shouted, tossing a mooring rope down from the prow to dangle into the water below. The helmet made his voice sound muffled and metallic but the others followed his example and began flinging ropes over the side. Savage lifted his shield and slung it by its strap over one shoulder. Then he grabbed the rope and leapt over the side.

He was glad to be wearing gauntlets as the weight of his chain mail turned his descent into a slide very quickly. In moments he was down the rope. He hit the freezing water with a splash and icy liquid was seeping through chain mail leggings and gushing down into his boots. He sucked in air but seemed unable to let it out as the shock of the cold gripped his chest. The sea was up to his waist and he had about twenty paces to struggle through to get to the beach. He could see Scotsmen leaving the barricades on the piers and running towards the beach to stop him and his men. The plan was working. Now he just had to get out of the water and avoid being slaughtered before he even made it to the beach.

Savage drew his sword and surged forward, sending up great waves and froth as he churned the water. It was hard going and in moments he was desperately out of breath. The helmet stifled his breathing further and he felt as though he were choking. He had to keep going though. Around him he heard other splashes and knew the rest of the men were following. As he waded for the shore he unslung his shield and slid his left arm through the loops in the back of it as he prepared for action.

As the water got shallower the going got easier and he caught his breath a little. Finally he stumbled onto the shingle of the sloping beach and stood, water running from him in torrents, as he prepared to meet the coming assault. Luckily the Scots' reaction had been one of panic and they were simply charging wildly in a desperate attempt to stop him and his men getting ashore. Rather than a coordinated attack they were arriving in ones and twos.

The first Scotsman came at him with a spear. Savage swept the attack aside with his shield and slashed with the scimitar. The blade cleaved the man's leather helmet in two and the skull beneath, coming to a stop at the bridge of his nose. As he collapsed, the next man threw his spear. Savage could only drop to a crouch. The spear missed him, just, sailing a hair's breadth over his head. Savage came up again, screaming as he rose, driving his sword up and into the man's guts. The blade smashed through chain mail rings, leather jerkin and drove through the soft flesh and insides beneath. Hot blood gushed down the blade, spilling over his hands and onto the shingle below.

A glance over his shoulder told him the rest of his men were arriving on the beach, splashing the last few yards out of the sea.

'Shield wall!' he ordered, pointing to his right with the bloody scimitar, then turning and pointing to his left and shouting 'Shield wall!' once more. The men arriving on the beach formed an arrowhead on either side of him, locking their shields together to form coordinated barriers against the still-arriving Scots. This gave them pause and they halted their advance for a moment. Savage was still breathing hard. His heart beat so fast he felt like it was about to burst out of his chest and he felt vomit at the pit of his throat. He stabbed his sword into the shingle, then tore angrily at the laces that held his helmet on. They parted and he ripped it off, sucking in welcome lungfuls of the chilly night air. Quickly he tied the laces of the helmet to his belt.

He didn't want to wear it but it was too expensive an item to simply throw away.

He knew they could stand there all night and as more and more men from his ship waded ashore he decided it was time to take the fight to the enemy. Barking orders, he sent one half of his men towards one pier and the other towards the second pier. They would attack the Scots from behind, which should allow the ships enough respite to dock. His shield wall parted as the two sides of it advanced in separate directions.

Savage moved to the centre of the phalanx of men who approached the pier where Syr Paschall's ship was struggling to land. They hurried across the beach, going as fast as they could without breaking formation. The Scotsmen who had broken off from the pier to try to stop them attacked bravely but there were too few of them to hope to make an impression. They threw themselves against the advancing shields but Savage's men locked shields, pushed forward and mowed them down, stepping over their bloodied, mangled corpses as they neared the pier. Some of the defenders on the pier looked around and saw the advance. They began shouting and gesticulating in their direction. Two of the crossbowmen turned around and loosed in their direction. Savage heard a cry and a man in the shield wall three along from him went down, grasping at the end of a crossbow quarrel that now protruded from his chest. He heard the angry hum as the second quarrel passed close overhead. He suddenly regretted taking off his helmet.

Some of the defenders on the pier abandoned the fight with the ship's crew and turned to face the new threat. As they did so it gave a couple of Syr Paschall's men the chance to finally scramble on the quay and desperate hand-to-hand fighting ensued. The clash of weapons rang in the air and the night was filled with the screams and cries of men.

Savage's contingent reached the landward end of the wooden pier and paused. Before them the pier jutted out into the sea. It was only about fifteen paces wide, less with the barricades that had been built on the seaward side, so there was not enough room for them all to advance in a line. This could negate their numerical advantage. Savage had about forty men with him, twice the number of Scots on the quay, but there was only room for four men to advance along it side by side. The Scots were already arranging a defence halfway down the quay and pulling men from the barricade to face the new threat. If they held fast the fight would be reduced to an even contest of four against four.

Among the Scots moved a man in expensive, highly polished plate armour. Over it he wore a blue surcoat emblazoned with a red chevron. His head was protected by a bascinet helmet and the visor was up so the orders he was shouting could be heard. He was gesticulating towards the end of the pier and Savage deduced this must be their leader.

'You there!' Savage shouted as loudly as he could. His voice was lost in the din of battle.

'Wait here,' he said over his shoulder to his men, then walked out in front of them. He began to walk down the pier, advancing steadily, but his sword arm was held by his side. He had gone three steps when he spotted a crossbowman levelling his weapon at him. Savage just had time to crouch behind his shield as the man loosed his weapon. There was a resounding bang as the quarrel hit the shield, the force rocking Savage back slightly. To his consternation he saw the point of the quarrel now protruded through the back of the shield a finger's length from his left eye. He stood up again quickly. There was little time before the crossbowman could reload.

Savage waved his sword arm above his head. 'You! In the blue and red. I want to talk!' he shouted.

Finally the Scots commander noticed him. He held up his right arm, signalling to his men around him to pause. Savage now got a good look at the knight's face. He was young and his features were slick with sweat. There was blood on his armour and his eyes had the faraway look of someone lost in the ecstasy of battle, the strange trance that sometimes overcame men in the heat of deadly fighting.

'Who are you? What do you want?' the Scotsman shouted.

'I am Syr Richard Savage, knight of Ulster and commander of these men,' Savage replied.

'Savage, eh?' the Scotsman said. 'I believe you have something belonging to my lord, Edward Bruce. I am Syr Neil Fleming of Argyle. I am entrusted with commanding the siege of this castle.'

'You've fought well, Syr Neil,' Savage said, 'but your battle is lost. Surrender now with honour and we'll let you all walk free.'

Fleming shook his head. 'I will never betray the trust my lord has put in me. Be gone, Savage. Get back on your ships and return to Dublin.'

'You'll all die. You're outnumbered five to one,' Savage tried one more attempt at reason. 'You don't need to do this.'

'If that's our fate then so be it,' Fleming roared back at

him, his eyes wide, spittle flying from his mouth. 'We will fight all of you. Men will see that we can die for our lord. Besides, my master is on his way. When he gets here it will be you who's outnumbered, not us.'

Savage narrowed his eyes, then turned and ran back to the end of the pier where his men waited.

'What do we do now?' one of them asked.

'You heard him,' Savage said. 'He wants to die. Let's not disappoint him.'

71

Carrickfergus Castle was a cauldron of activity. The arrival of the ships in the harbour from out of the darkness was as surprising to the garrison – probably more so – than to the Scots outside. The alarm had been raised and all able-bodied men who were not already dressed for battle rushed to pull on mail, armour and helmets and grab weapons from the armoury. They gathered in an expectant crowd in the outer ward behind the castle gate.

Strapping on his sword belt as he hurried to join them, Guilleme le Poer arrived and found Henry de Thrapston talking to MacKillen and the two other remaining sergeants of the garrison.

'We need to get out there and help the ships,' de Thrapston said. 'They're having real problems landing. We can attack the Scots in the harbour from behind.'

Le Poer nodded. He quickly surveyed the remnants of the castle garrison around him, noticing their gaunt, hungry faces, the way the chain mail and leather jerkins seemed to hang loosely on their starved frames and, above all, the paltry number of them. There were perhaps twenty-five altogether.

The expression on his face betrayed his thoughts.

'What is it?' de Thrapston said, noticing.

Le Poer took a deep breath then pulled the keeper of the castle aside by the arm. He did not want the men to hear what could be discouraging discussion.

'We're not sure how many men the Scots have left defending the siege works outside,' le Poer said quietly. 'It could be up to half of them. If this goes wrong we could end up losing so many men we won't be able to defend the castle. Worse, we could lose it in the fight.'

De Thrapston looked him in the eye for several moments; his face was grim as he considered the situation.

'We've no choice,' he decided. 'We have to sally out.'

Le Poer nodded. 'You're right. Let's go,' he said.

They took their place at the head of the band of men who shuffled forwards into the narrow entrance passage that went through the front gate tower of the castle. Crammed into the small space the men waited for battle. Some mumbled prayers while others simply stood quiet, lost in their own thoughts. A couple of them took fierce breaths through their noses, letting the inrush of air boil their blood and provoke their fighting spirit. De Thrapston gave the order and the air was filled with metallic clanking as the men in the tower above began to crank the portcullis up. Le Poer pulled on his cylindrical great helm. The world narrowed to his view through the eye slits as his breathing suddenly became loud in the enclosed space. His armour was chain mail and he hefted a wood and leather shield on his left arm as he drew his sword. Beside him the sergeant, MacKillen, gripped his own sword. His right leg jiggled nervously up and down as the iron-bound spikes at the bottom of the portcullis neared the top of the gateway. As it slid into the slot above the gate there came a loud rattling of heavy chains as the drawbridge was released. It fell with a deafening crash to span the sea-filled trench outside the castle gate.

With a blood-curdling roar, the men of the castle charged out of the gate and over the drawbridge. There was a short hill before them at the bottom of which were the line of siege works and trenches the Scots had built to cut the castle off from the town.

They started down the hill in a clump and something zipped by le Poer's head, humming like an angry hornet. A man to his right in the front ranks shouted in pain and collapsed to the ground. Two men running behind him stumbled over his body. A second man went down. Another angry buzz shot overhead.

'Crossbows!' le Poer shouted, spotting the men at the Scots' line of siege works who were using the shelter of the wooden screens to loose bolts in the direction of the charging garrison from the castle. They were still thirty or forty paces away from the defences and he knew they would lose more men before they got there.

Another loud roar came from below. Scots warriors came running out from behind the screens and pouring up from the trenches, pounding up the hill to meet the men coming down it. To le Poer's dismay it looked like there were as many of them as in the band who had left the castle. There was a knight leading them. He wore plate armour and like le Poer a cylindrical great helm. He bore a great two-handed sword, which meant he did not have a shield, though because of the plate armour he did not need one. To le Poer's surprise the surcoat the knight wore over his armour was white with a single, black, equal-armed cross in the centre of the chest, the symbol of the Teutonic Knights.

He had little time to wonder further. With a terrific bang something hit him somewhere near the forehead. His head snapped back and he staggered sideways, his forward momentum nullified by the blow. His hearing was engulfed in a high-pitched whistling that rang in his ears and he could see nothing but blackness. Completely disoriented, le Poer fell over, landing heavily on his right side and losing his grip on his sword.

For a few moments he lay still, unable to hear or see and wondering if he was alive or dead. He tasted blood and metal, his right cheek was sore and he felt a great pressure on it. The front of his helmet had been pushed in and now pressed into his face.

Deciding he was still alive, he prised the battered helmet gingerly off his head and sat up. A shattered crossbow bolt lay a few paces away on the cobblestones. What had happened to him became obvious. He had been shot in the head. With a careful, groggy hand he felt his way around his skull and everything seemed to be in place. His helmet had saved him. He was very lucky to be alive.

Dizzy and with his ears still ringing, le Poer staggered to his feet. He was vaguely aware of a familiar voice shouting somewhere nearby.

To his consternation he saw that the fighting was not going well. Two more of the garrison had been downed by crossbows. One lay still on his back, dead eyes staring up at the night sky. The second squirmed in agony on the ground amid a widening pool of his own blood. Le Poer felt a moment's queasiness at the thought that it could have been him as well. The rest were engaging the Scots in hand-to-hand fighting but another two of them already lay dead from stab wounds. The Scots had one man down. MacKillen was taking a swing at the German knight with his sword. The German easily parried his blow with the longsword, whirled around in a blur of motion and landed a blow on the sergeant that took his left leg off above the knee.

MacKillen screeched in pain and fell over, blood gushing from his severed limb across the ground and splattering the German's white surcoat with crimson. The German stepped forward, both hands on the hilt of his sword and drove the point down through MacKillen's screaming mouth and into his brain. The sergeant kicked his remaining leg violently then lay still. With practised movements, the German withdrew the blade from MacKillen's skull and swung again, this time at a man from the garrison who was locked in combat with another Scotsman nearby. The huge blade hit the Irishman at the bottom of his back, cutting him clean in two at the waist.

It was hopeless. The men from the castle were outnumbered already. Le Poer suddenly recognised the voice that was shouting nearby and realised that Henry de Thrapston had come to the same conclusion.

'Retreat!' de Thrapston bellowed. 'Get back to the castle.'

Le Poer, still dizzy, stumbled towards him. De Thrapston grabbed the younger man by the arm and pulled him back up the hill. The rest of the garrison did their best to disengage from their combats, then turned tail and ran.

It became a race to the gate. Le Poer knew if they did not get to the gate and close it before the Scots then the castle would be lost. They pounded up the cobbled hill as fast as they could go, lungs bursting, legs heavy, muscles burning from the effort. Moments later their boots were pounding across the wood of the drawbridge. They fell as much as charged through the threshold of the castle and de Thrapston yelled to the men above to drop the portcullis.

There was a rattling of metal and the heavy iron-bound gate, released from the catches above, roared as it dropped from the ceiling to seal the entrance.

A moment later would have been too late. As it was three of the garrison were left outside. They threw themselves in despair against the wood and iron grill of the closed portcullis. The Scots coming hard behind them slammed into them and the portcullis and before the horrified eyes of their comrades within the castle gate slaughtered the men left outside like they were sheep.

De Thrapston lurched to his feet. 'Raise the drawbridge,' he shouted to the men in the tower above. Three men began working a windlass in the floor, the chains began rattling and the drawbridge began to raise. The Scots at the gate were forced to run backwards or be crushed between the portcullis and the rising drawbridge, the last ones having to leap from the end of the drawbridge back down to the far side of the trench that separated the castle from the land. The men in the castle gate had a brief moment of vicious consolation from the sound of a Scotsman screaming as he missed the far side and fell into the trench.

The drawbridge slammed closed, doubly sealing the entrance to the castle. For a few moments all that could be heard was heavy breathing as the men tried to catch their breath.

De Thrapston looked around at how few men of the garrison were now left.

Le Poer's heart sank as his worst fears were realised.

'Those men from the ships had better get through,' he said. 'If they don't we're finished.'

72

Savage marshalled his men at the end of the pier. His plan was simple. They would form up with four men at the front and the rest behind them.

They advanced at a jog. The four men at the front had shields raised and locked together. All bore spears levelled and pointed directly forwards at the enemy. The rest of Savage's contingent came behind them. A couple of crossbow bolts were loosed at them but they bounced harmlessly off the upraised shields. The Scots down the pier arranged four men across it and prepared to meet them. As he'd previously observed, the narrowness of the pier negated the numerical advantage of Savage's men by forcing them to fight each other four against four.

Savage had no intention of obliging the Scots in this respect.

The Scotsmen locked their own shields together and braced for the initial impact, swords and spears ready to stab forward once the advancing warriors had been halted.

The two lines of shields clashed together with a bang that echoed around the harbour. Savage and the men following threw their shoulders into the men in front of them. Heaving forwards they turned their front rank into a human battering ram. The sheer weight of their numbers was impossible for the Scotsmen to resist and their shield wall came apart, the men behind it knocked backwards sprawling onto the pier.

Savage's men spilled forwards over them, delivering killing blows as they stepped on their bodies on the way past. The rest of the Scots turned to meet the new immediate threat, abandoning their battle to keep the men on Syr Paschall's ship off the pier. All semblance of ranks or sides dissolved into chaotic fighting. Blades sang as they clashed together, men roared in battle fury and screamed as they died. The wooden planks of the pier became slick with blood spurting from wounds and the iron smell of it tainted the air.

Fleming saw Savage amid the throng and with a cry of anger ran at him. Behind him Savage could see more and more men from Syr Paschall's ship pouring up onto the pier to join the fight. He knew they were on the verge of overwhelming the Scots but he would have to personally deal with Syr Neil. The Scottish knight swung his sword with both hands, a tremendous blow aimed at cutting Savage in two at the chest. Savage blocked with his shield. The impact of the blow jarred the shield and sent jabs of pain up into his left shoulder. He countered with the scimitar but it simply glanced off Fleming's superior armour, the blade skidding off his shoulder piece and scything down into the wood of the pier. He tried to pull it back out but it was stuck fast. Fleming swung at him again. Savage had to let go of his sword hilt and take shelter behind his shield. In a well-aimed blow, Fleming's blade connected with Savage's shield at the same place where the crossbow quarrel was still embedded in it. Already weakened by the earlier impact, the leather parted and the wood beneath split. The iron rim fell off and Savage found himself left grasping the useless handles as the shield disintegrated from his arm. He now had neither sword to attack with nor shield to defend himself.

Fleming grinned and spat at him. 'We may have lost,' he said, 'but at least I get the pleasure of killing you.'

He advanced, sword point levelled towards Savage's throat. Savage began to walk backwards away from the advancing blade. Without warning his left foot skidded in a slippery pool of blood and he lost his balance. Savage fell, crashing heavily onto the wood of the pier, landing flat on his back.

With a wicked shout of triumph, Fleming ran forward, stabbing down at Savage. Desperate, Savage moved sideways as best he could but he could not move far or fast enough. He felt the point of Fleming's sword breaking the rings of his mail and fiery pain erupted from his left shoulder as the blade entered his flesh.

Even as it did, Savage lifted both feet and planted them on Fleming's chest. The downward momentum of the Scots knight was checked and the sword's progress halted before it went deeper. Savage heaved with his thighs, forcing Fleming backwards and away from him. The sword was pulled out of Savage's shoulder again and now it was Fleming who staggered backwards, off balance and flailing wildly with his free hand for purchase in case he strayed off the pier completely.

Savage rolled on his right side and scrambled to his feet. He looked for his sword but it was still stuck in the pier and Fleming was between him and it. Pain blazed in his left shoulder and as he gasped and raised his right hand to his wound his left foot hit against something. Momentarily distracted, he looked down and saw one of the grappling hooks Syr Paschall's men had thrown onto the pier to pull their ship in and try to land.

Savage stooped, grabbed the hook and came up again, just in time to see Fleming, his balance regained, was coming at him again.

Fleming lunged at him but Savage danced to the side. His chain mail may have been less protective but at least he was lighter on his feet and the weight of Fleming's plate propelled him, lumbering forwards, following the momentum of his blow.

Savage swung the grappling hook backhanded at Fleming as he passed, holding the three-pronged hook in his right hand by its shaft. Two of the hook's prongs went through the open visor of Fleming's helmet. The points tore into his face, smashing through his forehead above the right eye and his right cheekbone into his skull.

Savage let go of the hook. Fleming gave a strangled, confused cry. He dropped his sword, his hands flailing to his face to grasp the shaft of the grappling hook that was now embedded in his head. The knight staggered sideways, his left foot stepped off the pier into space and he toppled over. Fleming fell from the pier. His body completed a full somersault before he landed in the water, sending up a tremendous splash that sent spray right up to splatter Savage on the pier above. The weight of the plate armour dragged Fleming straight under, the reddening sea closing over him in an instant.

Savage stood for a moment, looking down into the widening circle of blood in the water that marked where the Scottish knight had fallen in. His left arm felt like it was on fire and he felt blood running down it from the wound in his shoulder to drip from the finger of his hand. He was panting for breath and sweat dripped from his forehead, running into his eyes and stinging them.

He looked around. The remnants of the Scots defenders were being killed by the combined force of his men and the men from Syr Paschall's ship who were now scrambling in overwhelming numbers onto the pier. He felt an overwhelming weariness come over him as he realised they had won. The Scots on the other pier were now hopelessly outnumbered. They would land all of Syr Paschall's men then go over and deal with them, allowing de Mandeville's ship and the others behind to finally dock.

After that all that remained was to get to the castle and finally rescue Galiene.

73

Syr Paschall was distraught at being denied another chance to win glory. Savage told the seneschal what Fleming had said about Bruce returning with the army and so de Mandeville dispatched Paschall and the men from his ship to secure the town.

'We don't want any surprises,' de Mandeville had ordered once he was off his own ship. 'Perhaps you'll find a few more Scotsmen to fight on the way.'

It had not taken long to mop up the last of the Scots resistance in the harbour. The last two ships had docked and the warriors regrouped on the beach in the midst of the harbour.

De Mandeville looked up at the prow of Savage's grounded ship and shook his head. He turned and looked at Savage, an expression of half-reproach on his face.

Savage shrugged. 'It had to be done. Otherwise you'd still be floating out there.'

The seneschal nodded his agreement but he looked upset.

'I just hope this isn't a sign that God is angry with us for breaking the Peace of Easter,' he said. 'They seemed to be waiting for us.'

Savage tutted angrily. 'This has nothing to do with God,'

he retorted, grasping the hilt of his scimitar which, with some difficulty, he had prised out of the wood of the pier. 'It's just plain old bad luck. Or treachery.'

De Mandeville looked him straight in the eye. 'Thank you. If it wasn't for you we wouldn't have got ashore.' He suddenly frowned, pointing at the broken chain mail links around Savage's shoulder wound and noting the blood that still dripped from the fingers of Savage's left hand. 'That looks serious,' he commented. 'You should get it looked at by the surgeon—'

'Richard!'

Both turned to see Alys running towards them. Her cloak and breeches were soaked from wading ashore. Savage winced as she threw her arms around him. Hearing his sharp intake of breath she pulled back, noticing his injury.

'You're hurt,' she said. 'I need to treat that.'

Savage shook his head. 'Later. There's no time now.'

'You're no use in a fight now,' de Mandeville said. 'Why don't you take some men and start getting the food up to the castle.'

Savage nodded.

A man came running towards the beach from the direction of the town. He was shouting and waving as he came. All turned to see one of Syr Paschall's men approaching. He was sweating heavily and his face was ashen.

'Sire,' the man, panting from running, gasped to the seneschal. 'Syr Paschall sends word that the Scottish army is coming. We went to the town gate and climbed to the ramparts. We saw them by the torches they carry. There's thousands of them and they are almost here.'

A collective groan went up from everyone surrounding

the seneschal. De Mandeville himself rolled his eyes. He looked up at the dark sky for a moment, then, characteristically decisive, he began to give orders.

'The most important thing now is that the supplies get to the castle,' he said. 'Savage, it's now up to you.'

'I'll make sure they get there, sire,' Savage said, saluting with his uninjured arm.

'The rest of us,' the seneschal said in a raised voice so all those around him could hear, 'will go and meet Edward Bruce and his army. We'll go to the town gate and fight them there. That should buy enough time to get the supplies to the castle.'

The warriors collected their weapons and filed off the beach towards the town.

Savage told the twenty men he had been assigned to start unloading the ship and moving the supplies to the castle. He put his right arm around Alys.

'Come on,' he said. 'Let's get up to the castle and tell them it's safe to open the gates.'

They hurried up the hill from the beach towards the front gate of Carrickfergus Castle.

As they approached, Savage looked up and saw people on the battlements above the gate tower. Several of them seemed to be waving in his direction. They were shouting too but they were too far away to make out what they were saying.

'What is it?' he called back. 'You can open the gates. We come from Dublin. We've got food for you.'

'Very good, Savage.'

A new voice with a distinct German accent rang out across the night.

Savage and Alys halted. Men were filing out from the Scots siege works and trenches that stood between the town and the castle gate. These warriors were Scots. In their lead was a knight in full armour and helm, wearing the surcoat of a Teutonic Knight. Savage swore under his breath. They had been foolish and assumed all the Scots in the town had been defeated in the harbour. These men had been waiting for them to come to the castle. On reflection it was obvious. Why would the Scots leave the castle gates unguarded? The Scots spread out, forming a line of steel between Savage and Alys and the castle gate. The German, who seemed to be in command of them, signalled that they should halt. He walked forward a few paces alone then stopped. He pulled off his helmet and Savage recognised a familiar pair of pale eyes.

'Von Mahlberg,' Savage said, identifying the German. 'So you're fighting for Scotland now? What would your Lord Mortimer say?'

Von Mahlberg chuckled. 'Be assured, Syr Richard, my master approves of my actions here. Now. You and I have unfinished business. I demand a rematch of our duel in Bordeaux. Just you and I. Here before the castle.'

'He's injured,' Alys said bitterly. 'It won't be a fair fight.'

'It was not a fair fight the last time either, madam,' von Mahlberg said, his tone laden with mocking admonishment. 'Your husband cheated and robbed me of my deserved victory.'

Savage spoke to Alys from the corner of his mouth. His voice was quiet but insistent. 'Get back to the harbour. Get the rest of the men and come back fast as you can.'

'I can't leave you.' Alys looked horrified. 'You can only fight with one arm. You'll be slaughtered!'

'Thanks for your confidence in my abilities,' Savage said, trying to raise a smile. 'What are you going to do? Fight him for me? Go. It's our only hope. I'll try to stall him as long as I can.'

Alys looked dubious but nevertheless turned and ran off in the direction of the harbour.

'Even she deserts you in the end, Savage,' von Mahlberg said, drawing his sword and starting to advance. 'How unlucky you are.'

Savage took in the situation. He saw the figures on the top of the gate tower of the castle and understood now that they had been trying to warn him of the ambush. With a sudden shock he realised that one of them was Henry de Thrapston. Briefly he wondered if the gaunt skeleton-like face illuminated by the torchlight on the tower – so changed from the plump, hearty fellow de Thrapston had been the last time Savage had seen him – was actually a ghost, but he dispelled the idea as nonsense as quickly as it arose. Beside the keeper of the castle he spotted another familiar face in Guilleme le Poer and his heart leapt when he saw the girl with a mop of curly blonde hair at his side.

'Galiene!' he shouted, waving his right hand then breaking off to pull the left shoulder of his cloak down to hide his wound. 'It's me.'

The girl responded with a tentative wave.

She may as well have been a thousand miles away. The castle drawbridge was closed, opening a yawning, sea-filled gap between the land and the castle. At the bottom of the little hill that led up to that gap stood the line of Scottish warriors, blocking the way to the castle. In front of them was von Mahlberg.

'How nice. Your wife may have run off but at least your daughter will be here to watch you die,' the German said, walking ever closer.

He was approaching striking distance and Savage drew the scimitar so as to be ready for any sudden attack.

'What do you hope to achieve by this, von Mahlberg?' he asked. 'Even if you beat me you can't win. De Mandeville has hundreds of men in the harbour and all the other Scots there are dead. How many men have you got? Twenty? You'll be annihilated.'

Von Mahlberg gave a little chuckle. 'You are assuming I intend to stand and fight with them,' he said. He lowered his voice so as only to be heard by Savage. The Scotsmen standing ten paces behind would hear nothing. 'I have no desire for martyrdom. Once you are dead my work here is done,' he continued. 'My Lord Mortimer's purpose will be fulfilled. I have a boat hidden on the beach behind the castle. Once you are dead I can get away in that without going anywhere near the harbour. These Scottish heroes can fight and die for the castle gate.'

Savage opened his mouth, intending to relay what was just said to the Scotsman up the hill. He was cut off as von Mahlberg attacked. The German lunged forward, springing off his right thigh, sword extended. Savage jumped back, away from the blade. He struck down with his own blade, knocking von Mahlberg's sword aside. Savage stepped inside and swung at the German's head. Von Mahlberg, fast as lightning, pulled his forearms up putting his fists above his head and bringing his sword up to halt the scimitar's progress just above his forehead.

Savage tried to force his blade down further so it would cut into the German's scalp but he was only using one hand while von Mahlberg gripped his weapon in two. The blades sat locked together for a moment then it was Savage who felt his own sword being pushed upward by the German's superior strength. With a curse he pulled the blade away and jumped back beyond striking range.

Savage felt tired and slightly dizzy and he began to wonder just how much blood he had lost.

Von Mahlberg swung at him, this time a scything backhanded blow, his sword held in his right hand, aiming to take Savage's head from his shoulders. Savage ducked beneath the sword and came forward, intending to stab the German, but Von Mahlberg – with his free left hand – punched him directly on the wound in his shoulder.

Savage gasped as hot agony exploded. He staggered backwards, his sword hand reflexively covering the site of the blow as he tried to overcome the pain.

A huge roar echoed across the town. It was the sound of many men, all screaming and shouting in unison. It drifted from the darkness beyond the blazing fires around the harbour and marketplace. At the sound both Savage and von Mahlberg's heads whipped around in its direction. This could only mean that the Scottish army had arrived at the town gate and battle had begun.

'We will finish this now,' von Mahlberg said.

He lunged forward again, this time aiming lower. Savage turned his attention back to his attacker but too late. With a strange feeling of unreality, he saw the German's sword first burst the rings of his chain mail leggings and then slide seemingly effortlessly into the meat of his right thigh. He felt a tug behind his leg accompanied again by the ring of broken mail and realised the blade had gone right through his leg and come out the back.

Von Mahlberg, fully extended, came back up off his forward leg, withdrawing his sword back through Savage's leg and returning to a standing guard.

Savage looked at him for an instant then white-hot pain engulfed his right leg. He cried out, dropping the scimitar, both hands grasping for the wound. His leg crumpled beneath him and he collapsed onto the cobblestones.

74

O n the castle battlements, le Poer winced at the sight of the sword transfixing Savage's leg. Around him, the watching remnants of the garrison groaned as Savage fell.

'Can't someone help him?' Galiene wailed. She cast desperate looks around her, her face streaked with tears.

De Thrapston shook his head. His face was grim and there was a look of sadness in his eyes. 'If we open the gates the Scots will charge straight in. There aren't enough of us to hold them and we'll lose the castle. I'm sorry.'

Galiene was frantic. She looked from face to face around her but saw only the same expressions of pity and despair on them all. Suddenly her eyes widened.

'You!' she said, pointing to a warrior who stood nearby. Slung over his back by a leather strap was a crossbow. 'Can't you shoot the German?'

The man almost flinched under the intensity of the girl's gaze. 'It's too far,' he said. 'They're out of range. I might be just about able to hit the Scotsmen but the German is too far away. They deliberately built those siege works where they are because they're just outside crossbow range.'

'Can't you even try, man?' le Poer asked.

'I've only two quarrels left,' the crossbowman said; his

tone was apologetic and he turned to speak directly to de Thrapston. 'As far as I know they're the last in the castle, sire. Shouldn't I keep them for the Scottish attack?'

They could hear the shouting and screaming coming from the battle that had erupted around the town gates. From their elevated position they could also see the numbers of torches that burned in the dark outside the town and knew the size of the Scots army was substantial.

De Thrapston did not reply immediately. He bowed his head as he weighed up the options. He looked from le Poer to the crossbowman to Galiene and out into the darkness where the Scots were coming. Then he looked down the hill to where Savage lay writhing in pain on the ground. The German, his back towards the castle, stepped towards Savage, preparing to finish him off.

De Thrapston sighed. 'There's an army fighting its way towards us. Two crossbow quarrels won't make much difference to that. Have a go.' He nodded to the crossbowman.

Shaking his head, the man put his right foot into the stirrup at the front of his weapon. He cranked the windlass at the back end, drawing the string back until the ratchet clicked into place, holding the crossbow in the cocked position. He slid one of his remaining bolts into the groove then raised it to his shoulder.

Sighting it on the centre of von Mahlberg's back below, he took a moment to calm himself, then with a crack he loosed his weapon.

All on the battlements watched, breath held, as the bolt streaked through the night air, downward towards the German.

Another collective groan arose. The bolt was not going to make it. It lost momentum, its trajectory dipping until it clattered uselessly onto the cobblestones still ten paces short of its intended target.

'Waste of a quarrel,' the crossbowman said.

'No!' Galiene protested. 'Let me try!' She held out her hand for the weapon.

The crossbowman, his face a mask of consternation, looked to de Thrapston for guidance. The keeper of the castle just shrugged and nodded.

Galiene snatched the weapon from the crossbowman's hands and began spinning the crank to cock it. He held out his last remaining quarrel before she could grab that too.

Galiene slotted the bolt into the groove and took aim on the German swordsman who now stood directly above her father, his sword raised.

Le Poer laid a hand on her shoulder. 'It's too far, Galiene.'

'I have to try! I can't just stand here doing nothing,' the girl sobbed. She closed one eye then breathed out steadily, trying desperately to calm her thudding heartbeat and subdue the other emotions that threatened to disturb her aim. She knew she only had one chance. She prepared to loose the bow.

A hand closed over hers, preventing her from pulling the lever.

Surprised and angry, she looked around and saw Fergus, the rat boy. He looked her in the eye, then without saying a word took the crossbow off her. Galiene let him take it. She stood aside as he held up a finger to test the breeze, then he raised the weapon to his shoulder, closing one eye and taking aim. The point of the bolt was levelled at his target.

Suddenly the rat boy raised the bow as if he were shooting at something almost in the sky.

'He's aiming far too high,' the crossbowman commented. 'He's going to waste my last bolt.'

75

Savage gritted his teeth and tried to focus. While he could feel warm blood pulsing through the fingers he grasped his wounded thigh with, it was not gushing out in the way he knew would be the case if one of the big blood vessels in his leg had been severed. Relatively speaking, he had been lucky. His wound was not fatal. At least not yet, anyway.

Unfortunately it had been enough to put him at the mercy of von Mahlberg, and he doubted the German possessed much of that. He looked up and in the blaze from the bonfires and braziers he saw the German towering over him against the black night sky, an unpleasant grin of triumph on his face.

Grimacing from the pain and effort, Savage held up a hand towards him. 'Wait a moment,' he said. 'I need to ask something.'

Von Mahlberg reversed his sword so the point hovered above Savage's chest. He grabbed the hilt in both hands and positioned his feet shoulder width apart. 'Very well. Be quick though,' he said, shooting a nervous glance towards the market square to see if there were any sign of the approaching Scots.

'What is a member of the Order of German Brothers doing

working for Mortimer?' Savage asked. 'You're supposed to follow the commands of the Holy Roman Emperor and the Pope, not an English earl.'

Von Mahlberg chuckled. 'True. However I am an ex-member of that order, not a current one. My brethren found my eagerness to cleanse and purify the pagans of the east to be a little too fervent. They had the audacity to expel me. Luckily my first love was always the sword rather than God. A great lord like Mortimer has need of men with talents like mine.'

The brutality the Teutonic Knights had unleashed against the pagans of Lithuania was as legendary as it was indiscriminate and horrific, and Savage dreaded to think just what von Mahlberg had done to stand out from his brother knights.

'Enough talk. Goodbye, Savage,' the German said, raising both hands above his head, preparing to stab down and through Savage's heart.

Savage glanced around, hoping to see Alys returning with the others but there was no sign of her. He looked to the castle tower above the gate and thought of Galiene. What must she be thinking? Regret and pain surged within him as he thought about how she would have to witness his death. How he would never hold Alys in his arms again. How she and Galiene would be alone once more in the world.

He had failed them yet again.

He closed his eyes, hoping the end would be quick and painless.

Several moments passed.

Nothing happened.

Savage briefly wondered if he was already dead, but the

burning agony in his thigh told him that was not the case, or if it was then everything he had been told about the dead being made whole again in Heaven was a cruel joke.

He opened his eyes. Von Mahlberg still stood above him, sword raised above his head.

'What are you waiting for you bastard?' Savage said. Then he noticed the look of confusion in the German's eyes. He seemed to be struggling to say something but was unable to get the words out. He let go of his sword. As it clattered onto the cobblestones von Mahlberg suddenly dropped to his knees. He gave a sudden cough and Savage was startled as a gout of bright blood exploded from his mouth along with it. The German reached towards the back of his head with both hands, as if trying to grasp something there.

Savage decided not to waste whatever form of reprieve this represented. He sat up, pulled his right fist back then punched the German in the face as hard as he was able.

Von Mahlberg toppled backwards on his knees. He landed flat on his back and there was an odd wet tearing sound. His throat began briefly to distend, as if there was something under the skin trying to push its way out, then the skin parted and the barbed head of a crossbow bolt burst through. Blood welled up around the exposed bolt and began to pour down von Mahlberg's neck, forming into a dark, quickly spreading pool around his head.

Savage looked up and saw Galiene on the battlements. Beside her stood a strange-looking, pale-skinned, skinny boy who held a crossbow up in the air. He nodded to Savage, a serious expression on his face. De Thrapston and le Poer were grinning and slapping the boy on the back.

Savage quickly realised what had happened. The boy had

hit von Mahlberg from the battlements with his crossbow. It was an incredible shot. The bolt had struck von Mahlberg on the back of the neck, then when he had punched him the weight of the German's falling body had driven the embedded bolt right through his throat.

Von Mahlberg gave another cough then a strange low groan and his eyes rolled up into his head. His arms fell flat to either side of him. His body went limp. He was dead.

The line of Scotsmen who stood between him and the castle looked startled at this turn of events. However, they quickly got over their amazement and their expressions turned to ones of anger. Three of them had crossbows and Savage realised he had probably survived von Mahlberg's attack only to be finished off by these men.

76

A loud metallic clanking arose behind the Scots from the castle gate, the unmistakable sound of the portcullis being cranked open. Shouts came from the battlements and the Scotsmen turned around to see what was going on. Warriors on the battlements launched a volley of spears at them, possibly the last ones they had. The range was too long but it was enough to distract the Scots for a few moments. They all turned to see what was happening and a couple jumped aside as some of the spears landed short but skittered over the cobblestones towards them.

Something whizzed over Savage's head from the direction of the harbour. One of the Scots crossbowmen cried out and fell, clutching at a wound that had exploded in his guts. Savage and the Scotsmen all turned again and saw that finally Alys had returned, now accompanied by the remnants of his men from the ship. At least five of them had armed themselves with fallen Genoese crossbows.

They loosed the bows, causing more Scotsmen to fall, and then charged into them, swords and spears flashing in the light from the fires.

With a resounding bang, the drawbridge of the castle crashed open and the battered remains of the garrison once more charged out, de Thrapston and le Poer at their head, to join the fight.

The skirmish was brief and bloody. The men of the garrison unleashed a fury of pent-up frustration on the Scotsmen. The exasperation of being on the receiving end of months of punishing attacks was transformed into a furious whirlwind of aggression. Combined with the men from Savage's ship they outnumbered the Scots and the tables were quickly turned. Within moments more than half the Scots were hacked to death and the remainder threw down their weapons and cried to surrender.

'Richard Savage!' le Poer shouted as he strode to where Savage still sat on the ground. His face was bruised from the earlier crossbow hit but he wore a broad smile. 'Damn good to see you again.'

'Le Poer,' Savage acknowledged. He leaned forward on both hands, trying to push himself up to his feet. The pain that shot through his wounded leg made him collapse back down again.

'Need a hand?' le Poer said. He hooked his arm under Savage's and helped him rise, allowing him to lean on him and keep his weight off his injured leg.

'Richard!' Alys came running to him and flung her arms around Savage, burying her face in his chest. At the same time he spotted Galiene come running out of the castle gate. The girl, tears streaming, hesitated for a moment, then threw her arms round both her mother and father. Savage, wincing as his wife and daughter pressed themselves against his wounded leg and shoulder, gritted his teeth and put one arm around each of them.

For a few moments they stood like that, no one speaking,

then le Poer, still supporting Savage under one arm and involuntarily half-engaged in their group hug, gave an embarrassed cough.

'I feel like I'm intruding here,' he said.

'You need to get the supplies into the castle,' Savage urged as Alys took le Poer's place under Savage's arm and le Poer stepped away. 'Otherwise this has all been for nothing.'

Le Poer nodded and ran off to start organising the men to that task.

'Not completely for nothing,' Alys said, her eyes bright with tears as she ran her hands through the blonde curls of Galiene's hair. 'There were a few times recently when I thought I'd never see either of you again.'

'Can we go home, now?' Galiene asked, looking up at her father.

Savage exchanged glances with Alys but just replied, 'Yes.'

Men were now carrying barrels and crates full of food and weapons up the hill and into the castle. Standing to one side, the Savages watched, impressed at how quickly the cargo from the ship was moved. As they worked, the noise of battle from the town gate intensified, compelling the men to even greater speed.

Alys got to work tending to Savage's injuries. She pulled a leather belt from a dead man and tightened it around her husband's thigh to stop the bleeding, then she tore strips of cloth from other corpses' clothing to pack and bind his wounds.

Henry de Thrapston finally began to smile and Savage caught a glimpse of the old, congenial castellan he had first met in Carrickfergus the year before. 'We've enough supplies here to hold out for a while longer,' he said. There was a defiant bitterness in his tone that acknowledged that the mission had not succeeded in breaking the siege. It would be only a matter of time before the Scots army retook the town but they could take some consolation in the partial success of the supplies getting to where they were needed. 'We could do with a few more men, though,' he added, thinking of the meagre remnants of the garrison who survived.

'I think some of these fellows will have to stay with you,' Savage said, pointing to the men from his ship. 'We've one ship less than we arrived with.'

At that moment a great shout erupted from the other side of the marketplace. An armed man, bloody from fighting, stumbled from the main street into the light from the bonfires. Following him, a great confused tide of men erupted into the open area. They were Scots and Irish, mixed up and all fighting each other. The battle spilled across the marketplace and down onto the beach. Some men extracted themselves and began running for the ships. The fight for the town was coming to its bloody conclusion and it was obvious the raiders had lost.

De Thrapston's smile disappeared. 'We'll let as many of your men into the castle as we can, then we'll have to close the gates,' he said and ran off to start directing the process. 'Keep those supplies moving as long as you can!' he shouted to some of Savage's men who looked like they were about to set down what they were carrying and join the fray.

Savage caught sight of Thomas de Mandeville in the middle of the marketplace. He still wore his great helm but Savage recognised him by his armour and surcoat. He stood like a rock amid the chaos, his armour battered and blood-streaked, dealing blows with his sword left and right. Three Irish kerns fought beside him and as Savage watched he cut down at least three Scottish spearmen who came to attack him.

Horsemen burst into the marketplace and Savage knew the fight really was over now. They were knights, emblazoned with Scottish coats of arms. They rode through the throng of fighting men, mowing down whoever was in their path and striking killing blows on all sides with swords, axes and maces. Panic took hold among the raiders and many now began running for the ships or the castle. The battle was lost.

A horseman spurred his steed towards de Mandeville. He wore no helmet and Savage recognised the shaved head and blunt features of Gib Harper. De Mandeville raised his sword to protect himself but the big Scotsman rose in his saddle, standing in the stirrups and bringing the huge, two-headed axe he bore down. The blow was crushing, breaking de Mandeville's sword and smashing into his helmet. The armour held but was terribly dented. Savage saw the seneschal's knees buckle and he collapsed onto the cobblestones of the marketplace.

Another rider followed directly behind Harper. He wore a great helm, full plate armour and over it an azure surcoat embroidered with a rampant silver lion. It was Edward Bruce, Earl of Carrick and King of Ireland by conquest.

Bruce stopped his horse beside the fallen seneschal and swung himself out of the saddle. He sheathed his sword and drew a long knife from his belt. Savage winced and shook his head as Bruce went down on one knee and shoved the dagger through the eye slits of de Mandeville's helmet. The seneschal's body jerked violently then lay still. Bruce wiped his knife on de Mandeville's surcoat and climbed back onto his horse.

'Bastard,' Savage hissed through clenched teeth.

'There's nothing you can do about it,' Alys said. She felt the same anger but her tone was as hard as steel and she looked him straight in the eyes. 'Richard, we must get away or we'll all die here. This fight is over. We have to get to the harbour and onto one of the ships before it's too late.'

Savage looked at her for a moment. 'All right,' he said, resignation heavy in his voice, 'but we go this way.'

He indicated the dark beach on the opposite side of the castle to the harbour.

'Von Mahlberg says he hid a boat there to escape in,' he added, seeing Alys's look of confused uncertainty.

Alys bit her lip. Still unsure, she looked back towards the harbour. The fighting had already overflowed onto the beach and the piers around the ships. It looked like they would be lucky if any of the ships got away at all. The only other option was to flee into the castle.

'Let's go and get the German's boat,' she said, looking down at the corpse that lay nearby. 'He won't need it anyway.'

Alys and Galiene positioned themselves on each side of Savage, one under each arm, and helped him limp down towards the beach. As they climbed down onto the sand and their eyes adjusted to the dark, they made out the outline of a curragh sitting upturned on the shore.

'We won't get too far in that,' Alys said dubiously, looking down at the small, narrow rowing boat.

'We just need to get away from here,' Savage said. 'We stand a better chance of slipping away unnoticed in something small like this.'

Alys and Galiene turned the boat upright and slid it down towards the water. They helped Savage climb in, then both pushed it into the sea. As the freezing cold water got deeper Galiene got in then finally Alys pulled herself in over the back and settled into the rowing seat. She began to pull on the oars and the boat moved away from the beach into the surf.

Galiene looked back at the castle and in the firelight she saw the pale features of the rat boy looking down from the battlements. She raised a tentative hand towards him and waved. He waved back, then he was gone.

Behind them, amid the din of the closing battle in the marketplace, they could hear the rattle of chains as once more the castle drawbridge closed.

77

'Well who'd have thought we'd end up here, of all places?' Alys said, looking around at the desolate interior of the castle that had once been her home.

They had taken the rowing boat up the lough, leaving behind the battle as it raged to a climax in Carrickfergus. It looked like two of the ships managed to escape the harbour but more Scots had come across the lough in smaller vessels and continued to attack and harry the ships as they sailed away.

Galiene had joined Alys at the oars and they kept close to the coast, travelling up the lough until they reached the mouth where it joined the sea. With Scottish boats still patrolling to the south, they turned north. The countryside they passed by was dark and, it appeared, deserted. It was eerily quiet. No lights shone in the dark and no sound of animals came from the fields. This was not surprising. The land had been devastated by war, picked clean by the ravaging Scottish army and then drowned to mud by the constant rain that had brought the famine.

They had rested for a time on a little shingle beach beneath some towering black cliffs, then after the sun rose, with no better plan, continued north along the rocky coast.

They had not gone far when they reached the mouth of another inlet between low green hills.

'Vikingsford!' Alys exclaimed, realising that this was the entrance to the sea lough where Corainne Castle, her former home, stood. The year before the castle had been the first place taken by the invading Scottish army. Savage was asleep at the back of the boat and, wanting to see her old home, she and Galiene had rowed into the inlet.

The castle was actually little more than a fortified tower. It sat on the end of a long, sickle-shaped promontory that jutted out into the inlet of Vikingsford at one end of a natural harbour. As they approached in the early morning light they saw with dismay but no real surprise that the outside walls bore black scorch marks, the remnants of licks from angry tongues of flame. When they had first landed, the Scots had re-fortified the castle as it guarded their bridgehead on Irish soil. Once they had taken Carrickfergus, however, they had a proper harbour so had abandoned Corainne, setting it on fire as they went so it could not be reused by enemies.

Landing, Alys and Galiene found that the castle was not as damaged as its last occupants had perhaps hoped. The roof was gone and the top two storeys had been burned and were open to the sky. The room on the first floor was still usable, though the place had been stripped bare of everything from furniture to utensils.

They now sat in that room. It was as good a place as any to regroup and form a plan as to what to do. A fire burned in the grate and Savage sat on the floor beside it. Alys had picked medicinal herbs to pack his wounds. His great helm had been turned into an improvised pot. It sat on the fire, filled with sea water that bubbled, seething cockles and other shellfish that Galiene had collected on the beach. Alys stood beside an arrow-slit window, looking out at the empty, green-brown, washed-out landscape. It was, as usual, raining.

She was concerned about Savage. His wounds aside, he had evidently taken the defeat at Carrickfergus badly. He had hardly spoken since they boarded the rowing boat. His eyes bore a strange, flat look as if something had died within him. He now sat, silent, with his back to the wall, his head bowed.

'Such a wasted land,' Alys said, turning to Savage. 'Do you think Ireland will ever again be like it was when we were growing up? Do you think there will ever be peace?'

Savage grunted. 'Do you think there ever was peace here?' he said. His tone was bitter.

Alys frowned. She knew what was eating him. The same things worried her. There was so much unresolved. The war remained at a stalemate. Carrickfergus Castle had got enough supplies to hold out for longer but for how long? Edward Bruce still ruled half of Ireland. De Mandeville was dead. The pirate Tavish Dhu was still at large. What really was the truth about Piers Gaveston and was he connected with the mysterious "Leopard" in Tír Chonaill? There was worse to consider as well. Two of the most powerful men in Ireland – Mortimer and Edward Bruce – were hunting them and their daughter.

Alys sighed and left the window. She walked over and sat down beside Savage, taking his hand in hers.

'We're in a fine mess, aren't we?' she said. 'We're right in the heart of occupied Scottish territory. We've nothing but the clothes we're in. We've no horses and nowhere to go even if we did. The land around us is empty and wasted as far as the eye can see.'

Savage looked up, a bleak grin on his face that gave Alys a little spark of hope. 'At least we've got each other,' he said.

Alys returned his smile. 'And nothing else matters,' she said but then her smile faded again.

'What will we do, Richard?' she said, concern filling her eyes. 'Bruce and Mortimer won't leave us in peace until we're dead.'

Savage did not reply for a few moments. At last he raised his head and looked directly at her. His expression had changed, as if a plan and direction had suddenly come to him. Alys saw in his eyes a sudden fire, the determination she was used to seeing there.

'Aye,' he said, his lips curling into a wolfish grin, 'or until they are.'

Afterword

As mentioned at the beginning of the book, the historical events and many of the persons who appear in the story are real. The Battle of Carrickfergus is one of those events, as was the awful famine created by climate change that swept across Europe between 1315 and 1317, killing millions of people. Syr Neil Fleming's courageous and selfless act of defence was also recorded in a near-contemporary account of the war.

If you enjoyed this book I hope (if you have not already done so) you will also check out the first book in the series, *Lions of the Grail*.

For those interested in what happens next, there are many more tales to tell from this particular conflict. Richard Savage will return again.

Tim Hodkinson

About the Author

TIM HODKINSON grew up in Northern Ireland where the rugged coast and call of the Atlantic Ocean led to a lifelong fascination with Vikings and a degree in Medieval English and Old Norse Literature. Apart from Old Norse sagas, Tim's more recent writing heroes include Ben Kane, Giles Kristian, Bernard Cornwell, George R. R. Martin and Lee Child. After several years living in New Hampshire, USA, Tim has returned to Northern Ireland, where he lives with his wife and children.

@TimHodkinson

www.timhodkinson.blogspot.com